CALIFORNIO

a novel by

DARLENE CRAVIOTTO

Front Door
Books

Published by

Front Door
Books

Front Door Books
frontdoorbooks04@gmail.com

AUTHOR'S NOTE

This book is a work of fiction. The story's setting makes use of real locations, but the characters, events, and dialogue are all products of the author's imagination. Although some known names and events are employed, the related characters, incidents, and dialogue are entirely fictional, and any resemblance to actual people is purely coincidental and unintended.

For my Felipe

"If history were taught in the form of stories it would never be forgotten."

RUDYARD KIPLING

ROSA

She was the oldest woman in the world.

Or so my father always said about his grandmother Rosa.

When he was a kid, he and his twin sister, Esther, had to walk Nonie Rosa five miles into town every Saturday. My father wanted to play baseball with his friends, not waste his whole Saturday with an old woman who could barely move. But his mother told him it was good for his soul. "It'll help you get into Heaven," she said, pushing him out the door.

Reaching for Heaven made for painfully long Saturdays.

Nonie Rosa's back was bent from years in the lima bean fields, and her eyes never stopped looking at her feet, willing them forward just a few inches at a time. It took hours from the moment the twins first arrived at Rosa's house on the ranch, high up on the Mesa overlooking the Pacific, to make their way downtown to the Bank of America on State Street.

Nonie didn't trust the bank, and every week she made the long trek into town to make sure her money was still there. She couldn't read or write, but she could count in her own Rosa way by using pinto beans. She carried the beans with her in five blue velvet pouches—one pouch for each of her children and the accounts she kept for them—and when she got to the bank, she painstakingly counted out a bean for every cent of interest owed her.

My father and Esther went with her to help.

Nonie didn't speak English, so Esther would say those words for her to the bank teller. My father then used the old language to translate back to Rosa. With her red hair and blue eyes from her Scotch-Irish mother, Esther had no need to learn how to speak Rosa's language. But my father favored his father's side and carried the family name, so it seemed right for him to know those words from their past.

That's why Nonie had taught him the language.

When he was little, my father loved speaking Rosa's words. But something changed once he started school. Teachers would tell him, in the meanest of voices, "English only!" The playground became a place for battles, not for ball. And for the first time in his life, someone called him a "dirty spic." A "greaser." And there were more names after that, so many he soon lost count. He never shared any of this with Nonie because he didn't want to hurt her feelings. But one day she figured it out on her own.

That day was at the bank in 1927.

The bank teller was impatient. When Nonie started to speak the old language, my father's stomach knotted and he looked up at the man's face for understanding. What he saw instead was bitter and hateful. Nonie Rosa's words were different, and they made my father feel different in the world—like something other, something bad. While he could hide from Nonie the ugly names he'd been called at school, he couldn't hide this hurt he was feeling now.

Nonie watched as her grandson looked down at the ground and his cheeks blushed crimson. When it came time for him to translate back to Nonie, he mumbled the words, saying them in barely a whisper, without certainty, without connection, without pride.

What Nonie Rosa saw on his face she recognized at once.

Verguenza.

Shame.

Nonie didn't say anything while they were in the bank. But that afternoon, after the twins walked her back to her ranch, instead of wrapping up her homemade *chorizos* and sending them home with the children like she usually did, she asked my father and Esther to stay.

Firing up the wood-burning stove, Nonie made hot chocolate with cinnamon and fresh flour tortillas with butter and homemade strawberry jam. Once the food was ready, she took my father and his sister outside to sit underneath the big coast live oak tree, where handmade wooden tables were set up every Sunday for the big family barbecues. As they listened to the sound of the surf pounding Arroyo Burro Beach just beneath the bluff and watched the sun setting low over the Mesa, Nonie Rosa began to speak to her grandchildren about the people of the past. Her voice was strong and steady as she spoke in Spanish, with great pride, and she made my father say the words in English to Esther, so both children would understand.

"Every family has a story and this one is ours," she told them.

And that is how our stories began.

Rosa Garcia Gonzales de Adrian was the end of an era.

She was the last of our family who spoke Spanish exclusively, and she was the only one left who lived solely from the land. She grew the crops, slaughtered the chickens, kept the house, and brought up the children. She knew both the rough hide of a stallion's back and the tight pull of a Model T clutch. She outlived two husbands, one a tyrant and the other a man who taught her about love. Although she couldn't read or write, she could tell stories.

Those stories are what we grew up hearing.

We're an old-time Santa Barbara family that has lived in this coastal California town for generations. None of us have ever really moved away. We've gone off to attend college, or to fight a war, but somehow we've always managed to come back here to this patch of land between the rolling foothills and the cool blue waters of the Pacific. To settle down. To raise our children. To live our lives and to continue our stories.

We are Californios.

Some of us carry different names now, English-sounding ones, like Prescott and Beckom. But others still reflect our past in surnames like Sanchez, Ayala, and Garcia. What matters most is what we share: those special *enchiladas* at Christmastime made with hard-boiled eggs, onions, and cheese; the *pilillis*, with sugar and cinnamon, the butternut squash *empanaditas*; *tortillas*—flour, and never corn; and the special *salsa*—or what we call *sarsa*—that's always on the table at every family barbecue. And *vino*. Lots of red *vino*.

When I was a kid, I never saw any other families like our *familia*. Not on television or in the movies, and not in the living rooms or backyards of my friends. That was okay—I knew exactly who I was, where I came from, and why we did things the way we did.

I knew because of Nonie's stories—the stories that were passed on with pride from one generation to the next, to the children of the children who would never know Nonie Rosa's touch. Words spoken by her but never written down.

That's my job now.

I'm the bridge from Rosa to the distant past, to people I never knew—to Felipe and Petra, to Mercedes and Martín, and to all those whose photos never made it into our family albums. To the first families who came here and to the families who were here when they came. I learned about them all through Rosa's stories, as they were handed down through the years. I share them with my own family now and in the pages of this book. While it's true that I wrote these words that follow, the stories they tell aren't really mine. And it's not my voice that tells them.

It's Rosa's.

I

Felipe & Petra

❧ New Spain – 1774 ❧

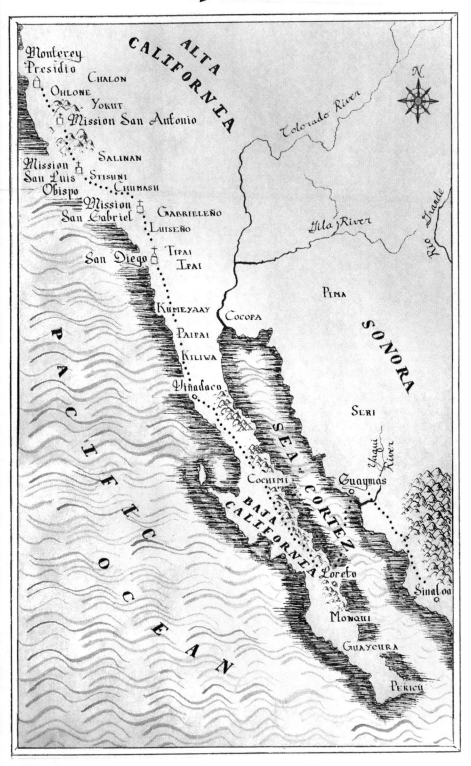

one

Once there was a man named Felipe.

A very good and simple man, and one you should always remember. Not just because he was a Garcia but because good men's stories should never be forgotten.

Well, maybe a few little parts.

But you can always skip over those.

The history books tell us that Gold, God, and Glory were what brought us here to this new land. They like to tell us who we were and what we were made of, but I will tell you different. We came here to survive. To get away from the poverty, and sometimes, yes, even death.

The year was 1774 when Felipe Santiago Garcia cheated death. The rains had been fierce that year. A *chubasco*—the meanest of storms—fell upon the people in the last days of May. The tiny village of Sinaloa, sitting just below the foothills of the Sierra Madre Occidental, was hit hard twice, first from the rain and then from the runoff of mud from the mountains.

José Maria Garcia had been waiting days for the clouds to part and the downfall to stop. He willed it with his heart while his wife, Lupe, prayed to the Blessed Holy Mother and his children looked to him for an answer.

The *chubasco* was stubborn, just like the land this family had worked so hard to claim. One year it had taken them to clear it, to dig the dry soil, to plant and to wait. The first crop of corn didn't take. The second, only half made it. José had been trained as a soldier, and he knew nothing about farming. This little piece of land was his retirement: a pension from the king. The Garcia men had all been soldiers—Castilian warriors who went where they were told and fought when they were asked—but none of them had lived long enough to own land. José had been the first lucky one.

This land was his life and the future for his children. It would bring a good husband for Teresa, who was almost fifteen. Another year or two, she would be married, and José could have a son-in-law, another pair of hands to help him—if only the land would do what he told it to do. Another strong back and broad shoulders could make the work go more quickly. He had a good son in Felipe, who was taller than most men and, at twenty, had the heart to work more hours than those twice his age. But José's body was slowing down. He needed a son-in-law to make up for what he could no longer do. Together, the three of them could tame the land, and a Garcia would never again have to take up the lance and become a soldier.

This had been José's dream.

Until the *chubasco* came and swept it away.

The crops had folded into the soil, and the rows overfilled with rainwater. The pens for the animals had broken apart; the pigs, chickens, and cows were swept away by the rising river waters. The family was forced to retreat to the safety of their *casita*. Protected by the powerful oak beam doorway overhead that José had cut and Felipe had carved, they huddled together and watched as everything they owned floated past them.

After the *chubasco* claimed the land, it came next for the *casita*.

Adobe walls of straw, mud, and manure, hardened by the sun and dried by the winds, began to crumble. As everything started to fall to pieces around him, José could only watch, knowing he was powerless to stop the destruction. And then his mind, too, began to crumble.

"What a fool is man to fall in love with life," he whispered, "when a jealous God can take it all away." The back of the roof fell in and Teresa screamed. Water rushed into the little house and swallowed up the family.

Felipe was in the floodwaters, paddling for his life, in what now had become an angry, rushing river. His sister's cries for help pushed him to swim faster, but the current against him was too rough, and by the time he had paddled in her direction she was under and unreachable. Her silence told him that she was lost. Frantically, he looked around for his parents, but they were nowhere to be seen. And the only sound Felipe could hear was the roar of the river. There was nothing he could do to save his family; all he could do was save himself. He swam with all his strength as the waters pushed him forward, slamming his body hard against a fallen tree that blocked his way.

That's when darkness overcame him.

And the river swept him away.

When the clouds finally parted and the sun came out to mock those who were still alive, Felipe awakened on a slope of mud, surrounded by scattered pieces of wood and bodies of the dead.

A village no longer living.

This is what Captain Rivera saw on the day he rode into Sinaloa. The people who had survived and stayed were starving. They were eating whatever scraps of garbage they could find that hadn't floated away. Rivera's job here in the village would not be difficult.

First he would feed them.

And then he would take what he needed.

ᏉWO

When El Capitán rode into Sinaloa, he was quite a sight.

Rivera, sitting tall on his white stallion, wore his red velvet riding coat that was ringed in eyelets and appointed with heavy silver buttons. A well-made musket sheathed in the finest of leather was strapped upon his mount, a dress rapier was at his hip, and a pair of the finest flared-barrel pistols was at his belt. His hair was tied back in a knot, and his head was crowned by a black felt hat marked by a single white feather.

Two mounted officers at his side wore short blue coats with matching breeches and the bright yellow shirts of the Catalonian Volunteers. Behind the officers walked a dozen mules, their coats wet with sweat, bound together by rope to the lead horses.

What hope they gave to the people of Sinaloa!

What fool would say he wanted to stay in that lost village when he could leave with a pledge that a new set of breeches, eight mules, five horses, five years of the king's food and lodging, and the gratitude of his nation would be his for the asking? This is what Rivera promised them that day in the village.

If they were willing to leave with him.

Gold, God, and Glory were the furthest things from Felipe's mind when Rivera faced the survivors in what was left of their village square and asked for new soldiers—recruits to travel to

Monterey, to the end of the world in El Norte. Without pause, Felipe was the first to step forward. He didn't do it bravely; he did it because he had nowhere else to go. His future would be in his father's past—to take up the lance in the name of the king and to become a soldier like all the Garcia men before him.

Whether he wanted to do it or not.

Stepping forward at the same time as Felipe, as eager to join the ranks of Spain's sons as his neighbor, was Tomás Luna, the younger of two brothers. He was the quick one, always curious, never looking before thinking, and often needing to be rescued. His step forward cast the fate of Martín Luna, his older brother. How could Martín stand by and watch his little brother take on such a big journey without staying close to his side, making sure he didn't fall hard on his backside, on his *culo*? He could not, and that made him step forward too.

When the two Luna brothers stepped forward, they gave no choice to their sister, Mercedes. How could she remain there with no brothers to watch over her and with only that sloth of a husband, Domingo, at her side? No, Mercedes would not stay behind, so she also took a step forward.

"Men only, stupid girl!" Martín said, sharply.

Never afraid of a good fight, Mercedes snapped back, "I have a man!" A sharp elbow to Domingo's flank called him to attention, so she could push him forward. "He can do my fighting for me. I will cook!" Martín reached out quickly, grabbing his sister by the wrist and pulling her back, as he saw Rivera shift in his saddle and start walking his stallion over to the Lunas.

"She makes good sense for a woman," Rivera said, liking Mercedes' spirit. If the Crown was looking for women to populate El Norte, these were the kind of women they needed.

Martín bowed to El Capitán, reaching up and grabbing the brim of his hat, as any good *soldado* would do to his superior. The gesture surprised Rivera.

"Where did you learn this salute?" El Capitán asked.

"My grandfather was a proud Catalonian Volunteer, like your own lieutenant and corporal," Martín answered, looking over at Rivera's two well-dressed officers. "He was a true son of Spain from the motherland!"

"You're an *español*?"

"*Si*, Capitán," Martín answered, proudly.

"Not like these homegrown *criollos*? Or these *mestizos*, these half-breeds?" El Capitán asked.

"The Luna blood runs Spanish pure, *señor*!"

Rivera smiled. "Not like me, then?"

These were not the words Martín was expecting to hear from an officer of España.

"This is where I was born and my father before me. I'm a proud *criollo*," Rivera said, his eyes locking with Martín's. "Spain may give me my uniforms and sometimes a few coins. But my children and I entered the world here. This is the land I protect. This land is my home."

Rivera didn't give Martín a chance to answer before pivoting his horse around quickly to face the villagers, leaving the proud son of an *español* to stare at the butt-cheeks of his mount. "We will take only the married men!" the captain said, addressing the people of Villa Sinaloa. "And your wives and children too!" A few of the men who had stepped forward left the line to search for their wives, so they could take them by the hand and bring them forward to join the group.

"If you have *una novia*, it's time to marry her!" Rivera called out to the men. "And as soon as we find a goddamn priest, we'll make sure he does the job!"

He spurred the stallion and galloped back over to his soldiers.

Martín was married, but Tomás would need to find himself a bride, and his older brother would need to help him. Tomás was barely old enough to have a beard to shave, and his body was soft and ill-equipped to become a soldier or a bridegroom. While Martín could teach him to shoot straighter and to stay longer on a horse, as a groom he would be on his own. Much would depend on the woman, and for this reason, Martín decided to pair his brother with the Ramirez widow, Beatriz.

Although she was in her early forties, Bea was still a handsome woman; big-boned, she stood a good head above Tomás—but he was still in his teens and hopefully still growing. In spite of her age, she was fertile, but her five children had all been swallowed up by the floodwaters along with their father. Bea had been overcome by grief since the loss, but in Tomás she would have a future and possibilities again. And besides, she would be more than happy to trade in the poverty of Sinaloa for the certainty of meals every day and a few blankets at night.

With Tomás paired up with Beatriz, and Mercedes and Domingo also set to leave, this left only Maria Petra Luna, the youngest of her family. Petra would soon be eighteen—a good age for marrying. But without a father to arrange such things, and no mother, may she rest in peace, Martín had been more than just a brother. He had raised Petra since she could walk, and she had followed him everywhere, always at his side. Life was sweeter with her smiles, with the touch of her hand and her eyes always seeking his. There was no child in Sinaloa that was prettier, and as a woman she had blossomed, breathtaking and unmatchable. No man deserved such an angel. How could Martín possibly give away his beautiful little shadow?

Petra had remained unbetrothed, without *un novio* in sight. With no husband to force forward to join Captain Rivera, Petra would have to stay behind in Villa Sinaloa with only the old uncles to watch out for her.

That did not sit well with Martín. He wanted her with him, at his side always. And for this to happen, he would have to choose for his sister what she had no right to choose for herself.

A husband.

Looking around at all the remaining men of the village, Martín wondered which one to pick. He needed someone who was kind. A good man who would not hurt Petra but one who also would never steal her heart. A man who wasn't the bravest, or even the smartest. An average man in many ways; a simple man without ambitions.

Martín's gaze fell on Felipe.

The Garcia boy was tall and sturdy, but there was still too much of the boy in him; his face was too gentle. Other men had more conviction, more muscles, more ambition. Felipe's father had always ruled the roost, and for some sons, this can destroy the spirit. What Felipe lacked was confidence in himself as a man. He never looked Martín eye to eye, never showed a flash of anger when needed, and never raised his voice. Instead, he spoke with few words in a quiet manner that most men viewed as weakness. No, Felipe was not a leader of men, as Martín was, and Petra would easily recognize the difference. She would always look to her brother for what Felipe could never give her. And that would be fine with Martín. This was the kind of man Martín wanted for his sister: someone who would never challenge him for Petra's heart.

"You will need a wife, my friend," Martín said with a smile as he sidled up to Felipe, placing a brotherly hand on his back. "I've got a good one for you. The best!" He nodded in the direction of Petra.

Now Felipe didn't know what to say. He had known Petra his whole life; he had memorized everything about her. The way her cheeks flushed in the late afternoon heat and how she would gaze deeply into a person's eyes, never the first to look away. How her beautiful black hair always found a way to fall when she wore it up, and how her slender fingers would brush it away effortlessly. The long slope of her neck, and the way she walked, gliding across the village square with grace and beauty. There wasn't one man who didn't want her, and yet they all knew they'd never be good enough to have her.

At first Felipe was sure this was a joke. The Luna brothers had never been friends with him, and now they were choosing him to be the husband of their sister? A quick yes would surely bring on their laughter; his eagerness would only show him to be a fool for thinking he deserved Petra. He didn't, and he knew it. But if wanting her made him have to play the fool, he would gladly take on that role.

"Yes," he said, looking for the first time directly at Martín. "I will marry her."

Martín didn't greet Felipe's answer with laughter. Instead, he grinned broadly, and offered his new brother-in-law-to-be his hand.

For the first time, Felipe understood that this wasn't a joke.

It was, in fact, a miracle.

THREE

When a woman is angry you do best to stay out of her way.

And Petra had never been so angry.

"How can you do this to me?"

"You want to stay here and starve?" Martín asked.

His attention was on the bundle of clothing he was packing up for his two sons and his wife. But no matter where he went, inside to gather up their belongings, or outside to stack up their saddlebags, Petra was at his heels.

"I don't want to be married to him!"

"It's the only way! If you want to leave here, to come with me, this is the way you do it!" Martín said, ending the discussion.

But it wasn't the end. Petra was just getting started. "He's a farm boy—a nothing! I can't spend my whole life married to a peasant! It will kill me!" She started to cry, and against this, Martín could not fight back. Her tears had always been able to reach him—he could never bear her sadness.

"Listen to me," he said, his tone softening. "You need to be patient." Martín reached out to her, pulling her close and comforting her, as he had done before she could even walk. He still could find the little girl inside who just needed to be held. "You are special, *mija*. You deserve the finest, and there is no one here who can give you that."

With her head on his chest, Petra listened to his heartbeat, and the rhythm of it slowed her tears. Martín knew her like no one else in the world, and in his arms she had always felt safe. If he had to leave Sinaloa, she had to find a way to go with him. She couldn't bear to live there or anywhere else if Martín wasn't with her.

"Use him to get out," he whispered. "Like a mule—he will take you away from here!"

"And what happens when we get out?" Petra asked. "How can I spend my whole life living with a mule?"

"He's too stupid to stay alive for long," Martin told her. "And when you're a widow, think of all the fine officers that will line up to court you. You can have your pick! And even they won't be good enough for you."

Martín kissed her gently on the forehead.

And Petra was no longer angry.

Once again, her brother had all the answers.

The night settled in, and it grew too late to start their journey.

Families did what they had been doing every night, finding shelter in the *cabañas* and lean-tos they had built out of the broken lumber and dried hides from the aftermath of the flood. Only Felipe slept out in the open, with no shelter to protect him and only the stars above to cover his head. Without his family, he was lost. He wanted no roof to stand between him and God—a God he no longer trusted. His heart ached for his mother, his father, and his sister, and he was eager to leave this place where, in the darkness, silence was the only company he had. There could be no greater hardships or more tears to shed than what he had found in Sinaloa. No matter what the journey in front of him held, he was eager to start it.

With Petra.

Felipe turned on his side and looked up at the Luna hacienda on the knoll above the village square. Large and sturdy, it was the only dwelling that was still standing. Its thick stone walls had shed the rain, and the floodwaters had not been able to reach it on top of the hillside. There was still room enough in that dwelling for all the Luna family. Deep inside of the house, in a room hidden all the way at the back, was where a family's pride slept— the women of marriageable age. Petra was there now, sleeping, and Felipe smiled when he saw that image in his mind.

It wouldn't be easy to win her, he knew this. She had gone out of her way to avoid him from the moment Martín had pledged her to him. As Rivera's officers had given out food supplies to the villagers that evening, Felipe had removed his hat and gone over to speak to Petra. But she had busied herself with Mercedes' girls, moving away from him to help the little ones with their bowls of *posole* that the women had cooked and were passing out to everyone. Later, when Martín was watering the mules and Petra was at his side, once again Felipe slipped his hat off and headed her way. But she had turned away from him by taking her brother's arm, and Martín did not encourage her to go closer.

What on earth could Felipe possibly do to stop Petra from stepping away from him? What words could he say to her that would bring her closer? To make her want him as much as he wanted her?

Only now, in the darkness, was Petra his. In his mind and in his heart, he could hold her close. And for now, maybe this was for the best. Maybe he didn't deserve her yet. Maybe he wasn't the man he needed to become. At least that's what Felipe said to himself so he could close his eyes and sleep a little. He would wait her out, he promised himself, as long it took.

Petra was worth waiting for.

FOUR

At the break of day, it was time to move out.

Rivera gave the command to begin packing up, and the people started tying their world up in bundles that would be strapped onto the backs of the mules the captain had brought with him.

Each mule had to carry a balanced load, one pack on one side of its rump and another pack on the other. Too much weight and the animals would have to be rested and watered too many times during their journey, and there was no time for that. They had to reach in a week the Santa Barbara Bay to meet up with the great Manila galleon—a ship that would take them across the Sea of Cortez to Loreto, where there would be more supplies, horses to ride, and cattle to take with them for fresh meat as they crawled north across Baja's eight hundred miles. But for now these few mules would have to carry all the women and also the packs.

The Luna family was given three mules: one for Martín, Sola, and their two boys; another for Mercedes, Domingo, their twin girls, and little Maria, the toddler; and the third for almost-newlyweds Bea and Tomás. With so many in the family, all three mules were fully packed with no room to spare.

And yet Petra's things still waited to be loaded up.

A small wooden trunk—the family's *arcón*, with brass hinges and an *L* branded black into its rich walnut wood—sat on the ground.

Domingo struggled with the weight of the trunk as he picked it up. "*Dios, mujer!*" he groaned, trying to hoist it onto the back of the mule.

But it was no use; there was no room.

"It doesn't fit!" Domingo said, dropping the heavy trunk back to the ground.

Mercedes bent down and tugged at the *arcón*. "What did you pack in here? The oven?" asked Mercedes, surprised by its weight.

"Only what I need," Petra answered, in the most innocent of voices.

Mercedes unlatched the top and opened the trunk.

Inside, spilling out gratefully now that they were free, were delicate silk gowns and the finest of embroidered satin dresses. Lace shawls—*mantillas*—were wrapped carefully together, surrounded on the sides by black satin pumps with real silver buckles, hand-painted ivory hair combs decorated with turquoise and jade, and velvet purses of different shapes and sizes. It was a wardrobe fit for a queen.

"Are you joking?" Mercedes laughed at all the finery. "You're not going to Madrid to meet the king!" She started to pull out the fancy dresses, unpacking the trunk.

"Those were Mama's!" Petra protested.

"Let them stay in Mama's village then," Mercedes said, paying no attention to her sister as she tossed the clothing to the side.

Petra was not about to let Mercedes tell her what to do. Even if it meant a fight between the two of them right there, she would not back down from her big sister. She gathered up the discarded gowns as quickly as Mercedes tossed them off to the side. Domingo, accustomed to these clashes between the sisters, took a seat on the ground and waited to see who would win.

"Who are you trying to impress, the mules?" Mercedes yelled, grabbing one of the gowns out of Petra's hands.

"You don't want me to take them because *you* can't fit into

22

them! You're too *fat!*" Petra yelled, yanking the gown back from her sister.

Domingo, on the ground, laughed. "That's true, *mi amor!*"

"*Cállate*, fool!" Mercedes snapped, telling him to shut up.

"There's no room to carry them, so why fight?" Domingo shrugged.

Before a winner could be declared, Felipe came to the rescue by leading his mule over to the Lunas. Removing his hat, he addressed Domingo. "With your permission," Felipe said, pointing to the small bundle on only one side of his animal. "I have room here for whatever more you want to take."

Domingo did not have to think twice about the matter. Since he was the only man of the family there at the moment, it was his word that counted. "Better to kill your mule than ours," Domingo said, pushing himself up from the ground and brushing the dirt from his hands.

But before he could lift up the wooden trunk, the ground shook with hoofbeats and Martín appeared on the back of a beautiful pinto mare.

"We don't need your ass, Garcia," said Martín, slipping off the back of the horse and standing face to face with Felipe. He said the words with a smile, even though smiling was not what he truly felt. Martín was not one to let you know the honesty of his heart, which he would only show to his family. Anyone who was not a Luna was never to be trusted. That was a fact.

Petra's eyes widened at the sight of the spotted pinto, and the fight with her sister was soon forgotten. She hurried over to the side of the horse, stroking the mare's mane and pressing her face into the animal's smooth flank.

"How did you manage to save a horse from the floodwaters?" Felipe asked, surprised to see a village animal alive and well. Putting a brotherly arm around Felipe's shoulder, Martín pointed up to the crest of the hillside and the grand, imposing Luna hacienda.

"While everything you owned washed away with the river, we stayed up high with our animals, safe and protected," Martín told him. "We will always be like that," he said, simply. "On top, looking down at peasants like you."

If Felipe had been a man quick to anger, he would've squared off and challenged Martín—been the cock ready for the fight. But anger was something Felipe did not want to taste and, for now, he would keep his silence.

If only to win Petra.

Martín patted Felipe on the back and moved over to his sister. Smiling, Petra took her brother's hand, and he lifted her gracefully onto the back of the mare. With great ease, he bent to pick up his family's *arcón*, placing it behind his sister and tying it securely onto the pinto. Looking over his shoulder, he gave a reminder to Felipe.

"She's still a Luna until we can find a priest in Loreto." Petra's honor belonged only to Martín—it was his pride to guard it and his duty to make that known.

Felipe had been warned.

"Until then, she travels with her family," Martín added, as he reached for the reins of the mare and led the horse away.

Petra sat majestically on top of the finely crafted leather saddle of the pinto. Over her shoulder, she cast a last glance at Felipe. There was absolutely nothing she could possibly want from this poor farmer-boy that Martín couldn't give her.

Felipe was a fool to even try.

Once the mules were all packed up, it was time to go.

The *parientes* being left behind—the family members too old or too weak to make the long journey—said their good-byes. There was no certainty that those who were leaving would outlive the ones remaining. The caravan was heading into the unknown, and more than one family crossed themselves, murmured El Credo, and offered a rosary or two to go with the travelers. For many, the faith they would carry with them was more important than anything in their packs.

El Capitán, on top of his white stallion, walked along the long line of travelers.

"Stay together!" he called out to them. "Never separate from the caravan without permission of an officer!" Rivera pointed to the two soldiers mounted at the front of the line. "Those are your two officers—Corporal Ortiz and Lieutenant Rios." They were opposites of each other. Ortiz, the corporal, was a bull of a man, dark in face and in spirit. The lieutenant, Rios, was all lightness, quick to smile, with honey-colored hair and an easy confidence. "It's their permission you will seek other than my own!" Rivera told them, looking down the long line of ragtag pilgrims.

It was this way they would travel—in a single line, with officers at the front and the people stretched out behind; women rode with their babies on top of the mules, and the men walked alongside with their older children next to them. This is how they would leave Sinaloa: with only El Capitán and God's grace leading them.

God was up to the task, to be sure.

But Rivera could only pray that he was up to it too.

"We stay together! When we march and when we stop for the day! What we do, we do as one! We are one family until Monterey!"

Felipe stood at the back of the line with the other recruits and several young boys, while the Luna family stood ready: Sola, Beatriz, and Mercedes, each perched on top of a mule, and Petra above them all, sitting on the strong back of the fine-looking pinto. They were the first family at the front of the line. As always, the Lunas came first.

Martín, with his brother Tomás on one side of him and his two young sons, Marco and Victor, on the other, had positioned himself directly behind the two officers. He knew his place in this world, and he was not shy about letting the world know it too. Without hesitation, he shouted for all to hear: "*Viva*, España!"

The other pilgrims followed his lead. "*Viva!*" they cried out, united in one voice.

Rivera snapped his reins, and the two officers spurred their horses. Together, the caravan moved forward.

The journey began.

FIVE

Fifty-two villagers set out that day from Sinaloa.

Only the two officers and El Capitán were trained soldiers and not strangers to this kind of journey. Lieutenant Rios and Corporal Ortiz, who sat on their mounts behind Rivera, were fighting men from the motherland, from Catalonia, with its salted cod and rich pork sausages. Volunteers who crossed the great blue Pacifico, they understood the hardships they would find once they came to this new world.

Rivera was the most seasoned; he had been one of the first to make this journey in '69 with Portolá charting the way. Now, in his middle years, the good captain had been shaken out of his retirement in Guadalajara. Spain had taken him from the comfort of his wife and his three sons, to send him again to El Norte to take charge of everything this time, to become governor of the people and *comandante* of the troops, as the Spanish way of life stretched across the countryside, one little mission and presidio at a time.

But most of the fifty-two villagers who now followed Rivera had never known any place other than their small village. They knew nothing about where they were going except that it was far away. They trusted they would be fed and clothed by the Crown, protected by Spain along the way, and when they got to Monterey—a promised land, to be sure—they would have fields to farm and homes they would build where they would raise their children. It was what the king wanted—to fill this new territory with *españoles* who would populate and prosper, living a good Spaniard's life, not just for themselves but for all those who came in contact with them.

That was the plan, at least.

That was what kept the caravan moving.

On this, their first day, Rivera would push them to see how much they could take: how long their backsides could manage the bumps on the road, how far they could go before thirst and hunger slowed their step. He would not stop for anything, not for the little boy who had to pee or for the squirming child in her mama's lap. The people had to keep moving, and Rivera had to be strong to push them to go farther. He measured their sturdiness by the sounds behind him. They were all quiet at first, but then the babies broke the silence, and the people started to relax. Children laughed, and fathers spoke in low voices. Mothers whispered words of comfort. Someone started singing and, before you knew it, someone else joined in. As long as Rivera could hear them behind him, he knew he could push the people farther.

With the promise of rain in the air, and with babies starting to fuss, the mothers who had a child tucked close to their bodies would shush them and coo to them and offer them the *teta*. Mercedes held Maria tightly in front of her while the little toddler suckled quietly at her breast. Looking back over her shoulder, Mercedes' eyes searched for her family.

Domingo brought up the rear of the caravan with the other men, barely able to keep up with their long strides and the pace of the travel. His two little daughters, impatient with their father's slowness, walked alongside Felipe and his mule, and when one of the twins stumbled, Felipe reached over and caught her, swinging her up into the air to the girl's delightful laughter.

Mercedes watched Felipe playing with her children, and she liked what she saw.

"He's not so bad looking, you know?" she called out to Petra, who rode on top of the pinto alongside her sister's mule. "Once he puts on some weight, he'll look more like a man than a boy. It might be fun to help make him into a man." She gave a low laugh. "I wouldn't shut my door to him!"

"*You* marry him then!"

"You're not the only woman to be in these shoes. Martín matched me with the first man who made him an offer, just so he could get me out of the house. I had nothing to say about it. Why should you expect anything more?"

"I'm not you. I don't want your life—I want something better."

"You're spoiled, *chica*. That's not your fault, that's Martín's. He made you think you're some kind of princess, just to stop you from crying, from missing Mama. That was a mistake. Now you're going to learn what it means to be a *mujer*, and it isn't going to be so easy for you."

Petra dismissed the words with the flick of her hand. Her sister knew nothing, only how to push out a baby and cook the meals. What did she know about the finer things in life? The most beautiful, the most honored. Nobility and grandeur. She would not settle for anything less, certainly not a farm boy from Sinaloa.

And she would not let her sister change her mind.

Not one little bit.

The caravan kept moving, and the hours dragged on. Soon the sun was setting and the land had changed. The mountains were well behind them now, and the river too.

Petra sat tall on her saddle and looked out on the new countryside. She had never ventured farther than the river, where the women would take the clothes and wash them. But they were long past their river now, and everything was different around her. They were out of the valley of Sinaloa, crossing unfamiliar flatlands and heading north. The sky seemed bigger and the smells stronger. Sage and anise sweetened the air. They were moving away from everything that had been comfortable. Petra was outside the walls of her life, and she was loving every step the pinto was taking.

But not everyone was like Petra.

Mercedes could only feel the roughness of the mule's hide on her backside. She didn't care about the new sights and birdsongs around her; only her little ones were what mattered. It was late, and they hadn't yet stopped to eat. Empty bellies brought tears, aching feet brought crying and whining. If her children weren't happy, Mercedes wasn't happy.

Still they kept going.

Rain started to fall. The people of the caravan wanted to stop and make camp. All were hungry. All were exhausted. All wanted to stop and rest.

And yet Rivera kept going. Snapping the reins of his horse, El Capitán picked up the pace. In front of him, the wide plain they were crossing was narrowing into an *arroyo*. It was in this direction Rivera rode at a quick trot, and the people had no choice but to follow.

Already struggling to keep up at the back of the pack, Domingo stumbled headfirst into the rocky soil. Still the pack moved forward, and Domingo scrambled back up on his feet hurriedly, to try to catch up. The rain, like Domingo, also picked up its pace.

The women, holding tightly onto the reins of their mules, pressed their babies against their breasts while lifting the end of their shawls to shelter them from the falling raindrops.

As the sky's darkness filled with flashing light and the boom of thunder rumbled across the plains, the caravan moved along, steady and unbroken, entering the *arroyo* behind Rivera, who leaned forward on his stallion, determined and unrelenting, like a man with the devil at his back. Out of the heavens, a sudden bolt of lightning cracked, striking a large boulder off Rivera's left flank. His horse screamed and reared up as El Capitán pulled at the reins, struggling to get control of the animal, while his two officers circled him to keep the horse from bolting.

Martín's two sons, Victor and Marco, grabbed their father's side, and for the first time all day little Marco, only six, showed his youth and started crying. Victor, at fourteen, was good at fighting his tears, as his father had taught him. But he couldn't control his face, as his eyes widened and filled with fear.

The people were terrified as they watched their captain struggling to gain control, digging his heels into the flanks of his horse and stroking his long neck. The thunder rolled again and Rivera's grip tightened on the reins, yanking hard at the bit to stop his horse from bolting. He needed to show the animal who was in charge. If he gave in to the horse's fear, the horse would control the man. And this would not do. Only through strength could Rivera lead and show that fear was not an option, running away was not a choice. It was in this way that Rivera took control again of his animal, and the horse gave in, following his lead and doing as he was told.

This, too, was how Rivera would lead the people.

What seemed like madness, or at the very least cruelty, made more than good sense to El Capitán. The people could survive a good soaking. What they might not survive was the *arroyo* that now surrounded them, with its tall cliffs covered in thick brambles and its boulders bigger than men—perfect hiding places for unseen dangers, for an unknown death in an unnamed place. The captain knew of these dangers firsthand, but the people did not.

Rivera rode his horse forward, without care for whatever discomfort it was causing the caravan, and headed quickly through the sheltered *arroyo* to its end, emerging once again to an open plain. Once they were back again to the land sprawling wide open and endless, Rivera raised his hand high, slowed his horse, and stopped.

And the caravan stopped behind him.

It was here they would make camp.

SIX

The tarps went up first.

As the rain poured down, the men worked quickly stretching out sheets of canvas, using ropes to tie them to poles that they slipped into the wet earth. Protected now from the rain, mothers stood under the tarps and stripped down their little children, unwrapping them from their wet clothing and bundling them up in blankets and shawls. The women would have to wait until the family tents were raised up and their privacy assured before taking off their own wet clothing. But for now there was work for them to do, and soaked or not, they had to do it.

The men kept to themselves and to their own duties.

While Felipe was finishing putting up one last tarp, Martín and Domingo unpacked the Luna mules and Petra's horse. Martín made it his business to take Mercedes off to the side, away from the family, to talk to her privately.

"Keep an eye on Petra!" he shouted through the pouring rain to make sure his sister heard every one of his words. "Keep her away from Felipe!"

"You should reach out to him, have him join us!" Mercedes shouted back at him. "Let the two of them talk and get to know each other!"

"She's my responsibility! You do as I tell you!"

"Petra's not a child anymore! She's not yours to watch!"

Martín had work to do, and Mercedes was wasting his time. "Enough! Do what I say!" he told her, ending the conversation.

Mercedes could never resist having the final word, and as her brother started to move past her, she grabbed his elbow. "Are you going to put yourself in bed with them too?"

If ever Martín had come close to hitting a woman, this was the time. His sister knew what words would hurt him the deepest, and she wasn't afraid to use them. Another day, another place with less people around, and Martín might have struck her. But for now he would do nothing except walk as far away from this devil-sister as he could.

Tomás had other worries.

Hurriedly, he searched through the contents of his saddlebag until he finally found what he was looking for: a small package wrapped in burlap. Running his hands over it, he checked to make sure it was dry. Unwrapping it, he revealed its contents.

A pistol.

Next to it was the horn of a bull, darkened with age and use, hollowed out inside, and with a tip of hammered bronze. Opening the end of it with his teeth, Tomás spilled out into his hand a pinch of black powder from inside.

It was gunpowder.

"Are you going hunting?"

Felipe's words—spoken just behind Tomás's back—surprised the young recruit, and he dropped the gun and powder horn to the dirt. Tomás was not the most comfortable with guns; they made him jumpy. But that was a secret he would never admit to anyone. Bending down to pick up the fallen weapon, he didn't see Felipe's smile or understand that his words had been said in jest. But even if he had, on Tomás the humor would have been lost. He took very seriously his role of being a man, and guns were a big part of that manhood.

"Martín says we won't be issued muskets until we're officially *soldados*," he told Felipe. "But I'm not waiting for permission to protect myself and my bride."

Felipe wasn't a man who would try to convince another man that his way was best. Better to let him find his own direction and stay clear while he was finding it. But Tomás seemed so much younger than the nineteen years he had, and Felipe could easily see him as a younger brother not sure yet which way to go. He liked him. And for this reason, he smiled again and offered his friendship.

"I think your bride needs a warm fire more than she needs your gun." Bending down, Felipe picked up the fallen horn of gunpowder.

"Tending the fire is woman's work," said Tomás, using words that Martín had taught him.

But Felipe paid him no attention as he found a spot underneath the tarp and began to go to work. He didn't need permission from a young man who barely shaved, or any man for that matter, to do what needed to be done. In spite of the rain falling around him and the damp ground underneath his feet, Felipe knelt down under the protection of the canvas tarp and did what he had to do. Without a mother or a father, his life depended upon being clever, on being smarter than the challenge in front of him. If a cooking fire was needed and there was no woman to make it, he would do it.

He pulled out of his pocket this thing and that. A knife with a good sharp blade. A piece of quartz he had found. A little dried grass he had been saving for his mule. He put them all together, and in his hands, they became magic: the strike of the stone against the blade, a pinch of Tomás's gun powder, and Felipe's own breath. Over and over again, he repeated the actions. He would not quit, not if it took him all night. With so much rain and water surrounding him, Felipe still did not take no for an answer. He only knew what he knew—that the women and children needed warmth. He saw that truth and followed it, and because he would not give up, he was rewarded with a spark: a small one at first, so tiny. But no matter how tiny, how impossible the task, still Felipe kept blowing, breathing life into that spark until one spark became two. His will, and his will alone, kept him going, until he was almost breathless. Still he went on! As he breathed life into those sparks, pretty soon they became a flame. A fire started where once there was none.

By now the men had all gathered to watch Felipe, as he coaxed the flames, nurtured them, and made them grow. It was a miracle. Who else could do this, surrounded by such mud and rain? Who else would even try? It was a moment that took them out of the storm and brought them together. When they were tired and hungry, without a home to shelter them—when all they could see in front of them was only night's darkness—Felipe had brought light to them. And the day's aching feet and stiffened backs were forgotten by the warmth of a fire.

Felipe's fire.

El Capitán was impressed by this new recruit of his, and he made certain to ask the men around him for the young man's name.

"Garcia," they told him.

And one of them quickly added his first name, "Felipe."

The man who spoke was Martín.

Standing at the side of Rivera, he watched Felipe with the other men. What he truly felt about Felipe, Martín kept to himself, carefully hiding it away from the captain. His feelings were not important. What he did is what mattered: making sure he was close to Rivera so he could prove his value by telling the captain what he needed to hear. That is why he gave him Felipe's name and looked proud while saying it. Even if it meant a nod now in Felipe's direction by the captain and even if it made the peasant boy rise above the others. Garcia's good fortune would serve Martín, of that he would make certain.

In the meantime, he would have to be more careful.

There was more to Felipe Santiago Garcia than what Martín had first seen. True, he was gentle and weak with kindness like a woman, but there was something strong in him too. And for the first time, Martín saw this.

Felipe was a man who might very well survive.

Once Felipe's fire had taken hold, dinner was prepared by the women working together, as women always do.

Supplies were low. Rivera and his officers had been traveling for two weeks before they arrived at Sinaloa, and by now the mule packs were down to only dried beef—*tasajo*—and a little flour for tortillas. Their *piñole*—the cornmeal that they ate—was almost gone. And there was hardly any chocolate left to fill up the pots for the morning. That would mean starting out at dawn on an empty stomach while the hot chocolate and *piñole* were made only for the children. There were no villages or *rancherías* along the way, and they would have to stretch the food as much as they could for at least four days until they arrived at the fort in El Fuerte. For now, the women would have to soak the dried beef in water and pound it to soften the *charqui*, heating it up in a big iron pot until the water took on some flavor and the beef was tender to eat.

When the meal was ready, each woman took her place behind the cooking pot and ladled out plates of the stewed meat for her family. Mercedes was the eldest woman of the Lunas, and she was the one who had the honor.

Felipe, out of respect, did not join the Lunas. Instead, he stood all the way in the back, by himself, waiting for his turn to be served last.

When it was Petra's time to receive a plate of food, Mercedes looked around to see where Martín was sitting. It was only after she was sure that her brother was busy with his own family, eating with Sola and their boys, that she dished out two plates of food and handed them to Petra. She nodded in the direction of Felipe.

Petra looked at the two plates but didn't take them.

"He's alone and he has no family," Mercedes whispered to her.

Still, Petra stood stubbornly in her place.

"Where is the little girl who found the fallen sparrow in the creek and begged us to save it?" Mercedes asked. "Where is that child with so much heart?"

Petra hesitated, but she still did not move.

"I'm not asking you to take the wedding vows, just take him dinner!" said Mercedes, thrusting the plates at her sister. Petra could do nothing else but take them.

"Martín won't like it." she told Mercedes.

"Don't let Martín see you." With a wink, Mercedes sent her on her way.

Taking care that her brother's eyes were not following her, Petra moved over to the back of the line where Felipe was standing. When she reached him, she stopped at a distance and stretched her arm out as far as she could, offering him the plate of food as one might feed a dog with rabies or a wild animal.

"This is from my sister," Petra said, without a smile.

"*Gracias,*" Felipe answered, removing his hat with respect. He had to stretch out his whole body and the length of his arm so his fingers could reach the plate of food. Once in his hands, he gratefully smiled.

"My brother could kill you if he sees you talking to me," Petra told him.

That was the end of Felipe's smile. He nodded his head, understanding the threat, and began to eat his dinner from the plate.

Petra watched him, sizing up his looks and his manners by the way he held his plate and how he scooped the stew up with his tortilla. He was slow and methodical, the way he ate and the way he moved. Everything about Felipe seemed gentle and easy.

"My sister says you have no one," Petra said to him, with not much care attached to the words. Felipe nodded again and kept eating, keeping his attention on the plate.

"I'm the last," he said softly, keeping his eyes on his plate and not on Petra, who stood there in silence. It was her silence that made him wonder why she still stood there at all and what he could do to make her stand there, close to him, forever. It was the closest he had ever been to Petra, and he wanted more than anything to look into her eyes.

And so he did.

"I won't marry you because your brother says I can," Felipe told her. "If you say no, I will honor that."

Petra was surprised by what he said and the kindness with which he said it.

"I have no choice," she told him, saying it simply without anger or regret. But what she felt and hadn't spoken could be seen there in her eyes—a sadness for a fate she could not change. It was the first time Felipe had ever seen Petra look unhappy.

"You have a choice," he told her. "With me, you do."

Petra wondered if he really meant it.

At night, they slept in tents.

All of the tents formed a circle with the mules and the horses tied together in the center so no one could sneak away with them and not be heard. The men slept separately from the women, with husbands, sons, and fathers taking turns in the doorways of the men's tents, on guard and watching for whatever dangers were in the dark— those outside of the caravan, and even those within. It was their duty to protect the honor of their women, and they would give up sleep to do it.

While their children slept together, with the cousins crowded next to one other, the women of the Luna family were inside their tent, settling in for the night. Finally out of their soaked garments, Sola, Bea, and Petra wore only their petticoats, as they unpacked fresh shawls and blankets for the night.

Mercedes was the last to peel off her clothing, but she seemed hesitant about undressing in front of the three women. She tucked herself into a corner of the tent and, turning her back to them, she removed her blouse. Kneeling down next to the wooden chest that was filled with their mother's clothing, she opened the top and searched inside.

"No, you don't! No, no, no! Those are for Monterey!" Petra said and hurried over to stop her sister.

"What good are they if we can't use them when we need them?" Mercedes said, reaching into the chest and pulling out a white silk blouse with lace ruffles down its front. Pulling it on, she tried to button it, but her bust was too large and the ends of the fabric wouldn't meet.

"When did you get so big?" Petra asked, as she watched Mercedes struggling to make the buttons reach the holes.

"I have a woman's body," said Mercedes proudly, as she slipped out of her damp skirt, pulling it down over her hefty hips and thick thighs. As she did, the top of her petticoat slipped at the waist, revealing a large belly that was round and firm. There was no way of hiding the baby that was growing there.

Petra was startled by the sight.

Mercedes put a finger up to her lips, making a sign to keep quiet.

"You shouldn't have come on this trip," Petra whispered, after looking over her shoulder to make sure Sola and Bea were not listening. "You need to be home, not on a mule all day!"

"I've had three babies already. I know what I'm doing," Mercedes said, clicking her tongue at such nonsense. "The fourth one can't surprise me with anything I don't know."

"What does Domingo say?"

"I haven't let him near me since he did this to me. Besides, he doesn't notice anything past his own big *panza*."

"You can't keep this a secret forever."

"Don't you say a word! Especially to Martín. We'll be in Monterey before this baby comes into the world, and I can practically deliver it myself by then. You keep this our secret."

Petra took a moment to think about it. There was no going back to Sinaloa for any of them, that was for sure. And what good would it do Mercedes if everyone knew, especially Martín? There was nothing to be done, so why not keep it a secret? Petra would have to make sure she took special care of her sister.

"You won't be hiding anything with your *tetas* hanging out," she said with a frown.

She tried to button her mother's silk blouse on Mercedes, but there was no chance of that happening. Removing her shawl, she slipped it over her sister's head, covering up her ample bosom with it.

The fit was perfect. This would be their secret.

At least for now.

෴

The men of the Luna family were crowded inside their tent. While Domingo snored loudly, Martín huddled at the entrance, blocking anyone from leaving. His pistol was there in his waistband with his hand on top of it, just in case he needed it.

Felipe lay asleep at the back of the tent. But Tomás, who was on his side close to him was wide awake.

"What will it be like?" Tomás whispered. "Do you ever wonder?"

Felipe's eyelids flickered and rose from sleep. "In California?" he asked Tomás.

Tomás took a long moment before answering. "To be with a woman."

Felipe smiled in the dark. "I think you need to have a talk with your brother." He closed his eyes and tried to get back to sleep.

But not Tomás. "Beatriz is a widow. She's had a husband, already. She knows what to do."

"Let her teach you then," Felipe suggested.

"But I'm the man!"

"A man who doesn't know what to do," Felipe reminded him.

Tomás thought about that for a moment. "That's true," he admitted quietly.

Felipe himself was no expert, but he had a few ideas. On those nights when his mind wandered to such things and kept him awake, he thought of the animals he had watched. The stallion mounting the mare; the boar on the back of the sow. He understood what needed to be done, but for him, he was sure it would be different. For a man and a woman had love, and somehow Felipe was sure that the love between them would be the difference.

"When a woman offers you a meal, she wants you to enjoy it," Felipe said, trying to figure it out as he said the words. "She doesn't care if you understand how she made the meal or how many times she has cooked it before. She only cares that you both enjoy the meal together. Let the woman cook for you, Tomás."

This somehow made sense to Tomás.

And for the first time all night, he didn't fight the sleep.

Eyes closed, he gave in to it.

seven

The morning began with the smell of rich chocolate.

The women were up before the sun was even awake, taking turns stirring the copper pots filled with powdered roasted cacao beans and cinnamon. On the iron griddle they threw the flour tortillas that their hands had patted into shape, round and flat, and just the right size for the little hands of the children, who waited their turn at the skirts of their mothers. If there were any tortillas left over, the men would eat them, along with their cups of strong chocolate. The women would wait and be the last to eat, whatever was left. And if there was nothing, well, they would offer up their hunger pains to the suffering souls of Purgatory and get on with their day.

But Petra would do things her own way.

When she took her turn at the griddle, she made sure that the tortillas were smaller and thinner, so that more could be made. While Mercedes handed them out to her girls and Martín's boys, Petra made certain to slip some extra tortillas under her shawl, hiding them from the others. Later she would hand them secretly to her sister while she helped Mercedes onto the back of her mule. Once the line began to move out, and everyone's attention was somewhere else, Mercedes could gratefully fill her growing belly, feeding the baby that was there inside of her.

Thanks to Petra.

With the rain gone, there was only sunshine and not a cloud above them as the caravan traveled forward. Even in the early morning hours, the air was warm and thick. By midday it had turned hot. Very hot. After hours of traveling, and with no breeze to ease up the heat, the people were starting to get sluggish and dazed. Many drank from their *botas*—the leather bags that were once plump and sweating from the water carried within them. Now they were flat and crumpled, with not much water left inside.

The land had changed into a desert before they had even noticed. Dry and parched like the people moving across it, there was little sign that rain had fallen here. The dirt their feet walked upon was cracked and packed hard. There were no trees for shade or thickets for shelter. There was only the heat, and it beat down on top of them without mercy.

The long line of travelers grew longer as those on foot fell farther behind, with Domingo bringing up the rear. Sweat poured out from him, soaking his shirt as much as the rain had soaked it the day before.

Felipe's mule, with both of Domingo's girls on its back, was slowing its gait. And even though Felipe took the reins of the animal at the front, and pulled at it to hurry it along, the mule did what he wanted, or at least what he could manage, and what he could manage wasn't much.

Rivera looked back over his shoulder at his people and saw them fading away with the heat. He signaled his corporal to ride closer.

"How much water do we have left?" he asked Ortiz.

"Only what's in the *botas*, Capitán."

"We need to ration the water."

"These people drink every time their mouths get dry," Ortiz shrugged, not caring to hide his displeasure with them. He'd rather be chasing heathens than playing nursemaid to a group of peasants.

"We need to make them stop drinking," Rivera said.

Ortiz didn't have to be told an order twice, especially one that meant more discipline and a stronger hand. Pulling his reins, he turned his horse around and headed down the long line of travelers. "Save your water!" he yelled, with not an ounce of kindness, not even for the women. "No more water! Put the *botas* away!"

One by one, the people did as Ortiz had ordered them, lowering their leather *botas* and stowing them away. Everyone did as they were told.

Everyone except for Domingo.

Not content with only one *bota*, he also carried an extra one for his children. That's the one he held up to his mouth and drank down as much as he could before having to put it away. But before he could lower it from his lips, a whip knocked it out of his hand.

Corporal Ortiz was at the other end of that whip.

"That's an order, *tonto*!" Ortiz spit the words out, from the saddle of his horse. He was calling Domingo a fool—an insult and a challenge. But the whip made the match uneven; Domingo did not have the power to square off with him. Ortiz knew this, and it made him smile.

"You follow my order—you fat pig of a *tonto*! Or you'll be feeling my leather on your back!" Ortiz snapped his whip again, close to Domingo's face, knocking him backwards and making him fall into the dirt. Spurring his horse, the corporal headed back up to the front of the caravan.

Domingo reached over for his fallen *bota* on the ground near him. The spout was still open, and all of the water now sat in a puddle in the dirt.

The water was gone.

EIGHT

A body can last longer without food than water.

The people on the caravan did not know this.

But Rivera did, and so did Corporal Ortiz and the lieutenant. They knew what the heat could do even to a *soldado*—to one who was trained and whose body was strong and disciplined. They had seen such men crumple into the dust, never to rise up again. And it could happen quickly, too, even to the strongest of men. But these people from Sinaloa were soft and untrained, without the grit of *los soldados,* and Rivera knew they could not last nearly as long.

It would hit the children first. They would lose their strength and walking would not be possible. With every step they took in the heat, Rivera could see the change coming over them. As more and more fathers began to pick up their small children and carry them, Rivera became worried. With no water going into their little bodies, no water would have to come out. The captain could see the children were in trouble when the little boys stopped peeing at the side of the caravan. And when the babies stopped crying out of weakness, with no water left inside them to make tears, it was time for Rivera to do something.

Martín's two sons had struggled to match the pace of their father as he walked at the front of the caravan, a leader for all the rest. Marco, the younger one, stumbled first, but Victor, his brother, caught him by the back of his shirt and stopped him from falling. A few more steps and Marco's legs gave out, tumbling the six-year-old to the ground. Martín scooped the boy up into his arms and carried him, as Victor matched his father step-by-step.

Rivera signaled his lieutenant to ride over to him. Rios pulled his horse up next to the captain.

"How far before the mission?" Rivera asked.

"Another two leagues, Capitán."

"At this pace, we won't get there until the sun is gone."

"The thirst is slowing the people down."

Rivera too was beginning to feel the heat, and he took off his hat and wiped his brow clean from the sweat. Pulling at the reins, he slowed his horse to a stop. Lieutenant Rios and Corporal Ortiz followed his lead. The people in the caravan slowed their footsteps and halted.

"Tell them they can drink now," Rivera said to his lieutenant. "They can drink as much water as they want from their *botas*."

"All of it, Capitán?" the lieutenant asked, surprised by the command.

"What difference does it make if there's still water in their *botas* but they're too dead to drink it?" Rivera answered. "These people need to pick up their pace and move faster. Or they will never taste the water at the mission."

The lieutenant pulled on his reins and turned his horse towards the caravan. Galloping alongside the people, he shouted to all of them. "Drink now! Drink as much water as you want! There's more at the mission up ahead!" Down the long line of villagers the lieutenant rode his horse and repeated the command for all of them to hear.

But the villagers just stood there.

No one made a move, and not one of them reached for a *bota*. Everyone stood as still as could be, with all eyes on Rivera. Their

46

silence is what made him turn, spinning his horse around to face them. And facing them, he saw why they did not speak.

Their *botas* were empty.

All of them had been thrown to the dirt.

Rivera signaled his two officers to his side. "Put the smaller children on the mules. Get them off their feet. Double them up, if you have to. If there's no room with their own family, put them on another mule. We need to move them faster!"

While the corporal and the lieutenant dismounted and started to move through the line of people, picking up the younger children and lifting them onto the backs of the mules, Rivera walked his horse over to the men and older boys at the back. He looked at them, sizing them up for strength. There were four boys in all—all of them big and strong.

"Which boy is the fastest here?"

Each shot up his arm high above his head, shouting to the captain to be noticed, pushing at one another, showing off, wanting to be chosen. It was what Rivera wanted to see—to measure the strength still left inside them. He would use this energy and their youth to push the people farther.

"Show me!" Rivera challenged them. "Come to the front and keep me company. Show these old men in the back what they don't have!" He taunted their fathers, making it into a game. A competition among men—the ones grown, and the young ones still growing. The boys eagerly accepted the challenge, and Rivera spurred his horse forward, alongside the boys who now raced one another for the front of the caravan.

Once in place up front, they jockeyed for position—to be closer to the lieutenant, the corporal, and—for one lucky boy— to be at the side of El Capitán.

That boy was Victor, who had left the side of his father to challenge the other boys.

"What's your name, *hijo*?"

"Victor Símon Luna, Capitán!"

"Think you can keep up with me?"

"I can lead you, if you want!" Victor said, with no hesitation and sounding just like his father. Rivera laughed at the boy's cockiness. This was what the captain wanted. This was what they needed to make them forget the heat: a boy without fear. Bold and brash. And too young to fear death.

"Come on, show me, then!" He beckoned to Victor.

Victor took the lead at the front of the caravan. Unafraid, he started walking with a faster pace than before. Steady and strong, he led the way, with Rivera on his horse at his side. The caravan picked up the pace now, with Victor showing them how. And the men at the back, not to be outdone by such a young boy, met the challenge and pushed themselves harder, matching Victor step-by-step.

Even Domingo found a second wind; pushed on by his nephew, he tagged along with the rest. As Victor's footsteps quickened their pace, Rivera, jogging along, spurred his horse to go faster and everyone followed.

Including Martín.

He would make sure to stay close at the side of his son, matching each one of Victor's quickening steps with his own. A Luna was destined to lead the people—Martín had known this in his heart his whole life. For right now, that leader would be Victor. But Martín's time was coming, he was more than sure.

If they survived, he would be the one to save them.

nine

The people kept going, trusting Rivera to lead them.

El Capitán knew this land as well as he knew the faces of his sons. He had traveled this path, on this *camino*, gathering up the Jesuits, and arresting them when the king had commanded it—and escorting the Franciscans into their place, when ordered to do that next. When the First People of these lands had grown restless and the command was to make peace with them even if it meant war, Rivera traveled this *camino*, learning where the streams were, where the rivers met the sea, and where the wells were dug deep.

Water was the heart and soul of this country.

Without it, the land was dead. Without it, there would be no Spanish footprints upon it.

This is what their maps showed them. Not just the shape of the land, or the names of the places. What mattered the most was where water could be found. It was the only reason they could live on this land at all. Or move from one place to another. Water would always have to be close. And with a map in hand, Rivera would never be lost in this wilderness.

That's why the people followed him.

The next stop on the captain's map was Cohohia—a tiny outpost put there by a Jesuit. There wouldn't be much at this place, just some modest straw huts and a small adobe dwelling that served as a church during the day and as a place for a *padre* to rest his head at night before going on to the next *visita,* the next group of converts, the next to be saved. But what was there at Cohohia was more precious than any cross a Jesuit might carry.

There was a well.

The only water in the area.

The caravan reached Cohohia before the sun had grown tired and slipped from the sky. The ground they walked upon was still hot from the day, and ahead of them, through the heat waves, they could see the outline of an adobe.

A great cheer went up as they saw it.

Rivera gave the orders for his lieutenant and corporal to gallop ahead and to start bringing up buckets of water from the well, and Ortiz and Rios raced forward on their mounts. As the caravan moved closer, the look of the ground changed. Groups of bent and broken reeds—dried out from the sun—lay scattered in piles. The huts, broken and empty, dotted the path on the way to the church, and the *ranchería* for the local tribe looked as deserted as the land.

The smell that filled the air told them why.

When they reached the church, they could see with their own eyes.

The walls of the small adobe chapel were blackened and charred. Parts of the back had crumpled into the dirt. The smell of fire was still strong, and ashes covered the soil. There was nothing left of what had once been a church and a dwelling place for priests. Rivera dismounted and walked closer to the ruins. He was puzzled by what he saw—everything had been fine when he had passed through on his way to Sinaloa just two weeks ago.

"El Capitán!" shouted the lieutenant from behind the adobe.

Rivera walked over to the back of the small church where Rios and the corporal stood.

Under the shelter of a charred wooden awning, there was a large stone-lined well. Ortiz pointed down inside and Rivera leaned in to take a look. Black eyes are what he saw first—four of them staring up at him. And flies circling around them. The stench was so strong Rivera had to cover his mouth. Two horse heads, large and bloated in death, were visible through the water, with the bodies of the animals submerged and a hoof here and there sticking out.

"The water's no good. They've tainted it," the lieutenant said.

"Goddamn heathens." Ortiz spit into the well.

"The Mayos have no reason to do this," said Rivera.

"The Yaquis maybe. Or a Seri raiding party stirring up the tribes?" The lieutenant looked to Rivera for some answers.

"What difference does it make?" Ortiz said angrily. "We should've killed them all when we had a chance."

"The people can't go on without water," Rios reminded his captain.

Rivera looked at the sun still hot above the horizon.

"We make camp here," Rivera told his lieutenant. "Put up the tarps and the tents."

It didn't take long for the word to spread among the people. They didn't need Rivera to tell them what one person had already whispered to another, passing it from family to family. They had been promised water, but there was none to be found at Cohohia.

When Rivera faced them, they already knew the truth. "We stay here for the night! Unpack the mules!" the captain shouted to the people.

No one moved.

Rivera was not used to his commands not being carried out. He didn't understand why they all just looked at him, but no one moved or did as he was asked. Maybe it was the heat, and they needed to hear more. "The sun won't be down for twenty minutes," the captain explained. "You need shade from the tarps!"

Mercedes stood with the rest of her family at the center of

51

the people. Her two little girls, Carmen and Imelda, sat on the ground in the shade of their mother's body, at the hem of her skirt. In her arms, she sheltered with her shawl little Maria, who was quiet now and not the active child she had always been.

This mother would not wait for the men to speak first.

"We need water!" Mercedes shouted. Murmurs among the people began, agreeing with her. They were exhausted from the long hours of traveling and weak from lack of food. But they were still strong enough to say no to doing what they were being asked now to do: to believe in Rivera, to follow blindly, to not ask questions.

Rivera was being challenged, and it was something new for him. The ranks of his *soldados* always did as they were told. But these people were different, and he wasn't quite sure how to make them do what he needed them to do.

But Ortiz knew how.

When the captain hesitated, the corporal reached for his whip and took a step forward. These people meant nothing to him. Half-breeds, most of them; not one was a Catalonian. Not a true Spaniard among them. Ortiz didn't need to be told their pedigree; the color of their skin betrayed most of them: dark like the savages living here. The Spanish they spoke was barely understandable, and their food made him sick. There was no difference between them and the barbarians they were trying to replace. He would happily use his whip on any of them.

Rivera ordered Ortiz to stand down.

"Put it away!" he commanded the corporal. These people were different, and Rivera knew that. *Soldados* did what they were told, but these people—women and children—needed to be handled with a softer touch.

"You can protest as much as you want, but it won't bring you water!" Rivera addressed the caravan. "What we need is shade. Put the tents up and rest. There's a river waiting for us just ahead, and there will be water tomorrow! But if you don't do as I tell you, then you will not see that river. And your children won't see it either!"

Rivera didn't wait for the people to answer. A true leader does whatever he has to do and expects to be followed. And what El Capitán had to do now was to show them that his life, like theirs, depended on action, not words. The mules had to be unpacked of the tents and tarps, so that is what Rivera started to do. He unbuckled the straps from the side of one of the mules and took down a rolled-up canvas.

"Ortiz!" Rivera shouted and tossed him the wrapped tarp.

The corporal had no choice but to drop his whip and catch the canvas.

Once the whip was dropped, the people began to step forward.

Together now, they all worked to raise up the camp.

The sun set, and the land began to cool.

There would be no fires that night without water for the cooking pots. And what the people ate was the last of what they had packed from Sinaloa for the journey. A few figs and some bits of cheese, if they still had anything left at all. For many of them, the thirst had taken away their hunger. Many of them simply slept, dreaming of the water waiting for them and praying that the night would give them the strength to make it to the river tomorrow.

But Martín was too impatient to dream.

His family was getting weaker. His little son who was always so filled with life, who was always trying to keep up with his big brother Victor, was quiet now as Sola held him. The little boy, who always struggled and squirmed, never wanting to be held by his mother, did not fuss now or want to be anywhere else except in her arms. His skin was burning up with fever, and there was nothing with which they could cool him down. When Martín's wife looked at him, her eyes were empty and without hope. But his son Victor looked at him with anger: How could his father simply watch and do nothing at all?

He couldn't.

Martín left the tent of his family and went to speak to Rivera.

"My son is dying," he said to the captain. "The little one— Marco. He's very weak. So are my sister's three little girls."

"The night is cool—that will help them," Rivera said, hoping it would be true.

"I can't live with myself if I do nothing. I'm telling you this so you understand my actions. I'm not yet one of your *soldados*. I'm not asking for your permission."

Rivera was puzzled by his words.

"Permission to do what?" he asked Martín.

While people slept silently in their tents, Lieutenant Rios helped Tomás tie down a few empty *botas* and several water jugs on the back of the pinto.

Sitting in the saddle, on top of the pinto, was Martín.

"We can bring more water if I go with you," Tomás insisted, looking up at his brother.

"One rider is more than enough. Stay and watch the family," Martín told his brother.

In the darkness, Felipe stood and watched. He saw the small group of men huddled around the horse with Martín mounted on top. He could guess what was happening. The river lay in front of them, and in the bright light of day, with all the heat that would come with it, the ride would be a long one. But one man traveling in the coolness of night, galloping at full speed, could reach the river more quickly. If he was truly a fast horseman, he could bring the river to them by morning.

Felipe stepped out of the darkness. Removing his *bota* from around his neck, he approached and offered it up to Martín.

"There's a little left. A few mouthfuls for the ride."

"Give it to my son," Martín told Felipe, refusing the *bota*.

Felipe held his hand up to Martín, offering it to him in friendship.

"*Buena suerte*," he wished him.

Martín accepted Felipe's hand, gripping it tightly. It was a moment of truce. And then he looked over at Tomás. "Watch out for this one," he told his brother, nodding in Felipe's direction. "And keep him away from Petra."

The last water jug was finally tied down, and the lieutenant pointed up to the sky. High above them the moon was big and stars filled the night. "Follow Polaris," the lieutenant told Martín. "That bright one, you see? You ride straight for it and never let it move its position. If it moves, you line it up again and follow it straight. North, you understand? North is where the river is."

The words had barely been spoken when Martín slapped hard the flank of the pinto and galloped off into the night, riding straight for the North Star. Once he vanished from sight, only the sound of his horse's hoofbeats told them he was still out there in the darkness, moving farther and farther away. Soon, not even the hoofbeats could be heard, and all was silent once again.

Martín was swallowed up by the night.

ᏀᎬᏁ

With Martín gone from the camp, Tomás would have to watch the family.

It was the first time that he had been left in charge. He made sure his *pistola* was close to him, tucking it under his shirt and into his pants. He would be the man Martín expected him to be, and his word would be the last one now.

"Where's Martín?" asked Petra when Tomás stepped into the family tent.

If Domingo had asked, he wouldn't have hesitated. Even Mercedes he could have answered with confidence. But Petra had a way of making Tomás feel small. You had to use the right words with her, or suffer her strength. And if you showed fear, she could destroy you.

"He rode off to the river to get water," Tomás explained, trying with all his might to stand tall, to face her and not apologize for it.

Petra couldn't believe what he was telling her. "Is he stupid?" she whispered low and urgently. "How could he leave us? We need him here! He's head of the family."

"I'm in charge. You listen to *me* now."

"You're a boy!" Petra laughed.

Tomás exploded at the words. "You women—you hold us

back!" He challenged his sister with anger, squaring off with her, unafraid. "We could all be galloping to the river right now instead of poking along on mules. A man can ride fast without women and children holding him back!"

"It was your idea to bring us out here! For what—to die?" Petra said, not backing down. Tomás pushed past her as he removed Felipe's *bota* from around his neck and moved over to where the children were sleeping. Petra followed him, not giving up. "Where did you get that *bota*?"

"Felipe gave it to Martín for the children. There's a little water left." He held it up for her to see. The bottom of the *bota* bowed outward from the water still inside of it. There wasn't much of it, not nearly enough for all five children.

"And which child do you give it to?" she asked him. "Which child do you save?"

Petra knew what his answer would be.

No answer at all.

Felipe was asleep at the entrance of the recruits' tent. A presence standing above him cast a shadow from the moonlight. When Felipe opened his eyes, he saw Petra standing there.

"Did you think this would save us?" she asked, holding out his *bota* for him to see.

Felipe sat up and took the *bota* from her. "For the children, it might," he answered her.

"Which children and how many? A little for all, or all for one little one? And who will decide this? You?"

Felipe stood slowly and faced her. Maybe it was the heat or the exhaustion that pushed her to go further. To not hold her tongue when faced with a stranger, a man who was not even her family. "What do you know about children? You don't have children. You don't even have a family!" she said to him angrily.

Petra's words hurt Felipe, but she didn't stop long enough to notice. "You should have gone for the water, not Martín," she told him. "*You* should have risked your life, not my brother! If you didn't come back, no one would miss you!"

Cruelty is a bitter fruit. You may not taste it at first, but the longer you chew on it, you can't taste anything but bitterness and you have to spit it out. Petra took a step away from Felipe, distancing herself from her words. Her anger cooled and, in its place, tears started to fill her eyes. "You and Martín make all the decisions, and we have nothing to say about it," she said, more softly. "You lead and we always follow. No matter what we want."

She didn't mean just Mercedes, Sola, Beatriz, and herself. Petra was talking about all the women who were there because the men had decided to go. If they died and the children died with them, it would not be on the souls of the mothers, sisters, and wives who had nothing to say about them being there.

Felipe understood this. But there was nothing he could say to make it different. Not wanting him to see the tears in her eyes, Petra turned away from him and hurried back to her family tent, disappearing inside of it.

These were the most words Petra had ever spoken to Felipe.

He only hoped they wouldn't be the last.

ELEVEN

When dawn came and there was no sign of Martín, Rivera kept his fears to himself.

The people started to wake up, and all eyes were on the horizon, searching it for some sign of hope. All thoughts were on Martín. Where was he and why wasn't he back?

Only Rivera knew how the easiest road could quickly change for the worse. A fall in the darkness. A bear at the river. *Indios* or *banditos*—an arrow or a bullet—each one was just as bad. There were many dangers that could cross the path of a lone horseman; a man who was unlucky could vanish forever.

It was too soon to say all was lost.

And Rivera would not be the one to say it.

But as the sun moved higher in the sky and the heat grew stronger, the people started to think it. How could they not? They looked at their captain, and they waited for his command. And he said nothing.

But inside he was thinking how long should he wait? The more time that passed, the more hours they were without water, robbing them of their strength. Should he keep them there, hoping and waiting? Or move them forward before it was too late to move them at all? Some of them were stronger and might survive if they went forward. It was a risk, but was it worth taking?

Finally Rivera shouted his command. "We move out!"

The tents came down and the canvas tarps, too, taking the shade with them. The people stood now in the naked sun, unprotected. The men packed up the mules, tying down the heavy bundles. For one of the animals, the burden was too great and its legs buckled with the heat. It was one of the Luna family mules—the one on whose back was tied the *arcón*. The weight of the wooden chest was too much for the animal, and the mule fell to the ground.

Tomás quickly grabbed the reins of the mule and yanked hard. "Up!" he shouted at the beast. "*Arriba!*" No matter how hard he pulled, the animal could not move its body; it was too weak. Yanking again, and prodding the hips of the mule with his boot, Tomás tried to get the animal to stand.

But it was hopeless.

Quickly, Tomás unbuckled the straps, freeing the pack and the *arcón* from the animal's back. All of the supplies of the family and the wooden chest fell off the back of the mule and into the dirt. Its back now freed from the extra weight, the mule struggled to stand once again, with Tomás using the reins to guide the animal up to its feet. Finally, the mule stood with weak and shaky legs but only for a moment. Then it crumpled to the ground once more.

In less than a heartbeat, a single shot rang out loudly. Blood seeped from a bullet wound above the animal's eyes.

"Move that shit to another mule!" Ortiz called out, as he lowered his pistol. The sudden violence stopped Tomás where he stood, and he couldn't move. Ortiz grabbed the recruit by the collar. "You want to bake your balls out here all day?" the corporal shouted, shoving Tomás to the ground where he fell among his family's things.

Felipe led his mule over to Tomás and helped him up. Together, they began to pick up the Luna belongings, strapping everything onto Felipe's mule. The *arcón* lay on the ground, with its latch broken and some of the beautiful silk clothing spilling out in the dirt. Ortiz's boots stepped on top of a pure white ruffled blouse, and the corporal looked down at the richly carved wooden chest. Bending, he started to pick it up.

Petra's hands got to it before his.

"This belongs to my family, *señor*," she told Ortiz, in the softest of voices. "Your filthy hands will never be fit to touch it," she said, adding a polite smile at the end.

Ortiz was filled with anger. "Are you going to let your whore of a sister talk to me like that?" he said, as he grabbed hold of Tomás by the neck, pulling him closer.

"Ortiz!" shouted the lieutenant, who was watching on top of his stallion. "Put the weapon away and mount up." Ortiz was not the best of men, but as a soldier he knew who ranked above him, and he did as his lieutenant ordered. Holstering his pistol, he mounted his horse, and with a snap of the reins, he galloped away.

As Petra bent down, gathering up her mother's clothing, Rios climbed down from his horse and moved over to help her. "I'm sorry for your troubles, *señorita*," said the lieutenant. "*Con su permiso*," he added, as he bowed to Petra, asking her permission to help her gather up the family belongings.

Petra's eyes avoided his, as was the custom of the day—for a woman was not to be bold and look at a man. But even as she lowered her eyes, nodding yes to him, she was more than aware that Rios was a good-looking man who wore the uniform well, and his manners matched the finest of *españoles*.

"Please forgive the vulgarity of my soldier," the lieutenant said, as he handed the clothing to Petra. He bent down to pick up the wooden chest. "This is much too beautiful to ride on the back of a mule." He wasn't just talking about the family's hope chest. The true beauty was not what he held in his hands but what stood there in front of him.

If Petra had any doubt at all about the meaning of the lieutenant's words, he quickly answered her uncertainty. "You are too much of a lady to be treated as anything less," he said gently. No sweeter words had ever been spoken to Petra. Damn the custom of the day, she had no other choice but to look at his face directly.

He had eyes the color of the sky.

Petra had never seen such a man as this one. Everything about him was golden—from the pale brown wavy locks that covered his head, to the fine yellow hairs on his sun-kissed arms. Rios was *rubio*—blond—in a country that was filled with darkness. For a moment, Petra forgot to breathe.

She liked very much what she saw standing there.

ᏇWELVE

The people struggled to go forward.

With every breath, they prayed it wouldn't be their last.

At the front, leading the way, Rivera set the pace, slower than before but still steady and sure. At his side, Victor walked, trying hard to keep up and to help lead the people onward. But sometimes the spirit is stronger than the body, and youth does not have the wisdom to know its limits. The task was too great for Victor, and his legs gave out. He fell to the dirt.

A shout from the caravan stopped Rivera, who turned to see the young boy on the ground. The captain was off his horse and over to Victor in moments. The boy lay unconscious in the dirt, as Rivera kneeled down close to him. As he stripped the shirt off Victor, the captain ordered the lieutenant and the corporal to stand over him to cast some quick shade. Fanning the boy with his shirt, the captain tried to revive him.

Yet Victor did not move.

Sola pushed her way through the soldiers to her son, kneeling next to him and crying when she saw how pale Victor looked. Taking his hands in hers, she pleaded with him: "Get up, Victor. *Por favor, mijo.*"

But even Sola's tears did not help her son.

Rivera could not stand by and watch the life slip out of this boy. Pulling his dagger from his belt, he rose to face the caravan. With one swift and certain move, he grabbed the lead mule and ran the blade across the animal's neck, severing its jugular and killing it where it stood. The body hardly had time to drop to the ground before Rivera entered the blade a second time in the belly of the beast, ripping it open. Plunging his fist into the abdomen, Rivera pulled out the bloody bladder of the mule; it was still plump and full. He carried it over to Victor, poking a hole in it with the tip of his knife and squeezing a stream of urine onto the boy's face and chest.

Victor startled at the touch of the hot liquid and groaned as Rivera continued to squeeze the urine from the mule's bladder onto his skin, trying to cool him down.

Petra and Mercedes knelt at Sola's side, as Sola held the hands of her son and prayed softly.

All of the caravan stood silently, watching as Rivera tried to stop this boy from dying. The only sound was Sola's soft crying and her whispered words to the Blessed Mary—one mother begging another to save her son's life.

But then Petra heard something else.

There was a sound somewhere off in the distance—a faraway rumbling and the slightest of vibrations. Looking out across the horizon, Petra searched for the source of it.

And that's when she saw it.

Dust swirling in the distance.

Standing, Petra raised her hand, shielding her eyes from the sun, watching as the large cloud of dust moved closer, growing louder, and heading straight for them. When she was sure of what she was seeing, she pointed and shouted.

"Martín!"

On the back of the pinto, Martín galloped with the speed of the angels. Five other horses, with the king's strongest *soldados* on top of them, tried to keep up with him. But Martín was the fastest of them all; master of the whip, he shouted and spurred on the pinto, pulling ahead of the soldiers and racing for the caravan. One by one, the people started to see them, and they rushed out to meet the horsemen. They knew what was on those horses and what was being brought to them. And they would not wait for it to reach them.

It was water. Barrels of it! And leather *botas*, plump and sweating.

When the horsemen and the caravan met up, the people's hands reached up to pull down those strapped barrels and *botas,* ripping them from their leather ties and fighting with one another to have the first drink.

Martín pulled out his *pistola* and shot up in the air. Not waiting for the soldiers to take charge, he began to give orders. "Make a line! Or nobody drinks!" Martín yelled at the people. He pulled the children up front, letting them go first, followed by the women, with the men all the way at the back. Only then would he let the soldiers begin to ration out the water.

Martín took charge and told the five soldiers what to do and when to do it; he did this because of who he was and what he had done. Felipe might have given them fire when they were cold and hungry, but Martín had brought them water in the desert. Because of him, their children would not die. Because of him, these families would have a future.

Martín had saved them.

GHIRGEEN

Victor was not there to give his father a hero's welcome.

He couldn't throw his arms around him or see the pats on his back or the smiles of welcome. The boy was weak, unable to move, and he lay on the ground silently, where he had fallen. When Martín did not see his family with the rest of the people he went looking for them, and that's when he saw Victor.

"He's not well," Rivera told him softly.

But Martín ignored the captain's words. When he saw the tears in Sola's eyes, he pushed past his wife and told her roughly to be still. He didn't like seeing his eldest son there in the dirt like some pig in a trough. Victor was a Luna, and he deserved better than that.

"Get up," Martín told his son. The boy looked up at his father, his eyes wide and uncertain. "You're not a baby. Don't make me treat you like one." Victor slowly tried to sit up. Too slowly for Martín. "Don't make me have to pull you up. Get on your feet!"

Victor tried with all his might to move his body, to push himself up, to stand. But no matter how hard he struggled, the sweat covering his brow, he could not obey his father's command. His legs would not hold him, his arms could not bear his weight. He was failing his father, and when the tears started to well in his

66

eyes, no matter how much the boy fought them, he knew how greatly he was shaming him too.

It was his tears that told Martín just how sick Victor was. His son would never humiliate him like this. A strong boy, Victor had always been his pride. Only death can make a man so weak he becomes a child. Martín scooped his son up in his arms like a little boy and carried him over to the line of people waiting to drink.

Felipe was already there, a *bota* in his hand. He removed the top and handed it quickly to Martín. Holding it above his son's head, Martín squeezed the sides of the bota and a steady stream of water found Victor's mouth. He drank quickly until he choked and started spitting some water back up.

"He shouldn't walk, not until he's stronger," Felipe said. No matter what he thought of this ignorant farm boy, Martín knew that Felipe spoke the truth. In a different place, at a different time, they could have stayed and waited until Victor was better. But that choice was not theirs. And Martín knew this too.

They needed to move on.

The five soldiers Martín had found at the river were part of a scouting party from the garrison at El Fuerte. They were tracking down the group of Seris who had destroyed the mission at Cohohia. The neophytes who had lived there in a *ranchería* of huts had been friends with the Jesuits and fought back against the raiding party. Two of the women and four children had been killed. They were Yaquis, and their people had never been friends with the Seris; they had fought with them over the years and feared their poison-tipped arrows.

With the Jesuits, and now with the Franciscans, the Yaquis had felt protected. That's why they had stayed at the mission. That's why they had let the *padres* teach them words they didn't understand and preach to them about their God named Jesus. That's why they had offered up their sons to be taught how to be good *españoles*. They had done all this, and in return the Spanish had protected them: the Spanish had guns and the Yaquis did not. Spanish bullets killed more Seris than Yaqui arrows ever could. But this last Seri raid had put a new fear in them.

"They ran off, every one of those goddamn Yaquis," the sergeant of the scouting party told Rivera, as he and his men readied their horses to move on. All of those years had come to nothing; all the prayers, the holy baptisms, and the Credos so patiently taught were now all forgotten. "They disappeared into the rocks like snakes."

"I have a boy with us who can't travel. He needs time to get better," Rivera said.

"Not here—it's not safe," the sergeant said, with a shake of his head. "We will escort you to the river." He put his foot in the stirrup and mounted his horse. "Too many people have died here already."

With these words, it was time to move out.

Whether they were ready or not.

FOURTEEN

With tent poles and canvas, the soldiers put together a stretcher for Victor.

They strapped the poles to the pinto—one on each side of its flanks. Victor was dragged on the litter behind his father, who rode now at the side of El Capitán. The captain recognized a true *soldado* when he saw one, even if that man didn't wear a uniform.

With Martín now riding the pinto, Petra had no choice but to ride on the back of Felipe's mule. It was the only animal without a rider, and like it or not, she would ride it. She and Felipe were betrothed—on her brother's honor—and she was duty bound to do as she was told. But Petra was the one holding the reins, and she knew how to use them. When Felipe got too close, walking next to her and the mule, Petra kicked the animal's flank, snapped the reins, and hurried to catch up to her sister and Sola. She would ride close to them and as far away from Felipe as she could manage. In this way, Petra did as she wanted and had her say.

With water in their bellies, the people moved more quickly. Soon the ground started to change; parched earth gave way to soil that was rich and sweet, quenched by some invisible stream underfoot. They could see plants and trees ahead of them, and these living things gave them hope. Their bodies could sense that water was near and that lifted their spirits, as well as their steps.

When you've known great thirst or hunger, it's not so easily quenched or the suffering forgotten. Even though the people of the caravan had drunk from the *botas* and the barrels, their bodies still thirsted—still wanted more water than their mouths had taken in. They had been moving for days; they had traveled long hours, their bodies ached and cramped. And when the promise of the river started to reveal itself, little by little, from the smell of moist soil and the shade of waiting willows, the people moved faster, reaching out for that promise.

And the river did not let them down.

Wide and full, the waters flowed, beckoning them into it.

Those who were walking did not pause, hurrying down the riverbank, the waters pulling them closer, drawing them into its coolness. The men at the back of the caravan ran quickly, diving into the waters. Even Domingo found his legs could move faster than he ever thought they could, and reaching the riverbank, he tumbled, belly-flopping into the water. The mules and horses stopped at the water's edge. Rivera watched on top of his white stallion as the people of his caravan took the time to know the river.

The bigger children held the hands of the little ones and let their feet touch the water. Mothers sat on the riverbank, holding their babies with one hand and, with the other, removing the soiled rags from around their bottoms. Splashing their *culos*, they washed them clean.

The soldiers waded deeper into the wide river; taking off their hats, they soaked them, and put them back on again, letting the water spill down their hot necks and broad backs. There was more water than any of them could ever use. And they sat in it, played in it, swam and splashed around in it. The people were feeling good again.

Even Victor looked better. This time when Martín offered him the *bota*, the boy was able to drink as much as he wanted, taking long sips and swallowing in greedy gulps.

On the banks of the river, the sergeant unrolled a parchment map and showed Rivera their route. "It's too dangerous traveling to El Fuerte. We go this way, on to Guaymas," he pointed off in a different distance. "West."

It wasn't what Rivera had planned.

But what can you do, when life is bigger than your plans?

You go to Guaymas.

FIFTEEN

The caravan traveled for two days and two nights.

By the third morning, the land started to change again. There were now lush grasses and chaparral, thick and green, growing more beautiful with every step they took. As the sun moved, they moved with it, until they saw rising up in front of them a big, dark mountain, like no other they had ever seen before.

One by one, you could hear as the people started to take notice. The little children giggled first, and the men all grinned. Before long, all the caravan was laughing, and even though the sight was not new to him, Rivera smiled as though discovering it for the first time. There in front of them in the distance, rising up to the sky, were twin peaks on the mountaintop that looked exactly like two teats. This was the mountain they called Teta Kawi—the Goat's Tits.

Rivera looked over his shoulder and beckoned to the caravan, pointing towards the mountain. This was where they were heading. At the foot of the mountain, there they would find Guaymas. Mercedes, with little Maria squirming on her lap, looked across her mule to Petra, "Just like a man to follow the *tetas!*" she said, with a laugh so big it rolled across the caravan.

It would take them the rest of the day to cross the wide plain leading to Guaymas. And the people were halfway across the flatlands when the fort came into sight. Perched on the foothills of Teta Kawi, the bright whitewashed walls of the garrison stood out against the rocky and barren mountainside. Huge, like the sun, it was a beacon for friends and a warning to foes. New and powerful, this fort had been built to show those who would challenge Spain that there would be no mercy, no compassion, and no peace without recognizing the strength of the *españoles*.

The largest fort in all of Sonora, it was built for the Sonora Expedition—Spain's solution to the *indio* rebellion. The Seris and Pimas, along with other allied tribes, had rejected peace, and had been terrorizing the land with fire and blood, attacking pueblos and ranchos, stealing livestock, burning down missions and homesteads, and killing the *vecinos*—men, women, and children— who lived here. Some of those they killed were their own people, neophytes who had found a place with the *padres* and who worked the fields of the missions for food and protection. The bloodshed had to be stopped, even if it took more bloodshed to stop it.

Spain fought back.

Soldiers were ordered up, eleven hundred strong. Highland Fusiliers from Mexico City, Catalonian Volunteers, and Spanish Dragoons from the motherland. Infantry of America from Louisiana and El Norte. Troops spread out across the provinces of Sonora, Ostimuri, and Sinaloa, stationed to defend against the rebels. Eleven hundred *soldados* against many thousands of *indios*—different tribes, different languages, but all with the same hatred.

Spain was outnumbered and outmaneuvered too.

The *indios* knew this land like a brother: knew where to hide, where to find water, when to attack, and where to stay low. They would hit hard, moving fast and striking in small groups, and then run away, disappearing like the wind. It was guerrilla warfare that took its toll on the *soldados* who were used to facing their enemies when they fought, not having them sneak up and attack in the dark after hiding for hours in thickets and rock formations. The *españoles* were hit hard at first, until they learned how to fight like the *indios,* swift and sudden.

Still, they were not able to beat the rebels.

The *españoles* needed help, and they soon found it in something they had never planned. The rebels who weren't killed by bullets started to fall sick from the diseases that found their way from the *españoles* into the families of the tribes. In the beginning, there were thousands of Sibubapas—more than the Piatos and Seris combined. But by the end of the fighting, after what the *indios* called the "yellow-vomit sickness" hit them, there were only a few hundred left.

With the deaths came peace.

The Guaymas fort was built to keep that peace.

Four tall towers at each corner watched out across the Guaymas plain—to the east, west, north, and south. The walls were three feet thick, made of the strongest adobe bricks. At the front were two large and heavy wooden gates with the coat of arms of Carlos III branded into the wood. It took six soldiers— three at each gate—to push them wide open for the caravan to enter. As they passed through the opening, with Rivera at the lead, the flag of Spain waved high above them on the tallest tower. This was as close to the motherland as any of these pilgrims had ever been.

Inside the fort, it was another world.

A village with everything you could possibly need: A granary for the storing of wheat and corn. Barracks for the soldiers. A chapel with a big iron cross on top. Vegetable gardens, and stalls for chickens, pigs, and goats. A commander's headquarters. Corrals for the horses. And a cemetery in the back.

The grounds inside were filled with life.

A blacksmith hammered at an anvil, while another shoed a horse. A wood-fired stone oven belched smoke as a soldier stoked it for the evening meal. A few men worked on top of roofs, patching them with mud and thatch, while groups of *soldados* stood in formation, muskets at their shoulders, with a salute for El Capitán and his caravan of new recruits with their families.

Petra had never seen so many soldiers in her life.

Everywhere she looked were men in blue coats and blue breeches, their collars and cuffs in scarlet red. Their short black boots were dusty with wear as they moved and worked or stood with eyes at attention, while in formation. Young men, handsome in their uniforms, outnumbered the fifty-two from Sinaloa. There were hundreds of soldiers, to Petra's eyes at least. Never had she felt so protected, so safe—and so watched.

These men could not help their eyes from watching. They had not seen an *española* in months, and as the caravan halted at the front of the compound, the women of Sinaloa were all that they could see.

And their eyes were hungry for them.

Not just for their beauty—for some of these women did not have great beauty—but each one in her long black skirt and long-sleeve blouse brought gentility into this place of men. The way the women moved as they were helped off the backs of the mules, their hands in the hands of their little children, keeping them close to their skirts, comforting them, the curves of their body, the softness of their skin: all this made them different, made them women. There was a calm they brought with their presence. Lust is not the only emotion held in a man's heart; so, too, is longing. For home. For family. For life. This is what the women of the caravan awakened in the men at the fort. And every man removed his hat at the sight of these wives, *novias*, and mothers.

For the Sinaloa recruits, this would be their first time as soldiers.

"Line up!" shouted Lieutenant Rios, and the men of the caravan hurried to stand abreast of one another the same way they saw the soldiers of the fort doing. Two lines of soldiers—the new and the seasoned—faced each other in the center of the compound.

They were a ragged group, these men of Sinaloa. Trousers were without belts and loose, a sign of the weight they had lost. Their tired faces were red and blistered from the sun. None of them looked like soldiers.

But Rivera did not treat them as anything else.

"Lieutenant Rios will be breaking you into groups," Rivera told them, as he walked along the line. "Each one of you will have a job to do—and, if God forbid, you don't attend to your tasks, you will answer to Corporal Ortiz."

Lieutenant Rios took a step towards the line and addressed the recruits: "You will be issued uniforms here and new ones in Monterey. Any man found out of uniform will be considered a deserter, arrested, and punished."

Domingo looked at Felipe standing next to him and whispered, "I hope they have something in my size."

"*Silencio!*" shouted the corporal, stepping in front of Domingo and facing him.

"Which of you knows how to read and write?" Rios asked the line of recruits.

The men all stood quietly. Only one hand went up.

It was Martín.

"You will be the Capitán's aide," Rios informed Martín. "You go with him now and stay by his side. Give your horse to the muleteers." Rios pointed to Domingo and Felipe, the closest recruits to where he stood. "You two will be muleteers," the lieutenant told them. "Take 1st Private Luna's horse to the corrals and come back for the mules." It was a simple order, one not difficult to understand at all. And yet something kept Felipe standing there. His brow wrinkled and his face grew pale. One look at him and you could see there was a problem. But it was not the lieutenant's job to make sure Garcia was happy.

"Move!" the corporal shouted, as he touched the top of his whip at his belt. Felipe stepped forward, reluctantly, and followed behind Domingo. Together the two of them started to walk over to Martín and the pinto.

With reins in hand, Martín led his horse towards them, meeting them face-to-face.

There was something in the way Felipe was standing that made Martín pause. He noticed Felipe's hunched shoulders and his head hanging low, how he didn't seem as tall anymore as God had made him. It looked as though Felipe was trying to use Domingo's size to hide behind him. Martín could always recognize fear—it made a person easy to beat. If Felipe was stupid enough to show fear, how could Martín not take advantage of it?

When Domingo reached out for the pinto's reins, Martín walked right past him and held out the reins to Felipe instead.

"Be careful with the pinto. She's not good with strangers."

Stepping away, Martín let the reins fall and Felipe lunged forward to catch them.

This was not the best thing to do.

Sudden moves spook a horse, and this pinto was no different than any other. She reared up on her back legs and squealed loudly. Her front hooves struck out at Felipe, pushing him backwards, and he fell hard on his ass, sprawling across the dirt.

All the recruits laughed, and the soldiers of the fort joined them.

The pinto reared again and this time Domingo lunged forward to grab the reins, but he just missed them. The mare, realizing she was free, bolted, with Domingo chasing her as best he could, while pulling up his pants as they threatened to slip down his legs. Felipe watched from where he lay, sprawled on the ground. The pinto had bested him, and worse than that, he was too afraid to chase after her or meet her face-to-face again.

The soldiers watched and laughed, and so did the women and children. Everyone except for Petra. She was embarrassed by the foolishness and shamed by Felipe, who was at the center of it and helpless to stop it. No one gave a hand or tried to help at all.

Not until the Red Sashes appeared.

Running out from the corral they came, the three Red Sashes, giving chase to the pinto and helping Domingo, who was clearly running out of breath. They were not *soldados*, these men. They wore the white pants and white shirt of a simple farmer, but what made you notice them was their long hair and the bright red sash each wore across his chest. The red sash told the world that these men were friendly to the *españoles* and were not rebels. They were *indios*, but their names and tribes were not important to the *soldados*; what was important was their red sashes, which meant they could be trusted. They were safe from the Spanish, and the Spanish were safe from them.

Two of the men wore boots, but the third, the one with white in his hair, was barefoot. He ran the fastest and was the first to reach the pinto. Squaring off with the mare, he kept his distance but faced her, looking directly into her eyes. When he was sure that he had the horse's attention, he lowered his head, bowing it to the mare.

The pinto stopped and watched the man. Slowly, the old Red Sash took a step closer towards her, never looking away. Focused only on her, he took one slow step after another, moving towards the animal.

The muscles on the pinto's flanks rippled, and a quiet filled the fort. All that could be heard was the sound of the horse's breathing as the old *indio* softly approached her, head bowed and eyes still locked on those of the animal. Slowly he moved closer but only if the horse let him. Carefully he moved, one soft footstep at a time. And when he was just a few feet away from the pinto's head, he stopped. Motionless, he stood in front of her. He was showing her he would not go forward; he was not to be feared. Bringing his hand up to his mouth, he licked it and put it into one of his pockets, to a stash of sugar hidden there. Then reaching back up to his forehead, he wiped the now-sugared hand above his eyes and across his skin. He looked directly at the horse and waited.

The pinto's nostrils flared and trembled. Her head lowered, catching a scent. She took a step towards the old Red Sash. The *indio* lowered his head, and the horse stretched her neck out, just within his reach. Still he did not move. The Red Sash respected where the pinto stood and he would not overtake her; he would not dare to claim her.

One more step, and the horse and man were face to face. The Red Sash leaned his head closer, and the horse stuck out her tongue and licked the sugar from his forehead. It was only then that the Red Sash moved his body next to the pinto. Horse and man rubbed gently against each other. The Red Sash ran one hand across her flank, and with the other hand, he took hold of the reins. With one swift and easy move, he suddenly mounted the pinto. It was a graceful and beautiful sight to behold.

Felipe watched all this, and he wondered two things.

Who was this man in the red sash?

And could Felipe ever be as fearless and confident as he was?

SIXTEEN

Most men and women have secrets.

They hold them close because sharing them is not a choice. Whether out of fear or embarrassment, they are not willing to risk being different, because in the eyes of those who watch them, being different means being less.

Felipe was terrified of horses. This was his secret—one he had kept close until that day in Guaymas. In our world, this secret might not matter. But in Felipe's world, horses were a big part of life. They were your partners that helped you build and work the land. They took you places, they helped you fight, and they helped you survive. From the time you could walk, you rode. A horse was as important to you as your own two arms and two legs. Being afraid of horses was like being afraid of yourself. It was shameful. And this is why Felipe kept it a secret.

Maybe if Felipe had stayed in Sinaloa, stayed a *vecino* hidden there in the village, his secret could have stayed there with him. No one might have known; it would have been his business and no one else's. He could have found ways to keep it hidden: used oxen for the plough, walked everywhere and never ridden. A secret can stay small in a small village.

Perhaps that's what Felipe's father had hoped for him. José had realized that Felipe was afraid of horses, crying at the sight of them in the corral. A father must decide whether to push a child or to wait him out. José had made a decision to teach the boy to ride, hoping that he would lose his fear. He worked with him every day, and finally Felipe could sit in a saddle and ride just like any other boy.

But horses always know when you are lying to them.

You have to be comfortable. The two of you have to find a peace, a way to trust each other. Otherwise you have problems. Fear inside of the rider gives fear to the horse, and as a young boy Felipe was still a little bit afraid.

That's why one day he fell, when he was about ten. Bucked off the back of a stallion as skittish as he was. It happened in a corral that was filled with horses. Felipe's stallion bucked and kicked and wanted to run. When a horse frightens, it can spread to the others. Soon all the horses wanted to take flight, but the wooden fences wouldn't let them. Their hooves struck the hard ground as they stampeded, and they struck Felipe as he lay on the ground. By the time his father reached him, Felipe was unconscious and covered in blood. They thought they would lose him that day.

But that was not God's plan. He wanted Felipe Santiago Garcia to stay alive to become a muleteer—a man of the horses. Sometimes we have to do what we don't want to do. Felipe had never understood this when he was young, but now he was at Guaymas; he had to do what he was told to do, and by God, he better learn how to do it.

This is why Felipe decided to watch the Red Sashes. They were invisible to the *soldados*, who never cared to look past the color of their skin and the features of their faces. Only Felipe noticed them, watching what they did every day.

Every morning, when there was work to be done—animals to be fed and groomed, fields to be attended, cooking fires to be built—the Red Sashes worked alone. At night, they slept apart from the others, outside and under the stars, not in the barracks.

Only when a scouting party was needed, and a Red Sash was made a guide or a translator, were they around the *soldados*. Only then did Felipe hear them speaking to one another. And only a few words at that: just simple words in Spanish, like little children talking for the first time.

But the old Red Sash—the man who had caught the pinto— never spoke at all. Not to the *soldados* and not to the other Red Sashes. They would tell him what to do, point and use words, and he seemed to hear them; he seemed to understand. But he never replied, never answered, not in the words of the *indios* and not in the words of the *españoles*.

"What's the matter with the old man?" Felipe asked one of the soldiers from the fort.

"Why do you care?" the soldier snapped back.

"I don't," Felipe lied, trying to fit in by not seeming too curious. "I just want to know if I can trust him around our horses."

"He's dumb!" the soldier said. "Dumb like an animal. Not once has he ever spoken." He spit on the ground, at the thought of it. "But don't worry, he won't give you any trouble. He's like a horse: we broke him!"

And that made the soldier laugh.

Felipe wondered what that meant—wondered how much it would take to break a man like a horse. He didn't have to think about this for very long because the next day he found out his answer.

The old Red Sash was in the corral, cleaning out the slop, and the heat of the day made him pause to take off his shirt. Felipe was there, too, brushing down the mules. He watched as the shirt came off the back of the old man, and as he turned away, that's when Felipe saw the thick, red welts crisscrossing the old man's back. He had been whipped, and the whip had left its marks deep and wide. Not one place on his back had been untouched by the leather. As Felipe stared at the scarred flesh, the old Red Sash turned his head and his eyes met Felipe's.

They were as black as a starless night. And just as paralyzing.

"Calixto!" One of the Red Sashes saddling up the horses called out.

It was the first time Felipe heard his name.

The old man was called Calixto.

SEVENTEEN

What the old man noticed first was how tall the *español* was.

And how his face was still that of a boy's, with the same curiosity upon it.

How could he not notice him? Everywhere he went the boy/man followed. Always there, just at his heels—but careful when he was in the corral with the horses. Keeping his distance but still watching. This one was who the *españoles* had laughed at. But what the old man saw in the eyes of this boy/man was not funny. It was fear.

Calixto had seen it many times in his lifetime. Too many times, in too many eyes that haunted him still. He only wanted to forget those eyes and how helpless his hands were then and how hopeless his heart was now when he remembered them.

But here it was again, in a boy/man of an *español* who simply would not go away, no matter what Calixto did: turning his back on him, staring him down, paying no attention to him at all. Still the boy/man watched him with the horses, even while he kept his distance. Silently, with no words between them. They didn't need words to understand each other. One was in need and the other could help.

Fear could be mastered. Calixto knew this. And he knew he could teach this to the boy/man.

But why should he? Why should he help this *español*? When everything inside of the old man had turned to stone, hardened and died. Even his heart. Especially his heart. And his words too, gone now, along with his caring. He was frozen inside—the words frozen there too. He had nothing more to share, no more feelings for anyone or anything.

Except those eyes that still haunted him, and now were there, in the eyes of the boy/man watching him. Always watching. And refusing to go away.

Calixto did not have the words to tell him no.

How could he tell him? And which words would he use? Not those of the *españoles*, which would stick in his throat and choke him. Not the words of his people, his home, his family. Those words would come screaming out of him, bleeding from within, not killing him, but ripping him apart while he went on living.

How could he tell the boy/man about Cmaam, his beauty, his woman? What words would he use for his little ones—Zaah, Iizax, and Hax—the sun, moon, and water of his life? There were no words he could use and no way to tell him. No words to match their beauty. Their innocence. Their youth. Their trust. How could any words make the boy/man understand—that everything had been taken away from him. His pride. His leadership. His love. His honor. His future. His people. They left him his body but took away everything else. And what good is a body when it does not crave life?

Even the whip couldn't make him care.

Or make him want to fight back.

Fighting had once been his answer. He would not be bridled like their horses. He would not give up his people and their land. Strike hard and run was his way. Hit them first! Conquer them before his people could be conquered! This was what he wanted and what he had told them. They were people on the move because of him.

Because they trusted him.

We keep moving, hiding when we have to. We know this land and it will shelter us, protect us, if we ask it.

The men followed him—they were strong and willing to fight. Ready to hunt the *españoles*. Striking fast like the puma jumping on the rabbit. Swift and unseen, hidden by the land before the pounce. But what about the family of the puma? What happens when the hunter goes off to seek the prey? How can the women and children be left alone with the old ones? With no protection, no warriors to guard them?

We bring them with us.

And the families went with them, moving and hiding as the warriors did. Wives, mothers, sisters, and all the children. They all went, following their leader. Following Calixto.

Because they trusted him.

They hid in the thick brush, day in and day out. The thorns ripped their flesh and pressed them low to the earth. The women and children moved when the warriors moved, hiding with them when the *soldados* came close. Keeping the little ones quiet and swaddling the babies to hush their cries, as the men readied their arrows and pulled back their bows. They watched from the thickets as the *soldados* fell, and when their guns shot back the bullets did not know who was the warrior and who was the baby, the child, the woman. The blood that seeped into the earth was the same. The soil knew no difference.

Still they stayed, hidden in the arms of the brush.

When the *soldados* rode off, beaten for the moment, dragging their wounded on the backs of their horses and leaving the dead for the buzzards, the warriors came out from hiding. This was their victory and they would celebrate it.

But not for long.

Because after the *soldados* were gone, they found their own broken and bleeding, the lifeless bodies of their own people. Many of them were not warriors. And that was when sound filled the thickets again; those who had been quiet now wept and wailed and clutched those who had fallen, many of them the little ones, the old, and the women.

Calixto could not stop them from crying. There were times when he was certain the tears of his people would never stop. But he had to keep them moving. Moving on to the next rock crevice and thicket, to any part of their earth that would welcome them, shelter them, and keep them hidden. He moved them onward, still holding their loved ones, to the next hiding place and the next battle.

One by one—family by family—he saw them perish. From the bullets of the *españoles*, and at times from the sicknesses that came from hiding, from moving without rest, with little food and whatever water, fresh or bad, they had for drink.

Calixto was lucky. His family survived longer than most.

Until one day the torches of the *españoles* found their thicket.

The fire was fierce, and it spread quickly. No one could outrun the flames, with the thorns holding them fast. Cmaam, his woman, his wife. And the sun, moon, and water of his life: Zaah, the baby Iizax, and Hax. Each one faced the flames and each one fell where she stood, the baby in Cmaam's arms, and the two little girls pressed tightly against their mother's side.

When the fire became embers, Calixto searched and searched, burning his hands and the soles of his feet. Endless seemed his searching, and hopeless too. He could not tell the ashes of his own family from the ashes of the others. He only knew they were gone by the screams he had heard, the screams that he recognized as his own life dying, the screams that he still heard: screams that took away his voice, took away his words, and burned his heart into ashes.

There were no words, no way to tell this story. Not to the ones left behind, his own people, and certainly not to the *español* boy/man. Without words, the old man had hoped that the memories would eventually fade away. But the eyes of his people would always be remembered, and their fear would always haunt him.

Here in front of him, he recognized that same look in the boy/ man. And he decided to do something to make it go away. Holding out the reins of the pinto to the boy/man, Calixto beckoned him to come closer. He would teach him how to master fear.

Maybe then Calixto could be forgiven.

EIGHTEEN

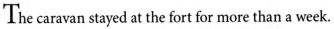

The caravan stayed at the fort for more than a week.

There was still no sign of the Manila galleon that was coming to pick them up, and the *comandante* had not received word when the ship would be on its way up the coast from Acapulco. The summer storms had been brutal on the Pacific, and there was no telling how long it would be before the caravan could take its next step across the fickle waters of the Sea of Cortez to the shores of Baja.

But to the people of Sinaloa this did not matter.

They had everything they needed there, as much water as they could drink and enough for the women to fill their cooking kettles for the thick stews and rich soups they now could make for their *familias*. There was plenty of fresh meat from the cattle, chickens, and rabbits that were kept within the safety of the thick adobe walls of the fort, and there were vegetables from the gardens. There were none of the hardships they had faced traveling from Sinaloa. Bruised and aching feet could heal while bellies were filled up, clothing was cleaned, and the sick recovered.

Victor got stronger and soon he was pushing away his mother's comforting hands, impatient with her fussing over him, eager to be back up on his feet again and racing with the other boys to show his strength. Maybe he ran a little bit slower than he did before, that's true. But if he felt weaker, he kept it to himself only. Time would heal him, he was sure. No one had to know this, especially his father.

Martín was too busy becoming a soldier to notice.

On their second day at the fort, all the men of Sinaloa were outfitted as *soldados de cueras*. From the heavy boots on their feet to the wide-brimmed black hats that covered their heads, they wore the uniform of Spain. Dressed in blue pants and blue shirts, with their collars and cuffs in scarlet red, a black kerchief around their necks, and a cape of royal blue, there was not much difference between them and the *soldados* of the fort. Except for one very important part of their uniform.

The *cuera*.

The men from Sinaloa were cavalry, and what separated them from other soldiers was the long, knee-length leather jacket called the *cuera*. Several layers of thick, rough buckskin, sewn together and held around a man's waist by leather straps, protected him in battle. Roughly made, its looks were not what mattered. Its thickness is what counted and the way it stopped an arrow from piercing all the way through to a man's heart or to his belly. If any men needed to be reminded of this, they could see it in the roughly sewn leather patches here and there on these old and well-used *cueras*.

Tomás's finger found a hole in his that went all the way through, and when he inspected more closely, he saw a reddish-brown stain spreading out from the hole. It was dried blood from the *cuera*'s previous owner. Crossing himself quickly, Tomás asked for another.

The women stood across the parade ground and watched as their men became soldiers. "Look, how noble!" Mercedes said to Sola, Bea, and Petra. But while the eyes of the other women sought out their own man, Petra's attention was not on Felipe.

She was watching Lieutenant Rios on top of his mount.

As an officer, he was dressed richly, with yellow collar and cuffs and real silver buttons. The insignia of his rank he wore on the shoulders of his blue coat: epaulets of silver lace outlined with rich yellow silk. His saber, sheathed in its scabbard, accented his trim waist and slid down the whole length of his long, muscular leg.

It was hard for Petra to look away.

And it's a good thing that she didn't. She might not have seen what happened next. A turn of her head too quickly and she would never have seen the lieutenant, handsome on his stallion, turn his head in her direction. The two looked at each other and the world fell away. For one brief moment, no one else existed.

And then Rios smiled.

While the men went through training, the women were kept busy watching the children and tending to the meals that they served three times during the day.

The two cooks of the fort were also Red Sashes. They shared their clay ovens with the women of Sinaloa, but the women pushed them away, unwilling to share their cooking fires with men, and in this way the ladies took charge. And, by God, the men of that fort ate meals so home cooked and delicious they could close their eyes and swear they were home by the side of their own families again, whether only a few miles away or miles across the ocean in Manila or Spain.

Lieutenant Rios always made sure he went to the kettle where Petra was dishing out the day's *posole* or rabbit stew. More than one portion he would ask for, just to be able to be close to this woman who was, without a doubt, the most beautiful woman in the caravan. And possibly of all the women he had ever seen there in Nueva España.

The smiles between Petra and Lieutenant Rios did not go

unnoticed. Mercedes saw it first, before Martín did. And how could she not say something to Petra?

"You need to save those smiles for the man you will be marrying," Mercedes told her sister.

"No one is asking me to say vows. I don't see a priest anywhere."

"Felipe is one of our own—a *criollo*. You knew his family, his sister. You know more about him than you know about this man with the shiny buttons and the sword."

Petra reached out and patted her sister's belly, which looked even bigger now than it did before.

"Take care of your own henhouse. Don't tell me how to watch mine." Petra always knew how to shut up her sister.

Mercedes covered her belly with her shawl and, for once, kept quiet.

"What is your youngest sister's name, Luna?" the lieutenant asked Martín as they sat together, finishing their supper.

"Maria Petra," Martín told him. "We call her Petra."

"'Petra' is female for *Peter*," Rios said. "And 'Peter' means *stone*."

"She's very headstrong, that's true." Martín laughed.

"Petra doesn't fit her," the lieutenant replied softly. "She's not a stone at all."

Martín was not so sure he liked the familiarity with which the lieutenant was talking about his sister. Or the way this man said her name gently, as though he owned it.

"She's not married, Petra?"

"Betrothed," Martín said, pointedly, hoping to end the conversation. The lieutenant looked over at Martín, waiting to hear the lucky man's name. "To Garcia," Martín added.

"The tall skinny one? The one who was knocked down by the horse?" The lieutenant laughed.

"They've known each other many years from the village. His father was a *soldado*. He fought in the same company with our father." Martín was feeling as though he had to defend not only Petra's honor but himself for the choice he had made by promising her to Felipe.

The lieutenant smiled and just shook his head. "That's the best you could give her?"

"She needs a husband."

The lieutenant shrugged. "That's a decision that shouldn't be rushed," Rios said to Martín, sounding more like an officer to a private, giving an order more than an observation. The lieutenant didn't wait for a response from Martín. Instead, he tossed the little bit left of his meal into the dirt, rose from the table, and left Martín alone to figure out if the lieutenant's words were an insult.

Or simply a wish.

NINETEEN

Felipe did not notice the lieutenant's interest in Petra.

He was too busy with Calixto, caring for the horses and learning everything he needed to learn to get back in a saddle again. This was no easy task. Just being in the corral took all of Felipe's efforts not to bolt, not to go running away as far as he could go. And in the beginning, that is just what he did, bolting and jumping over the gate, running like hell to the other side of the fort. Felipe just could not stay in that damn corral.

Calixto spent a whole day running after the boy/man, dragging him back and making him stay there to face the horses. At first, he had to tie Felipe to the wooden slats of the fence and let him twist and kick, like a wild pony. But the more time he stayed tied up like that, with the horses watching him, the more Felipe started to get used to them—to their smell and to the sight of them. Pretty soon, he started to calm down, and he stopped fighting to get free.

Once that happened, Calixto knew he could begin to work with the boy/man. He untied him from the fence and threw a rope around the neck of the pinto. Tugging at the long leash, he pulled the horse closer to Felipe. And the boy/man stayed where he was. This time he did not bolt.

Only now could he learn. Only now could Calixto teach him.

Slowly, the old *indio* showed Felipe everything he knew, all the tricks to calm the pinto, connecting with her to make her trust and follow. Fear disappears when two connect as one. The eyes meet in silence. The connection begins. Without words getting in the way, you have no choice but to trust. To forget your own fear by connecting with another. By the second day, Felipe could stand at arm's length and face to face with the pinto. The longer he stood there, the more comfortable he felt. The less he wanted to run, the more he wanted to stay. His fear went away and with it went the pinto's fear too.

Nothing now stood between them.

Nothing stopped them from moving closer to each other. Side by side they stood, so close they were almost touching. Felipe could feel her chest move with every breath she took. She could feel the warmth of him next to her. And when the pinto lowered her head, nudging his shoulder gently, it did not surprise him. Felipe's hand reached out slowly and answered her with his touch. Before he knew it, he was on top of her.

The two were now one.

El Capitán was impatient to move on.

To travel all the way to Monterey before the rains came, he would have to get his caravan moving again. They had months of traveling ahead of them before they reached what they would call their new home. The Sea of Cortez stood between them and the rest of their journey. One way or another, they had to cross it.

When the wind changed, it was time. Rivera could see it in the way the flag now moved, high above the fort, the fabric with its colors blowing towards the southwest. In the direction of Loreto.

The orders went out—it was time to pack up.

Out of the corrals, Domingo led the mules with their empty saddlebags hanging low on their flanks. Ahead of them all, and leading the way, was the pinto with Felipe on top of her, looking taller than he had ever looked before. Everyone's attention turned in Felipe's direction. No one could believe what they were seeing. How could this be the same man they had all laughed at? Felipe made sure they knew that it was. Walking the pinto proudly in front of them, he pranced and cantered her, picking up speed until he was galloping her gallantly across the grounds, one hand on the reins and the other holding his hat up high for all those he knew were watching him.

More than anything he wanted Petra to see him. To see he was a man who would never give up, even in the face of fear. This was one truth Petra could always count on. And he wanted her to know this. This was why he looked for her—searching the faces of the people in the caravan, looking from family to family for a sign of the Lunas. And pretty soon he saw them, packing up their belongings, with Petra among them. Galloping the pinto as quickly as the horse would carry him, proud to show her everything he had learned, Felipe raced to her.

Petra was busy with the children, holding Marco's hand in hers and juggling little Maria on her hip. But when the pinto raced up behind her, she turned around quickly to see who was the rider.

The sun was just behind Felipe, and his face was in darkness.

Even though her hand went to her forehead to block out the sun, Petra still could not see who it was. The swiftness of the ride told her the man in the saddle was skillful. Petra's thoughts were of the lieutenant—a fine horseman to be sure, one of the best in the caravan. She greeted him then with the warmest of smiles, welcoming the sight of him. Had Felipe's heart stopped at that moment, he would have died the happiest man in the world. But that was not to be. Instead, he climbed down off the saddle and the sun was no longer in Petra's eyes.

She saw the rider was Felipe. Knowing that took the smile away from her face. And Felipe's joy went with it.

He waited for her to speak—to say something was better than hearing nothing at all. It would not replace her smile, but he longed for something that told him she saw him. That he was there, a part of her life. Even if her words were harsh or angry. The words did not matter. Her voice alone was enough. But Petra was not kind enough to give him this. She answered him only in silence. Turning back to the children, she led them away. There was packing to do and she was eager to move on.

Felipe hoped that no one had noticed this.

But someone had.

Calixto.

TWENTY

The caravan headed for the sea that very same day.

It was an easy ride from the fort to the sands of the great bay overlooking the Sea of Cortez. Six Red Sashes on horseback, with Calixto among them, led the way for the single line of travelers, with Rivera and his *soldados* near the front and the families following behind. The mules came next, with Domingo and Felipe on their horses bringing up the rear.

They had only been traveling for an hour when the shape of the land started to change. Instead of the dry rocky hillside that had sheltered the fort, the land flattened out and became green. There were now salt marshes and mangrove swamps surrounding the caravan. It was like entering a little forest as they walked their horses under the canopies of mangrove trees. Above them, the branches were full and low, while beneath them, the hooves of their horses sunk into the moist earth. Their path narrowed and turned west, as they headed for a clearing through the dense marsh grass.

They could smell the sea before they saw it. Ocean breezes brought it to them. They could taste the salt in the air and their noses filled with the scent of sea life.

Martín, at the front of the caravan, was just behind Rivera. While his son Victor rode a tall black stallion next to him, little

98

Marco shared the saddle in front of his father. With every step their horse took and the closer they came to the water, the more frightened Marco became.

"I don't like the sea!" he protested.

"What do you know about it?" Martín laughed.

"It stinks!" Marco said, wrinkling his nose.

"You are very lucky," Martín said to his son. "Not many boys get to do what you are doing." Marco curled his lip up, not really caring. But Martín went on. "To go on an adventure on a great big ship! Bigger than anything you have ever seen before! Only the best boys go on a galleon—like the one your gran-mama went on many years ago with your papa. All the way from España on the great Manila galleon."

"You've been on a ship, Papa?" Marco asked, suddenly interested.

"Of course! Only the brave boys get to go!"

Marco sat up a little straighter. "I want to go!" Marco cried out, wanting now to be like his father. And since his father had survived, the sea must not be a bad place after all. "I like the sea," the boy admitted, reaching up and touching the roughness of his father's face.

The clearing in the marsh grass widened and gave the people of the caravan their first look at what lay beyond: the brilliant blue bay stretching out and meeting the Sea of Cortez. While the waves crashed roughly against rocky shores bordering the inlet, the water in the bay was quiet and calm. The winds blew gently and the water rippled softly.

It was a perfect day to sail.

And yet, no ship was in sight. No Manila galleon was anchored in the bay, and not one ship was on the horizon. The Sea of Cortez was empty. The only sight was a lone *soldado*, running out of breath and headed up the rocky shore towards the caravan.

It was Tio Pepe.

When he reached El Capitán and the other *soldados,* they could easily see he was not only out of breath but also drunk.

Watching him fall face down in front of them made them certain of this. It was nothing new for Tio Pepe. Looking for ships and drinking all day is how he lived his life. There was nothing to do on the beach and no one to do it with. His one and only friend was the agave plant that he used to make the milky white *pulque* he drank morning until night, and night until sleep.

Rivera had known Pepe when he was a young soldier, as someone better than what he had now become: a retired *poblador*, with no woman to keep him in line or children to stop him from being a fool. But when the ships were anchored there—when it was time to work, to unload the supplies or to make ready a launch—everyone knew there was no better workman than Tio Pepe.

"Has there been any sign of the ship?" El Capitán asked him, as Pepe lay sprawled on the ground at the hooves of Rivera's mount.

"*No, señor!*" was his answer, as he struggled to rise up from the ground.

"We are heading to Alta California, sailing on the supply ship that will be anchoring here," Rivera told him.

Pepe hiccupped and steadied himself on his feet. Reaching around to his back, he found his *bota* hanging over his shoulder and brought it around front. Unscrewing the tip, he held the sheepskin bladder up above his head, squeezing it tightly and drinking the long stream of milky white *pulque* that squirted into his mouth. Pepe tried to focus his eyes as he looked down the long line of the caravan. He wasn't sure at first what he was seeing, for what he saw was shocking to him.

"Are those women and children?" he asked El Capitán.

"Families of my recruits," Rivera answered him.

"*Ay, Dios!*" Pepe shook his head and crossed himself. Then he spit on the ground and squirted out another stream of *pulque* from the *bota* into his mouth. After a long drink, he took a step closer to Rivera's mount, stood on his tiptoes to stand as tall as his small, wiry frame would stretch, and he whispered to El Capitán.

"You think they will survive all the way to California?" he asked Rivera, in confidence.

"A ship would help" was Rivera's reply.

And he wasn't kidding.

Tio Pepe backed away. He was all business now.

"My eyes are a little bit clouded at the moment," he said to Rivera. "But even they can see the water is too still, and what little wind that blows . . . " Pepe wet one of his fingers and held it up in the air. "That little nothing of God's breath is blowing south. The north-easterners are gone for now. Won't be blowing that way for a while. No ships coming here soon."

"We need to cross that sea," Rivera said, looking out at the water. And then, turning back, he looked at Pepe with great purpose. It was a challenge he was offering. And he knew that no one loved a challenge more than Tio Pepe.

"That I can do," Pepe nodded, with his eyes now focused. "I can get you there!"

And for that one moment, Tio Pepe looked sober.

Just south of the bay, the Yaqui River emptied out into the Sea of Cortez.

This is where Tio Pepe led the caravan.

Too drunk to sit high in a saddle, he walked in front of them, leading the way. Pointing just beyond a bluff, he beckoned them to keep going—it wasn't far. And when they reached the top of the bluffs, they looked down and there they saw the river's mouth kissing the sea. This was where the packet ships would sometimes wait to transport supplies across the sea to Loreto. When there were no ships, the smaller boats, the *lanchas* with oars and a single sail, rested on the riverbanks, waiting for their bellies to be filled and to feel once again the water underneath them.

Four *lanchas* waited there for the caravan.

These four small sailboats would be a tight fit for the people and all their supplies and belongings. Four of the Red Sashes would also have to go with them. They knew this sea. Their people were fishermen; at home in their *balsas* made out of reeds, they paddled the sea, searching for sea turtles and diving for oysters rich with pearls. The caravan would need them to navigate these boats and man the sails, to bring them safely back to land—to the shores on the other side of the sea.

Rivera gave the order to dismount, and the people climbed off their horses. The packs on the mules were untied and belongings were loaded into the boats. The *arcón* was lifted from the back of the pinto, and Felipe struggled with the weight of the chest.

"Careful with it!" Petra said, as she stood off to the side.

"It's very heavy," Felipe said, with his finest of smiles.

"For you maybe," Petra shrugged.

The lieutenant soon proved Petra's point by coming to Felipe's aid and lifting the chest from the recruit until he held it easily in his arms.

"It's so beautiful!" Rios said. "Just like the woman who belongs to it."

"I had a good grip on it," Felipe said to his lieutenant, not wanting to be seen as the lesser man.

"Go grip something else," Rios ordered Felipe, with not the kindest of voices. Felipe bowed low to Petra and moved over to the other recruits. "This will sit with me," Rios told Petra, as he stood as close to her as her honor would allow. "I will guard it with all my strength, as I will you, if I am so fortunate to sit in your presence."

Petra had a feeling deep inside of her that she had never had before. Something burned low, deep in a place she had never known. Looking into his eyes was when she felt it, and looking away from him was not an option.

Until Mercedes came along.

"Get in the boat!" she yelled at Petra. "We don't want to lose you." She took Petra by the arm, leading her away, but not before throwing a glance in the lieutenant's direction, wagging a finger at him and letting him know he was pushing the limits.

While the *soldados* unloaded the mules, the corporal separated the people into families, watching them as they climbed into the boats. Ortiz wasn't the most patient with them. The women struggled with their skirts, while holding their children, as they tried to climb into the boats. Many of them stumbled, but Ortiz just watched and did nothing to help.

This did not sit well with Mercedes. She struggled right in front of the corporal, holding Maria in her arms, as she lifted up her petticoats. She clearly needed a boost up into the boat.

"Are your arms broken?" she asked the corporal.

Ortiz looked at her but did not speak.

"Are you too weak to lift these children? To help them into the boat?" Mercedes asked, hoping to embarrass the corporal into action.

Ortiz smiled at what could only be a jest. "They have mothers for that," he told her. "They're your brats, not mine." Ortiz moved away to supervise the loading of another launch.

Mercedes was about to shout after him, but Petra stepped up and shushed her. Taking Maria from out of her arms, she held up her sister's skirt, and Mercedes climbed over the side of the boat, tumbling into it.

Calixto, with two other Red Sashes, loaded a second launch, working alongside several recruits, with Felipe and Domingo among them. "Speed it up!" Ortiz shouted, as he came up behind them. The two younger *indios* made an effort to hurry up their work, but Calixto did not even look at Ortiz as he slowly packed up the boat. "You move too slow, old man," the corporal said. Calixto did not turn or say anything at all. "I said move!" Ortiz pushed Calixto from the back. The old *indio* fell forward into the boat. The corporal laughed and watched as Calixto slowly pulled himself out of the launch, standing up again to face the corporal. "When I tell you to move, you move. You hear me?" Calixto stood silently in front of Ortiz but he did not say a word. This did not make Ortiz happy.

"What's the matter with you, old man?" The corporal reached for the whip on his belt.

Felipe and Domingo stopped loading up the boat and watched the corporal and Calixto as they faced each other.

"When I speak to you, you answer me. You understand?" Calixto did not answer.

Felipe waited for someone to speak up—to say something. But all the *soldados* kept their heads down and did their work. No one wanted to stand up to the corporal, not with the whip in his hand.

"He can't speak," Felipe said, the words tumbling out of him before he could even stop them. Now the corporal turned his attention to Felipe.

"What do you know about it?"

"I worked with him. He's good with the horses."

"The other heathens speak," the corporal said, moving over to the two nearby Red Sashes. "You speak, *comprendes?*" Ortiz unfurled the whip at their feet, snapping it.

"*Si, señor!*" both of the *indios* answered quickly.

The corporal smiled and moved closer to Calixto. "You see? That's how you do it. You speak—it's very simple." Ortiz ran the tip of the leather lash in the dirt around Calixto's feet. "Now, you do it. You say it for me: '*Si, señor!*' Say it pretty like that for me."

"He can't do it, *señor.*" Felipe said.

"I didn't ask you! *You* speak too *much!*" the corporal shouted. Felipe quickly took a step backwards, removed his hat, and bowed his head to the corporal with respect.

But Ortiz was not interested in Felipe's respect. He wanted it from Calixto, and if the old *indio* wouldn't give it up to him, he would simply take it. The corporal's hand slashed out, like a snake on its prey, and grabbed Calixto by the throat, pulling him closer.

"Ortiz!" shouted Lieutenant Rios, standing at the side of one of the nearby boats and watching Calixto with the corporal. "Let the man work!"

The corporal let go of Calixto at the sound of the order.

Everyone got back to work.

Including Calixto.

The afternoon was finished by the time the boats were all loaded. Only the horses and mules stood on the sands, while the families filled up the four small boats. Rivera handed the reins of his white stallion to Tio Pepe. "Make sure he gets back to the fort. When I come here again I don't want to find out you sold him."

"*No, señor!*" Pepe said.

"Or someone ate him!"

"*No, no, no, no, no!*" Pepe answered, quickly taking the reins from the captain.

Felipe and Domingo tied the reins of the other horses together to make it easier for the two Red Sashes to lead them back to the fort. There was the pinto at the front of the group of horses, and Felipe stopped next to the mare to run his hand along her smooth flank. He took her reins and started to hand them over to the Red Sashes. But someone reached in and stopped him.

It was Martín.

Taking the reins out of Felipe's hands, he reached up to the pinto's neck and removed the bit from her mouth, along with the saddle. With a loud yell, Martín slapped her rump, waving his hat to spook the pinto, and chasing the horse away. The pinto bolted, racing across the sands and hurrying off to the bluffs.

Inside the boat, the Luna family watched as their pinto raced away from them, out of their lives now, forever. Sadness filled their faces, and Petra was in tears. Martín walked back to their boat and climbed inside, joining them.

"Why did you do that?" Petra asked sadly. "She would have been safe at the fort. She has no one to take care of her now."

"She was ours," Martin said, stubbornly. "Better for her to die alone than to have a savage care for her."

Petra turned to look back up at the bluffs. They were empty now.

The pinto was already gone.

GWENGY-ONE

The four *lanchas* glided into the Sea of Cortez.

With much panting and groaning, Tio Pepe and the two Red Sashes took turns pushing off each one of the boats from the safety of the sands into the arms of the deep blue-colored sea. As each vessel hit the waves, the bow of the boat rose up, pointing high to the sky. The people, crowded together, held onto the sides and to one another so they wouldn't be thrown out, as the spray hit their faces and the salt water soaked their skin. Sailing over the surf, the four boats righted themselves; the wind caught their sails and pushed them out farther away from the land.

A Red Sash in each of the boats worked a single canvas sail at the front, while the families and recruits were crammed tightly together with what remained of their lives from Sinaloa tied up and packed at their feet. In the lead boat, El Capitán sat in the front, and in the fourth boat, the last one at the end, Corporal Ortiz was in command.

Felipe and Tomás sat near the oars at the center of the second boat. The Lunas almost filled up the middle of the boat, with Beatriz, the families of Martín and Mercedes, and Petra. Behind them sat Lieutenant Rios, with the family's walnut chest sitting on his lap. At the front of the boat, Calixto stood holding a line that moved the sail—this way and that—as it caught the wind and pulled them forward.

This is how they traveled for the rest of the day.

The air was so clear that their minds played tricks on them, and they thought they could almost see the distant shore. Eighty miles they would have to travel, and if the winds were kind, it would take them three or four days. If the winds were not, well, that was another story. Ships had been known to take weeks to cross these eighty miles. The winds could be cruel—soft and loving one moment and then brutal the next—like a woman wronged. There were times a boat would have to turn back, and sometimes they were even lost, disappeared all the way to the bottom, taking the sailors with them, without a trace of them ever being there at all. This was what the Red Sashes knew, and Rivera knew it too. But not so the people of Sinaloa.

Thank God. They had enough burdens to carry, enough fears to keep them company; they didn't need to know the truth.

They had to do everything on these tiny boats and live their lives like they were on land. When they would get hungry, they would eat. But with nowhere to cook, it was a little bit of this and a little bit of that. Dried fruit. Dried meat. And only a few sips of water every now and then from their *botas*. The water would have to last them for the length of the voyage; there were no streams out there in the middle of the sea. No wells. No rivers. When they were tired, there were no beds to welcome their aching backs; they slept where they sat—in the heat of the day or the middle of a sudden rainfall. They could not run from the weather; they covered their heads with shawls and capes. They sat in those little boats and they took it. And when it was time to relieve themselves, there were no trees to cover them, nowhere they could go to hide. The men would stand and turn their backs to use the sea, but the women were not so lucky. There was a bucket and a blanket that was held up to give each other some privacy.

This is how they traveled. They didn't need to know anything more, anything that would give them more worries, give them more fear. To make them wonder if they would ever make it to land again.

That first day had been calm and the water smooth; they glided along the sea for hours.

And then the sun began to set.

They watched it slip slowly from the sky, touching the water and turning the whole world golden orange. It was a sight so beautiful it filled them with hope—for a better life in a land called California. A future ripe with possibilities. Not just for their lives but for the lives of their children sitting there in their laps and for all the children yet to come.

But then the darkness came.

The light slipped out of day and the night arrived cruelly. High above them, the stars were shining with all their tiny spots of light. But one thing was missing: a moon. Without it, there was no moonlight for them to see, and everything around them disappeared. They couldn't make out the boat in front of them or the boats behind, and even the faces of their families could not be seen in the darkness.

Sounds kept them company. The slapping of the sail by the wind, the splash of water on the hull, the noises of the people: the snores, the coughs, the crying—all reminders that they were not alone.

In the dark of night, people found ways to comfort one another. Children lay across the laps of their parents, and with every fidget and little twitch as they slept, mothers and fathers felt safe themselves, knowing their children kept them from being alone. Families held loved ones close, arms around one another, hands clasping hands.

It was in this way that Petra's hand found the hand of another. In the darkness, she could not tell whose hand it was. But she didn't care. It was a strong hand, yet gentle too. With fine long fingers that had reached out to her in the night, awakening her, as the boat had rocked her to sleep. Wide awake at the touch, Petra had stretched out her fingers for those that had reached for hers. And this is how she spent the night, holding onto a stranger's hand in the darkness.

It was a man's hand, to be sure. Long fingers and a wide palm. A ring circled one of those fingers—the little one of the right hand. It was a simple band: Was it silver or was it gold? There was no light to tell the difference. But on top of it, there was something smooth. A jewel perhaps. Or a stone. She could feel it there with her fingertips. She wondered who was this man who sought to comfort her. Or who sought comfort himself in her touch. She wanted to whisper, to ask him, but her family was close, and to do so would betray the man's touch, forbidden for her and only possible in darkness.

Besides, she didn't need to hear him say his name.

She named him on her own.

She knew him in her heart. She pictured him in her mind. And in the darkness, she clasped his hand in hers, grateful for his touch.

If love is possible this way, without words, without a name, or eyes to gaze into, with only one hand holding onto another, then this was how Petra found love. It helped her get through that first night, and in the light of day, it made the hours pass quickly as she prayed for darkness to hurry back to her. Though her body was trapped in that small boat, with the stink of the unwashed people around her, the sun beating down all day, and the movement of the sea making her sick, her mind rescued her by promising her darkness. And the touch of a hand soon to come.

That second night she waited for it. And in those late hours, at that time in darkness when the soul is sure it is all alone, it came again.

That touch. That hand in hers.

Petra held onto that hand and she knew.

This was a man she could love.

TWENTY-TWO

On the third day the winds died.

The sail went flat and no matter how Calixto turned and twisted the canvas, it would not fill. There was not even a little breeze to move the boats along. And without the wind to cool down the sun, the heat filled up the day.

The four *lanchas* sat still in the water.

For the first time in two days, Calixto let go of the sail and sat down to rest. Turning his back to the sun, he shut his eyes to the world. He had not rested once since first stepping into that boat and taking the helm. No one there knew what he knew: how to read the stars, or the movement of the wind; how to look at the sun and find the land. No one could keep these people alive on the sea like he could. But he was weary now. He needed to rest.

That rest was not for long. A shout went out from the lead boat far ahead.

Rivera at the stern cupped his hands and shouted across the sea: "Oarsmen at the helm!"

Lieutenant Rios went into action, moving his way through the people and over to Calixto. "Man the oars!" he told him.

Slowly, the old *indio* pulled himself up. He made his way over to one side of the boat and, finding the long wooden oar at the bottom, he pulled it up. His shoulders and arms ached from working the sail; his face filled with pain. But he pushed forward and kept going, his hands trembling as he attached the oar to one side of the boat and moved over to the second oar on the other side.

Everyone watched him.

No one helped him.

At first, even Felipe watched on. What could he do? He knew Calixto to be stronger than most men. For long hours they had worked together in the corral, and he knew the old man was tough. There were times when Felipe would quit because he needed to drink water or to take a little rest. Calixto always kept going and would never quit, no matter how hard the work. But this time was different. Felipe could see the look on the old *indio*'s face, and he knew that the man's strength was gone. Calixto couldn't do this by himself. And Felipe could not sit back and just watch.

He hurried over to Calixto.

Rios confronted him. "What are you doing, Garcia?" Ignoring the lieutenant, Felipe helped Calixto lift the long oar up and slip it into its place on the side of the boat. "I asked you a question, Private," Rios said, squaring off with Felipe. "Who ordered you to help this man?"

"No one, sir. But I think he is exhausted."

"You do not think, recruit. That's not your job. You follow orders—*that's* what you do. This man knows more than anyone here about sailing these waters. These people are like mules. They can work until they drop."

Felipe did not hesitate or hold back his words. "If Calixto drops, I think we will be the next to drop after him." What Felipe said made sense. The lieutenant was smart enough to know this. He was not an officer so vain as to punish a *sol-dado* for speaking the truth, even when speaking was not his place. Knowledge was important to the lieutenant, and he valued wherever it might come from, even if it came from a lowly recruit. He took a good look at Calixto and noticed for the first time just how old this man appeared.

"Is this true? Do you need to rest?" Rios asked. But Calixto refused to answer him. "If you're tired, old man, I want to hear you say it." Calixto would not answer the lieutenant. Instead, he took a seat at the oar, with his back to Felipe and the lieutenant, facing the rear of the boat. Wrapping his hands around the handle of the oar, he tried to go back to work.

"Tomás! Man the other oar!" Rios called out, looking over in the direction of the young recruit. Tomás hurried out of his seat and took his place on the other side of the boat, sitting backwards, the way Calixto faced. "Trade off and take turns," Rios ordered Felipe and Calixto. And then the lieutenant reached down and put a hand on Calixto's shoulder. "We need you." Rios went back to his seat, and Calixto began to row. Tomás, across the boat on the other side, followed his lead. Slowly, the boat began to move forward again.

Felipe sat behind Calixto, waiting his turn to take the oar. He bent down low so that only the old *indio* could hear him. "Why don't you speak?" Felipe pleaded. "You understand us, I can tell. Why don't you answer?" Once again, Calixto held his tongue. He kept his back to the young *español* and just went on rowing.

That was the only answer he wanted to give.

The wind was stubborn and did not return for the rest of the day.

Nothing moved the boat but the slow sweep of the double oars working together, with Martín and Tomás trading off on one side, and Calixto and Felipe doing the same on the other.

When darkness fell, there was still no wind.

But the moon came back to visit. A little sliver of it hung high above them. And the light from it outlined all the people. You could see them, sitting together in families, all clothed in black.

You couldn't make out their faces, but their shapes you could see. Black figures in the darkness.

Petra watched and waited for the stranger to come to her side. She wanted to reach out and touch his face, to memorize him in the night for the daytime to come. With the wind quiet, she listened for his movement, wanting his closeness, willing him next to her. To see the shape of him. To feel him there beside her. But no one came that night. No hand reached for hers in the darkness. And in time, the sound of the steady oars began to lull Petra to sleep.

A loud crash in the water woke her with a start.

Water sprayed across the bow, and everyone was soon awake. Another splash at the back of the boat and one more at the side. Everywhere they turned there were loud splashes and water exploded all around them.

Tomás was the first to leave his oar and look over the bow.

What he saw he could not believe.

"Look!" he shouted. "Look at the water!"

Around the boat the water lit up like it had swallowed the moon. There, in the middle of the light were fish, hundreds of them swimming, schools of them, and as they moved, each move lit up the water and the sea glowed even brighter.

Another splash, this time close to the boat, and one more soon after. All eyes could see it now, could see the splash and what caused it: birds were falling from the sky. Pelicans diving, fishing in the night. And with every new splash from a diving bird, the sea filled up with light.

Never before had the people seen such a sight.

Beauty and magic in the darkness of night.

The sky was raining birds—big fat pelicans with long beaks to spear the fish and plump cheeks to swallow them. Diving into the water they went, scooping up a meal and rising out of the light, back into the night, only to be followed by another bird diving into the sea. And all around them the splashes exploded into brilliance!

Parents held up their little ones, sleepy-eyed toddlers and babies, showing them the sight. It was something so incredible it would always be remembered. They would tell their unborn children about it one day. And the children in their arms would tell this story to their children too.

For Calixto, this sight was nothing new. He had seen it when he was alone and fishing off the shore of his people's island— Tahejöc—just north and across from Guaymas. It had always given him a thrill, and if he was quick, he could catch the fish before the birds did, using nets to pull them into his tiny *balsa*, while fighting off the pelicans with his paddle. He knew the size and strength of these birds, and he understood that if he was not careful they could knock him into the sea.

But to the people of Sinaloa, who knew nothing of these waters, this sight was a miracle. To come at such a time, with darkness all around and no sight of land in front of them, it was surely a sign of God. What else could it be? And more than a few of them made the sign of the cross and thanked God for showing his presence.

Petra sat as still as she could, afraid to move, afraid to wake herself up from this incredible dream. This was what she wanted her life to be. Not stuck in a village with days and nights the same as the ones that passed before them, living the expected and the ordinary. Petra wanted more from life—magic and brilliance! She wanted to feel her heart racing. To be thrilled. To be excited. To feel alive!

Marco scrambled over Petra's lap to get closer to the sight, reaching his hand out over the edge of the boat.

It was then the bird struck him.

It knocked Marco forward and over the edge of the boat, and the boy fell into the sea. Petra reached out but too late. Sola's scream brought Martín, but before he could jump after his son there was a large splash over the side as someone dived into the water first.

Felipe was in the waves before anyone else could even move. He was a good swimmer, he knew that. It had saved his life in the flood. But even though he had survived, he hadn't been able to save his family. He couldn't bear to let that happen again. He would drown first before he would let the water take Marco.

And that's why Felipe dove into the sea that night.

When he reached out for the little boy, he was reaching out for his sister, Teresa, and for his mother and father too. He couldn't bring them back, but this boy was still within reach. Using the light from the fish and the birds splashing down around him, he followed little Marco, slipping farther down into the sea, out of the light and into the blackness. With Felipe's arms stretched out and his legs kicking fast and hard, he swam to the little boy, trying to grab him as he kicked and struggled with all his might, sinking lower and lower into the depths of the sea.

The people on the boat watched and waited, looking through the light below them, as Felipe swam deeper after the little boy.

Martín dove into the water after his son, and Tomás followed his brother.

Below, all three of the men swam after Marco, with Felipe in the lead, as they tried to reach the boy.

Up above, as the people watched, the light in the water began to dim as the fish began to swim away, deeper into the sea, moving away and taking the light with them as they moved. So too, the birds followed after them, and soon the water around the boat turned to darkness once again.

Silence filled the night.

A breeze began to blow.

The sail trembled with its touch.

The surface of the water started to ripple.

Bursting out from the waves came Felipe, with little Marco in his arms. Martín and Tomás followed after them, and with Felipe leading the way, they swam to the front of the boat. Calixto reached down and helped bring the little boy out of the water. Marco's eyes were closed and his body was still.

Calixto laid the boy out on one of the benches, face down,

shores of the first island, and then the second, and there, on the backside, covering the rocks, were sea lions—*leones marinos*, hundreds of them stretched out, watching the boats as the people in the boats watched them. Great big bulls roared and bellowed, barking to the people of Sinaloa, as the sails of their boats brought them closer to the shore.

The seabirds too came out—the gulls and the sandpipers—flying overhead and showing them the way.

The air filled with the promise of land, and the smell of earth pulled them closer.

Ahead of them, the shoreline curved: a bay with the smoothest of waters appeared with sands bleached white from the sun. The four *lanchas* followed the shoreline and entered the bay, and when the wind slowed to a breeze, the oars came out and the men rowed the people the rest of the way into the shore.

This is how they landed in Baja California.

There was no one there on the sands that day to meet them. No one to help them pull the boats up on the shore or to unload the four *lanchas*. No horses or mules were there to carry them, no one to welcome them or to show them the way. They climbed out of the boats with their bodies still feeling the movement of the sea. That made them laugh and hold onto one another a little bit more, to find a way to stand, to move around, and to walk again.

They loaded up their shoulders and arms with all their belongings, the Red Sashes carrying the most, with packs tied to their backs. The women and the children, too, carried as much as their arms would hold, and if a woman had a baby on her hip, well, then, her man would have to carry even more.

Petra made sure she was at the side of Mercedes, taking little Maria from her, so her sister would not have to carry so much weight. Still, Mercedes lagged behind. The sea journey had taken much out of her, and she rested a moment at the side of one of the boats. Leaning her head over the sand, she retched, and Petra reached in to hold her hair back, away from her face. Domingo's arms were filled with belongings and he could barely see over the top of them, but as he passed by his wife, he saw that she was sick. He was not used to Mercedes looking so weak and vulnerable.

"Come on, woman!" he called out to her. "The longer you take, the more time I have to carry this shit!"

Mercedes did her best to pull herself together.

"What's the matter with you, woman?" Domingo asked her, not out of concern but to get her mad and to get her going. "When did you get so weak?"

"Five moons ago!" Mercedes shouted at her husband. "When I should have kicked you in the *huevos* and told you to roll over!" Finding her strength again, Mercedes grabbed Maria out of Petra's arms and carried the little girl away, moving down the beach to join the others.

Domingo paused a moment where he stood, wondering what the hell his wife was talking about. The words meant nothing to him. So he shrugged and went on his way.

When all the people had gathered on the beach, El Capitán led the way. His new recruits and two Catalonian Volunteers were at the front, the families came next, and Felipe with Domingo, Calixto, and the Red Sashes brought up the rear.

They did not have to walk far to get to Loreto. It was only a half-hour journey following a stretch of sand all the way towards the mountains. They only had to walk the well-worn path from the beach to find the pueblo. Rivera knew the way well. At one time he had been stationed here—El Capitán of the presidio—*comandante* and military protector to the Jesuit *padre*. Loreto was to be just a brief stop in Antigua California—old California—before they kept moving on to the new California in El Norte. Stranded on a stretch of sand, without grass, without many trees or much shade at all, this was not the land of milk and honey filled with golden riches that the books had promised was California. El Capitán knew he would be much happier leaving this place than he was arriving.

But the people from Sinaloa, who knew no better, looked upon the pueblo and saw Loreto's gifts. Fresh food and plenty of water. Clean clothes and supplies to keep them going. And rest for the weary—not just for the body but for the soul too. For what these people hungered for was not so easily hunted or made by hand. They needed something more to keep them going, to keep them reaching out for their future.

The sound of church bells ringing in the distance called out to them.

This was the true beauty of Loreto.

The Sinaloans had not heard a Mass—they hadn't received communion or the blessings of a priest—in almost two months. There had been prayers and some hymns along the way, a rosary now and then, but these people needed more, and here in Loreto they would find that. The church bells quickened their footsteps, hurrying them towards what they knew would be waiting there for them at the end of the sandy path.

Our Lady of Loreto.

Many had tears in their eyes as they gazed upon the soul of the pueblo.

Built of stone and mortar, the church was surrounded by thick walls of white stucco-covered adobe that protected it like a fortress. The bell tower stood high above, watching over all of the pueblo: the presidio across the way, also protected by walls, and the rest of the town spread out at its feet, from the storage grounds for grains, drying of meat, and gathered supplies, to the guardhouse and barracks for the unmarried soldiers.

A dozen soldiers lived in Loreto, each man waiting for his chance to get out. To go north, where the future was growing. Most of the pueblo was filled with huts made out of dirt for the hundreds of natives living there—young and old, men and women. Families, all of them. Close by, on a *mesa* overlooking it all, three dozen bigger huts were scattered every which way across the sand, looking not much better than cowsheds. This was where the married *soldados* lived, as well as the sailors and the tradesmen—a carpenter and two blacksmiths—along with their wives and children. *Españoles*, all of them. Each family had a hut, and each hut had one room only, with a dirt floor and a cowhide for a door.

This was all that filled the pueblo known as Loreto.

The capital of California.

ᏨWEᏁᏨY-ᖴOUR

It was on a Sunday when the people of Sinaloa arrived in Loreto.

A young son of the land—a Cochimí—was hunting lizards on the rocks of the slope of the *mesa* in the hot afternoon sun. He had just snagged a big fat one with a bit of string, using it like a noose to catch it by the neck, when the church bell began to ring and the boy forgot about the lizard and looked out.

The path to the pueblo was filled with strangers.

Frightened by the large group, the boy ran to the safety of the *padre* within the adobe walls.

Inside the church, Mass was just ending, and the priest was giving the final blessing. But this meant nothing to the Cochimí boy who was not yet baptized and knew no words of Spanish or Latin. Racing down the aisle, the boy jumped up on the altar, the words of his people spilling out of his mouth as he pointed to the church doors. The priest made a quick blessing over the rows of people in front of him, lifted up his robes, hurried off the altar, down the aisle, and through the doors.

Outside of Our Lady of Loreto, the people of Sinaloa spilled into the church grounds.

The priest pushed open the massive wooden doors of the church, and as soon as he saw all the strangers in front of him, a huge smile spread across his face.

"Welcome, pilgrims!" he shouted to all the people gathered outside his church. Moving into the center of them, he bent down to pick up one of the little boys, scooping him into his arms. Even though the boy struggled and kicked, crying out for his mama, this meant nothing to the priest, and he only pressed the child closer to his breast, giving him a loud kiss on his forehead.

Behind the *padre*, the people of Loreto started to file out of the church. First the *españoles*, and then the natives— Cochimís, Monquis, and all of the converted. Each of them was dressed in their finest Sunday clothing. The *españoles* who were *soldados* were in their uniforms, and the men who were civilians were wearing silk stockings and velvet jackets; the women were in lace dresses and *mantillas*, their hair pinned back with colorful ribbons. Even the newly converted neophytes were dressed in European clothing, which the *españoles* had given them: white cotton shirts that were matched with blue-flannel pants for the men and blue-flannel skirts for the women. All of Loreto now stood behind their *padre*, gazing on the strangers in their midst.

The people of Sinaloa were quite a sight. The clothing of the women and the children had been ripped and patched and bore the stains from weeks of travel. The new recruits looked ragtag in their old *cueras*, some without stockings for their shoes and with jackets too tight or too large. They were a pitiful-looking group.

But to Father Moraga the look of them did not matter at all.

"We've been expecting you!" he said, locking eyes with every man and woman who now surrounded him. He saved his biggest hello and a firm embrace for Rivera. "Welcome, Capitán! Welcome back to your home!" The little boy in the priest's arms continued to cry and squirm, but the *padre* seemed not to notice. "You're early!" Father Moraga said to Rivera. "We did not expect you so soon!"

"The sea was kind to us."

"Thanks to God!"

Rivera took the little boy out of the *padre*'s arms just to stop him from crying. He understood the boy's discomfort: El Capitán also was not fond of Moraga. The priest was too eager and too sure of himself, using his robes to push his way through life. It pained Rivera to admit he needed this man. But he did.

"We need a good cooked meal," Rivera told the *padre*. "And after that, we need a priest."

The *padre*'s face lit up, and he clapped his hands to his breast with excitement. Rivera was afraid this man would drop dead with joy.

And sorry when he didn't.

The priest said two Masses that Sunday.

After the people of Sinaloa were fed—thanks to the generous sharing of Sunday suppers by the good people of Loreto—a Mass was said once again, this time with great importance.

"Among our honored guests, we have four couples from Sinaloa who are betrothed and whose names I will read to you now as the public banns of marriage are announced."

The priest looked out at the rows of people that filled up the church. There were so many of them that even the back of the sanctuary was crowded with men who stood, having given up their seats for the women and children of Sinaloa. The Luna family was in the first row, with Tomás and Beatriz sitting next to each other; to their right sat Petra and Felipe, with Martín sitting on Felipe's other side.

"We do not have the luxury to wait three Holy Days of Obligation before these weddings take place," the priest explained to the people. "These four couples, because of their travels, seek the blessed sacrament of marriage before continuing their journey."

At the back of the church, Rivera watched on, with Lieutenant Rios at his side.

"If anyone knows why any of these four couples should not be wed, say it now, after I speak their names." The priest read from a leather journal he held in his hands: "Antonio Luis Beltran and Maria Rosa Arrellaga, Pedro Alberto Castillo and Carmen Louisa Arce, Tomás Diego Luna and Beatriz Amada Buelna, Felipe Santiago Garcia and Maria Petra Luna."

The priest looked out at all the people in the church and waited.

Felipe's eyes searched Petra's face, hoping for a smile.

But Petra's gaze was on Martín, trying to catch his eye and hoping for a last minute reprieve. Martín did not look at her, but sat straight and sure. At the back of the church, Lieutenant Rios watched on.

All was quiet.

No one said a word to the priest.

ᏔWENᏔY-FIVE

The wedding was to take place the next day.

It was a good reason for the town to celebrate and to have a *fiesta*. That night the cooking fires were busy as the women baked for the festivities. One of the steers was slaughtered, along with three pigs and two dozen chickens, in preparation for a big barbecue. Beans were washed and soaked. Corn was ground and flour made ready for the tortillas. Chiles were roasted, and yes, brandy and wine were put up in jars for the next day's communion and wedding toasts.

The men of Sinaloa sneaked a few drinks that night too. They passed around their own jug of *mescal*—one that the *padre* knew nothing about or he would have stopped them from passing it. They drank with the grooms-to-be as they set up their bedrolls on the *mesa*, camping out with the presidio's unmarried *soldados*, who had given up their cots to the women and children of Sinaloa.

Inside the barracks, the women settled in for the night.

The Luna women were making ready for the next day, setting out the wedding clothing for the two brides—Beatriz and Petra.

"You must wear Mama's dress—the black satin with Chantilly lace that she wore on her wedding day," Mercedes said, as she tried hard to keep the mood festive for her sister. "She has a fine tortoiseshell comb with a beautiful pearl inlay. Hand-painted from Manila!" Mercedes looked through their tied-up belongings, moving blankets and clothing every which way as she searched for the family chest.

"Where did you put it?" Mercedes asked, turning to Petra. "Where is the *arcón*?"

Petra knew exactly where it was. Or more importantly, who had carried it last.

"Domingo forgot to bring it here. I'll go get it," she said.

Her eagerness gave pause to Mercedes. "Should I be going with you?" she asked Petra, filled with suspicion.

"I'm about to be a married woman. I'm not a child who needs to be protected."

Mercedes was not so sure. "I will give you a few moments," she said to Petra. "But if you take too long . . . "

"What will you do? Send me to jail?" Petra asked, with sarcasm.

"I will send Martín to find you. That's worse than jail."

"He *is* my jail," Petra said softly. And with those words, she was out of the barracks, not caring if Mercedes heard what she had said or not. Petra stepped out into the darkness and the night surrounded her. For a woman to be alone in public at night like this was close to being a sin. It was something most would never think of or dare to even try.

But Petra was different from the rest.

The farther she walked away from the barracks, the happier she felt. There was no fear inside of her. She was not alone—she was free! The stars above kept her company, and the sound of her own heart beating quickly made her feel strong and brave. With every step she took, it was a step away from Martín, away from Mercedes, and yes, away from the whole family.

She was not a Luna.

She was just Petra.

She heard only her thoughts and no one else's. She felt only her feelings and cared not about anyone else's. She knew the taste of her own desires and forgot everyone else's. That's what pushed Petra deeper into the night—that first kiss of freedom awakened her inside, and at last she felt alive. Petra had no idea where she might find Lieutenant Rios, but she knew that she had to stay hidden, that darkness was her friend, protecting her from being discovered and having to go back.

The laughter of the *soldados* could be heard up on the *mesa*. Rios would not be among them, Petra was certain of this. He was different, like she was. Gallant and noble. Drinking with the troops would not be where she would find him. Her eyes searched across the pueblo, looking towards the presidio grounds.

That's when she saw the *comandante*'s quarters.

Candlelight flickered inside of his adobe *casita*.

And that's exactly where Petra headed.

It was custom for Loreto's *comandante* to entertain the officers who arrived there on the peninsula. But this occasion was even more special. Capitán Rivera was replacing the commandant, Felipe Barri, as governor of California. The power had shifted to El Norte—to Monterey—and Barri could not think of a better man he would want to see as the new governor. They had celebrated with a dinner in honor of Rivera, and Barri had toasted him many times as a man that he respected. The officers—Rios and Ortiz—along with the presidio staff had been there to raise their glasses and to share a meal. But once the officers had been dismissed after dinner, Barri could really speak his heart. "Serra's getting too big for his britches, outgrowing those filthy robes of his," he told the Capitán. "Only a strong military man like yourself can remind those fucking Franciscans who's really in charge here in California."

Barri had been careful to say this in private, and not in front of Ortiz and Rios. He didn't trust the Catalonian Volunteers.

"Too many run back home with their tails caught between their balls," he told Rivera. California was rough, and it could break a man. "Better to leave the work to the sons of this land than to bring over those panty-waists from Sevilla," Barri said to Rivera.

But Rivera was not so choosy.

He would take his soldiers from wherever he could get them, whether they spoke Castilian Spanish or the Spanish of the *criollo, mestizo,* or *nativo.* There wasn't much difference, in Rivera's mind. Death comes to all men the same.

Barri raised his cup of wine and toasted El Capitán.

"To the future of California!" he said.

"To the Californios." Rivera held up his glass. "Whoever they might be!"

Rios did not see her at first when he came out of the *comandante's* house.

She had waited until he was alone, after Ortiz and the other officers had headed off to the *mesa,* to their troops and their *mescal.* When the others were out of sight, she appeared in front of him.

For a moment, he wasn't sure Petra was real.

A woman all alone in the night did not belong there. This, more than anything, frightened him. Still, the fear did not manage to turn him away. There was something fascinating about seeing Petra there in the darkness.

He moved closer to her, slowly.

Petra could not find her voice at first. She could only look into the lightness of his eyes and pray that this moment might go on forever. Loreto disappeared around them. There was no Martín, no Felipe, no one to come between them.

"You must go back," Rios told her, keeping his voice low. But Petra did not move.

"You were kind enough to carry our family's *arcón*," she said.

"I gave it to Domingo—he has it with him," Rios told her. "I'll make sure he brings it to the barracks for you."

"My sister wants me to wear the black lace wedding dress that my mother wore, for my wedding tomorrow." Petra hesitated and waited. Hoping he could save her.

"There was a blue dress I noticed when the *arcón* fell, which spilled out with the others. That was very beautiful, that dress," Rios said to her. "You would look like an angel dressed in that one." If his words were not enough to move her, his smile as he said them gave her the courage to step closer to him.

"Do you want this?" she asked him, in a voice that was no longer timid, no longer afraid of his answer. "I'm to be married tomorrow, and there's nothing I can do to stop it." She said the words carefully, making sure he understood the full weight of them.

"Your brother has sanctioned this, and sealed it with his honor," Rios explained, trying to help her in the only way he could. "You're from the same village as Garcia—you've grown up together. The familiarity will do you well in a country where everything will be new to you."

"Do you want this?" she whispered, saying the words even more slowly, making sure he answered her not with reason but with his heart and soul.

Petra's boldness made him pause.

He was not used to a woman looking so deeply into who he was and what he believed. There was a strength in Petra that one did not usually find in such beauty. There was a courage within her that forced him to match her with his own strength and to bravely face the truth between them.

"We are not finished, you and I." He said this to her in the most tender of voices. "Go and marry Garcia, but remember that I've said this to you."

Somewhere in Loreto a guitar was being played. The laughter

of the *soldados* filled the night. The air was sweet and cool. But Petra and Rios knew only of each other.

"Always remember this," he said, watching her closely. Standing there and facing him, Petra wanted more than anything to be in his arms. To know his touch. To disappear within him. But that was not to be.

Not for now.

A bonfire on the *mesa* lit up the night.

The recruits from Sinaloa were gathered around, as two freshly slaughtered pigs were wrapped in palm fronds and lowered over glowing briquettes into a pit in the ground. Tomás was part of the group and so was Felipe. All the men were liquored up, as Martín passed his jug of *mescal* from *soldado* to *soldado*. He reached Felipe last and thrust the jug at him. "Come on, Garcia, you've got to catch up with us!"

Felipe shook his head and raised his hand with a smile.

"Not for me. I want to keep my head clear for tomorrow."

"The big head is not the head you have to worry about, my friend. It's the little one you hope won't let you down!" Martín said, grabbing his own crotch to make his point. The soldiers all laughed at his crudeness. It was the night before a wedding when men sought the brotherhood of other men and drinking became a sport.

Martín was clearly leading the way as he bolted back shot after shot of *mescal* from the jug that he carried. He was much drunker than any of the others, hungry for it like a man in a hurry or one who was just trying to forget. The thoughts and images that fill the mind the night before a wedding were not what Martín wanted to be picturing. He wanted to shut himself off inside. No pictures. No feelings. No thoughts. Nothing to remind himself that Petra was getting married in the morning, that she was being taken away from him.

"Come on, Garcia! The least you can do is toast your bride!" he shouted.

Martín took the jug and slammed it against Felipe's chest. He was egging him on, challenging him to keep up, drink for drink, the way the others were doing.

But Felipe would have no part of it. He turned his back on Martín and moved away into the darkness. Martín followed after him. The two walked side by side, matching each other's steps, away from the others now and bolder with each other.

"You have the most beautiful bride of them all, you know that, don't you? I'm the one to thank for that. The least you can do is to drink with me."

"You know she doesn't want me," Felipe said, simply. Not looking for sympathy or anything at all from Martín. It was a fact, and both men knew it. "You know this," Felipe said it once again, and this time it was an accusation more than anything else.

"What difference does it make?" Martín said. "These are women's concerns. It has nothing to do with being a man. Unless you're less than a man." Martín laughed, trying to best Felipe.

"It's very convenient for you," Felipe said, stopping to face Martín. "You will never be replaced, and that's what you want. This is the only way you'll ever keep her for yourself."

Martín's hand shot out and grabbed Felipe by the throat. Both men were on the ground and Martín was on the top, his fingers squeezing the life out of Felipe. But Felipe showed no fear. He looked into Martín's rage and spoke the truth.

"Kill me," Felipe said, in the calmest of voices. "Go ahead and do it. Let her go off with Rios. He'll take her back to Spain, and if you're lucky, you'll get one letter a year from her. You'll never see her again."

It was true. Without Felipe, Rios could step in and ask for Petra's hand. And there was no guarantee that a true son of Spain would ever want to settle here, in such a wild and untamed land as this one. Whatever faults Felipe possessed, his poverty and his breeding would work to Martín's advantage. Felipe had nowhere else to go. He would never run back to Spain or capture his sister's heart and take her along with him.

And this is why Martín let Felipe live.

Swallowing his rage, he loosened his grip from around his future brother-in-law's throat. Their fates would always be tied together in their love for Petra, whether Martín liked it or not.

They would be family.

GWENGY-SIX

At sunset the next day they were married.

The four couples from Sinaloa stood on the altar in front of God and all of Loreto. It was time for the last of the single men and women to join hands and to become couples. To begin their new families. All of the women were dressed in black, the custom of the day. Some with lace around their shoulders and a touch of satin at the collar.

Except for Petra.

Blue was the color of her dress.

No matter how many words Mercedes had spoken or how many times she had insisted on Mama's own beautiful black lace wedding dress being worn, Petra would not hear of it.

She would be her own woman.

And she would wear blue.

It made no difference to Felipe. Standing at Petra's side was the proudest day of his life. It did not matter to him—not at this moment—that she did not want him. His heart was so full with joy, just to be standing next to her, that there was no room inside of him for regret. There was nothing anyone could do to stop him from feeling blessed.

But for Petra, it was a different matter. She could only hope that the tears that welled up in her eyes would be mistaken for joy.

135

And not for the death she was feeling inside of her.

It is not common to have four weddings at the same time. But the priest had no other choice. Time was running out, and if they wanted to get to Monterey before the rains came, they had to do this quickly, so the priest had to make do and get on with it.

One Mass for four couples.

It could be done.

For the ceremony itself—the words between man and wife— well, one by one, each couple said them. First, Tomás and Beatriz— the bride, taller in size and greater in age than the groom, but no matter. Tomás's voice shook as he said the words: "I, Tomás, take you, Beatriz, to be my wife . . . " But Beatriz calmed her bride-groom with her smiles and with the way she looked at him: he was the only man in the world for her, and her eyes let him know that. Next were the Beltrans-to-be, followed by the almost-Castillos, and last came Petra and Felipe, with his eyes searching for hers as he said the words: "I, Felipe, take Maria Petra . . . "

But Petra could not look at him; she was afraid her eyes would reveal the truth. When it was time for her words to be spoken, she said them in barely a whisper.

"I, Petra, take Felipe to be my husband."

Once the vows were said, the *arras* came next—the thirteen wedding coins passed from bridegroom to bride. They symbol-ized the husband's vow to always protect and provide for his wife. Each couple needed their own set of coins, but this was a problem for the four couples.

None of them had coins.

The wealthy would have used thirteen gold coins, and the tradesmen would have used silver. Even the poorest would have copper coins for their *arras*. But the people from Sinaloa lost everything in the flood; they had no coins at all. Instead, they would have to share what the priest kept in the church sacristy: thirteen copper coins from Spain kept in a black velvet pouch and loaned only to the poorest of couples.

The first couple said their promises to each other and then passed the coins back to the priest. The next couple received them, and after their vows were said, the coins moved on again. It was in this way that the *arras* were shared among the four couples from Sinaloa. Felipe and Petra were the last to be handed them. The priest spilled out the thirteen coins into Felipe's open hands as he said the words: "Lord, bless these *arras* that are given to Felipe and Petra. Pour over them an abundance of your goods."

When the last of the coins settled into Felipe's waiting hands, he looked closely at them. Copper was not what he wanted for his wife. Not for Petra. She deserved much better than this. He made a vow—silently, right there—that someday he would turn this copper into gold. And only after his heart had vowed this did he turn to face his bride and say to her the words of the bridegroom.

"Petra, receive these *arras* as a pledge and a sign of the goods that we will share."

Petra held out her hands, slowly opening them, just below Felipe's. Felipe let go of the coins and all thirteen of them spilled into Petra's waiting palms. She had no choice but to play the role as it was written. To say the words that she had to say.

"Felipe . . . " His name caught in her throat. It was not the name she wanted to be saying. It tasted wrong. This wedding was wrong. But she had to go on. There was no way of stopping this. "I receive these *arras* as a pledge of God's blessing and a sign of the goods that we will share together."

Petra lowered her head and gave in to the tears that she could not hold back any longer.

Felipe understood why she was crying, but even though he knew he was the reason for her tears, he could not help but want to comfort her. He laid his hands over hers, touching her gently.

That's when Petra saw it.

The ring on his finger.

She recognized the feel of it at once. The cool touch of the gold band and the smooth stone on top—a bright piece of turquoise she could now see in the daylight. But she did not need to see it; she knew every curve and bend, every dip and vein in this stone. Her fingers had memorized it in the dark from the nights on the sea when she'd felt so alone. In the daylight, Petra had looked for some sign of a ring on the lieutenant's hand. Once or twice she had thought she caught a glimpse of gold there on his finger. But she was never allowed to be close enough to him during the day to really know for sure.

Only now did she see it.

This was the hand that had found hers, holding it until the fear had passed. Felipe had been the one who had comforted her—the one who in her heart she knew she loved. He wasn't the man she had pictured in her head, the man who she'd wanted it to be. And yet, his touch had calmed her and given her peace. And filled her with love that made sense to her, that felt right and good. The sight of the ring on Felipe's finger shot through her, and her hands began to shake.

The coins all tumbled to the ground.

ᏭWENᏭY-SEVEN

There was quite a *fiesta* that night in Loreto.

Everyone celebrated the four weddings. The *indios*, too, were part of the festivities—the neophytes who had been brought to the Lord and even the ones who still followed the old ways. By torchlight they feasted, and the wine flowed as the spirits lifted. Life was hard for these people. And if this was the way they could taste a little bit of the promise of Heaven, well, the priest could look the other way just for one night.

There was dancing too. Guitars and mandolins played with a violin to keep them company. The night was rich with music: waltzes from Europe and fandangos from the motherland—music that had crossed the great Pacific and settled here, to be remembered, to be changed, to be made fresh by this new place and its people.

The newly married couples were at the center of it all, danc-ing every dance and holding each other for the first time as they began their lives together. It was a way to get to know each oth-er's bodies. A little taste of what was yet to come.

And so it was for Felipe and Petra.

They danced along with the rest, with Felipe's arm around her waist and Petra's arms around his neck. The wine had loos-ened them up, and the music kept them dancing and pressed against one another. And when they changed partners, they went from each other to another couple, swinging from one dancer to the next. Petra twirled and spun out of Felipe's arms and over to Tomás and finally into the arms of Rios.

For the first time on her wedding day, Petra's face filled with a beautiful smile.

And this was what Felipe saw—the joy in Petra as she felt for the first time the arms of Lieutenant Rios. She lingered with him a moment too long, unwilling to move on. Until at last, she knew that she must. And she returned once again to her rightful place—into the arms of her husband.

That's when her smile faded.

The night grew longer and the party went on.

One by one, each married couple sneaked away from the *fiesta* and found their way into the darkness. This would be their first night together, and the barracks would not be where they would spend it; they sought a privacy that only they could find. Making their way into the darkness, they followed the path down to the beach to the shelter of the *tinglados*—thatched roofs held up by small tree trunks buried in the sand, with an opening that looked out at the sea. Here only sea turtles would be watching them, and the sounds of their couplings would be covered by the waves.

The Beltrans were the first to sneak out of the fiesta, husband leading wife by holding her hand. They had known each other since they were children being bathed in the river and had been promised to each other for years. They were eager and happy. So too were the Castillos, newly betrothed but happy to be matched. They followed second.

Tomás would have kept dancing all night. His love for the grape and his fear of the wedding night made him want to keep the party going. But Bea would put an end to that by leading the way. Seeing that the Castillos and Beltrans were already gone, she grabbed Tomás by the hand and dragged him away from the light.

Felipe and Petra were the last of the couples to remain. They were the center of attention now of all the dancing couples. One by one, the people shouted and clapped, encouraging the new man and wife to get on with it. To leave them behind and to go forward with the rest of their night.

Too many eyes were watching them, and too many tongues would be wagging the next morning if Felipe and Petra did not leave the *fiesta* together. Whatever they did not have between them was for them to know and not for others to find out. Petra did not want anyone to know her business—this was the curse of living in a village, and she would not fall prey to it.

For this reason alone, she reached for Felipe's hand.

And the two of them hurried off into the darkness.

They moved down the path to the beach, and every step they took led them away from the sounds and the lights of Loreto. They were alone now, and the truth of that slowed down their footsteps and made them uncertain. They didn't know where they were going or what would happen when they got there. They were in no hurry to find out or to go forward.

They stopped a moment.

And Petra let go of Felipe's hand.

There was no one watching now, no reason for Petra to be holding it. The moon was half full and it lighted their way. Waves broke on the shore not far from them. They followed the sound until they were walking on sand. Felipe was just ahead of her, and Petra tried to keep up with him.

The *tinglados* were spread out across the beach in front of them. A patch of palm trees off to the side had a shelter of tall ferns below them. One of the couples could not wait for a *tinglado*, and the sounds of their coupling there, among the ferns, filled the night air.

Embarrassed by the sounds, Petra ran past Felipe and down the beach.

Felipe ran after her.

Past the *tinglados* and down to the wet sand of the shore, Petra kept running and Felipe followed after her. Only the breaking surf stopped her, and she sought the shelter of the rocky shore that spilled out and met the sand. She ran over to the rocks until they blocked her way and she couldn't run any farther. There was no way for her to escape this. She had no choice but to turn and face him, as Felipe walked up the beach to her and stood close.

"Whatever you're going to do to me, do it quickly and get it over with," she said to him. It was more of a command than anything else. She would not show him her fear. "I won't fight you," she added.

"And what would you expect me to get from that?" Felipe asked her.

She was surprised by the question.

"I would be giving you my love. A gift," he explained.

Petra looked away, embarrassed by his words.

"But what would you be giving *me*?" he wanted to know.

She didn't speak right away and that alone was answer enough for him. He turned away from her and started back across the sand, on his way to one of the empty *tinglados*.

She watched him go inside of it.

And then she followed after him.

The moon lit up the waves as Felipe sat inside of the *tinglado*, looking out across a calm sea. Petra appeared at the edge of the shelter and looked inside at him.

"Nothing is what I would be giving you," she said to him, simply. "I can't give you love. I don't feel it for you."

"I love you," he told her, simply. "I can't help it."

Petra knew this from the way he always looked at her, every time they were close. With the words he spoke to her and with the words he didn't speak. But this was not her doing—she hadn't made him any promises. Or offered him something she couldn't give. It was Martín's doing; he put them together like this. And yet, though the fault rested with someone else, Petra was the one who now was hurting him. For this, she was truly sorry.

"I understand," she said. And there was a tenderness in the way she said it.

It was this moment that gave Felipe hope.

"I'll never take from you what you don't want to give," he told her.

Felipe would not settle for anything less. He didn't want her unless she wanted him too. Petra would be safe that night; there would be nothing between them, he assured her. Just a night's sleep together, that's all they would share. Nothing more. It was a peace between them that he was offering her. And she was glad to take it.

Petra slipped into the *tinglado* and sat next to him.

Slowly, Felipe removed his *cuera* from around his chest. Rolling it up, he laid it down behind Petra. And then he moved away from her and back outside to the sand. Lying down, he stretched out his long legs and put his hands behind his head, gazing up at the sky.

Petra lay down in the *tinglado*, using the *cuera* as a pillow for her head. She stretched out on her side to face the sea.

Together they listened to the waves rolling in.

"What is it about Rios that makes you want to love him?" Felipe asked, his eyes still looking up at the sky.

Petra did not hesitate before she answered.

"I don't know him," she said. "He's different."

It was true—Rios was not like Felipe or any of the men in Petra's life. Not only in his looks—the lightness of him—but he didn't share the same past as she did. He had never drunk from the same well, or shared the warmth of the same summer sun, or tasted the bitterness of floodwaters, or known the stench of death on his soil. He was not part of her memories or something she wanted to forget. She did not know him at all.

"He's not from Sinaloa," she said, hoping he could understand. But Felipe was not sure that he did. And as the silence separated them, sleep came to them both.

The wedding night was now over.

TWENTY-EIGHT

In the old times, a wedding could go on for days.

No one seemed to get tired. And if they did, they would sleep a little, and when they woke up the party would keep going. The women cooked for days, and in between they danced with their men. They sang songs they had grown up singing, and they told stories that were written in their hearts. And everybody drank *vino* until they forgot what it was they were celebrating. Then they cracked open the brandy and remembered once again.

In Loreto, the celebration of the four weddings lasted only one night.

Rivera was in a hurry.

He was in a race with winter. They had three months before they would reach San Diego and miles in front of them before they could end their journey in Monterey. If they took too long or stopped too many times, winter could catch them and they might not survive the journey.

The safety of these pilgrims was in Rivera's hands.

And more than that.

Spain was impatient to take land that had been flirted with but never claimed. Now Russia had shown an interest, had teased and penetrated California's shores, and Spain had become a jealous lover and wanted to possess her.

Rivera would be the one to help make that happen.

To take claim meant more than just soldiers protecting the soil with guns and swords. Women and children were needed to make the land a place worth living, taming it and gentling its wildness. These families would bring with them their Spanish way of life, bringing order to a land where they saw no order, planting fields with crops where there were none, and making clothes and shelter where warmth and protection was never guaranteed. These fifty-two people from Sinaloa would be the first to help fill this land, from San Diego all the way up the coast to Monterey Bay. Joining the groups of *soldados* already there, they would make up less than two hundred *españoles*, surrounded by hundreds of thousands of native Californians—tribes and clans that were already living there and doing just fine.

Until Spain came and told them they weren't.

California would find its future in these first pioneers. In the sweat of their labors and in the seeds of their children. But Spain wanted more. What good is land if you can't own it? If you don't own it, someone will come and take it away from you. The land—like a woman—had to be claimed.

And the tribes that were there?

Well, they would have to be claimed too.

Whether in black robes, grey, or brown, the priests would take their souls and Spain would own their bodies. The hands of thousands can build so much more and do it so much more quickly than the hands of only two hundred. Together, the *españoles* and the native Californians would build this promised land of California. And all would be good.

That was the plan, at least.

These fifty-two people from Sinaloa were the beginning of that plan. They were a precious cargo, and Rivera would not risk their safety or use their journey to make his name bigger. Let Anza be the one to do that, to end up in the history books for finding a quicker way to the new California.

Only months ago, Anza and his *soldados* had set out to do just that, traveling north on the mainland all the way up to Tubac. From there, he and his expedition moved westward, clearing their path with pick, shovel, ax, and crowbar, hacking and cutting their way to the Colorado River, where they crossed its wide banks, braving the threat of the Apaches, only to crawl across the sand dunes of the desert, until finally showing up starving at San Gabriel.

But at least they made it.

Anza was a hero.

Soon there would be families following him. He would lead them to Monterey and even farther, to the bay of San Francisco, and into the history books as they settled there. But for the moment, the very first families were too precious to gamble on a trail so new and so dangerous.

Instead, they would follow Rivera and the well-worn path that El Capitán knew like the sound of his own breath. The road they would be traveling on—the Camino Real—was Portolá's, and Rivera knew every step of it because his footsteps were the ones alongside Portolá when this road was carved out of the steep mountain passes and the rocky *arroyos*. Make no mistake, this was not an easy road, but the threats that were there were known and not new. And there were missions along the trail that held promises of food, fresh mounts, water, and survival.

Let Anza find fame. Rivera only wanted to survive and go home. He longed for that time when he could return to the arms of his family, where he could enjoy the sunsets over his farm, and the company of his sons. Let Anza and the others claim the glory. Rivera was ready to retire and rest.

But first he had a future to bring to Alta California.

All he had to do was keep these people moving.

And this day, after the four weddings at Loreto, they were moving much too slowly.

"Wake them up, Ortiz! Get them going!" Rivera shouted to

his corporal, as the captain sat on top of his fresh new mount—a chestnut stallion—and watched the people of the caravan slowly packing up their belongings outside of the mission's walls.

Ortiz was quick to reach for his whip.

"Not with the whip!" Rivera ordered.

El Capitán was not fond of this corporal. The soldier was too quick to hurt instead of lead. There was a cruelty inside of Ortiz that was always hungry and needed to be fed. Pain and fear were the only things that could fill him up: the sharp snap of leather ripping skin and the black helplessness in the eyes of those who fed him. The corporal was not interested in leading but only in the power that came with each stroke, each blow, each cry for God's mercy. This taste for blood and degradation could only lead to his destruction. For this reason, Rivera paid special attention to this corporal, for the man's own safety, as well as the safety of his caravan.

"Use words, not leather," Rivera commanded, as he pressed his horse against Ortiz's mount and firmly grasped the wrist of his corporal who held the whip. "This is the future of California that we are privileged to be escorting, and you will treat these people with respect."

Rivera waited for Ortiz to answer him, to retreat a little with a salute or a humble nod even. But the corporal stubbornly remained silent. He was not fond of taking orders from a man who had never even set sight on the motherland, a dark-skinned *criollo* who was barely above the heathens he was too stupid to command.

"It's a long walk to Monterey, my friend," Rivera reminded him. "I would hate to see you make the journey in leg irons."

The threat was enough to loosen the corporal's tongue. "*Si, señor,*" he answered, even though his heart was not in it. Slowly, he put back his whip.

But no matter what commands would be shouted that day, or even if Ortiz had been able to use his whip, the people from

Sinaloa could not move any faster than they were already moving. It had been a long night for all of them. Their heads hurt and their stomachs ached from too much of a good time. Good food. Good wine. Good dancing. And a good night for sinning.

That is why, at dawn, the people all had to go to Mass.

The *padre* made certain of this with the loud tolling of the mission bells, ringing out with the rising of the sun. All of the people in Loreto had struggled out of their cots, drawn to the mission and the promise of salvation.

Hungover—*crudo*—or not.

Even the brides and their grooms, the *señors* and new *señoras*, bid good-bye to the soft white sands—their wedding beds—and arrived back at the mission for Holy Communion and to break the fast and pack up their things.

Felipe and Petra had been the first to show up on the path from the beach. Dawn was just waking and the bells of the mission had not yet rung when the two came back to the gates of the presidio. Mercedes was already awake sitting outside at the back of the barracks, as she breastfed Maria in her arms. She saw her sister and Felipe come into the presidio grounds and watched as the two separated and went their different ways, Felipe heading off to the corral and Petra off to the barracks and her family.

Impatient to hear all the details of the wedding night, Mercedes moved out to the marching grounds to meet her sister, with little Maria still feeding at her breast.

"How did it go?" she asked Petra, in a whisper.

"How did *what* go?" Petra answered, pretending innocence just to get her sister's goat, while the two of them walked in the direction of the barracks.

"Don't make me beg you," Mercedes said.

"What do you want to know that should be your business?"

But to Mercedes *everything* was her business.

"I'm your sister. I have a right to ask. If we don't talk, how will you learn?

149

Petra had no answer for that.

And it didn't matter if she did because Mercedes just kept talking anyway.

"It gets better," Mercedes advised her, with great authority. "*Maybe* it can get better. It depends on how the first time goes—the first time tells the tale. Even if it wasn't so good, even *that* you can get around, if you like the way he looks. And if you don't? Well, you close your eyes and pray the deed goes quickly." Mercedes reached out for her sister's arm, taking hold. "So how was it?" she asked, anxious to know the answer and hoping for the best.

"Better than expected," Petra said with a wink.

When Mercedes opened her mouth to ask for more details, Petra turned away from her and went into the barracks. More than that she would not tell her sister.

And for the moment, that would have to be enough.

The Beltrans were the next couple to return to the pueblo, and after that, the Castillos soon followed. Tomás and Beatriz were the last to arrive—running back to the now already packed-up caravan that met the couple with catcalls and whistles. And God help him, Tomás could not hide his joy or the big smile on his face. He made a point of finding Felipe, who was leading several of the mules over to the caravan.

"You were right!" Tomás said to him, excitedly. "It was the most delicious meal I have ever had!" And he pumped Felipe's hand with great gratitude for the little talk they had together that first night of the caravan. "And you?" Tomás asked him, lowering his voice, out of respect and so no one might hear him. "How did it go for you?"

Felipe half-smiled but did not answer. He took the mules by the reins and walked them down to the end of the long caravan line. Tomás could think whatever he wanted to think. And so he did. Nothing could stop him from smiling that day, and he hoped for Felipe it was the same.

The caravan now had grown in size. Horses had been added, along with *burros* instead of mules. These donkeys were smaller in size and did not have the fortitude of the horse within them, but they were strong and would do the job. Cattle, too, for fresh meat, would be driven alongside them; a small herd was assembled, with Domingo, Calixto, and Felipe on horseback, keeping them together and moving them forward.

Everyone rode on horseback now. Without wagons to sit upon or covered carts to ride, the women sat on top of leather saddles, sidesaddle, in heavy cotton skirts with only their shawls to give them shade. The young children rode smaller ponies alongside the horses of their mothers.

Marco refused to share a mount with his older brother. He was a big boy, he reminded them, ever since the sea had tried to claim him and he had beaten it. This had made him impatient with always being within his mother's reach and drew him closer to his father. But Martín had his own duties as Rivera's aide and shooed the boy away from the front of the caravan where only Martín would ride at the side of El Capitán. Absent his father's desire to keep his son close, Marco found a place at Felipe's side, riding his little pony next to his new uncle at the back of the caravan.

The four Red Sashes also joined the caravan. Having proven their worth by navigating the *lanchas* safely across the sea, they were now expected to travel with the Sinaloans all the way to Monterey. More *indios* from Loreto joined them. All of them had been baptized by Father Moraga, all good neophytes; they were Cochimí and they knew the language and the land where the caravan would be traveling. Rivera would use them to interpret, and the *indios* would serve as guides as the *españoles* moved deeper into their people's territory.

The long line of travelers stretched out across Loreto from the mission to the far end of the presidio. All of the people of the pueblo and the governor, too, came to see them off. The *padre* stood at the side of El Capitán, with his arms raised high in benediction, as he blessed all the people and the journey they were about to take.

"In the name of the Father, the Son, and the Holy Ghost!" The *padre* crossed himself, and everyone in the caravan did the same.

Someone in the back of the line began to sing.

"*Alabado y ensalzado . . .*"

"Praised and exalted" is what they sang.

"*. . . sea el divino Sacramento.*"

". . . be the Sacrament divine."

More people began to sing the Alabado—a hymn of the people. Always sung without guitar, without mandolin, and with only the people's voices to carry it high to the heavens. All of the caravan knew the words, and everyone began to sing them together.

Rivera removed his hat and raised it high above his head. Turning in his saddle, he looked back at the people and raised his voice so all could hear him.

"*Adelante! Siempre Adelante!*"

Forward, he told them. Forward always!

And with Rivera's command, the caravan moved out of Loreto.

II

Siempre Adelante!

ᏩWEᏁᏩY-ᏁIᏁE

Calixto was not interested in moving forward.

Siempre adelante! made no sense to him at all. The *españoles* were never happy with what they had or where they had it. They were a restless people who wandered simply to wander, not to look for food or to find water; they moved with no reason or sense. Guaymas had plenty of everything, and still they had kept moving. Loreto had a big warehouse filled with supplies; there was water, there was food, there was clothing and shelter—and still they were moving. When would they stop? When would the land be good enough, plentiful enough, to fill them up inside?

They were an empty people, these *españoles*.

Not like the people Calixto had come from. You moved only when there was no food; you moved only when the water was gone and you had to find more. You traveled only when your survival depended upon it, no other reason than that. You followed the fish because they were plenty. You hunted the turtle, and the turtle took you where you must go. You gathered up the fruits and the seeds that the land offered you. You did not stick the seeds into the ground, forcing them to stay when the wind wanted to carry them away. You did not need to claim the land with your crops that could be flushed away by *chubascos* or scorched by the sun, leaving you with nothing. The land would

155

not be conquered by owning it. The wind, the rain, and the sun had power over the earth, and they were the ones that owned it. The *españoles* did not understand this.

And so they just kept moving.

But Calixto wanted to stop.

They were traveling away from the sea, moving inland. And with every step that took him farther away from the water, the voices of his people told him to turn around and go back.

The caravan had been traveling for two days, heading west from Loreto. The coastline was gone. The sand no longer was under their feet. The path had turned rocky and rough as the long line of the pilgrims followed a dried creek bed through a cactus-filled *arroyo* at the foot of new mountains. The trail led higher, steeply twisting its way upwards. And the hooves of the horses stumbled at times, trying to find their footing along the rugged way. Riders had to hold tightly to the reins, spurring their mounts to keep climbing.

It was not right for Calixto to be there.

These mountains were not for his footsteps or for any of his clan. He was from the Turtle people and needed the waters to always be close to him. Calixto knew these mountains from the clear days when they were visible from the far shores of Tiburón Island—his people's island. Tiburón is what the *españoles* had called it, from all the sharks that swam there in the waters. From their island, the people could see the mountains of Baja rising up, looking like giants—*xica coosyatoj*. Sierra de la Giganta, the *españoles* called them: the mountains where giants once lived. These giants were the ancestors of Calixto's tribe. Many of them died in a great flood years ago, and the ones who had survived became the rocks, animals, and plants now living there.

It was a sacred place, these mountains.

The Ancient of the Pelicans created it this way, along with the Turtle, Moon, and the Sun. These were the gods of the ones Calixto called The People—*his* people. This was the truth as he knew it, the world explained to him by those who came before him.

Calixto did not belong in these mountains. Neither did any other Seri.

It did not surprise him when the sicknesses fell upon them.

It was the giants telling them to go back.

ᏦᎻᏆᎡᏖᎩ

The sickness did not hit all the *indios* at once.

Slowly, it found them, one by one.

Maybe it was what they ate—so different from the meals of the caravan. Not liking the food of the *españoles,* the *indios* ate the seeds they found along the trail or the fruits of cactus and other plants they gathered along the way. If they had meat at all, it was a lizard or two, or a rabbit or rat they had trapped at the camp. If it wasn't the food, perhaps it was the water from one of the creeks they had stopped at, or the rain that pelted down on them that whole second day, soaking them to the bone but never stopping them from moving on. Whatever the reason, the sickness came when it came.

The fevers hit on the third day.

And only the *indios* were felled by them.

Three of the Cochimís became ill in the morning and one more was stricken by dusk. One of the Red Sashes could not eat by the time the night had fallen, and the second Red Sash was sick soon after. In all, six *indios* were ill by that third night.

Calixto attended to the two Seris with a tea he made from the gum of the cholla plant—a plant he knew well from Tiburón—that grew in the heart of the island. He made his tribesmen drink the hot tea even if they did not want it. All night long, Calixto did this, and for this reason, the fever did not come as hard as it had come to the others. By morning, the Red Sashes could travel once again, still weak but stronger because of Calixto's tea.

But the Cochimís did not do as well. The fevers raged on and overcame their bodies. One of the men died that night. And in the morning the *españoles* awoke to find that sickness had found their caravan. The mothers tried to keep their children away from the *indios,* moving as far from them as they could. The men, too, kept their distance. They had seen this kind of sickness before, and they knew that it could spread among them like a fire hungry to burn.

Only El Capitán and his two officers found the courage to move closer to the sick Cochimís, who still lay in their bedding on the desert floor. "Get one of the men to bury the dead one," Rivera told Rios, pointing to the Cochimí who had died overnight. "And make litters for the rest. We can't afford the time to stop and wait for the illness to pass."

Rios turned to look at his recruits, gathered with their families at a safe distance away from the *indios.* He did not hesitate choosing the man he wanted for such a horrible duty. "Garcia!" he called, looking over at Felipe who was standing next to his new wife. "Grab a shovel!"

Felipe had no choice but to do what he was told to do.

ᏭᎻᏐᎡᏐᎩ-ᎾᏁᎬ

It took hours for Felipe to dig the grave.

This land was stubborn, baked hard by the sun, and the shovel was no match for it. The body of the Cochimí, now wrapped in canvas, waited patiently as Felipe sweated and grunted his way deeper into the soil. While he worked, the lieutenant looked on from a distance. It gave Rios pleasure to watch him. To know that he had power over him.

Not just because of Petra.

"That's deep enough!" Rios shouted to Felipe. "In this heat he will be bones before you know it. And no one cares if the coyotes find him."

Felipe stopped and wiped the sweat from his forehead and he pulled his shirt off over his head.

Still, Rios watched him.

Pulling himself up out of the grave, Felipe went over to pick up the canvas-covered body, cradling it in his arms and carrying it over to the grave. The lieutenant turned away and went back to his troops.

And Felipe dropped the body into the ground.

That night Felipe slept alone.

The newlyweds from Loreto had each been given their own tents, for privacy. When supper was over and all the families had gone off to bed, Domingo and Tomás stood in front of the canvas flap of Petra's tent. When Felipe arrived, they blocked him from entering.

"The women are nervous," Domingo said. "You know how women get." He shrugged, running out of words.

Tomás said what Domingo couldn't. "They don't want you sleeping here with Petra," he said quickly, without apology. "Not with the sicknesses in the camp. You have to sleep somewhere else."

"I'm not sick," Felipe said.

"You touched the dead."

"I had to bury him."

But this was not open to discussion.

"You spend too much time around them," Tomás said, impatiently, sounding more like Martín than himself. "You don't keep your distance like the rest of us. And they're filthy, just like the animals. That's why they're sick." Tomás turned around and picked up a blanket that was sitting at the entrance of the tent. He dropped it on the ground in front of Felipe, not wanting to risk touching him by handing him the blanket.

"Just for a few nights, to make sure you don't get sick," Domingo explained, trying to be kind. "To keep the women happy." Domingo gave him a grin.

Felipe picked up his blanket and walked away.

The *indios* had set up their own camp away from the caravan. Their cooking fire was still aflame and the light of it could be seen across the way from the *españoles*. More of the Cochimís had fallen ill, and they lay close to the warmth of the cooking fire. The Red Sashes were across the way, sharing the heat from the other side of the embers.

Calixto used the flames to heat up a pot of water, and when he was sure it was boiling, he wrapped his hand in a cloth and took the pot from the flames. Pouring the water into a cup filled with the crushed-up cholla plant, he made the same tea he had given to the sick Red Sashes the night before. This time he offered it to the sickest of the Cochimís, holding their heads and helping them to sit up and drink it.

In the darkness, Felipe lay on his blanket at the foot of a patch of agave not far from the *indio* camp. He watched Calixto with great curiosity as the old man cared for the sick. Moving from Cochimís to his own Red Sashes, the old man cared for each one of them with the same compassion. It did not matter who they were or if they were different than he was. What mattered was healing them. Treating each man the same as the other.

Felipe watched Calixto do this all through the night.

And he learned what it meant to be a good man.

CHIRCY-CWO

The next morning Calixto was gone.

He was smart enough to not flee alone. He left in the company of two of the Cochimís: two of the strongest, young and impatient, dressed like *españoles*, in cotton breeches and sombreros. They spoke their words and did as they were told, but they were only recent neophytes—baptized but not believers. There was nothing to keep them there now that death was reaching out for them. These *españoles* were doomed, the Cochimís were certain of it. They trusted this land they walked upon more than they did these strangers who were trying to claim it.

While trying to claim them too.

Calixto had noticed the two men speaking quietly with each other, while the other Cochimís and Red Sashes slept. When they left the campfire, just the two of them, he followed them to where the horses had been corralled. When he saw them untie two horses and climb on them, he didn't ask their permission but followed by jumping on the closest stallion and riding after them.

The Cochimís did not make him go back.

And the three of them escaped into the night.

A scream at daybreak told the caravan there was trouble.

Ortiz spared the whip but used his fists instead, smashing them hard into the face of a young Sinaloan recruit.

"No one falls asleep on guard duty!" the corporal shouted, matching every word with a blow as he struck out at the *soldado*. He was just a boy, this recruit; Juan Vargas was a close neighbor of Felipe's from the village. No more than fifteen or sixteen, he looked much younger, and they called him Juanito.

"I'm sorry! *Lo siento!* Forgive me!" The boy sobbed with every word.

Still, the corporal beat him.

But blows were not enough for Ortiz. Reaching back to his belt, he pulled his knife from its sheath, running the blade at the boy's neck, one side to the other, and freeing a thin red line of blood from his throat.

"Three good horses we lost because of you! Because you slept!"

He would have killed that boy right then and there, dug the blade deeper and done the deed, but the recruit screamed like a little fox. And Ortiz was smart enough to put the knife away and throw the boy to the dirt.

All the caravan was now awake.

Rivera and Rios came running, and the men, women, and children gathered around outside their tents, watching as the news was told.

"This fool—*pendejo!* He was asleep, and three of the savages took off! With three of the horses, two saddles too, and blankets! *Cabron!*"

Ortiz kicked the boy where he lay in the dirt. The sight was too much for the mother of Juanito and she ran out to him. Kneeling next to her son, she shielded him with her body and would not move.

All eyes were on Rivera.

It was one thing to discipline the troops but not in front of the families. Especially the women. These people of Sinaloa could not understand the seriousness of what had happened. It was not only the question of theft—although that alone was a sin to be reckoned with. Every horse was needed, every item important to the journey and their survival. But more than the theft, the *indios* had broken a code. They were joined together, all of this caravan, as one people, in good times and bad, and when one thought differently than all the rest and acted on that—doing whatever he wanted—that violated the bond needed among all of them to survive and go forward. The escape by the *indios* was an insult not only to Rivera but to all of the caravan. Their leaving said to the people that they cared nothing about the *españoles*, only about themselves.

They had to be caught and punished.

As a lesson for all.

"Take two men and go after them," Rivera said to the corporal, without hesitation. He knew Ortiz was the man for the job; he would do what needed to be done, swiftly and out of sight. The caravan understood this. More importantly, every *indio* they had brought with them on this journey would understand it too. The message would be clear to them: stay with the caravan or suffer the consequences. Order must be kept, and it was Rivera's job to keep it.

"We move out tomorrow morning, one way or the other," the captain said quietly to Ortiz. "Be back by then. And I want to see three horses with you. I don't care how you get them back."

Ortiz smiled. He was more than confident he could handle this command. "Garcia!" he called out to Felipe, who was standing with the *indios* and separated from the rest of the *españoles*. "Saddle up the horses for us!" he ordered.

Felipe hurried to the corral, and as he did, he thought of Calixto. He did not understand this man at all or why he would run away. Everything he needed was there with the *españoles*, not in this wild and untamed land. The caravan had food and fire, tents for the weather, and weapons for protection. Calixto had turned away from all that and the security that they had offered him. Together they were strong. But Calixto had traded all this for a horse and the company of two *indios* he barely knew. Felipe could only hope that Calixto was far away now—from Ortiz and the punishment he would face when they caught him. Felipe thought all of these things as he saddled up three horses, readying them for Ortiz and the two soldiers who would join the corporal in the search for Calixto.

"Have you ever used an *escopeta* before?" Felipe turned to see who was asking this question.

The words came from Ortiz, standing there with Martín, outside of the makeshift corral. In his hands, he held an *escopeta*—a long rifle—and he was aiming it right at Felipe. "He's a farm boy," Martín said. "Farm boys know nothing about anything except fucking sheep."

"Well, then, he's about to learn."

Ortiz cocked the trigger, and that's when Felipe finally understood.

He would be the third soldier to hunt down Calixto.

CHIRCY-CHREE

There was nothing Ortiz loved better than the chase.

Whether it was rabbits on the Catalonian plains when he was a tiny boy, or bighorns on the slopes of the Pyrenees when he sported his first beard, this was what he lived for—the hunt and the kill.

It was much sweeter though when it was a man he was hunting.

It took more time, that's true. But it was a fairer fight—man-to-man—and when Ortiz would win (as he always did), it made his manhood swell with pride. It wasn't just the kill but the catch: overpowering another man and besting him. Seeing him destroyed—crumbling in pain and fear, reeking of sweat and shitting his pants—witnessing this loss of control is what Ortiz craved. To watch it happen right in front of him, to know that he was responsible for it—this is what filled him up inside and made him feel like a man. More than any woman ever could.

It was a skill he was good at. It made his name mean some-thing here in this godforsaken land of heat and heathens. The people were at peace because of men like Ortiz—soldiers who pushed forward, without water, without food or rest. When all hell was raining down on top of the provinces—on Sonora, Sinaloa, and Ostimuri—it was men like Ortiz who made it through the flames.

He did it better than the rest, everyone knew this.

The hunter learned from the hunted. The *indios* were his teachers. When they struck the *español* troops hard, appearing like phantoms out of nowhere and then running like the wind and escaping the fight, the other *soldados* called them cowards. They could not understand an enemy like this, hitting hard and fast and then evaporating like the mountain mists that had once sheltered them. But Ortiz watched and learned from these *indios*. He learned to track them by their own way of tracking. From the captured and the wounded, he was taught their ways. And when other *soldados* grew tired and their feet and backs hurt from the heat, Ortiz stripped down like the Pima, the Yaqui, the Seri; naked now, like they were, he pushed forward. When marshes stopped their horses, he climbed off his mount and crept forward. And when the *indios* hid in the thickets too overgrown for the soldiers to march through, he remembered their *rancherías*—their own homes—that they had burned to the ground to confuse and to stop the *soldados* from following them. Ortiz learned from this, making his own fire and setting flame to those thickets, the same thickets that shielded the hunted. The hunted were to him just like the rabbits on the coastal plains of Catalonia, hiding away from a little boy with a knife who was waiting patiently for them to run.

But the *indios* did not run.

They stayed deep in those thickets. And Ortiz stood by and listened to the screams of their children dying in the flames. That is how he got to be known and how his name found meaning. By not caring.

"You think they can be your friends, but you see now that's not true." Ortiz spoke to Felipe, as the young recruit rode his horse next to the corporal, and they followed the hoof tracks of Calixto and the two Cochimís.

"We should have killed them while we had the chance!" Martín added. Ortiz looked over at Martín, riding on his other side. Of all the *criollos*, this one he hated the most. For his ambition and for the way he kissed anyone's ass that was above his.

"Were you there?" he asked Martín, not waiting for an answer. "Were you with us in '68 when we were drinking our own piss for water? When the Yaquis slaughtered our farmers, the Pimas killed our horses, and the Seris insulted us with sneak attacks, pretending friendship with one hand and cutting our throats with the other? Were you there when the blood of the *españoles* paid for this land?"

Once again, Ortiz did not wait for an answer.

"You were still sucking at your mama's tits," he told Martín. "You *criollos* don't know half of what you think you know. We're outnumbered here with these savages, and when we get to San Diego and beyond, it will be even worse. If you make friends with these people, you will end up dead. If you let down your guard, you will be letting down your people. And you can kiss California good-bye."

These last words he spoke directly to Felipe, for the sin of this recruit was greater than all the rest. It wasn't one of stupidity but of kindness. And kindness could get them all killed.

"I'm not his friend," Felipe said softly.

After he said it, he wondered why he needed to say it at all. Better to be like Calixto and not speak a word than to say only what a man like Ortiz wants you to say.

And yet Felipe had said it.

"Good to know," Ortiz said, with a furrowed brow. Already his attention had moved on. His eyes were back on the tracks they were following, and his mind grew focused on the men they were hunting. "I will keep you to those words." The corporal snapped his reins and galloped forward.

And Felipe and Martín, good soldiers that they were, followed after him.

Calixto was tired but still they kept riding.

He had no choice but to keep going and to follow. This was not his land; as a stranger here, he needed help from the Cochimís. They knew where they were going, where there was water, where it was safe to stop and rest, and where others could help them. Calixto needed them for that knowledge.

But what the two Cochimís didn't know was that it was Corporal Ortiz who was coming after them. Ortiz, the relentless hunter. And because they didn't know this, the Cochimís did nothing to cover their tracks or to hide the droppings of their mounts as they rode across open plains, racing for the safety of the mountains ahead of them and then climbing up the rocky sides to the *mesa*—the flat land—at the top.

They moved fast, never stopping.

But the loose rocks along the ridge of the mountainside caught the hoof of one of the horses, and it stumbled to its knees and fell. The Cochimí riding on his back was thrown hard to the ground. The horse had trouble getting up, and the three *indios* worked together, taking the reins and pulling on them to get the animal to stand. When the horse was finally able to get up, they could see the split on the horse's right front hoof. Part of the hoof had been stripped away, and the horse could not put his weight on it. He was lame and could not be ridden.

Calixto quickly stripped the blanket and saddle from the back of the horse. Tossing the saddle over the edge of the mountainside, he threw the blanket onto the rump of one of the other horses. He mounted the horse and offered a hand up to the Cochimí that was thrown. Taking hold, the man pulled himself up on the back of the mount, behind Calixto. Together, the three *indios*, now on only two horses, galloped off, leaving the lame horse behind them.

Ortiz slowed his horse down as he entered a ravine, waiting for Martín and Felipe to catch up from behind. When they joined him, the men took a moment to drink from a shared *bota*, which Martín passed from one man to the next. Looking up, Ortiz's eyes searched the rocky cliffs of the mountainside to his left. That's when he heard it. A horse whinnied in the distance. Ortiz looked farther along the ridge in front of them. Something caught the sunlight and sparkled among the rocks.

The silver buckle of a leather saddle.

Higher in the mountains, the land evened out onto a *mesa* that was flat and rocky with no trees in sight. Just a patch here and there of shrubs covered ground that was dry and bleached by the sun. Calixto and the two Cochimís slowed their horses, walking them a little before stopping and letting the animals nibble the manzanita at their hooves. The three *indios* climbed down off their saddles. Calixto shaded his eyes from the sun as he looked across the flat land in front of them.

One of the Cochimís reached into his boot and took out a knife. Moving over to a clump of cactus nearby, he ran the blade across the stem of one of the red fruits, slicing it off from the plant. Carefully, he poked a hole into it with the tip of the knife and brought it to his lips, drinking from it, as the nectar dripped down from his mouth. The other Cochimí joined him and cut another fruit from the plant. Slicing it into two halves, he held out his hand and offered one half to Calixto, just as a sharp sound of a loud crack cut through the air. The white-shirted chest of the Cochimí exploded in red and he fell backwards into the dirt. Dead.

Ortiz stood at the top of an outcropping looking across the *mesa* at the *indios* who were exposed there in front of him in the barrenness of the land. With his rifle reloaded, he shot again.

What happened next happened fast.

Calixto's horse, frightened by the shots, bolted, and the other Cochimí scrambled on top of his horse as fast as he could. Martín and Felipe appeared on their horses as they scrambled up from the mountainside onto the *mesa*. Calixto took off running.

The Cochimí on top of the galloping mount looked back behind him as Calixto ran for his life, trying to catch up with him and to climb on the back of the fleeing horse. Holding his hand out to Calixto as far as he could, he nodded for him to keep running and to jump as he slowed the horse a little, trying to help Calixto escape.

Another shot rang out from Martín's pistol as he rode his horse, chasing after them.

The bullet flew close to Calixto—he could feel it in the air as it whizzed by him and almost hit the horse. He looked up into the eyes of the Cochimí who still held his hand out, still reaching to help him. The *indio* nodded his head again, encouraging Calixto to jump, to grab hold, to save himself.

That's when Calixto stopped running.

He would not see this Cochimí killed because of him. Not another person would die because of his actions. Stopping where he stood would set this Cochimí free to escape as fast as the horse would carry him. With no one holding him back at all. The Cochimí understood this and looked away from Calixto. Taking the reins in both hands, he snapped them hard. And the horse took flight.

Martín whipped his mount and chased after the Cochimí, bolting past Calixto.

Felipe slowed his horse down when he reached the old *indio*. Calixto turned around to face him. Standing still and strong, he did not cower, nor did he move. He simply waited. Slowly Felipe, on top of his horse, circled Calixto, keeping him close and not letting him escape. Working the reins, in control of the animal, Felipe was master of his horse.

Just like Calixto had taught him.

GHIRGY-FOUR

Of the three hunted, Calixto was the one most wanted.

And now Ortiz had him.

The corporal circled his horse proudly around the old Seri. Calixto waited and showed no fear. What would happen next would happen. In many ways, he welcomed it. Peace had been far from his reach, and in this way, he would find it again. It was worth waiting for.

Ortiz would do his best to make him wait. For the corporal, the anticipation could be as sweet as the act. He had no reason to hurry this. The day was still young and the caravan was close. Ortiz had hours to do what he wanted to do, and he would make sure to savor each one of those hours. "Tie up his hands and feet," he ordered Felipe, his eyes never moving away from his prize catch.

Felipe hesitated.

"He won't be able to walk," he said to the corporal.

"He's not walking anywhere," Ortiz said flatly. The corporal climbed down from his horse.

"How will we bring him back to Rivera?" Felipe asked.

"Why do you care?" Ortiz said, squaring off with his recruit. Standing chest to chest with Felipe, the corporal's attention was no longer on Calixto. "Why do you care so much about this fucking savage?"

173

"I don't care," Felipe answered, afraid to say anything different.

His words did not convince the corporal. Ortiz knew that Felipe liked this heathen, and he understood that Calixto was not the only one who needed to be punished. Both men had to be taught a lesson, and Ortiz was eager to do the teaching. "Tie him up," the corporal ordered again, not moving from where he stood. Face to face with Felipe, he reached over and slowly unbuckled the leather belt from around the recruit's waist. Slipping it out from his uniform, he handed it to Felipe.

Felipe looked over at Calixto. And at that moment, Calixto did the worst thing he could possibly do: he looked back. His eyes connected with Felipe—those eyes, so wide and dark, and yet eyes just like any other man's. Felipe searched Calixto's face for some kind of difference, for something that made him less than a man, for a reason that might let him do what the corporal was ordering him to do. A reason not to care about him and to treat him worse than an animal might be treated. Felipe searched Calixto's face, but he could not find that reason anywhere in Calixto's eyes.

Impatiently, Ortiz reached over to the back of his saddle and took down his whip. He ran the tip of the leather like a threat across his open palm. "Tie him up, Garcia," Ortiz said.

Felipe did not hesitate a moment more. He took his leather belt and wrapped it tightly around Calixto's wrists, binding them together. Ortiz threw Felipe some leather straps from the side of his saddle.

"And his feet too!" the corporal ordered.

Felipe did as he was told, tying up Calixto at his ankles.

"Stand him up against the cactus," Ortiz told him. Felipe took hold of Calixto by his bound hands, and the *indio* did not struggle as he was brought over to a tall patch of cactus.

"Now, take his shirt off," Ortiz commanded.

Felipe paused.

"Take it off!"

Felipe did as he was told, unbuttoning the cotton shirt that Calixto wore. But as he did, his hands began to tremble. He did not want to be doing this, and if his words could not say that, his hands would show it. After it was done, he stepped away, wanting to distance himself from what was about to happen.

But Ortiz had something else in mind. As Felipe started to walk past the corporal, Ortiz held out his whip.

"Fifty lashes, Garcia."

Felipe was stopped by the words. Ortiz snapped the whip in Felipe's direction.

"His back or yours, Private. Makes no difference to me."

Slowly, Felipe reached out and took the whip from the corporal. Ortiz grinned and walked over to Calixto. Facing him, he leaned in as close as he could. "Your time is over, *viejo*," Ortiz said, enjoying the sight of the captured *indio*. "You lost! You're too stupid to understand that, aren't you?"

Calixto heard the words and understood every one of them. But he would not give the satisfaction to the corporal by showing that he did. He would not waste his voice on such a man as this. Instead, his eyes focused on Felipe, who now stood with the whip in his hand.

Stepping back, Ortiz gave the command. "Teach him, Garcia."

Felipe's eyes never moved past those of Calixto's.

"Do it!" shouted Ortiz, and pulled his pistol from his waistband. Pointing it at Felipe, he cocked the trigger. "*Puto*, do it!"

The words were barely out of the corporal's mouth before Felipe snapped the whip. The leather tip reached out and found its mark—striking Ortiz sharply on the wrist. The pistol flew out of his hand and the eyes of the corporal widened with rage. But before his brain could tell his hands and feet what to do next, the whip was pulled back and was lashed hard against the corporal's chest. Ortiz was knocked backwards to the ground. And still, the whip did not stop. Before he could right himself, the leather lashed against his face, and when he doubled up in pain, Felipe hurled the whip again and again and again. Over and over, Felipe snapped the whip, moving closer to the prone corporal, like a madman striking out in rage. But before he could hurl the whip again, his hand was stopped.

Calixto stopped him.

Though bound at the feet and hands, he had dragged himself over to Felipe, throwing his body against his to stop the whip. While the corporal lay sprawled in the dirt and stunned, Calixto worked quickly. He held up his hands for Felipe to untie them, and Felipe did what he asked. Once untied, Calixto reached down to his feet and freed them from the leather straps at his ankles.

Now, he could run.

"Go!" Felipe told him.

On the ground, Ortiz began to stir. Calixto reached down to pick up the pistol lying in the dirt, pointing it at Ortiz. One shot echoed across the land.

The corporal fell back to the dirt, dead.

With pistol in hand, Calixto moved over quickly to Felipe and pointed it at the young *español*. Felipe waited. But not for long. Calixto smashed the *pistola* against the side of Felipe's head—knocking him out.

Running over to the corporal's horse, Calixto jumped on the back of the animal and galloped away across the *mesa*, disappearing into the mountains.

ᏩᎻᏆᎡᏩᏯ-FIVE

The sound of the gunshot brought Martín back to the *mesa*.

He had been close on the heels of the fleeing Cochimí, when the crack of the pistol stopped him. Something about that sound told him there was trouble. Ortiz would not be so quick to kill the captured savage. He would want to have his fun with him first, playing with him the way a bobcat chases a little squirrel to tire him out before he snaps his neck.

One shot was for killing, not for playing.

Martín waited for a second crack from the pistol. More than one might mean Ortiz was having his fun, killing the beast one bullet at a time. But when no other shots were heard, Martín knew he had to turn back. Something was wrong. Pulling on the reins and turning the horse around, he headed back—back to Ortiz and the captured Calixto.

It didn't take long for him to see it.

Two bodies were sprawled across the ground.

Martín saw them from a distance, and even from afar, the blue of their uniforms told him who they were. He whipped his horse to go faster, and by the time he reached them, he could tell: one of the bodies would never rise again, and the other was already starting to sit up.

The wrong man was alive.

Martín paid no attention to Felipe as he jumped from his saddle and went to look at the fallen corporal. Touching him with his boot, Martín pushed him over until he could look into his eyes, still open and staring. Blood covered his neck from the bullet that had ripped open his throat. Death had been quick.

There was no question who was at fault. The corporal was dead and beyond blame. The soldier who somehow had managed to live, when any other would have surely been slaughtered simply for wearing the uniform, was a man who had befriended the very savage who had done this intolerable deed. Felipe had been spared.

For this, he would be judged.

And he would face the consequences.

At dusk, they returned.

The caravan was not prepared for the sight of only two returning *soldados.*

At first, Domingo, watering the horses in the corral, was not sure what he was seeing. He shouted for the lieutenant to come and take a look. Rios joined Domingo at the edge of the corral and looked off where the private was pointing. Across the wide *arroyo,* coming down the rocky side to the flat land below, was a lone rider, and behind him, with a rope connecting him to the back of the saddle, walked a man with his hands tied with leather straps. The rider was Martín and behind him, on the back of his saddle, was the body of the corporal. Felipe, with his hands tied, stumbled along behind them.

A prisoner.

Ortiz was buried within the hour. Before the sun set, his body was slipped into the earth, and one of the travelers—a carpenter from Sinaloa—tied together a cross with the corporal's name carved into the wood.

It would not last the winter.

The grave would be lost to rain and sleet. The wooden cross would come undone, the leather straps would dry out in the summer heat, turning to dust over the years, and the wood would crumble, until nothing was left to mark the grave of Corporal Ortiz. No one would ever come to mourn him or say a little prayer. And perhaps the shallowness of the grave that was dug by Domingo and Tomás was not an accident. The coyotes could thank them for the ease with which they had found the scent and dug up the remains, enjoying the taste of Ortiz for many days and sharing the bounty with the buzzards. The corporal's problems were over.

Felipe's were just beginning.

Rivera did not wait for the corporal to be buried before bringing Martín and Felipe into his tent to hear the story. With his hands still tied, Felipe stood in front of the captain.

"Why does he still live? If that savage killed Ortiz, why not him too?" Martín spit the words out angrily. "Because he was his friend, that's why! He must have helped him escape!"

"Why are you still alive?" Rivera asked, standing face-to-face with Felipe.

This Felipe could not say. He did not understand Calixto's actions, just as he did not understand his own. How could he explain what he had done? What words could he possibly use to make the captain understand why he had helped Calixto? How could he tell him that in Calixto he saw someone who deserved to be spared—a man like any other man and one worth saving. He could not hope to make the captain understand this, not with any words that Felipe knew how to say. And now he understood why Calixto's tongue never spoke. Sometimes the only answer is silence, when words are not enough.

This is how Felipe answered Rivera—as Calixto would have done.

"I don't have time for this," Rivera said, impatient with Garcia's silence.

But Martín could not stay quiet. He was the son of a soldier, and he knew better than most that discipline meant nothing unless it was enforced. One of his own first memories as a child was standing in the village square, watching as two soldiers were publicly hanged. The one for murdering the husband of his mistress, and the other—only sixteen—for sodomy. Justice had to be swift on the frontier. It served as an example, not just for the soldiers but for all of the *españoles*.

"Capitán, this man needs to be punished! He failed while on duty."

"Are you running this caravan now?" Rivera snapped, stopping Martín from saying more. "We have no time for an inquest, not to mention a trial. We have to get to San Diego before the weather changes. That's my only concern, and it should be yours too."

Martín touched the brim of his hat, saluting the captain. He did not want to further anger Rivera and risk his position as his aide.

But that was a worry Martín did not need to have.

"I'm promoting you to corporal," Rivera told him. It's true, he was not fond of Martín, but his choice was limited. "I have no one else who wants it as badly as you do," Rivera said to Martín. "Whatever happened out there is only known to Garcia and God. The only truth we're sure of is that we lost a corporal—a bad one, at that. Consider yourself lucky and move on." Rivera faced his new officer and looked Martín straight in the eye. "But don't you ever walk too close to my boots again."

A little ambition was fine, but too much was no good.

Rivera dismissed Martín with a salute and waited until he had left the tent to face Felipe.

"I don't know what happened out there, Garcia, but you put me in a difficult position."

The captain took a moment to study Felipe's face. This recruit was young, and he knew nothing about the world. But this journey would teach him. Rivera was certain that by the time they reached Monterey, Garcia would not be so young anymore.

"I had high hopes for you—that you could be a good leader for these people," Rivera told Felipe. "We'll need that where we're going, where there are so few of us. You've shown great determination and courage on this journey. When others quit, you kept going. You made fire in the rain, giving us warmth and safety at a time when these people needed it—when all they had were their own fears, their own doubts, and nothing to pull them together. You saved that boy from drowning. Now, we are one caravan, united as we go forward. You helped make that happen."

Rivera took a moment to let his words settle and for Felipe to understand them.

"I will never look upon you with the same trust," said the captain. "Once doubt is added to a man's reputation, that's a tough skin to shed. I need every recruit on this caravan, and I don't have the luxury of stripping you of all responsibilities. But I warn you: one misstep might be overlooked because we have to move on, but if you ever make another, there will be hell to pay."

Rivera took his knife and cut the leather bonds from around Felipe's wrists. Felipe was a free man again.

But at a price.

ᏆᎻᏆᏒᏒᎩ-SIX

Calixto was never seen again.

Felipe knew nothing about this man he had helped, but he had seen on Calixto's face that he was the most comfortable when they were crossing the sea in the little *lancha*. As the caravan moved further inland, it gave Felipe great pleasure to think of the old *indio* on a small reed raft, spear in hand, fishing—free now to do what he wanted, to go back to his home again.

Although El Capitán didn't punish Felipe, Martín found a way to do that on his own.

The new corporal did his best to color Felipe as a coward and a traitor to everyone on the caravan. At meals, people kept their distance from him, not truly knowing what had happened on that *mesa* or why and how the corporal had been killed. They wanted nothing to do with Felipe, at least when Martín was around. They did their best to turn their backs to him and leave him alone.

Well, for a day or two. Maybe three.

Ortiz had not been a well-loved man, and no one was crying that he was gone. Because with him also went his whip.

And as for Calixto? An *indio* who escaped from being forced to work day and night? Live and let live is what many of the villagers would say. The people from Sinaloa did not have the same needs as the *soldados* and the priests to tell the *indios* what to do and how to do it. Truth be told, even if there were those who wouldn't admit it, some of the villagers shared the same blood of many of the *indios*, even though they called themselves *españoles*. What mattered the most to these people was *familia*.

And the rest you didn't talk about.

Within a few days, no one bothered to turn away from Felipe anymore. Even Tomás and Domingo shrugged and got on with their lives. Within a few days, they were bringing plates of food over to their brother-in-law, sent there by Mercedes and Beatriz, and since they were already there, they shared a word or two and passed around their special *bota*—the one filled so tightly with *vino*. With the wine warming their bellies, Domingo and Tomás saw no reason for Felipe to sleep away from his and Petra's tent anymore. The *indios* who had been sick were well again, and Felipe showed no signs of their sickness. It was time for the bride and bridegroom to be reunited, so said Domingo, his mind made up by all the wine he had drunk.

But Petra wanted no part of it.

It was bad enough that she had to marry this farm boy, but now her future was forever connected to her husband's. If he drowned, she would sink with him. If his reputation became soiled, Petra's name was dragged into the mud too. He had already lost Rivera's trust, and one more mistake would be her mistake too.

"Maybe he shouldn't come back to the tent," Martín advised her, as they walked together along a stream during one of their stops. "Was the wedding night successful?" he asked, not brave enough to look at his sister's face while she answered.

"For me, yes. But not for him," Petra said, hoping she didn't have to explain more than that. Her brother, of all people, knew that she could not be a real wife to a man she didn't love. And Felipe was not the kind of man to force himself on a woman.

"This is not a marriage then," Martín told her.

Petra could only hope that he was right.

"Make him sleep outside your tent, while you sleep inside of it. And make sure everyone sees this," Martín told her. "When we get to Monterey, I will speak to the priest and make sure that the marriage can be ended. Annulled."

Petra, for the first time, could see herself as a free woman again.

Once more, Martín had the answer.

The caravan moved on through the mountains, following the *camino* as it snaked back down to the flatlands below. The pack train stretched out long and slow across an arid countryside covered in brush, with yucca and cactus in between.

The days were long as they traveled.

The sun beating down on them and the constant rhythm of the horse's hooves made them sleepy, lulled them until they nodded off, their heads snapping them awake only to fall again into dreams where the faces of their loved ones came to them and they saw their future in their eyes.

Life went on, even on the *camino*.

Children needed to be tended to, to be watched, to be protected from snakes and scorpions and from wandering off to be eaten by a cougar or a bear. There were meals to be prepared, clothing to be mended, firewood to be gathered, tents to be set up, dishes to be cleaned—all by the end of the day.

But still, they found time for each other.

Late at night, they would reach out, or if they had children, they would take a walk alone together. And those walks would lead them to privacy, some trees perhaps, or an outcropping of rocks, and even a cactus or two to hide them. There they would get to know each other all over again.

Tomás and Beatriz made the most of their small tent, disappearing as soon as the light left the sky. Sometimes they could be heard as they celebrated their new marriage. Sometimes more than once on some nights. This would give ideas to the others. And pretty soon, there were many couples celebrating their marriages too.

It had been a long time for Domingo and Mercedes. Traveling all day could be tedious, and one's mind would wander to other thoughts. But every time Domingo approached his wife, she would slap his hand as it circled her waist, or she would push him away as his body sought hers late at night.

"The children!" She would say this in a hushed voice that made him want her even more.

"*Mujer*! A man needs his comforts!" Domingo had said to her, as the two of them lay in their bedding one night. He had rolled over to face her, but Mercedes turned her back to him.

"There's no privacy with the children around all the time," she told him, reaching for any excuse to keep him away from her growing belly.

But one night this excuse did not work.

Domingo had other plans.

"I sent the children to sleep with their cousins!" he told her, with great pride.

There were no more excuses. And the two of them lay down together.

"We have all the privacy you want, *mi mujer*," Domingo said, with a smile. And he pushed his body against her back. Mercedes could feel that he meant business. Domingo wrapped his arms around his wife and cupped her breasts.

"Ummm," he sighed. "These are bigger than I remember." Sliding his hands lower to her belly, he had trouble making each hand meet the other. Domingo laughed at the size of his wife. "I'm losing my big *panza* with all this damn walking, but yours is getting bigger!" A sudden ripple across Mercedes' belly stopped Domingo's laughter. He was serious all of a sudden, as the child within her reached out and touched its papa.

"*Dios,*" Domingo whispered, and his eyes widened. Mercedes turned to face him. She didn't need to keep the baby a secret from her husband any longer. And she could only hope to see happiness in his eyes for the deed they had done and the life that was now growing there between them.

"I think we are not alone in this bed," Domingo said, looking to Mercedes to confirm the truth—that what he felt moving inside of her belly was not indigestion but a new life growing there.

"You must not tell the others," Mercedes said to him with an urgent whisper.

"But you will need help with the birth."

Mercedes reached out and silenced him with a finger to his lips.

"If El Capitán finds out, he will make us leave the caravan in San Diego, while the rest of the family goes on to Monterey." She told him this, and Domingo now grew quiet. "We will have nothing in Alta California—no land or home. Everything we own fits on the back of two *burros*. Family is all that we have. Family is where our home will be. We must stay together!" Domingo knew that Mercedes was right. And he let her know this by holding her even tighter.

"This baby will be coming at Christmas," she assured him. "And not a day sooner. We will be in Monterey, celebrating with all of the family. As it should be!" Domingo kissed the tip of her nose.

And for the first time since the caravan's journey began, Mercedes was happy that her children were sleeping with their cousins and that she could be a bride again.

The nights had their pull on Felipe and Petra too.

It was not difficult for Petra to keep her distance, just as her brother had told her to do. She didn't even have to ask Felipe to stay away. Each night, after setting up a bedroll inside the tent for his wife, Felipe tipped his hat to her and went outside where he slept in his own bedroll until the morning sun woke him and it was time to take down the tent and for them to move on. Petra was his wife in name only. Until she told him differently, he would honor her by keeping his needs to himself.

For this, Petra was grateful. It made her feel safe and strong to know that Felipe understood; that when she told him her feelings, he listened. He was not like her brother who made her do whatever he told her to do, no matter how much she wanted to do something else. It was always Martín's way, and what Petra said or thought had no meaning to him.

But Felipe was different. And she wondered why.

At night, she would watch him, just outside their tent, as he stretched out his long body, finding a place there on the ground that welcomed him and brought him sleep. She could watch him sleeping there in the moonlight through the slit in the opening of the canvas. He was so close she could hear his breathing, and it brought her some comfort just listening to it. No longer did she feel alone, with Felipe just within reach. And those first nights they had their own tent and they slept in this fashion, sleep had come to her quickly just because she knew he was there.

Then something strange started to happen to Petra.

Sleep did not come to her so easily every night. While she watched his chest rise and fall with his every breath, slowly she started to feel an ache deep inside of her. There were feelings she had never felt before, coming to her every night now, overwhelming her body until, at times, with every breath Felipe took, they took away her breath with them. Petra didn't understand what was happening to her. Every night, with her bedroll so close to Felipe's, these feelings of Petra's spread across her breasts and found their way lower.

And in the daytime too, they started to come.

After hours of riding in the saddle, when her eyes fixed

themselves on the broad back of the lieutenant as he straddled his horse at the front of the caravan, the ache would grow stronger, until sitting on a horse all day became almost painful. Was it something she had eaten, she wondered? The dried beef and the hard tortillas were certainly not the fresh meats and vegetables they had eaten back in the village. Could she be ill perhaps? She felt feverish at times, that was true. But only when she caught sight of Felipe asleep at night or of Rios in the daytime as they rode in the long line of the pack train together. On the off chance that her hand would touch the lieutenant's during a meal when plates were passed, or especially when Felipe would help lift her down from her horse. Oh, those times were sweet agony! She would grow light-headed and a pain came so fierce between her legs where the ache took root and would not let her go. Later, when she would seek shelter to relieve her water, she noticed the wetness would not go away. It saturated her, dripped from her, and if she touched it she discovered a warm wound that led deeper into her body. And an opening that seemed to grow with the wetness.

Petra realized that she was not well at all.

In fact, she thought she could be dying.

What else could it possibly be?

ᘓᕼIᖇᘓy-ᔕᕿᐯᕿᑎ

It was called El Camino Real.

The King's Road.

It stretched the length of Baja, from Loreto to San Diego, cutting through mountains separated by deserts, with a sun so fierce it burned the skin and took the joy out of living.

"If this *chingada* road was made for a king, he was one mean son-of-a-bitch!" Domingo said, as he and the other recruits put their muscles to good use trying to clear a passage of the trail that was blocked from last winter's storms.

They had been traveling well on the *camino*—ten miles a day and the road had been straight and clear all the way from Loreto. Into the mountains it had taken them and out again, zigzagging its way up the steepest grades—the *cuestas*—that the Jesuits had built cutting to and fro, this way and that, for an easier climb.

They had struggled at El Inferno, outside the mission at San Ignacio. The *arroyo* the *camino* had led them into grew narrow and deep. The pack train was soon forced out of the wash by a trail that led upwards onto the left shoulder of a steep bank where God had thrown so many rocks it looked impossible to climb. It was so steep that you could not look straight up at it without your head spinning. Everywhere you turned you saw boulders, and when the noon sun high above shone down on

189

those boulders, they turned dark red in color from the heat. It was like trying to climb hell. This was the worst pass on the *camino*, and they had to climb it to keep going.

Slowly, they picked their way around and up the slick boulders lining the slope all the way to the top. Using their reins and spurs, they prodded their animals with shouts and curses to keep them going.

One of the horses buckled at the knees and fell, throwing off a woman and her young son. The horse tumbled down the side of the mountain, all the way to the bottom of the *arroyo*. The horse was dead as soon as it hit the rocks below, the fall breaking his neck.

Rivera realized the climb was too risky, and he gave the command for all to dismount. The pack train was stopped halfway up the steep slope; the supplies were taken off the backs of the *burros* and horses, lessening the burdens on the animals. Once freed, their hooves were lighter and they were able to climb higher as the men led them to the top by their reins, leaving the women and children to carry the heavy supplies and packs in their arms and on their own backs.

It was a hard day for the caravan, but they persevered and went forward. Once out of El Inferno, they were headed northwest, and it was smooth traveling for a while.

Until the land forced them to stop again.

Two steep mountainsides faced each other, with a river running between them. The *camino* had been built at the site where the river's silt stretched along its side. Rocks had fallen from the steep slopes, and the road was partially blocked, with no room for the wide caravan to pass. There was no other way to move forward, and the *camino* was the only connection the *españoles* had to one another, up and down the Californias.

They had no choice but to stop and get to work.

"*Chinga* this *puta camino!*" Domingo shouted, as he slipped and fell to the ground.

The men of the caravan were covered in sweat, working to push the rocks out of the way.

"Stop your *pinche* whining, Ruiz! *Chingate!*" Acevedo, the middle-aged baker from Sinaloa, spit the words out at Domingo.

It was an insult that needed to be answered.

"*What* did you say to him?" Tomás confronted Acevedo.

"I'm tired of hearing it—all his piss and moaning about this thing and that! Shut up, why don't you? And work!" Acevedo pushed Tomás aside to confront Domingo.

That was all it took. One shove, one man touching another. That's when the fighting began. Someone threw a fist and another man caught it. Right in the face.

Now all the men on the work detail threw down their picks and their shovels and concentrated on beating the shit out of one another.

Had there been a priest traveling with them, this would not have happened. But without one, it was a free-for-all, with every man fighting just to show the others his strength. For almost three months they had been on the road, and their patience, like the fallen mountainsides in front of them, had also crumpled, stopping them right where they stood.

And the men weren't the only ones.

"It's about time someone told that lard-ass to shut-up!" The words were spoken by Luis Machada's wife, Lydia, who was known to be Sinaloa's biggest loudmouth. It was always her opinion that counted the most, even though it only counted to her and to no one else.

"The only work Ruiz does is when he's shoveling food into his mouth!" She told the women this with a laugh as they all were washing dishes on the banks of the river, and they could see their men fighting across the way.

Mercedes would have been forgiven if she had taken the first swing, defending her husband. But the extra weight of the baby inside of her held her back.

CALIFORNIO

Beatriz took her place.

The slap caught Lydia off-guard, and Bea took advantage of that, pushing her hard so she understood that the first blow wasn't an accident. This one sent Lydia backwards into the river, and she sank like a rock. Her friends had to grab hold of her before the water took her for a long swim.

Petra could not help but laugh as she put her arm around Beatriz to congratulate her on her prowess. Bea was usually the quiet one, but this time her anger did the talking, and Lydia, half Bea's height, was no match for her and didn't fight back. Instead, her two friends Lucille and Christina spoke up.

"What are you laughing at, *puta?*" Lucille called out to Petra.

The word stopped Petra in her tracks. No one had ever called her this before—called her a whore. At least, not to her face.

By now, the fight between the men had been stopped by the officers separating them, pushing them apart and ordering them to stand back. This was how it was done with men. They had officers to keep them in line, to control them if they found a reason to forget their journey or the rules in their lives. It was easy for the men to obey this way.

But for the women it was different.

They only had one another to keep order—to make sure all the women followed all the rules. When someone did something out of the ordinary that challenged all their lives, that woman needed to be called out.

"Who are you to call me a *puta?*" Petra faced Lydia and her two friends, and her eyes started to fill. She didn't like confrontation. It always brought tears to her eyes when what she really needed was to fight back.

Mercedes put her arms around her sister and turned her away. "Leave these cows alone. They're stupid, let them be." Mercedes walked Petra away from Lydia and her two friends.

"We're not in Sinaloa anymore!" Lydia called out to Petra. "You don't live up on that hill like your shit doesn't stink! You

Lunas are no better than the rest of us. If you don't want to be called a whore, don't act like one!"

This was more than Petra could take.

"Why do you say this?" She turned quickly and faced the women.

When they didn't answer her, she walked back to the river to confront them.

"Why do you call me a whore?" Petra asked, and she willed herself this time not to cry but to face them with as much strength as she could find deep inside of her. "I want to know this!" She spoke defiantly, not backing down this time.

"What other kind of woman, if not a whore, makes her husband a cuckold while her eyes search for another man?" Christina spoke these words—the youngest of the three women. She was Petra's age but already the mother of three small children. Petra had always thought of her as a friend, but that was in Sinaloa—and this was not Sinaloa anymore.

"You can't hide what you're doing. We see everything, we're not blind. You aren't sleeping with your husband—he's outside your tent every single night," Lydia told Petra.

"That's between my husband and me," Petra said, not backing down.

"Not when you walk around here like a cat in heat!" Christina sneered. "We see you—the way you keep to yourself when we're setting up the camp. You're too good to talk with us, but you have no problem speaking with the lieutenant."

"I saw her one night talking with him at Loreto." One of the other women farther down the river had shouted this.

Petra looked down the bank at the woman. She was Tia Anita, a grandmother, one of the oldest traveling in the caravan. She was not known as a gossiper; she was a woman who many looked up to and respected for her gray hair and a long life of minding her own business.

"A woman alone in the night with a man who is not her

husband is not a good woman," Tia Anita said, with a shake of her head. "If you don't want to be called a whore, don't give us a reason to call you one."

With those words, the fight between the women ended. They all went back to the river's edge, back to washing their dishes. But they had said what needed to be said. A woman who would not welcome her husband into her tent and into her body could bring trouble to them all.

Petra had to be told.

And she had to be stopped.

THIRTY-EIGHT

The passage was finally cleared, and it was time to move on.

But the damage to the caravan was not so easily fixed.

The men had worked hard together, but when the night came they separated into their own small families again. Each family stayed only to themselves. Sides had been taken—family against family.

Rivera could see the difference at supper that night.

The caravan ate in silence. No one laughed, no one started to sing a song or bring out a fiddle and play a tune. Even the little children did not run around, playing with one another the way they had when the caravan first started out.

Trust was gone; friendship was nowhere to be seen.

The Lunas all sat together, stretched out on a tarp spread across the ground. When little Marco wanted to run off to play with the Acevedo twin boys, Martín grabbed his son and pulled him back to sit down.

"Stay with the family!" Martín ordered, and Marco knew better than to challenge his father. "Which one of those cows called you a *puta*?" Martín asked Petra, spitting the word out like a bitter root, his eyes staring at the other women in the caravan.

"It wasn't just one," Mercedes corrected him.

"What difference does it make if it was one or all of them?" Petra said, not at all happy. "Why shouldn't they say it? They have eyes—they see what happens every night. They know what's not happening in our tent!"

"Let them see it! It'll only help you when we talk to the priest in Monterey," Martín told her. "They're proof that you're telling the truth."

"What I do is no one's business!" Petra said. "Yours or anyone else's!" She spoke defiantly, not caring if any of the families were watching or listening to her.

Martín thought a moment and then looked across the way where Felipe sat by himself, finishing his meal.

"Garcia!" he called out to his brother-in-law.

Felipe rose and came over to him.

"You're on guard duty tonight," Martín ordered him. "I don't want you sleeping outside your tent anymore. You do guard duty every night until we get to Monterey. That's an order."

Felipe looked over at Petra, but her eyes avoided him. Her brother had spoken, and as corporal, he had issued a command. Felipe had no choice but to obey his order. Touching the brim of his hat, he saluted Martín before going back to finish his meal.

"There!" Martín said, looking over at Petra, with a smile. "Now they won't have anything to talk about."

And that was how the matter was settled.

Felipe welcomed being on his own at night.

Guarding the caravan kept him away from Petra, and for this he was grateful. He could not bear the closeness of her anymore. To awaken in the middle of the night and to feel her presence on the other side of the canvas was more pain than he could take.

He wanted Petra. But he had no idea what that meant.

Felipe was not even sure what to do with a woman. True,

he had some idea. He had watched the livestock—the bulls and the horses. But in his soul, he knew that men were not livestock and that there must be another way to do what the animals were doing. For the life of him, though, he did not know what that was. During the day, on the long stretches of traveling, he thought about this. And by evening, all he wanted in this world was to be with Petra, to mount her and to do with her, yes, what the stallion he had seen had done with the mare. Luckily, Petra wanted nothing to do with him. And he was a man, not a stallion, and as a man he could hold himself back. But there she lay each night—a hand's reach away on the other side of the canvas, wearing lace and petticoats, as much clothing as she could possibly wear—protecting herself in the night. Clothing he wanted to rip away. With a quick sign of the cross, he would turn his back to the opening of the tent, and thank goodness that the roughness of the day's ride rewarded him with sleep.

On some nights, though, sleep would not come. And it took all of Felipe's strength not to push forward and to follow the urges he felt at the sight of his sleeping wife. On those nights only the saying of the rosary helped, and perhaps a walk away from the tent, away from the caravan and out to some bushes for shelter, a patch of cactus for privacy. There he could find some relief. But lately, even after touching himself while seeing Petra in his mind, and after that sweet release, just going back to the tent again and lying outside of it, still so close to her, made him want her all over again. And how many times can a man walk into the woods by himself before he has to find another solution.

That is why the night watch was so welcomed. Felipe could still keep an eye on Petra's tent from where he was stationed. But from afar—above the caravan, on the slopes of an *arroyo*, or the small rise on a desert floor—and his heart did not quicken as it did with her body stretched out so close to him, separated only by a canvas flap. With the moonlight, he could watch over her from a distance. In his heart, he could still be close.

As the nights stretched into weeks, the caravan crawled north up the length of Baja. The moon melted away in the sky until it disappeared completely and there was no light at all shining down to reveal Petra's tent or any of the tents. Darkness swallowed up the sights.

It was on such a night as this when it happened.

A sound broke the silence. Something was moving in the distance.

It was late, and the other soldier on guard duty with Felipe was asleep close to the campfire they had built to chase away the desert chill. The second shift was Felipe's—the one that would bring dawn with it when it was over.

The tents of the caravan had been set up at the bottom of a long-ago forgotten riverbed, while Felipe and the other guard sat on a rise overlooking the camp across from a large patch of tall cacti, so many of them it was like a small forest. The limbs of the cacti stretched skywards, so they looked like a giant army marching across the desert, arms raised in surrender. At dusk, Felipe had watched as the figures of the cacti disappeared slowly into the night, along with the vision of the caravan tents that were stretched out beneath them.

Now, in darkness, there was only sound. The crackling of the campfire. A coyote in the distance.

And something moving out there in the darkness.

Felipe could hear it near the caravan, close by. An animal perhaps was moving in the night. A big animal, by the sound of it. A cougar perhaps. Felipe listened more closely and the sound grew louder—footsteps were walking in the dark, crushing the pebbles of the riverbed underneath them as they moved, heading from the direction of the tents and over to the forest of cactus.

Reaching into the campfire, Felipe pulled out a piece of

kindling—a slender branch with the end of it red from the fire. He held it in front of him and let the light lead him into the darkness, down the incline to the flatland, following after the footsteps.

As he moved forward, the red glow leading the way, the footsteps began to quicken and Felipe hurried after them. Removing the kerchief of his uniform from around his neck, Felipe pressed the embers of the branch into the cloth, wrapping it around the burning wood until the cloth burst into fire. The flame lit up the darkness as Felipe hit the edge of the cactus patch. The shadows of the plants were cast down upon him, surrounding him like an angry mob rising in the night. Twirling his body around, Felipe threw the flaming spear of fire in the direction of the now fleeing footsteps that were moving deeper into the forest of cactus.

The fire exploded into sparks, lighting up the night as it hit the center of the cactus patch, and the sudden brightness lit up a figure as it fled.

The colors of his uniform were brightened by the flame. Blue pants. Yellow shirt—brilliant as the sun.

It was Lieutenant Rios.

And he was running away into the night.

Ꞇꞅiꞅꞇy-niꞑє

They were quickly approaching the last mission in lower California.

Nuestra Señora del Rosario was called Viñadaco by the Cochimís. Five hundred of their tribe lived in reed huts that were built there after the Dominicans had come that year to claim their souls as well as their land. Five hundred souls was not a lot for the Dominicans to claim, but they had found something else on that land that was even more valuable. There were fresh water pools, and when the good *padres* had their neophytes dig even deeper, they tapped into a flowing spring that led to a river only two miles away. Viñadaco was a fine place for a mission, the last mission before the month-long journey to San Diego.

A journey without guarantees of any more supplies.

And very little water.

When Rivera and his people arrived at Viñadaco, the men got right to work setting up the tents, while the women took the children with them to help bring the water jugs to the stone-lined aqueduct filled with spring water.

Mercedes, Sola, and Beatriz unpacked the bedrolls from the *burros*, as Petra took down the water jug from the side of her horse. Placing it up on her shoulder, she started off for the aqueduct.

But Mercedes stopped her.

"Don't go alone," she warned her sister. Mercedes grabbed Marco by the hand, pulling the little boy over to them. "Go with your Aunt Petra," she said to him.

"I don't want to go!" Marco cried out.

"Be a man! Protect your aunt!" Mercedes told her nephew, giving him a little swat on his *culo* to make her point.

Marco was not the happiest of little boys at the moment, but he had no choice if some day he wanted to be a man. Protecting the women in the family was part of the job; his father had taught him that. Like or not, he had to do this. Taking Petra by her hand, he pulled at her.

"Let's go!" he said, sounding like a little Martín.

When they got to the aqueduct, Petra and Marco had to wait their turn. And because little boys sometimes get impatient, Marco could not stand waiting, so he ran off with the other children.

"Would you like some help?"

Petra knew that voice without having to turn and look. She knew it from her dreams that woke her up at night with unexplained yearning. She knew it from her days when, even from a distance, she could hear him shout to his *soldados* or answer a command from his captain. She did not dare to turn and look at him, for fear of betraying a heart that was beating so quickly the whole world might hear it.

It was the lieutenant.

"We can't be seen together," she whispered without turning to look at him. "The caravan is talking, making up lies about me."

Rios moved closer, standing just behind her.

"They're jealous, these women," he spoke softly. "Like the stars hating the moon, they hate you because your beauty out-shines them."

His words touched Petra, and she wished that she could turn around and look at him, to gaze into his eyes and ask him to say more. His voice was as welcome to her as this spring water, so fresh and so cool.

"You don't belong here in this dried-up land," Rios whispered. "You should be in Barcelona with the scent of orange blossoms filling the air, where there is music and dancing and long walks in the moonlight, where you will turn the head of every man and fill the heart of every woman with envy. Every *cortèjo* will be vying for your honor, but only one will be good enough to call you his own."

Petra could feel his soft breath brush across the nape of her neck.

"I will be that man for you, *mi amor*," Rios promised.

Some of the women at the aqueduct were now watching them, staring at Petra and the lieutenant who stood so close behind her that they were almost touching.

"Please, no more," Petra whispered, feeling the heat rise to her cheeks and knowing it would betray her with a blush.

Rios called out to the women.

"Would you like some help, ladies?" he asked, and with a big smile, he walked over to them.

The women all gathered around the lieutenant, welcoming the help and attention of such a handsome officer, one so quick with tender words for every one of them. Rios was good with women. He understood them: they were like little dogs that needed only to be petted now and then to tag along at your side, so loyal and so loving.

One by one, Rios helped each woman with the water jugs, taking them and filling them up from the bucket that he lowered into the aqueduct. And for each bucket and every woman, always he had a smile and a sweet word or two. The young women flirted with him, and the older ones once again felt young, just by looking into the blueness of his eyes. More importantly, they didn't trouble themselves with Petra. She faded away from their attention with their eyes so full of Rios.

Once the water jugs were all filled, the women were happy to move on.

"Now they can talk all they want," Rios said to Petra, with a wink, saving her water jug for last and filling it slowly at the cool spring waters. "I have filled all their heads with pretty words, and now they can't say I've singled you out."

Marco came running back to Petra's side once the other children had left with their mothers. Petra's little chaperone was now ready to do his job. "We have to go back!" Marco announced in a strong big-boy voice. Standing next to his aunt, he took Petra's hand protectively as he stared up at the lieutenant.

Rios reached down and touched the boy's hair gently. "I need a brave *soldado* to be scout," Rios said to the boy. "Someone must run ahead and make sure we are safe!" These words were more powerful than any that could ever be said to a little boy with machismo running through his veins.

"I'll do it!" Marco shouted. He ran off like a flash of lightning back to the camp.

Petra was alone once again with the lieutenant.

"I *have* singled you out," Rios said, as they started to walk back slowly to the tents. Petra could not help but stop and look at him. No one was watching them now. Their eyes could finally meet.

"From the moment you smiled and captured my soul," he told her, not looking away.

"I'm a married woman."

"I want no more than you can give me, no more than your husband is willing for me to take," Rios said, in all honesty.

Petra didn't know what words she should say to him—to encourage the lieutenant or to stop him? She could only tell him the truth and let his heart decide.

"Felipe is my husband in name only," she confessed to him. "When we reach Monterey, my brother will ask the priest to petition for an annulment." Rios smiled, and for that moment, their eyes only saw each other.

Petra wanted more than anything to feel him on her lips.

For this reason she turned away.

And hurried back alone to the camp.

FORTY

The caravan headed west, and this part of the *camino* was a new direction for Rivera.

When he first traveled the road in '69 with only his *soldados* to keep him company, they had pressed forward into the mountains at this point—the highest of the mountains in lower California—Sierra de San Pedro Mártir. They struggled against the huge granite rocks of those towering mountainsides, climbing thousands of feet into the clouds, only to climb back down again, crawling like snails clinging to the earth. It used to take them twice as long to get to San Diego.

The *camino* now changed directions just like the *españoles* who had built it.

Five years ago, the Jesuits had been kicked out by the king, no longer the fair-haired boys of the Crown. The Dominicans had replaced them, and they would build more missions in the coming years—five of them in the next twenty-five. But mountains are no place for a mission. This land was for billy goats to scramble across, not for men on horses carrying hundred-pound packs.

A new route was found. The one that the caravan now traveled on.

Smooth and flat, with not a rock in sight. A peaceful stretch that was easy on the horses' hooves and the backs of the *burros*.

In front of them, the land started to rise slowly, ever so gently. And as the caravan followed this new direction, the sun moved with them. No longer bearing down on top of them, hot and blinding, the sun perched at their shoulders and they carried it along at their side, bringing it with them.

The land no longer threatened them. Not with its heat. Not with its emptiness. Not with its endless challenge. There were no more rocks to climb on this path, to slow them down and fill them with dread and doubt. This land was welcoming. This land was their future. Something just ahead of them told them this. They could feel it, pulling them and pushing them too. To come closer. To come home.

They heard it before they saw it.

A great thunder in the distance.

The sound repeating itself, over and over, drawing them closer, not with caution but with curiosity. It called out to them: "Come to me! Come know me!" It made the people want to go faster, hurrying their horses to carry them there, as the sound grew louder with every hoofbeat. *Adelante! Siempre Adelante!*

The dream was just within their reach. Their ears were hearing it, and finally, their eyes could see it too. One minute it wasn't there, and then the earth seemed to bow to it and they could see now what lay there in front of them.

The ocean.

The magnificent Pacifico.

Stretching out endlessly, a violet blue kissing the feet of the sky.

A shout went out from all the people. The men lifted up their sombreros and waved them high in the air. And the sea breezes flung back the long hair of the *señoras*; the happiness in their eyes was brighter than the sunshine falling on their cheeks.

It was a moment like no other.

And it stopped the caravan right there.

High above the crashing waves and mountains of rocks spilling out into the water, on top of the highest of bluffs, the caravan had stopped not to rest, not to make camp, not to cook a meal. They had stopped simply because their hearts were so full.

After traveling in a single line along the bluffs, high above the ocean, the caravan descended downwards to the rocks below, to a spit of sand that met the water; and with every step of their horses, the sand grew wider into a long white beach. There was no reason to stop, but Rivera knew his people. He was a good captain, and going forward could wait. Raising his hand, he stopped the caravan and turned in his saddle, shouting to the people that followed him.

"*Viva* California!"

He did not need to say more than this. The people climbed quickly from their horses, and with Marco and the other children leading the way, they were in the waves and splashing in the surf before you knew it. The men flung off their *cueras*—tossing the heavy leather vests onto the beach—shedding the *soldado* and becoming men again. Like boys, they dunked each other and pulled one another into the water.

Only Martín stayed seated on his mount. He had no time to play these kinds of children's games. If he was to be a corporal— *un cabo*—he would take the job seriously, while the others were being foolish. He didn't trust this land like they did. Let them play, but he would always be vigilant. Walking his horse along the long line of the pack train, he guarded it and their belongings from any stragglers and thieving *indios* among them.

At the very end of the long line of *burros*, still making his way on top of his horse and trying to catch up, was Victor.

Martín rode out to meet his son.

"What're you doing all the way in the back?" he asked, with a frown.

Victor looked pale and winded.

"I'm a little tired, Papa."

"You keep going no matter how you feel, you understand?" Martín snapped at him.

Victor nodded and started to dismount.

But Martín stopped him.

"Stay on your horse!" he told him sharply. "I don't want you playing around with those *bobosos* in the water. You're on patrol with me."

Once again Victor nodded, doing as his father said.

"When we get to San Diego, I'm putting you in uniform," Martín told him. "You're getting soft!"

Martín slapped the side of his horse and went forward. But he didn't get far. A scream rang out from the pack train. And all hell was let loose.

The horses reared up on their back legs, and the *burros* brayed as they pulled at the ropes that tied them together. The mounts that were not tied to one another and the cattle that were not corralled went running every this way and that, some of them racing into the waves, struggling in the water and trying to swim away.

The people of the caravan could only watch from the shoreline, not understanding the sudden craziness that was taking over their livestock. Packs of their belongings flew off the backs of the *burros* and went flying across the sand as the *burros* stumbled and crashed into one another, biting and kicking and trying to get away.

The men ran from the waves and out onto the sands, reaching out to grab hold of the ropes that bound the *burros* together. Felipe and Domingo chased after the horses that struggled in the water, and Felipe tried to grab the loose reins to pull the animals to safety as the waves crashed over their heads and pulled some of the horses under.

The children clung to the sides of their mothers, watching as their world—the one they had known as home for these last three months—was flung about in front of them. Bedrolls, cooking pans, clothing, tents, and food supplies went flying, while their clay water jugs crashed and broke, spilling precious water onto the beach.

What had happened? What had caused such terror?

The people didn't know; they couldn't see the answer.

But there's always one person who wants so badly to know the truth they run into the center of danger instead of running away. It doesn't matter how afraid that person is or if it's wise to go forward when the danger is not yet known. They go forward anyway.

Tomás was this kind of person.

He was always the first to step forward, quick to make a move before all was known. Tomás did not wait for anyone to tell him what to do next. He grabbed his pistol at his side and pulled it out, moving into the pack train and into the center of the struggling animals. While the other men tugged at the ropes that tied the burros together, Tomás hurried along the sand until he found what he was looking for—the reason for the stampede.

A *burro* lay dead on the beach.

Buckled at his knees, his heart had stopped, dropping him there on the sand and posing him like a priest at prayer. At his hooves seeped the red stain of life. And there, deep in his flank was the messenger of death.

One single arrow.

FORGY-ONE

Tomás was quick to take action.

"*Indios!*" he shouted. Pistol in hand, he turned around quickly.

That's when he was hit.

A rock struck him in the face and he fell backwards, blood pouring from his forehead. As the *soldados* scrambled to put back on their leather jackets, they too were hit: on their backs, their chests, and their faces. The children held tightly to their mothers and the women sheltered them with their skirts, hiding them and keeping them close.

Felipe gazed high up at the bluffs, as he looked straight into the bright sun.

On top of the bluffs, their shapes dark and shadowed by the sun behind them, stood a long line of powerfully built men—the Tipai of the Kumeyaay. Naked except for the deerskin loincloths wrapped around their waists, they stared down upon the caravan, their bows and arrows pointed at the beach while two of the younger ones—boys no older than twelve —threw more rocks at the *soldados*.

The caravan was frozen in fear at the sight.

All except for Martín. Pulling his musket from the side of his saddlebag, he raised it up and pointed it at the bluffs above.

"Hold your fire!" Rivera commanded, pulling his horse up next to his corporal. "I know these people." Up on the bluffs, one of the Tipai stepped forward—the tallest among them and the one who the others now watched and followed. His name was Zegotay, and the paint decorating his face told whoever looked upon him that he was a leader among men. Raising his hand, he shouted to the young Tipai who were throwing the rocks at the soldiers below, and his word made them stop.

Rivera walked his horse closer to the foot of the bluff and stared up at the Tipai. He recognized Zegotay as one of those who had welcomed Portolá and his expedition in '69, when they had come to build the presidio and mission at San Diego. The Kumeyaay had met them in peace back then—with their women and children at their sides, their bodies painted in bright colors of red, black, yellow, and white. They brought to Portolá and his men gifts and much friendship. Zegotay and the other chiefs had given long speeches of welcome, along with barbecued sardines and mussels and bright-colored fishing nets to help them hunt the waters. And Portolá had given them, in return, colorful beads and yellow brass buttons from their uniforms. They had all shared a meal together and promised each other their friendship.

But that was five years ago, before the land that the Kumeyaay harvested—from mountain to seashore—was taken over by these strangers who knew nothing about the land or how to accept its gifts without killing it. They had no cycles of harvest, these *españoles*, never moving with each season to the most plentiful of places. They stayed in one spot only, forcing the land to do whatever they wanted it to do, like they forced everything else that they met along their path.

These men with sticks of fire came into their pine-nut groves in the sierras and cut down the precious piñon trees, destroying the place there that was so sacred—where the Kumeyaay celebrated their dead in their festival called Waheruk. Their women, too, had suffered, taken by the soldiers and known in the most violent of ways. And when their chiefs went to them—speaking to the ones in grey robes to protest such things—they were told: "Be patient." Their Creator named Jesus would make everything good again, the Robes had said to them. "Let us shelter you here, and you will never want again." they were promised.

But those who left their villages and moved closer to the *españoles* found bad food, or little food at all, water that was rank or scarce, and work like none they had ever done before. They spent all their days building, not hunting, staying in one place where sicknesses could come and find them to take away their spirit forever.

There were thousands of Kumeyaay living high in the sierras all the way down to the beaches at Rosario, north beyond the river, beyond the place the *españoles* called San Diego. Thousands of Kumeyaay and only a handful of *españoles*—no more than twenty-five. They were strange men who could not walk on their own two feet but sat on the backs of their animals; they were a people who only knew the world in their own image, renaming the Kumeyaay "Los Diegueños," using their tongue to claim what was never theirs and building what they wanted to build by destroying what was already there. So few took so much from so many, and with each year's passing, there were less and less of the Kumeyaay.

Their loss now pulled them together.

The tribes in the north, the Ipai, joined the Tipai from the south. The men who stood on that bluff that day were united not by their families or the villages they shared in common but by their hatred for the strangers living among them.

The *españoles*.

Now there were more strangers coming, and women and children this time. This was something new, something the Kumeyaay could not understand. They had always believed that the *españoles* were a people that did not have women. Why else would the soldiers take the Kumeyaay's women and take them with such force, if they had their own? No women of these strangers had ever been seen before in the five years the *españoles* had been on their lands.

Until now.

That day the men of the Kumeyaay looked down on the beach at Rosario and wondered at the sight in front of them. Were these the women of the *españoles*? And how could they be sure? Covered up with cloth from head to toe, their bodies were hidden away like some great secret. But it was the children that gave them away—the children clinging to them and the babies that they sheltered in their arms. The truth was found in the sight of them and by the way their young bodies clung to the ones who were protecting them. These were mothers. These were women.

For this reason alone, Zegotay held back his arrows.

He shouted down to Rivera, using the words of his people and not the Spanish the Robes had been trying to teach them. The words fell down from the bluffs and echoed across the white sands, the language known by the land but foreign to those strangers standing at the shoreline.

Rivera called out to the Cochimís and the Seris who were part of his caravan.

"What is he saying?" the Capitán asked them.

The language was Yuman, one that the Cochimís also spoke, but the Seris did not know it at all. These words of the Kumeyaay were strange, even to the Cochimí, and only a few words were like theirs; the rest were new and they did not understand them. The accent of Zegotay was one they had never heard before. They could not help Rivera with its translation, and so they stood there silently, as much of a stranger to these words as the *españoles* who had brought them there.

Rios spurred his horse, galloping over to the caravan's group of *indios*. He singled out one of the Seris, the youngest, who had ridden with them all the way from Guaymas. His name was Simon, given to him by the priest when he was baptized.

Dark and slender, looking more like a boy than a man, he was small and agile, with a strength not easily seen on the outside. Dressed in the white cotton blouse and pants that neophytes wore at every one of the missions, he wasn't barefoot as Calixto had been; instead, he was wearing a fine pair of leather boots just like the *soldados* wore.

"Speak up!" Rios snapped at Simon. "What does he say?"

"I don't know all of these words," Simon protested.

"Tell us the words you know."

Simon hesitated.

" . . . 'Women' . . . He says the same word for 'women' that the Cochimís speak." Rios waited for Simon to go on, and he spoke harshly to him when he didn't.

"What else does he say?"

"'Go.'" Simon looked up at the lieutenant who sat high above him in his saddle. "He is saying we should leave this place."

Up on the bluff, Zegotay held his bow out in front of him so that all those on the beach could see its size and strength and understand the power he held in his hand. The other Kumeyaay at his side did the same, and all of them began to shout and whoop the most terrifying of sounds. Suddenly they all turned quickly and ran off, disappearing from sight.

This was not a good welcome.

It was no welcome at all.

FORTY-TWO

What a cruel day it was for the people of Sinaloa.

Feeling hope for the first time and then having it snatched away was worse than never feeling any hope at all. In the middle of such beauty—with the blue Pacifico at their backs and the sea breeze caressing their skin—now there was deep despair. Everything they owned had been thrown across the sand. Trampled on, ripped, and crushed by frightened hooves, shit upon by the cattle, *burros*, and horses. Broken pieces of their lives had been cast aside with no meaning. And what little they had was made less.

What a fool is man to fall in love with life.

When a jealous God can take it all away.

So said Felipe's father as he had watched the *chubasco* drown their future.

There was nothing greater than God. Forgetting this was the ultimate sin. The fault was not in life but in the living. For wanting too much, needing too much, being too much of this world. All of their lives lay broken in front of them because their desires made them choose living over God. And for this, they were punished.

So they had been taught. This was what it meant to be *español*.

The weight of this truth kept them all silent now and unable to move.

Except for Petra.

She scrambled across the sands, searching for what was hers. Desperately she pushed out of her way the broken pots, ripped tents, and empty flour bags. These were useless to her, common and ordinary. Petra was looking for something finer, something greater than the shards and pieces, the broken and the soiled. She hurried down the beach to a section of the sand that was littered with strips of wood, smashed timber that was spread all around. Mingled among the wooden ruins there was cloth, dirtied by the filth and blood from the animals.

Petra fell to her knees and began to dig.

Underneath the scattered remains of broken wood and dirtied cloth were brass hinges attached to a studded leather top: the rounded cover of a chest. It was the Luna family's *arcón*. Petra hurried to pull the chest free from everything on top of it. She worked frantically, tugging at it and trying to loosen it from where it was trapped.

Felipe hurried over to help her.

She did not pay attention to him at all; his presence did not slow her hands.

Mercedes was at her side now. "Leave it," she told Petra. "It's ruined."

The words did not slow Petra. She clawed at the sand, at the broken pieces of their world, trying to reclaim the chest with all its splendor.

Felipe, at her side, helped her, pulling away the shards of wood, the broken hinges, the strips of leather. And when they got to the top of the *arcón* and pulled it free, it broke into pieces. Nothing was there, the bottom of the chest was gone, spread across the sand at their sides, broken all around them.

It was only then that Petra looked closer at the clothing spread out all over the beach: dirtied, ripped, and stained. She reached out to pick up one of them, holding it gently in her hands. White lace with ribbons of satin was woven through the fabric; it was a torn jacket of the finest brocade needlework. Within Petra's reach, she spotted another piece of clothing and picked it up—the delicate blue gown she had worn for her wedding; the arms ripped now, the bodice was stained and smeared with bright red blood. It was her mother's clothing.

Petra began to cry as she held the dress tightly. Mercedes knelt down and wrapped her arms around her sister.

"They're just things. They don't mean anything, *mija*."

But Petra's tears still came and they would not stop. Mercedes shushed her and held her close. "Don't waste your tears," she whispered. She stroked Petra's hair gently. "God gives you only so many tears, you can't waste them. What will you do when you really need to cry? When the loss is so big you want to fall down and die?" Mercedes used the hem of her skirt to wipe at her sister's eyes, clearing away the tears. "A Luna doesn't cry," Mercedes reminded her. "You keep yourself busy so the tears never come."

Petra nodded her head yes. It was true. No matter how much she wanted to cry, she had to fight it. It was her family's way of not giving in. Of never being beaten down. And never losing, no matter what life throws at you.

Mercedes bent down and started to pick up all the dirtied, ruined clothing.

"Help me pack up!" she shouted to the rest of the family, standing off to the side. Sola, Beatriz, and all the children came running to help pick up the scraps of their family belongings that had littered the beach.

They had miles to travel before they could rest.

And they needed to be kept busy.

FORTY-THREE

Much was lost that day on the beach at Rosario.

Three of the *burros* were trampled to death. Eight of the horses ran off, and the caravan spent the rest of the day tracking them down, only to be able to bring back two of them. The fifteen cattle they had been bringing with them were gone. Six had escaped, and the other nine drowned along with two of the *burros*.

Most of the bags of flour had broken open as the packs on the back of the *burros* were flung across the sand. Other food supplies too were now ruined, and all the water jugs had broken on the beach, their water spilling into the sand. They had only whatever water still filled the *botas* they carried, which was not much water at all.

And San Diego was still two hundred miles away.

Rivera took charge with a new passion. He had not brought these people so far to lose them so close to finishing his job.

"We have to move quickly! No more rest breaks!" The captain addressed the caravan on the beach from the saddle of his mount. "When we stop to make camp at night, it will only be for a few hours. At the first sight of the sun again, we move on!"

The people listened in a way they had never listened before. Their survival depended on it.

"No more water or food until I tell you to drink or eat!" Rivera commanded them. "Women and children will double up on the horses and only the officers will ride. All of the *soldados* will walk the rest of the way to San Diego. Half of them in front, half at the back. We will get fresh horses and more supplies in San Diego, but until then we will ration, and we will keep our eyes open and our weapons ready!"

Removing his *sombrero*, he held it up high, shouting to one and all to move forward.

Siempre Adelante!

The days that followed were long and painful.

Their bellies ached with hunger, and their bodies were sore from the pace of the traveling. It was only when they were sure they could not take one step more and that their thirst would consume them that Rivera let them drink, and then the little water they received spurred them forward.

As rough as the days were, the nights were even rougher. When the sun went down and camp was set up—with families doubling up together in the few remaining tents—the food was rationed, and there wasn't much. The flour ran out within a day, and there were no more tortillas after that. They shared the dried beef and whatever kernels of corn they had salvaged from the beach. Eating took no time at all, and the rest of the night hours were spent with the thought that tomorrow they would have to do this all over again. But what filled their heads the most was what filled their hearts with so much fear: the images of those men in deerskin loincloth with naked bodies covered in paint. The Kumeyaay who had faced them with so much anger and arrows pointed directly at them had filled the caravan with a fear they had never felt before. They were strangers in this new land, without the comfort of home to protect them, and for the first time since they left Sinaloa, they ached for their old lives and a village that had been their friend. Sleep only came now because they were exhausted. Many wondered if they had the strength to continue.

Some didn't have that strength.

Three of the Cochimís ran away the night after the Kumeyaay appeared at the cliffs at Rosario. The natives of this land were strangers to them too, as they were to the *españoles*. And yet the Cochimís understood some of what the Kumeyaay had said, and their words had been frightening, filled with an anger that the Cochimís both understood and shared. As long as they stayed with the caravan, they too were at risk. They too were the enemy. Better to take their chances by themselves in this foreign land than to stay with the *españoles* and remain the enemy.

The Seris stayed a while longer. They were too far from home, and the tribes here did not speak their language; there would be no allies among them, and like it or not, their hopes were tied to the success of the caravan and to the survival of the *españoles*. This truth didn't hold them long, though, and three nights later, every one of the Seris, except for the one called Simon, ran away when two more Cochimís left in the dark of night.

Something had to be done.

Rivera added more *soldados* to stand watch at night and to guard the sleeping caravan. And after he did this, the nights were quiet and uneventful.

Until one night, just before dawn.

"Halt!" A shout rang out in the stillness of the dark. It was more of a scream, really; the young recruit was nervous on this night, his first night of guard duty. His voice had cracked high, and he shouted again.

It was loud enough to awaken Felipe, asleep at the camp-fire. He had stood guard during the earlier hours, and this was supposed to be his time to sleep. This young recruit, José Villa, was skittish like a young colt, though, jumping at every shadow, every bump in the night—unlike Felipe, who was used to guarding the caravan in the darkness of night. It seemed to Felipe that Villa had spent most of his time at guard waking up Felipe: "My mistake! The *burros* moved in the corral!" "It's nothing! Go back to sleep!" "Sorry!" The nervous Villa had apologized every time he had awakened Felipe. And each time Felipe settled back into sleep again.

But this time, the unlocking of the trigger on Villa's musket told Felipe it was time to get up.

Villa had his rifle raised, pointing it off in the direction of a thick growth of tall manzanita plants at a distance from the tents of the caravan.

"Halt!" Villa shouted once again, staring out into the night.

Felipe was on his feet with his hand on the pistol at his belt. The moon was big above them, and it was easy to see out across the land. But the thick growth of brush near the bottom of the hillside across the way made it difficult to tell if man or beast was there or simply a part of the undergrowth.

Felipe did not hesitate to move forward. Using the moonlight to show him the way, he pulled out his pistol from its holster and held it in front of him as he moved towards the brush.

"I will shoot!" Felipe shouted. "Hands above your head!" He commanded the bushes directly in front of him, not afraid to look like a fool if nothing was there at all.

But something *was* there. Hands went up quickly, and from out of the bushes stepped a Seri.

It was Simon.

Standing away from the protection of the brush, Simon was trying hard not to be afraid, but his hands held above his head trembled just enough for Felipe to notice.

"What are you doing out here?" Felipe asked him.

Simon's eyes darted—looking off into the darkness.

"Are you running away?" Felipe asked him, still pointing the pistol in his direction. He would not make the mistake again of being blamed for letting another *indio* get away. "They will punish you if you run!" he told Simon.

"I'm not running away!" Simon said quickly.

"Why are you out here then?"

"Who is it?" came a shout behind Felipe. And when he turned, he was facing the lieutenant in the darkness.

"Who do you have?" Rios asked again, with anger.

Felipe stepped away so the lieutenant could see.

"What are you doing out here?" Rios asked Simon.

"He's one of the Seris from Guaymas," Felipe said.

"What are you doing here in the dark?" Rios raised his voice.

Before Simon could speak, the lieutenant's hand rose quickly and came down hard against the *indio*'s face, knocking him to the ground.

It was a hard blow.

Simon lay on the ground, his lip bleeding, and his eyes began to fill. Whether it was pain from being hit, or the humiliation that came with it, tears found their way down his cheeks. This was more than Rios could stand. Reaching down and grabbing hold of Simon's arm, he pulled him up, dragging him to his feet.

"I don't think he was running away," Felipe said quickly.

"It's not your job to think!" Rios snapped.

The lieutenant firmed his grip on Simon, pulling him roughly by his arm and dragging him away, back to the camp and off to the corrals. Without turning to look at his recruits, Rios shouted his command.

"Go back to your posts!"

Felipe and the other *soldado* did as they were told.

But Felipe couldn't help wondering: Why was Simon out there in the dark?

FORTY-FOUR

Their food ran out two days later.

The rations they had been eating had only been enough to stop them from fainting from hunger, but now they had nothing at all. The children fussed and the babies cried; the breasts of the young mothers dried up. The women grew quiet and could barely stay on top of their horses, because their heads were so light and spinning. The hunger slowed the steps of the *soldados*, now weighed down by the packs that the missing *burros* once carried for them.

In spite of it all, the caravan kept going, following the *camino* and letting it lead the way. Trusting it to take them where they had to go. The road turned inland and cut through a marshland that was lush and green. A stream ran through it, on its way to an outlet and the ocean beyond.

The caravan stopped and the people drank from the stream; the sweet waters filled up their empty bellies and made them forget the stews and *posole*, the freshly slaughtered beef, the *frijoles*, and yes, the *tortillas* and hot chocolate that had greeted them each morning. They filled up their *botas* and they drank long and hard, each swallow a nectar that calmed them and made them stop wanting.

It allowed them to keep going, out of the marshland and

223

across the land. And just when they thought they couldn't take one more step, the *camino* brought them hope again. On the crest of a hillside, they looked down and saw the Pacifico once more, and this time there were islands sitting in it.

The Coronados. Four islands so close to one another they looked like one. San Diego was just within reach.

That was when the Kumeyaay appeared once again.

Not warriors this time but women and children. A few at first—five or six—and then more: fifteen, twenty. With mothers holding the hands of their young ones, they watched the long line of strangers descending to the flatland below. They watched the caravan from a safe distance, from the clifftops overlooking the *camino*. The women were naked except for a sealskin skirt and necklaces of seashells across their breasts. The bigger children ran naked at their feet. And when the caravan moved forward, the Kumeyaay women tagged along behind it, crawling down from the cliffs with their children and following these new strangers at a careful distance.

Tomás, at the front of the caravan, his forehead still bandaged from the stoning at Rosario, slipped his hand down to his waist and kept it there on the handle of his *pistola*. He would not be surprised again, nor his blood shed as it was before. This time, he would be the first to spill blood, or be damned for not trying.

He was not the only recruit to reach for the comfort of his weapon. No one felt safe here. No matter that these were women and children that were following their footsteps; they were different these people, *indios* not *españoles*. And their difference is what filled the people of the caravan with fear and distrust. Yes, and anger too. They could not forget the supplies that had been lost, spilled across the wide white beach, and the wasted food that their empty bellies now longed for. They had been shamed and humiliated—the rocks that had pelted their husbands, their fathers, their sons did more harm to them than just to their bodies. And those wounds, which had bled from them trust and friendship, were still raw and open. There was no place in their hearts that day for kindness.

Rivera understood this about his people. And he was careful to keep them under control.

"Go down the line and make sure each man has his hand on his weapon," he told Rios, who rode at his side. "But tell them this: if any man shoots without my command, I will personally flog him myself."

Rios turned his horse around, moving down the long line of the caravan, speaking to the recruits and telling them to be ready but to hold back with caution. A false shot would be worse than no shot at all. Ahead of them, the land started to rise as they made their way from the flatlands, away from the sea, heading inland once again.

And still the women and children of the Kumeyaay followed them.

The sun was high above when the caravan finally reached the river. The banks were covered in tule reeds and cattails; the river became narrow enough for the caravan to cross over, shallow enough for only the hooves of the animals to get wet. They traveled along the bank, and the river widened the farther they went on. The *camino* curved and followed the water, and the caravan went forward. Through the opening of an *arroyo* they passed, and the river started to grow in size, widening and getting deeper.

Before you knew it, the children of the Kumeyaay were running past the caravan as fast as they could, scrambling up the sides of the *arroyo* and disappearing out of sight. Rivera on his horse followed after them, and all the caravan did too. When they reached the top, they stopped and looked down.

A vast valley spread out on the other side of the *arroyo* cliffs.

In the center was the river, its banks watched over by shedding sycamores and weeping willows. Wild strawberry bushes and honeysuckle grew lush and plentiful, fed by the rushing water at their roots, and their scents were heavy in the air. Meadows stretched out all around, filled by wildflowers, blue lupines, and orange poppies, with bright yellow sunflowers standing tall among them, taller than the children of the Kumeyaay who now ran past them, too familiar with this beauty to pause or even look.

But to the Cochimís and to Simon, the last remaining Seri, these sights were more than they could bear. Their hunger hurried their steps, until they too were running, scrambling down the side of the riverbank to the strawberry bushes below, where they stripped the ripe and ready fruit, devouring them whole, one fistful after another, their lips turning scarlet red and the juice dripping warm and sweet down their chins.

The people watched as Simon and the Cochimís feasted on the fresh berries. The children in their mothers' laps reached their hands out, crying with hunger at the sight. But Rivera did not halt or give the command to stop moving forward. There was a far better prize waiting for them than berries at the side of a river. Smoke rising ahead told him they were close. Standing taller in his saddle, the captain could see it.

A large settlement of tule huts was clustered together just up river. Hundreds of Kumeyaay were standing there, in the village that was called Nipaquay. Overlooking the widest part of the river, the men, women, and children were all dressed in the clothing of *españoles*, gathered together outside their *ranchería*—their native home. All eyes were on the arrival of the caravan.

The people of Sinaloa had finally arrived at Mission San Diego.

FORGY-FIVE

The first to spot them was the blacksmith.

Dirty pants, no shirt, streaks of charcoal on his broad chest and lined face, he stood at his forge at the side of the mission chapel, pounding the hell out of a horseshoe. The children running across the fields in front of him did not catch his attention at all, but the sound of horse hooves lifted his head.

"Holy Christ," he said, when he saw what was coming, his face filling with surprise.

There on the horizon in front of him was the caravan, stretched out in a long line as it moved closer to the grounds of the mission.

Four adobe buildings stood close to one another, surrounded by a protective stone wall that circled the church grounds. The adobe looked freshly built, the church having just been moved inland, farther away from the lust of the presidio *soldados* and closer to the natives whose souls needed to be saved.

The job would turn out to be more than one priest could handle.

And that is why on the day the caravan appeared, two priests came rushing out of the chapel, their simple grey robes of wool kicking up the dirt at their feet, as they hurried to see the miracle arriving at their doorstep: not just supplies but women and children too.

"Welcome, Capitán!" said Father Jayme, the older of the two priests and the taller one, as well. He lifted his hands up to Rivera, and the captain grabbed hold of them in brotherhood.

"You are a welcome sight!" added the second priest, Father Alphonso, who was larger than the first, with a *panza* that stretched the limits of his robes.

"I hope you have some food for us, Fathers!" said Rivera.

Even the Capitán could only think of his belly at this moment.

"Everything we have is yours!" said Jayme with a wide smile. "We are blessed to have you! And to see our women and children here, praise God!"

The people felt such happiness. They had made it safely this far after four months of travel. Summer had been new when they left Guaymas; now it was gone, and autumn was beginning to fall. But all they could think of was the meal they hoped would be waiting there to fill up their bellies.

"Father Alphonso will prepare a wonderful feast for all of you. *Un barbacoa!* " Jayme said to the travelers. "There's not much beef, I'm sad to say," he apologized to Rivera. "But we have plenty of chickens!"

"To be honest, we were hoping you were bringing us a cow or two," Father Alphonso added. "It's been awhile since we've had fresh beef."

"We were going to change that for you, but the cattle had their own ideas," Rivera explained. "They ran off, thanks to the Tipai, who were not very welcoming. We lost some of our horses too—we'll be needing fresh ones."

"We only have ten horses, and those are for the guards," Jayme told him.

Rivera was surprised by such a low number.

"How many *soldados* do you have here?" he asked, looking around the grounds for some sign of men in uniforms.

"We have seven. One is retired, our blacksmith. And another doubles as our carpenter."

Rivera frowned at the number. The priest could see Rivera's concern, so he tried to ease his fears.

"Not to worry, there are plenty at the presidio—twenty soldiers, at least. And more too at San Gabriel, another ten, perhaps," Father Jayme said, while helping Mercedes off her horse and taking little Maria from her mother's arms and into his. "Our natives are all good people here, receiving the Lord and doing His work. We don't need more soldiers at our mission." The priest smiled as he gazed into the wide eyes of Maria. "This is what we need more of—our sweet little children. The future of España!"

Jayme looked past the caravan and saw the Kumeyaay gathered together—men, women, and children—all standing at a distance, away from the *españoles*, but watching with curious eyes. Their circular huts—made of dried reeds with a round top—were behind them in a *ranchería*, their village just outside the mission wall. Surrounding the *ranchería* were fields of corn, wheat and barley, peas and beans.

Those fields were a beautiful sight for the caravan, and they could not take their eyes off them.

The priest beckoned the Kumeyaay with his hand to come closer, to join the pilgrims in their midst. One or two took a hesitant step in the direction of the strangers, wide-eyed in wonder at the sight of women *españoles* for the first time. Still, their curiosity did not overcome their need to hold back.

It was the children who moved closer to one another, without care, without fear. Once gathered and facing each other, it didn't take long for them to run off together to the orchard, the Kumeyaay children leading the way to the apple and pear trees that were full with fruit and ready for the picking.

The *soldados* freed their backs from what they carried.

"Don't get comfortable! We eat and then we move on!" Martín called out to the men.

The old blacksmith approached as he watched the recruits at work.

"From where do you come?" he called over to Martín, who was unbridling his horse.

"Sinaloa!" Martín replied, on his way from his horse to a nearby well at the front of the mission.

"I have people in Sinaloa," the blacksmith said to Martín, as the corporal was passing him by. "Two sons and two daughters." The old man scratched his beard that was speckled in grey. "But the last one—I'm not sure she made it." He said it like a fact of life, like someone talking about the weather.

Martín stopped and turned to look at the old man.

"She lost her mother—God rest her spirit," the blacksmith went on, crossing himself. "Died giving birth to her. I don't think she was strong enough to make it. She was so tiny when I held her in my hand, like a tiny bird fallen from the nest."

Martín took a few steps towards the old blacksmith. "You left before you knew if your daughter lived or died?" He asked this in a voice that was slow and hollow.

The old man shrugged.

"I was a soldier. I had my orders. I had to leave."

Martín took a step closer to the old man, standing so close that he could feel the blacksmith's breath on his beard.

"How could you not want to know if your child was alive or dead?"

The blacksmith's body tensed. He did not understand the proximity of this stranger or why he was being questioned.

"Who are you to ask me these things?" the old man said, readying himself for a challenge, physical, if necessary.

But fighting was the last thing on Martín's mind. A burn lodged in his throat, as if he had swallowed the hottest embers of a raging fire. It spread to his eyes, and that's when they filled and grew wet—tears were coming to put out that fire. Damn this feeling! Martín would fight it and not give in. But the tightness in his throat took away his words; he dared not speak or he would lose this fight. Silence was all he could give this blacksmith. But it was his silence that spoke the loudest, more telling than any words he could ever say.

The old man stared at the corporal in front of him, and it was his own image he saw staring back. He knew the truth in an instant, and his face filled with a wide grin.

"Goddamn," he whispered.

And then the old man laughed.

"You're one of them!" Wrapping his arms around Martín, he held him tightly against his breast. "Goddamn!" he shouted for all to hear. He pushed Martín away and studied his face, his body, everything about him. "Look at you! You're me—twenty years ago! The same wide chest, the same thick arms! Mine got bigger, look!" He held up his arm and flexed his muscle—a big one—for Martín to see. This old man was as strong as a bull and proud of it too. "That's from work, pounding iron. Real work! Not just holding my dick to take a piss." The blacksmith pulled Martín closer. "Which one are you? Are you Martín?"

Martín nodded, like the little boy still there inside of him.

The blacksmith kissed him hard on his neck.

"Where are the others? Are they here?" The old man looked over at the caravan. "Where are the blessed children of Victorino Cesario Luna?" he shouted for all the Sinaloans to hear. "Come out and meet the man who gave you life!" Slowly, one by one, Mercedes, Tomás, and Petra stepped out of the caravan group and revealed themselves to their father. Victorino could not believe his eyes. His children were gone, replaced by the people who now stood in front of him.

"Goddamn." He said the word softly this time, almost like a little prayer.

To Petra, this man was no more than a stranger. Never having known one, "father" was only a word to her. There were no memories of him to make this man real.

"Who is he?" she asked Mercedes.

But Mercedes remembered him, and she could not answer her

sister because her heart was so full. She forgot everything about who she was and who she had become. No longer Domingo's wife or the mother of Maria and the twin girls, she was a five year old again, and like a small child, she ran as quickly as her aching legs would carry her to the old blacksmith who waited to receive her with wide open arms. She almost knocked him to the ground as she wrapped him in her embrace.

He freed himself and held Mercedes at arm's length to get a better look.

"Jesus, you got fat!" Victorino said, with a whistle.

For once in her life, Mercedes did not try to best a man with her words. She was crying: whether she was a Luna or not, the tears came, and she did not try to stop them.

Laughing, Victorino pulled her close again, and this time as he wrapped his arms around his daughter, he could feel the reason for her bigness. The baby within her kicked, and Victorino could feel his grandchild.

His eyes widened. "When are you . . . ?"

Not wanting him to spill the secret, Mercedes grabbed him quickly by the hand and dragged him along. "Come meet your other daughter—the beautiful one!"

But Victorino did not need to meet his daughter. As he caught sight of Petra, he stopped in his tracks, dropped Mercedes' hand and could not go a step farther. The blood drained from his face, and his body trembled.

He was seeing a ghost.

"Josephina." He whispered her name, the love of his life. Paralyzed by the sight of her, there on the face of his daughter, Victorino could not move. He stayed where he stood.

It was Petra who moved to him, slowly, and only with curiosity. There was no love for this man she had never known. Gratitude, perhaps, for him giving her life, but the umbilical cord between father and child comes after birth, when the mother no longer protects the baby within her body. That's when the father takes over, guarding and guiding with his words, his deeds, and his love. That cord was never formed for Petra. And when the man in front of her now began to cry, nothing stirred within her. No more than seeing a blind man begging outside the Sinaloa church, someone she would give a coin to and a quick, kind word. But nothing more than that. And certainly not an embrace or a place in her heart.

This man who said he was their father was someone Petra didn't know; no words of his ever reached back to Sinaloa to check on his children, to bond him to Petra or to any of them. For twenty years he had disappeared into the world, and so he was dead to them. To now be alive, here in front of them, meant nothing to Petra. And in truth, she wondered who this man really was? Certainly not her father and absolutely not a Luna— because Lunas never cried.

And this man was now sobbing on his knees in front of her.

FORTY-SIX

The priests at San Diego put on one hell of a barbecue.

The chickens who gave their life for that meal will be sainted in Heaven, that's how tasty they were. There was zucchini and corn and tomatoes, onions fresh out of the ground, fresh *salsa*, and—hallelujah!—*tortillas* once again. Flour *tortillas*! The caravan had not eaten so much food since the weddings in Loreto.

It was such a perfect day, that day.

The Lunas sat in the shade of an oak grove, away from the caravan, closer to the *ranchería* than the mission walls, and they ate as a family together, young and old. And in the middle of them all was the man who called himself their father.

"Eat up, everyone!" Victorino told them, acting like the host of this *fiesta*. This was his family, his big *familia*, and it filled him with a big pride. Little Marco sat with his mother on one side of his newfound *abuelo* and Victor sat on the other, with the twin girls of Mercedes on Beatriz's lap nearby. All of the children gobbled up the barbecued chicken, its juices running down their chins and onto their necks and chests as they chewed.

Victorino watched his grandchildren, eating them up with his eyes, with pride.

"Don't you feed these little ones?" he called over to Martín and Mercedes. "You need to fatten them up!" He took the meat off his own plate, ripping it apart, and plopped the chicken pieces on the plates of Victor, Marco, and the twins. Reaching over to the baby, Maria, he took her from Mercedes' lap, picking her up and running his beard on her cheeks until she giggled and squirmed in his arms. Kissing her belly, he blew kisses and bubbles on her skin, and all his grandchildren laughed at his antics.

But Mercedes, Petra, Tomás, and Martín were stone-faced and silent. Until Mercedes could not hold back her tongue any longer.

"Look at you! Such a way with children," she said, shaking her head with amazement.

"Children love me!" Victorino smiled, with pride.

"Too bad you didn't stick around for us," Mercedes added, not trying to hide her sarcasm. Or a little bit of her anger.

"Oh, come on now, don't be mad," Victorino laughed. "How can you be mad at your own Papa?"

Martín was the only one brave enough to answer.

"It would have been good to hear from you sometime over the years."

"For what reason?" Victorino asked, quickly.

"To know you were alive," Mercedes offered.

"You didn't hear I was dead, did you?" Victorino asked them.

He looked from one child to the next, and each one gave the same answer—if not in word, then in a shake of the head: no, they hadn't.

"There! You see!" He reached for his jug of wine where he sat and popped out the cork. "If you didn't hear I was dead, then you knew I must be alive!" Putting the wine jug to his lips, he drank down a long gulp. Wiping a hand across his lips, he grew quiet for a moment, weighing something heavy in his mind—whether he should keep carrying it or put it down forever, freeing himself from ever carrying it again.

"You know," Victorino said softly, "your mother's family never let me know that my child lived. All they could see in their hearts was that I was the one who put the seed in their daughter, and that's what killed her. That's how they saw me; it's true. No more than a stud bull was Victorino. Forget about *my* loss; their tears were the only ones that mattered. I never heard one word from her family. So all right! The gate swings both ways, you know?"

Reaching over to Martín, Victorino offered the wine jug to his son. A peace offering, perhaps. The only way he knew how to make things right.

Martín shook his head no. Reaching past his eldest, Victorino offered it next to Tomás, who followed his big brother's lead and said no too. They would not drink with this man. But Petra surprised all of them as she reached out for the jug, and Victorino laughed as she swallowed down a long drink of the wine.

"Finally! A real Luna!" Victorino grinned.

Petra offered the wine back to her father, and he took another swallow. Setting the jug back down next to his side, he looked once more at his children.

"Well," he asked, "how do I look?" He puffed out his chest and held his head high proudly.

"You look like you got old," Martín told him.

For a moment there was only silence. And then Victorino laughed as loud and hard as anyone has ever laughed.

"That's my blood talking!" he roared.

His children did not laugh with him.

But Domingo did. That caught Victorino's attention, and he looked over at the two son-in-laws.

"Who are these two *bobosos*?" he asked his children.

"I'm the husband of Mercedes," Domingo said, choking a little, with his mouth full of chicken.

"She feeds you well, I see," Victorino replied, looking away from Domingo and over at Felipe, who sat a little bit away from the family. "And what about this string bean of a man? What's your name?"

Felipe put down his supper plate and looked Victorino right in the eyes.

"I'm Felipe Santiago Garcia," he said, with just the right amount of pride. Looking straight into the eyes of Petra's father, he showed no fear, nor did he back down to make himself less than what he was.

"Your husband?" Victorino looked over at his daughter.

Petra was careful not to show her feelings. She was not about to reveal anything of herself to a man she did not really know. If this was her father, he would have to earn her trust. For now, he didn't have it.

"We were married in Loreto," she said simply and added a smile as a newlywed should. "He's from Sinaloa."

"The son of José Maria Garcia," said Victorino, before anyone else could say the name. He looked closer at Felipe—at his hands, the cut of his shoulders, the promise of who he might become—sizing him up, comparing him to his father and to the future that might follow him. "He was at my side when we battled the Yaquis in '40. A good fighter, your father."

"He preferred farming," Felipe said softly.

"And what do you prefer?" Victorino asked.

Felipe did not even need to think before he spoke.

"A long life and a big family."

Victorino smiled at Felipe's answer and looked over at Martín.

"I like this one. He knows what he wants."

The grove of oaks started to fill then with Kumeyaay children, running and playing among the trees. Two of the smallest girls rushed ahead of the rest, as they ran after one of the boys, a big young man, his chest and legs naked and browned from the sun, wearing deerskin at his loins, and his feet free of shoes. He ran swiftly from tree to tree, hiding from the two little girls until they found him, and then running off again. The children called out to him in the language of the Kumeyaay, and their voices carried throughout the grove.

Victorino's attention now turned away from his family, and

he shouted something back in the words of the Kumeyaay to the children playing in the grove. They called out to him, and once again he spoke, using words his family did not understand. The two little girls ran to Victorino and he rose to meet them half-way. Bending down, he scooped them up into his arms.

The church bell began to toll in the distance. Supper was ending; the barbecue was finished, and it was time now for all to go to Mass.

Victorino carried the two little girls over to his family, and the rest of the Kumeyaay children followed after him. They were fascinated to meet face-to-face the strangers who were among them, and Victorino spoke to them in words they understood, coaxing them to come closer, to meet these strangers and to see they were just the same as they were, no different, no better, no worse.

"How did you get so good with children?" Mercedes asked; it was hard for her not to feel a little bitter when she said the words. So many years had been lost, so many moments without a father. But this was a man who truly had a gift with children, and they, in turn, surrounded him, and the little girls in his embrace circled their arms around his neck, playing with his hair that curled at the back of his head.

"These are mine!" Victorino said with a laugh. "These two little sweet ones in my arms—Josephina is four, Isabella is three, and their *mamacita* is already big with another one." The Luna children just sat there, stunned. No one seemed to breathe, no one moved. It was like learning of a death.

But for Martín it was something more. Whatever battle had been raging inside him about his father was now ending—and his father had lost. If forgiveness had ever hoped to grow inside of Martín, the roots of it now withered and died.

"Take the children and go to Mass," Martín said to Sola, in a voice that no one would dare challenge. Sola quickly gathered up Marco and Victor and took along the twin girls of Mercedes too. Beatriz followed after her, carrying Maria in her arms.

"We'll all go together!" Victorino called out, but Sola knew better than to listen to anyone other than Martín, her husband. She led Victorino's grandchildren away from him through the grove, back to the mission; she didn't wait for him to get a kiss or a hug from any of them.

"Come and meet your sisters," Victorino said to Mercedes, Martín, Tomás, and Petra. "They're Lunas, just like you!"

Mercedes looked at her father with eyes that were starting to fill.

"Are you going to leave them too?" she asked quietly.

"No more soldiering for me. I'm a blacksmith now. A family man, can you imagine?"

Mercedes did not want to hear anymore. She took Domingo by the hand and pulled him away as Tomás and Beatriz followed. Together they headed out of the grove and back to the mission. Petra hesitated a moment, a part of her curious about this man they called father. But the cold look in Martín's eyes told her not to stay. And she followed after her family, with Felipe at her side.

Now only Martín and Victorino faced each other.

"Too bad! Too bad for them!" Victorino said, trying hard not to be angry in front of his small daughters in his arms. He said something in Kumeyaay to the older girl, and leaning down, he let them scramble out of his embrace. The younger one began to cry, trying to hold on to her father. But her sister took her by the hands and picked her up, carrying her back through the grove.

Victorino faced Martín, the anger inside of him growing.

"They're your sisters. You should get to know them."

"They're your bastards. We want nothing to do with them."

"I'm married to their mother, church wedding and all. Each was baptized. Good Catholics!"

Martín had heard enough. He turned away from his father.

"I want you to meet my wife," said Victorino.

"I don't need to meet your bitch." Martín moved away from him, starting through the grove.

"You're a fool!" Victorino said, following Martín. "What was I supposed to do? Be like a priest the rest of my life?"

"You don't dirty what's pure."

"I don't give a fuck about pure! This is the future right in front of you—those two little girls. It's not just the blood of the *conquistadores* that lives here. This is not España—this is California!"

Martín hurried his steps; he would not listen.

"Your mother was the same way—the fruit doesn't fall far from the tree." Victorino said to Martín, and when his son showed no sign of listening, the father reached out and grabbed him, forcing Martín to face him.

"Do you think Cortés kept his dick pure—that he never knew a beautiful native girl? That all his children were filled with only Spanish blood?"

"We're better than that! Catalans!" said Martín, spitting out the words in his father's face.

"I'm not! Maybe your mother was, or tried to be, but not me! You know, they sent her back to España when she was pregnant the first time, back to Catalan, just so the baby could be born on true Catalonian soil. It was her first child and that was so goddamn important to her and her family that they risked a sea journey that was long and dangerous just so the first one would be a true *español*."

"That was me!" Martín said, proudly. "I am Catalan pure, and I will always honor and protect Spanish blood."

"That baby died on the ship coming back," Victorino told him. "You were her second. Born at the fort in El Fuerte, on the River Sinaloa with your mother screaming every second of the birth. And the hands that pulled you into this world were those of an old Yaqui grandmother. *My* grandmother!"

The revelation was barely off Victorino's lips before Martín lunged at his father, knocking him to the ground. "You're lying!" he shouted, and his hands found their way around his father's throat. But still this did not stop Victorino from letting his son know the truth.

"You don't know who you are," the old man said. "You're a *criollo*—a *mestizo*. No matter how pure your mother was, you are a Luna too. And Lunas are from this land—a land that hasn't been pure since the *españoles* took their first shit on it!"

Martín wanted to kill him, right there and then. In truth, his hands began to wrap more tightly around the old blacksmith's throat. If it had been any man other than his father, he could have done it, snapped the life out of this old man. But even though Victorino was old, his strength had years of practice to it, and he could match the fight within his son. With Victorino's age came a wisdom that was more powerful than any muscle strength. It allowed him to understand a man's vulnerabilities, where to find the softest spot to thrust the blade. Martín had not had the advantage of growing up with Victorino, and he had never learned this from his father. And because Victorino had struck him with the words that would hurt the most, Martín had been weakened. He could not fully grip—or ever break—the neck of the man who not only had given him life but who knew him better than he knew himself.

Within a heartbeat, Victorino reached back and grabbed his son's *pelotas*, squeezing them hard until Martín let go of his father's throat. Once he did that, Victorino flipped him over quickly and was on top of him. Besting him and pinning him in his place.

But the fight was still in Martín. "If you ever call me a *mestizo* again, I will silence your voice forever!" Martín threatened his father, no matter that he was now on the bottom and Victorino was on the top.

"You got a lot of me inside of you," Victorino said, impressed by the fight he saw in Martín. "Goddamn!" Smiling with pride, Victorino released his grip and let his son go.

Martín scrambled to his feet and rushed out through the oak grove. Moving farther and farther away from his father, back again to his own life and who he wanted to be.

No matter the truth.

FORTY-SEVEN

Without confession, the Mass means nothing.

Even before the adobe bricks of the mission walls had dried, the confessional had already been built. Made of oak, it looked like a tall windowless box; inside, a thin wall separated it into two sections, each one barely large enough to contain one person. A small window between the two cubicles was covered with a thin bit of cloth, giving privacy so one side would not see the other. It was dark in there, and God was the only one who could see the sinner. Confessor and priest were like strangers, and only their voices were known to each other. Sins took flight like little birds, on the wings of words spoken softly in the darkness. And by speaking them, wounds were healed, burdens were lifted, and the soul was set free.

But this was something the *indios* could not understand.

The priests couldn't teach them this; they could only show them, in manner and deeds. When the *padres* Jayme and Alphonso went into the confessional, taking turns hearing each other's sins, they were showing the *indios* what they needed to do to cleanse their souls and make them ready to receive the Lord.

Still, the *indios* did not understand.

These men in grey cloth were not like them. Without women and children for their own, they lived apart, separate from all that life was about. They were different, and this difference was not to be trusted. The *indios* did not understand the cramped black box or why they had to sit in darkness inside of it. They didn't trust speaking to these men in grey, hidden away and without eyes to gaze into, to see if the truth lived there inside of them.

Without confession, there could be no forgiveness. And without forgiveness, there could be no real conversion. Baptism alone was not enough. It was only the beginning—the first step to reaching the Lord. But there are many steps to trip upon while traveling through life, and without confession to forgive those stumbles, a soul could never truly be saved. The *indios* would forever be damned.

Or so said the priests.

It took the people from Sinaloa to come and show them the way.

For the first time, there were not only men making confession—men in grey who told the *indios* what to do, and men in blue who forced them, with whips and muskets, to do it. Now, there were families—women with children—and this the Kumeyaay finally understood. When Petra, Mercedes, Beatriz, Sola, and all the rest of the women lined up, taking their turns and entering the black box, the Kumeyaay watched and wanted to know more. When the women emerged out of the darkness, unharmed and unbroken, the fears of the Kumeyaay started to go away.

Finally the priests had a way to reach them.

That day in San Diego, when women walked into that confessional, Spain truly claimed this new territory. There was no room for more than one way of life there on that land, or so said the king, and the uniform alone could not win over the will of the native. Men alone could not conquer California. It took the women from Sinaloa, as they walked into that black box, to reach the Kumeyaay and show them the way.

As Petra, Mercedes, Sola, and Beatriz went inside the confessional, first one, then the next, the *indios* stood and watched, intrigued. But what the women could not tell them was that what they were witnessing was not as simple as it looked. The words spoken in darkness hid greater secrets inside of them. "Father, forgive me, for I have sinned" were words that only held half-truths. The easy sins were spoken, but the ones deep inside, the ones that claimed the soul, could not be uttered.

I do not want this child could not be spoken by Mercedes to any man and certainly not to a man of the cloth.

My body hungers for one I cannot have were words impossible for Petra to say.

And how could any of them ever dare to speak what was in Beatriz's heart? *I rage at you, Lord, for what you've taken away from me.*

These were anguished cries that would never be heard.

I hate my husband, I hate my life, I hunger for what I want and hate myself for wanting.

Forbidden words hidden not only in a woman's heart but deep inside a man's too, an officer perhaps, and one with too much to risk by revealing secrets, if only in the darkness and to a priest, unseen.

Men, too, kept their silence.

And yet they all went to Mass.

They opened their mouths and received the host, content in knowing that some things were between themselves and God alone. And the priests be damned, for they would never know the whole truth.

The mission's chapel was barely big enough to hold all the people that day. The doors were thrown open and the *soldados* stood shoulder to shoulder in the back as the women and the children filled up the rows, with the *indios* there among them.

Victorino and his two little girls sat in the front pew, with his wife squeezed tightly against him—his future there beside him. Behind him was his past.

Mercedes and Petra sat on the pews with Victorino's grand-children, while Martín and Tomás stood by the door of the chapel. Not once did they look at Victorino. The only man they would now called father was the one standing tall on the altar in front of them, dressed in his simple grey robes.

It was a proud day for that father—Father Jayme—standing in front of the congregation. Four of his finest students, the bright-est of the Kumeyaay children, acted as altar boys. They had been eager to learn, even when they did not understand the language, whether Latin or Spanish, and were the first to be baptized. They did what they were told to please the good *padre*, a man known for his kindness. Quick to offer a bit of food or a gentle smile, Jayme had patience with all his children, the ones that were so curious, the ones he would find at the seashore or in the oak grove. Whenever he found the young boys hunting hares or fishing at the river, or the little girls gathering up acorns, he would reach into his deep, magic pockets and pull out a sweet or a bright button or two, tiny trinkets that tempted the young child to follow this man in the grey robes back to the mission, back to a new life and into the arms of the Lord.

But sometimes an older child would run away back to his village. That's when the *soldados* would take over.

The king's soldiers did not have Jayme's patience. Nor did they have his big pockets filled with sweets or shiny trinkets. They only had their whips and ropes, and muskets too. If treats and trickery did not do the job, well then, they would chase after the children, tie them up, and throw them on the back of a horse. It was their job to protect and support, to make sure the rules were followed and the lessons learned.

This was not Jayme's way of doing things, and when he saw this, he stopped it. No child would be harmed, no boy or girl hurt, not at Jayme's mission. Maybe that is why the children loved him, followed him, and did what he asked them to do. Maybe that's why they stayed at the mission or why the ones who went home spoke of seeing kindness in the good father. Some of them even returned, bringing their families with them. There was food at the mission and shelter, and the man in grey was caring. Why shouldn't they stay there with him?

The villages of the Kumeyaay started to get smaller. All it took was one curious child who did not run away when coming upon the man in grey. A little boy who had never been on the back of a horse before, until Jayme put him on top of one. A little girl who had never seen a satin ribbon or tasted sweet chocolate, until the *padre* opened her eyes to such treats. Jayme showed them the magic in the puff of smoke from a musket barrel and let them watch as the speed of an unseen bullet struck down a buck. The curiosity of those children is what Jayme cultivated, just like he cultivated the fields of corn and wheat he toiled in every day.

There was always one child whose curiosity was stronger than his fear. That child would tell another and once the children followed, their families would follow next. And for the ones who wouldn't come, well, that's when Jayme packed up the mission and came to them. To their village of Nipaquay. There could be no running away after that. Mission and village would become one. And all would be good.

Or so it seemed.

But like the sins unspoken in the confessional, there were also words not spoken that day in the Mass. When the people of Sinaloa were among the Kumeyaay of the mission, when Jayme looked out upon his congregation, with full heart and a smile of pride, he saw only what he wanted to see. He saw *españoles* and *indios* sitting together and praying as one body in Christ.

But the good *padre* did not see the whole truth.

The confessional was not the only place where Jayme was in darkness.

FORTY-EIGHT

It was late when Mass was finally over.

The sun was low in the horizon, and the caravan hurried to mount up so they could reach the presidio and set up camp before night would fully fall on them. It had been a long day, and the children were tired from too much play and so much to eat. It was hard for the mothers to hold onto sleeping children in their laps with one hand, while holding the reins with the other.

Marco was too tired to walk alongside his uncle, so Felipe picked him up in his arms and carried him. Exhausted, the boy did not resist, and his eyes closed as soon as his head rested on Felipe's shoulder. The presidio was two leagues away, and the promise of fresh horses and setting up camp hurried the steps of the caravan. By the first grey light of the beginning of night, the outline of the presidio walls finally came into sight.

There were twenty-two soldiers at the San Diego presidio, and with their help, the tents of the caravan were quickly set up.

Few words were shared among the Lunas that night. They were fed up with traveling, tired of sleeping in different places on land that had no meaning for them. But tonight was the worst of all the nights. Victorino had stolen something precious from them: their spirit and their strength.

Of all of them, Mercedes seemed the most lost.

The baby in her womb weighed her down more than ever before, and she felt each kick as nothing more than a burden she had to bear. Joy had been taken from her, as she had lost her father all over again. Better it would have been if she had never seen Victorino, if in her heart the memory of him could have been left untouched and cherished. But to see him with a new family, with daughters he adored, was more than Mercedes could bear. It made her feel weary to her bones, and when she lay down in the tent that night she dreaded the morning, wishing only she could rest there forever.

It was Sola who put the twins to bed for her that night and cradled Maria to sleep. Beatriz shooed away Domingo from his wife's side, so that Petra could lie down with her sister. This was more than a husband could understand or fix. Only another sister, only Petra, could comfort her.

Petra had never seen Mercedes like this before, without a quip or a sharp word to protect her, like armor, from the world. Her heart was hurting, and there were no words to heal it. Instead, Petra stretched out next to her and wrapped her arms around her sister tightly, holding Mercedes and rocking her gently. Until finally Mercedes closed her eyes, and tears gave way to sleep—the best comfort in the world.

Four sentries guarded the presidio, with Felipe among them.

It was a quiet night, and in the distance the water lapped at the shores of the bay. An owl hooted high in a nearby cypress tree. The presidio, on top of its hillside, was quiet. The view to the west looked out across the coastline; to the east were the fertile fields and valleys bordering the river. The night was black but the sky was filled with bright stars—the only light that pierced the darkness.

Until a few hours past midnight.

When the night changed.

It was only a tiny dot of light at first, so small that not one of the sentries spotted it. The smell is what was noticed at first. A wind was blowing from the mountains, down the valley and to the coastal shores. The wind is what caught it, carried it, gentle at first, bringing it all the way down river to the hillside where everyone slept.

Felipe was the first to catch the scent, as he sat outside the presidio walls at a corner overlooking the coastline. He wasn't sure if it was real or if his mind was being cruel to him, bringing up memories of his mother in her apron, stirring a kettle for a family meal. When the smell grew stronger, Felipe got up and looked over the presidio wall to check on the cooking pit in the grounds. But it was out, and the embers were cold and grey.

Still the smell grew stronger. Felipe realized then that this was no memory.

Somewhere there was a fire.

Hurrying along the edge of the presidio wall, Felipe approached the sentry on duty at the other corner. "Do you smell it?" he asked urgently.

The sentry was dozing, but the words woke him up.

"Smell what?" he asked, yawning.

Felipe left him and hurried to the other side of the presidio that overlooked the valley and the river beyond. That's when he saw it. An orange glow in the distance that seemed to be growing. The smell grew stronger, and smoke began to show. Flames silhouetted what they were now destroying.

The bell tower of the mission.

The attack had started in silence.

No shouts or cries gave anyone a warning. Torches glowed in the black of night and quickly fire took flight on arrows from mighty bows, finding their marks in thatched roofs of dried tule reeds. The wind did the rest, exciting the flames and making them grow as they fed fast on everything they touched.

The sleeping men in grey robes awoke in their room that was now filled with smoke. Father Jayme arose quickly and threw open his shutters for fresh air, but then fell backwards from the heat. Flames surrounded all the buildings.

And only when Jayme had been seen at his window did the men in darkness step out into the light.

Out of the flames they seemed to come, hundreds and hundreds of them: Kumeyaay warriors from villages in the south. They were Tipai; their bodies were slicked down with seal oil, their loins were covered with deerskin, and their faces were streaked with paint. Only now did they raise their voices as one, shouting and screaming their war cries. They raised their arms, revealing bows, knives, and *macanas*—war clubs that could kill a man with one blow. Spreading out, the warriors surrounded the burning mission buildings—the granary, the chapel, the sanctuary, the smithy, soldier housing, and priest quarters. The voices of the Tipai were loud and filled with anger as they pressed forward, wanting to destroy.

Inside the priest quarters, as thick smoke filled the room, Alphonso began to tremble and cry, frozen where he stood. But Jayme moved quickly, reaching for his robes and throwing them on.

The smoke grew thicker.

Alphonso pissed his pants and fell to his knees. He threw himself on the floor and began to crawl to the door. Jayme tried to give him courage.

"Be strong!" he shouted to Alphonso, trying to pull him back to his feet. "We have to go out there and talk to them!"

Alphonso slapped away Jayme's hands and got to his feet, bolting out through the door.

Inside the soldier's quarters, Victorino, half-dressed, struggled through the smoke-filled room to find his children in their beds. Gathering them in his arms, and with his wife at his side, he struggled to get to the door.

Outside the chapel, a *soldado* raised his musket to shoot, but an arrow found his throat before he could pull the trigger. The Kumeyaay holding the deadly bow lowered it and used a hand to signal the others to go forward into the chapel. The flames, growing around him, lit up his face. It was a face that was well known at the mission.

It was Zegotay.

Once they were sent forward, the Kumeyaay began to tear apart whatever was in their path. They entered the burning buildings, ignoring the flames and hungry for revenge. Inside the chapel, they tore down the velvet curtains, smashed the confessional, knocked over the statues of the Blessed Mother and Saint Diego, and ripped with a blow from their bows the paintings that hung on the walls. The granary was raided, and all the stored corn and wheat was tipped out from its barrels and strewn on the floor. Kegs of wine were thrown to the ground, bursting open and spilling like blood flowing from an open wound.

Destruction was what the Kumeyaay wanted, and as the flames grew, so too did their hatred for anything that was *español*. Their food. Their clothing. Their idols. Their trinkets. Their strange words and their grey robes. The Kumeyaay wanted to kill or destroy everything about them. For every child taken, every family that left a village, every one of their women who had been fouled and broken by the soldiers. For all the leather lashes against the naked backs of the Kumeyaay, for every awful deed done to them and to their way of life.

Into this hell walked Father Jayme.

The priest came out of his quarters to face them, to hold his hands up with a Bible in one and a rosary in the other. He came in peace to speak to them, with love and gentleness.

"Good people!" He faced them with a bravery that bordered madness.

The Kumeyaay responded to him, stopping where they were to watch.

"I come to you in peace! Do not destroy the blessings that have been given you!"

Jayme began to speak with their words, using the language of the Kumeyaay to reach out to them. "The Lord loves you and provides!" he told them so they understood.

Their response came quickly. Before he had even finished.

The first blow upon him came from a shaman, Oroche, from the village Magtate. He hit the priest hard against his face, followed by a blow to his body by Yquetin of Apusquel. The look that filled Jayme's eyes as he stared at his attackers showed that he had no understanding of this violence. He knew not from where it came. Sadly, he would never comprehend it.

They fell upon the priest, and blow after blow came fierce and steady.

And the flames grew out of control, burning everything around him.

FOR&Y-NINE

It was almost dawn when help finally arrived.

They had ridden as fast as they could—the *soldados* from the presidio and the recruits from Sinaloa. Wearing their *cueras* around their chests, with their muskets and leather shields in hand, they had followed the growing orange glow of the spreading flames and readied themselves for battle. On sweating mounts they had approached the mission, Rivera and Rios leading the way and the fastest horsemen, Martín and Felipe, at the front. The flames were out by the time the rescue party arrived. Only the embers remained, turning into ashes. The roofs had disappeared, eaten by the fires, and the adobe walls stood cracked and broken but too stubborn to burn completely.

Rivera was the first to dismount and hurry to the priests' quarters, barely recognizing the building for what it was. The others soon followed after him, climbing down from their saddles and taking their muskets with them. Ready to face the enemy.

But no enemies remained.

The Kumeyaay were gone.

Only their destruction was left behind.

Father Alphonso was found in the root cellar of the granary. That's where he had hidden in the thick of the attack, and that's where he now crawled out from, sobbing and covered in soot and dirt. His hair was completely singed and his body naked, smeared in his own excrement. But he was alive, trembling and mumbling his prayers.

He was one of the lucky ones.

They found Father Jayme dead on the bank of the river.

Dragged there after he was beaten, his body was one large wound from head to foot. Covered in his own blood and mud from the waters, his face was gone, stripped away completely. He was unrecognizable.

Six of the *soldados* who were at the mission were found sprawled across the grounds; four had arrows in them, and two had been cut by knives and were near death. The wounded ones were put on litters to be taken back to the presidio. There were *indios* too who had been hurt—beaten for just being there. For giving over their lives to the *españoles* and forgetting who they really were: Kumeyaay in blood and name.

The presidio *soldados* went from one burned building to the next, looking for survivors.

They found Victorino with a pistol in his hand at the foot of his forge. After making sure his children and wife were safe in the huts of the *ranchería*, he had gone back to the smithy to save his tools from being stolen and to protect his forge. Without it, he would have no way of making a living for his family. He had to go back to save the smithy. That is where the Kumeyaay warriors had fallen on him and crushed his skull with the thick, hard wood of a *macana*. He had fallen right there at his forge, but stubborn old bull that he was, his eyes were open and he was still clinging to life.

Martín found him, just in time to watch him take his last breath. And at least his son had the decency to reach out and close his father's eyes for the last time before taking his pistol out of his hand and slipping it into his own belt.

As Martín walked away from the ruins of the smithy, it was

Rios who came up to him and asked with concern, "How is your father? Is he safe?"

Martín looked at him without emotion.

"You are mistaken. I have no father here."

And Victorino was never spoken of again.

FIFTY

The caravan was never told about what happened at the mission. The *soldados* had ridden back to the presidio, and no words were ever spoken about what they had found there or what their own eyes had seen. Nothing was said to their wives, and only the other soldiers there at the presidio were told in hushed whispers about the brutality and the violence of the Kumeyaay attack.

The women were smart enough not to ask questions. They saw the wounded carried back on litters, their bandages soaked in blood, and they knew enough not to ask how or why. They could tell by the look of their men that something bad and unspeakable had happened. It made the men a little bit harder. They grew angry at the slightest irritation, impatient and quick-tempered. The wives saw this and kept their distance, withdrawing from their husbands, careful of what they asked of them.

But with the children it was different. They could not understand what their fathers and mothers were not saying. And when the little ones got cranky, no mercy was shown. Discipline was harsh, judgment and sentence was swift. God help the children who did not learn the rules, remember them, and do what they were told. It was a quick swat on the *culo* for them, sometimes with the switch—a leather strap or the leafless branch—against the thigh or buttocks. This was how it was done in those days. Life was hard and lessons were rough; children could not stray from the path.

And neither could the *indios*.

The natives of the land had been told they were "children of God," and like all other children, they had to learn the rules and do what they were told. Or punishment would be swift for them too. In this way, God's love would be known. So had said the missionaries, and their word was the word of the land.

Until Zegotay said differently. And when he did, the *españoles* heard him loud and clear.

It changed them—toughened them—and as the men grew harder, their women and children followed along, growing tougher and stronger in their own ways.

It changed Felipe too. But not like the others.

His eyes began to open and he started to see: the way the *indios* walked and rode separately from the *españoles*, ate not what they ate, slept not where they slept; how they were kept apart from the whole, separated from the caravan. And yet they did the same work, walked the same *camino*, suffered the same heat, the same thirst and long hours. Their feet blistered just as those of the *españoles* did; their faces also burned red from the sun, their bodies knew the same aches and grew just as weary. When the mountains cooled at night, they shivered in the open while the *españoles* shivered in their tents. They shared together the harsh ways of the *camino*—the fifteen hundred miles carried the same hardships, the same fears, the same dangers.

But one thing was different.

Felipe had chosen to be there. He had chosen to travel the *camino*, and so had the rest of the people from Sinaloa. Each family wanted to be there, had chosen to be on that road, with bundles of their life on the backs of *burros*; and their families were together, man, wife, and children.

But the *indios* were alone. Men without women, and no families to comfort them, no children's laughter to fill up their hearts, giving them a reason to take the next step. They were young men, with strong bodies, able to work hard, and that's why they had been chosen. The old *indios* had been left behind.

Calixto, with his white hair, had been the only one to come with them. But Felipe had watched Calixto as the old *indio* worked with the horses, and he had moved like a young man—quick and easy. When Felipe had looked more closely at Calixto's face, he had noticed that it was still a young man's face. And it had made him wonder: What had put the white there in Calixto's hair? What had taken a young man and turned him so old?

Calixto's eyes held the answer: dark as a day without sun. There was something there on the other side of that darkness. Most didn't see it because they never looked. Who cared enough to look deep inside a man's eyes when that man was an *indio*? What *español* would do such a thing?

Only Felipe.

He had been the only one of the *españoles* who had something he wanted to learn from Calixto: the *indio* knew horses, and Felipe had watched him so he could learn. He had studied everything about the way Calixto moved, and when he had looked at his face, he saw those eyes, so dark, so filled with something he couldn't name.

Only now did he know what it was.

Felipe recognized it that night at the mission in San Diego. When he saw the burning embers and the priest's quarters still in flames. He could see it in the bloodied wounds, in the arrows pressed deep in the flesh of a *soldado*'s chest, and in the red slash across a dead corporal's throat. It was there in the ripped church paintings and the spilled-out grains and the spoiled food trampled by hundreds of naked feet. Thick in the smoke that hung over the ruins, it carried a scent so pungent, he could almost feel it pressed against his skin, choking his breath, stinging his eyes and bringing tears along with it.

It was rage.
That's what he had seen in Calixto's eyes.
And now, for the first time, he understood it.

III

Californio

FIFTY-ONE

The skies opened up and rain began to fall.

San Gabriel was only a day away, and Rivera kept the caravan moving.

The clouds were thick with darkness, and thunder rolled across the land as the *camino* turned away from the ocean and headed inland. Flashes of light filled the foothills, but still the pack train and the travelers pressed onwards.

They had stayed at San Diego longer than Rivera had planned. A search party had been put together; the rebels who had attacked the mission were to be hunted down. The Sinaloa recruits joined the presidio soldiers and together they traveled from the Tipai *rancherías* in the central grasslands to the coastal villages of the Ipai, searching for the ones with blood on their hands.

After a week, they found no one. There had been too many rebels, and as the recruits and soldiers went from village to village, none of the Kumeyaay would say the names of the men who had caused such bloodshed. These men were not rebels to the Kumeyaay; they were simply warriors protecting their people.

Rivera needed to move on before the rains came.

Monterey needed more men. Once the presidio and mission were staffed, he could deal with the *indio* problem in San Diego. More punishments would need to be handed out, if that was the only way to persuade the Kumeyaay to give up the rebels among their people. Father Jayme's way had not worked. He had been weak and too kind for the Zegotays of the world. If Spain wanted to keep this land, it would have to rule with a stronger fist. This would be the only way to convince the heathens to cooperate. The *indio* was incapable of being an ally or of sharing the land. A man does not trust another man unless he fears him. Rivera, as the new governor of Alta California, needed to be swift and stop the rebels, or the hundreds of them would turn into thousands. It would become a war again, just like it was against the Seris and Pimas, the Yaquis, and Apaches. Alta California needed to show the strength of its *gente de razon*—its people of reason—*los españoles*. And once he got these damn settlers to Monterey, Rivera would return and show these *indios* just who was in charge here.

But the rains did not cooperate.

They came early.

Lightly at first, but it wasn't long before the skies opened up. By midday the river they followed raged, and the waters reached the top of the banks. Mud oozed through the hooves of the horses and *burros,* the animals slipping and sliding on the trail as they tried to keep their footing.

Everyone was soaked through, and still the rain fell hard upon them.

It was rough for the men to see their families like this. Domingo watched as Mercedes rode in front of him, with little Maria pressed tightly against her body. His wife held her shawl above their little daughter's head, trying to shield the girl from the falling rain. But nothing could protect her as the storm beat down relentlessly. Domingo nudged his horse to go forward until he pulled up next to Mercedes. Pulling off his sombrero, he handed it to his wife to hold above Maria's little head.

"We need to stop and put up the tents! The children are going to get sick!" Mercedes shouted to her husband, above the noise of the storm.

2) 52" ⟩ 4"x4"

36" ⟩ 2"x4"

32½" ⟩ 2x4"

44" ⟩ 2x4"

olives

Domingo nodded and spurred his horse forward.

Up at the front of the caravan, Martín rode at the side of Rivera.

Domingo pulled his horse up next to the captain. "This rain is too much for these people!" he shouted.

"Get back to your position!" Martín called out to his brother-in-law.

"We stop at San Gabriel tonight and not before!" Rivera yelled.

Domingo turned his horse around and went back to his position. He did not have the courage to look at his wife or his children as he rode to the end of the caravan.

Rivera was in charge, and they had to let him lead. He knew that these storms could go on for days, and after San Gabriel there were no other missions or presidios until San Luis Obispo hundreds of miles away. It would be weeks of traveling by themselves, with no help within reach. There were more tribes farther north, some of them friendly and some of them unknown. It would be a lot of land to cover with no certainty of safety for these women and children. Even now there was danger. They were not yet out of Kumeyaay territory or away from the Liuseños. And as they moved closer to San Gabriel, there were the Tongva people: Gabrieleños, Fernandeños, and Nicolerios.

The women and children being soaked by the rain was only an inconvenience. Rivera would not risk a greater sacrifice by stopping, just to keep them dry.

They moved on, and the rain continued to fall.

The caravan arrived at San Gabriel in darkness.

Everyone was chilled to the bone, their wet clothing clinging to their bodies.

It was the first time Mercedes needed to be helped down from her horse.

"Your baby is kicking the shit out of me," she told Domingo, as he struggled to help her off the back of the animal.

"A boy, maybe?" he laughed, with hope of finally getting himself a son.

"Or a girl with big feet," Mercedes grunted, as she clung to her husband and he shakily helped her dismount.

They had barely settled into their tents for the night and fallen asleep before it seemed that dawn came and it was time to be on the *camino* again. The sun looked down on them for the first time in two days, and hope filled the air, which was sweet and fresh from the storm.

It took both Petra and Domingo to help lift Mercedes onto the back of her mount.

"Jesus, woman!" Domingo groaned under Mercedes' weight, as he boosted her by the butt onto the horse.

"You should stay here," Petra said to her sister. "Martín will understand if you tell him about the baby. It's too far for him to send you back to Sinaloa."

"And if I'm left here, who will help me deliver this child?" Mercedes asked, with a whisper. "What women are here to be at my side? To help this little one get out?" She looked over at the soldiers as they helped the caravan load up the *burros*. "There are only men here!"

It was true. There were no *españolas* there among the soldiers at San Gabriel. But there were plenty of *indios*; you could see them working out in the fields. There were hundreds of them. Many were women.

Petra pointed them out to her sister.

"There are plenty of women here."

Mercedes just shook her head. "I don't know those women or how they bring babies into the world."

"I'm sure it must be the same way we do it," Petra said.

She was worried about her sister. Traveling on the back of a horse all day was not good for a woman about to give birth. If

Mercedes could stay there to have the baby, she and Domingo could come to Monterey later and rejoin the family.

"Archuleta's wife is a midwife, and she is three horses to my right," Mercedes told Petra. "Tia Carrera, just behind me, helped ten grandchildren into this world. These women are our friends, *mija*. Babies are brought into this world by the people in their lives. These women in the fields are not our people. They're strangers. They're not like us." She reached out and touched Petra's cheek gently, trying to take away her worries. "I promise to keep my legs closed until Monterey," she said with a grin.

And that was the end of the discussion.

Neither one of them would speak another word about the baby.

Petra would honor her sister's wishes.

FIFTY-TWO

After a week, the caravan was not even halfway to San Luis Obispo.

The *camino* had gone inland after stretching out along the oceanside for days. The Pacifico had been the bluest of blues, and the tribes living there—in tule huts that were clustered together at the seashore—were not hostile. They simply kept their distance and let the caravan go on its way. The people were sad to see the ocean finally disappear as the land started to rise. The caravan soon found itself on the top of cliffs, with the *camino* turning and heading into the mountains.

It was slow going for the horses and the *burros*, as the weight of the people and their packs grew heavier on their backs. The *camino* narrowed and the animals slowed their pace, their hooves barely staying on the slender path. One misstep would mean a fall, and it was thousands of feet to the bottom of a canyon.

The height made the people dizzy, and their stomachs started to turn.

Mercedes, on top of her horse, closed her eyes and would not look down.

But Petra found joy looking outwards and beyond, at the rounded tops of the hills that lay in front of them. Covered in a fresh green coat from the recent rains, meadows separated them and stretched out to the horizon, as far as you could see.

It was a beautiful sight.

Even Mercedes found some courage and opened her eyes when Petra called out to her and begged her to look. Her mouth dropped at the sight, and her eyes widened at the beauty around them. God had surely leaned down and touched this part of the land. It was as close to Heaven as the earth had ever reached.

Felipe, too, saw what they saw. At the back of the caravan, he sat higher in his saddle so he could see all of it: the perfect blue sky, the rolling green hillsides with oak trees to shade them, and a wide creek to quench their thirst. For the first time since Sinaloa, Felipe felt a stirring within him: he wanted to stay. He wanted to stop the journey and never travel again. He remembered the look in his father's eyes when the first growth of the little seeds began to show on their land. When the corn started to poke through the soil and the wheat chaff began to appear. He understood now that joy in his father's smile when he brought his family out to the fields to witness such a miracle.

Life was beginning right in front of them.

Like God Himself, they could plant a seed, nurture it, and watch it grow. It was a power that could make a poor man rich. The land that stretched out in front of the caravan was lush and fertile, and Felipe felt it pulling him towards it, reaching out to him and letting him know that this was a good land. A good land to build a life, and to call home. The pull of it was great, and even the child inside of Mercedes felt it, shifting within her, pressing its head down at that great gateway into the world that dwells inside every woman.

Giving her power. But also pain.

This baby inside of Mercedes was getting ready to come out.

And Mercedes knew it.

She started to hiccup and she couldn't stop. This was what she did every time a child of hers was making ready for that magic journey into the world. Mercedes knew this as clearly as she knew the face of every one of her children. She felt a tickle down there in that precious space between her legs and knew the baby was kissing her, saying, "Hello, Mami. I'm here! I'm coming soon to meet you!"

The hiccups lasted for hours.

Since she was riding on top of her horse, not too close to the others, no one heard her, so no one knew. Mercedes figured she had a week, no longer. Her first babies—the twins— had taken three weeks after the hiccups had come, but little Maria had come quicker. Less than a week. This baby would not make it all the way to Monterey before it pushed its way into life. Mercedes smiled at the thought and hoped to God it was a son for Domingo, a big, strong boy who would come to them at San Luis Obispo, and if he didn't come right away, well then, she would finally tell Martín her secret so they could all stay a few days more at that mission, waiting for the baby to come. Her brother would be angry at her for slowing them down and hiding the child from him, but the hell with his anger. He would be an uncle again, and there would be one more *español* born to seal España's claim to this land. Martín would forgive her because he would be proud— this child would be a new Luna, the first to be born in El Norte.

Mercedes looked out at the beauty of this land, and she was happy. San Luis Obispo would be a good place to have her baby. The blessings of Saint Luis would be on her son. A boy is what she would have, for sure! And just as that thought came to her, she looked ahead at the hillsides, and there she saw a group of deer crossing down a slope, with a doe at the back and her baby close to her side.

This was a sign; Mercedes was sure of it. A birth at San Luis Obispo—that would be the plan!

But babies sometimes make their own plans.

As the caravan crawled down from the mountains and onto the flatlands, the cramps started to come. The baby stopped moving inside of her, and within hours a wetness spilled out from between her legs. It was just a little trickle at first, a slow leak. But the cramps started to grow stronger. As the hooves of the animals moved along the rough and rocky *camino,* water gushed out from Mercedes, and her skirt stained dark and wet.

The caravan kept moving. No one knew.

Mercedes tried to focus, to figure out what to do. The contractions by now were coming stronger, faster, tightening her belly and squeezing her insides until she wanted to call out to all the saints and beg them to stop the pain. When the next one hit her, coming so quickly she could barely take a breath, she had to bury her face into the back of little Maria to smother a scream that, like the baby inside of her, wanted to come quickly, right then and there. Once it had passed, Mercedes snapped the reins and rode her horse over to the side of Petra, who was on her own horse, a few riders ahead.

"Take Maria," Mercedes told her, through gritted teeth.

"What . . . ?"

"Take her now!" Mercedes spoke quickly, lifting up little Maria and holding her out to Petra, who reached as far as she could to take the little girl into her lap. Mercedes gave a quick kick to the flank of her mount and galloped away.

Petra knew immediately.

Martín, at the front of the caravan, saw a horse galloping out of the line of riders and across the grasslands, heading for a grove of oaks near the creek.

"Hey!" he shouted out to the rider, until he saw that the rider was Mercedes.

Petra rode quickly to Domingo at the back of the caravan. "Take Maria!" she told him as she held the little girl out to her father.

"What's the matter?" he asked, as he took hold of his daughter.

Petra kicked the flank of her horse and raced after her sister, calling out as she rode off quickly across the grassland, "Señora Archuleta! Come quickly!"

Mercedes was off her horse and hunched over the rocks at the bank of a flowing creek, in the shade of a grove of oak trees. She was vomiting into the water as Petra rode up behind her, scrambling down from her horse quickly and rushing over to her sister's side.

"The baby's coming." Mercedes spit into the water as she spoke.

"No, no it's too soon."

"I can't stop this. It's coming!" Mercedes said, starting to pull her blouse over her head.

Petra reached out to help her sister, but a big contraction hit Mercedes and she gasped, grabbing her sister to steady herself as she tried to ride out the pain.

"Archuleta's wife is coming. Hold on!" Petra pleaded.

As the contraction built, Mercedes put her hands on her thighs and squatted at the creek bank, bearing down and moaning loudly. Petra got behind her, holding her, keeping her steady and on her feet, supporting her sister. She grabbed Mercedes' skirt, pulling it up and out of the way, baring her legs and hips. As the contraction left her, Mercedes tugged at her skirt, wanting to be rid of it, and Petra helped her pull it off. Another wave of pain grew quickly, hitting Mercedes harder than all the others, and she screamed out as Petra sat behind her, taking her sister in her arms and holding her as she bore down with the pain, gritting her teeth and grunting, pushing with all her might.

Martín appeared on horseback, the first of the caravan to reach the creek. He was off his horse in a moment and ran over to Petra and Mercedes.

"Get up!" he yelled at them angrily. "We've got to keep moving!"

Mercedes let out a yell as another contraction overcame her.

This was something new for Martín. He had never seen such a sight as this.

"What is she doing? Is she ill?" he wanted to know.

"What do you *think* she's doing!" Petra screamed at him.

Mercedes pushed her back against Petra as she sat in her sister's lap; digging her heels into the rocks for support, she squatted low and bore down.

Several of the women from the caravan appeared, leaving their horses at the oak grove and hurrying over to Petra and Mercedes at the creek bank. Archuleta's wife, a small slip of a woman, led the group and spared no time before taking her position at Mercedes' side. The other women were quick to move Martín away, leading him back to his horse, and pushing him from sight. This was women's work and no place for a man.

That is when Martín finally understood. The color drained from his face and he bolted, jumping on top of his horse and racing like hell back to the caravan.

Archuleta's wife crossed herself.

Slowly, she pulled open Mercedes' legs.

FIFGY-GHREE

Screams echoed across the green meadows.

There was nothing the men could do to help Mercedes, so they went to work setting up the camp and putting up the tents, gathering firewood and watering the livestock.

Still, Mercedes went on screaming.

It was more than Martín could stand.

He hurried to find Felipe and Domingo, who had been sent to a meadow to tend to the livestock. When he found Domingo, he grabbed hold of him and let his fists fly, beating the hell out of his brother-in-law.

Felipe tried to step in and stop it.

"Keep out!" Martín bellowed, and one quick punch to Felipe's jaw jolted him backwards. Turning back to Domingo, Martin beat him some more, and the poor guy tried to free himself, too frightened to even throw a blow. He screamed, matching the screams of his wife down at the creek, but the louder he screamed, the harder Martín hit him. Only when he begged, when he broke down and cried, did Martín get his belly full and throw him to the ground.

"I didn't know! I didn't know! I swear it!" Domingo sobbed, and the tears flowed from his eyes. His nose was running, with blood streaming down to a split lip. "She was like this in Sinaloa!

274

She didn't tell me! We would have stayed, if I knew! God's truth! I swear to Christ!"

Martín wanted to kill him. He wanted to kill *somebody*, that's for sure. Those screams from his sister pierced him and filled him with a fear he could never show. Anger was his only friend, the only thing that pushed away the fear.

Mercedes screamed again. Even Martín's anger could not stop him from hearing it. Turning away from Domingo, who lay there in the dirt, Martín hurried off to his horse, mounting it and riding away.

And not one of the men blamed him for leaving.

Archuleta's wife, kneeling on the ground, stroked Mercedes' naked legs with wet cloths, cooling her down and giving her some comfort, as Petra held onto her sister from behind.

Mercedes looked exhausted.

The other women of the caravan all had their jobs to do. Some of them were in a group together saying the rosary, while others stayed close to the creek, rinsing out cloths and then soaking them in the water to hand back to Petra, who used them to wipe the sweat from her sister's face.

Archuleta's wife was used to attending births; she had been doing this for the last twenty years, after her first baby at fifteen. She was the midwife of Sinaloa, and nothing surprised her about bringing a baby into this world; even the slowness of this birth was not throwing her. Calm as a Sunday morning, she put her head down low, holding back Mercedes' knees, as she checked for some sign of the baby. Seeing nothing at all, she rolled back her sleeve and reached her hand deep inside, until she found what she was looking for and then she nodded.

"The baby's right there. One more big push."

Mercedes shook her head. "I can't do it," she whispered, exhausted.

"Come on! This one's shy, kick him out!"

"I need to rest," Mercedes said, but before she could finish saying it, another contraction began.

Archuleta's wife pushed down on the top of the mound of Mercedes' belly. "Push!" she yelled, as she tried to move the baby down lower in the womb, so Mercedes could push the baby out.

Gritting her teeth, Mercedes bore down with all her strength.

"It's moving!" Archuleta's wife shouted, feeling some movement at the top of Mercedes' belly. Quickly, she bent down low, pulling apart Mercedes' knees so she could look once again for some sign of the baby. "I see it!" she cried out. "This one's got lots of hair!" Archuleta's wife said with a big laugh. "Keep pushing!"

Mercedes pushed again, harder and longer.

Archuleta's wife reached her hand inside of Mercedes, trying to find the baby's shoulders. "Push! Push! Push!" she said, and with each word, she tried to pull at the baby.

Mercedes' face turned red as she bore down and pushed.

Archuleta's wife called for assistance, and several of the women hurried over to her, grabbing her by the waist to hold her there, as the tiny woman pulled with all her might.

Gasping as the baby was being pulled, Mercedes could feel the suction of it as it moved within her. With one final tug, Archuleta's wife pulled the baby out, and she fell backwards into the arms of the women behind her.

The baby, covered in blood and the slime of birth, was clasped tightly in the arms of Archuleta's wife, who smiled as she reached into her waistband and brought out a small dagger. Holding the baby up by its heels with one hand, she used her other hand to cut the umbilical cord free. As she held the child high by its heels, the sex of the baby was there for all to see. Swollen by the birth, and by being inside of the womb, there was no mistaking what this child was.

Mercedes' face lit up with a big grin.

It was a boy!

One big helluva boy.

FIFTY-FOUR

Domingo came running as soon as he heard the women shouting for him.

The baby had already been cleaned up and swaddled in a blanket, lying quietly in Mercedes' arms as Domingo hurried down to the bank of the creek, out of breath and with his face still covered with dirt and blood.

"What the hell happened to you?" Mercedes asked, taking one look at her husband and his beaten-up face.

"Oh this? This is nothing." Domingo shrugged it off, trying to wipe his face clean with his sleeve.

Petra handed him a wet cloth to use to tidy himself up.

"I fell off my horse," he lied.

Domingo was not good at lying. Mercedes knew this about her husband, and she looked over at Petra—the two sisters trading a look that said they knew exactly what had happened. Martín was their brother, and they knew how quick he was to use his fists before his brains. They had spent their whole lives knowing his anger and recognizing its marks.

"I hope you hit that horse back," Mercedes said softly. "I hope you hit him so hard it knocked the meanness right out of him. For your own pride and honor, you must always stand up to that mule of a horse."

Domingo's eyes could not meet hers. His face flushed with shame. Mercedes' heart hurt seeing her husband so beaten in body and spirit.

"Do it for your son," she told him.

She said that word Domingo had waited so long to hear. He had a son.

He could not believe his ears, and he looked at Mercedes to make sure it was really the truth. His wife smiled and Domingo kneeled down at her side, looking at the baby in her arms. She held the child out to him.

"You did it right this time," she kidded him. "You got yourself a boy!" Domingo took the baby into his arms and gazed into his son's eyes.

No man was ever happier.

No woman ever felt such pride.

The women left Mercedes, Domingo, and the baby at the side of the creek while they went back to the caravan to prepare the evening meal. They would all spend the night there, and in the morning they would move on. San Luis Obispo was still a three-day ride, but with Mercedes having just given birth, they would need to move a little more slowly the first couple of days, and it could take longer.

When the sun was low and had almost slipped away from the sky, Martín appeared at the creekside with a litter he had built out of wood slats and canvas. It was time to move his sister back to the caravan. Mercedes didn't say a word when she saw her brother, and Martín was quiet himself. Domingo, sitting at his wife's side, was a silent reminder of Martín's rage, and his beaten and bruised face was more powerful than anything Mercedes could have said to her brother to give him shame.

Martín was not a man of apologies; he didn't know how to

say he was sorry—no one had ever taught him. He could only seek forgiveness in the deep love he felt for his family and for the actions he took to protect them, shelter them, and keep them safe. This was how their brother showed them that he was sorry—by building a litter to carry his sister further in their journey. It was strong, and there was nothing fancy about it; raw and sturdy it was, just like Martín.

Mercedes raised her hands out to her brother, allowing him to help her stand. Taking her by the arm, he guided her over to the litter where she stretched out on top of it. When Martín turned, there was Domingo facing him. With his newborn son in his arms, he held the baby out to his brother-in-law, a surprise that Martín did not expect at all. A man who is beaten by another man always keeps his distance, but Domingo was no ordinary man. He matched Martín's rage with gentility and kindness; to Domingo, what mattered the most was family. No matter the problems, the secrets, the misunderstandings, or the cruelty. The world offered much worse. And *familia* was the only sanctuary that could offer healing. At every birth. Every death. Every wedding. At every celebration of life.

Martín looked into the face of this brand-new Luna resting in his arms, and he searched for the loved ones gone but not forgotten—there in the tilt of the eyebrows or the shape of the nose, the curve of the lips, or the look deep in these newly born eyes. Here in this little face, Martín could see the people of the past, and he recognized this boy, knowing him at first glance from the faces of the ones who had come before him.

"His name is Josep Antonio," Domingo said, proudly. "For your mother, Josephina."

Martín's eyes started to fill with tears.

And there was absolutely nothing he could do to stop them.

FIF5Y-FIVE

Mercedes died the next day.

No one expected it. Death came to her like the coward that it is—cruel and without warning, while hearts were still happy from the birth of little Josep. The litter that she lay upon had been attached by poles to the flanks of Domingo's horse, and he had ridden so carefully on the *camino* that next morning, pulling that precious cargo: his wife and his newborn son.

The night before, they had all celebrated.

With Rios, so handsome as he stroked his mandolin, everyone sang the songs of the old country—the lullabies, love songs, and yes, the Alabado, in praise of God. The whole caravan welcomed this new little boy, as Mercedes lay on the litter close to the campfire and nursed her son. The men wanted to carry her to her tent so she could rest, but Mercedes wanted to sleep outdoors to show her newest child the stars. Domingo, little Maria, and the twin girls spread out their bedrolls next to their Mama, and all the family lay down there together, looking up at the night sky and watching those stars twinkling until they twinkled all of them to sleep.

The caravan moved out at dawn.

Mercedes took only the smallest sips of hot chocolate that day. "For the baby," she said as she offered him her breasts, but turned away her own face for anything to eat. Little Josep was good at the breast, latching on from the first moment he saw that *teta*.

"Just like his father!" Mercedes had smiled and winked at Domingo.

Petra offered to hold the baby during the first part of their ride. But Mercedes had shaken her head no, not wanting to be separated from this baby at all.

They would soon enough be separated.

And maybe she knew that or had a feeling somewhere deep inside of her. Who can tell for sure? She never said. She never spoke one word, never complained or said she felt bad, or needed to stop, to rest at the side of the road. She was tough, Mercedes. Maybe a little too tough for her own good. She just smiled and kissed her children, settled back in the litter like "a queen," that's what Domingo had called her.

"Don't get used to this!" he had kidded. "You're too mean to be a queen!"

And later he would cry for having said it.

It was late afternoon when the caravan stopped at the river. The horses and *burros* were covered in sweat and so, too, were the people from Sinaloa. They would camp here and use the water to cool themselves off, before going on. The children already were running for the riverbank, stripping off their clothing as they ran.

Petra handed little Maria to Beatriz, and the twin girls ran after their Tia Sola with Marco and Victor by their sides.

That's when Petra heard the shout.

All the way at the back of the caravan.

She hurried towards it, and as she did, she could see all the way at the end of the line, past the stopped horses and the *burros* yet to be unloaded, all the way to the end, to Domingo and his horse and the litter with Mercedes on it. It was Domingo who was shouting, like an animal in a trap with no way to get out. So wounded. So much in pain was he. And he was pulling at something, pulling at that litter, pulling at Mercedes, trying to get her up, trying to pick her up, and trying to hold onto her. But she was sleeping, sleeping so quietly, so soundly.

Petra was sure of it.

Mercedes' body was limp, and Domingo couldn't hold onto her, so peaceful and asleep was she, not hot and sweating like the rest of them, not tired and aching, but so calm and peaceful.

Closer and closer, Petra ran to her as Domingo's shouts turned into screams, and she wondered how could her sister sleep through such screaming? Why wasn't she waking up and giving hell to her husband for the racket he was making? Over and over, Domingo screamed, and as Petra got closer, she saw the tears now streaming down his face as he pulled at his wife, begging her to get up, to stand, to keep going.

But Mercedes would not wake. She would never wake up again.

Her eyes were shut tightly, and her mouth, so peaceful, hung open. So quiet she was, not a sound did she make. Petra had never seen her so quiet. Or so pale. Her face was white, and when the baby started to cry there in the litter, and her sister did not reach out for him, did not lower her blouse and offer her breast—when she just kept on sleeping—that's when Petra knew the awful truth.

Someone grabbed Petra then, and she held on tightly, crumpling to the ground, not wanting to see, not wanting to be told, not wanting to know this world would forever be without her sister, without Mercedes' smile, without her life, her strength. This was more than Petra could bear. She buried her face into strong arms that held her tightly, that pulled her close, into the safety of his chest, and her screams vibrated deep inside of him.

Felipe held Petra tighter than he had ever held anyone before.

FIFTY-SIX

Never have so many tears ever been shed.

Not just by the Luna family but by everyone in the caravan. A piece of them had slipped away that day; their world had forever changed. Their Sinaloa had lost the one woman with more piss and vinegar in her than any of them. Mercedes had been the first woman to step forward to take this journey, risking everything to find a new home, a better life, and a safer place for her family. Even the ones who didn't like her, the women who gossiped and talked about her behind her back, still respected her because they knew she could kick their *culos* if they didn't. If God could choose to strike down someone with such power, such taste for life, any one of them could be the next to follow.

Death had shown up to remind them he was waiting for every one of them.

But the Luna family cried because Mercedes was not there to tell them to stop crying, to remind them that each one of them was a Luna—that they needed to move on, no matter what. She couldn't tell them this, and so they gathered around her body and didn't hold back their tears. The people of the caravan kept their distance, leaving the family alone. And after the tears of the Lunas had been shed, they did what every other family has had to do.

They moved on.

Martín picked up his sister and carried her in his arms. Domingo was barely able to stand but Tomás walked at his side, helping to hold him up and guiding him along the way. Little Josep, in Petra's arms, was blessed with his youth and did not understand. But the twin girls at Petra's side knew, and when one stumbled and fell in her grief, the other twin helped her up and they held hands and walked on together. Felipe carried little Maria, who wrapped her arms tightly around his neck, looking like a lost little lamb as she searched the faces for her mother. Sola and Beatriz followed at the rear, with Victor and Marco at their sides.

The caravan turned away in respect, letting the *familia* do what they had to do. Leaving them alone, together.

They buried Mercedes under the tallest of oak trees on top of a hillside. It pained them all that there was no priest, no blessings, no holy water to cleanse Mercedes for her new journey, one she never wanted to take.

El Capitán said a prayer and read from the Bible he always kept in his saddlebag for all the souls he carried with him. Mercedes was not the first to die on one of his journeys, and she wouldn't be the last. But the ones who had died in the past had all been *soldados*, and death was always a risk when a man took up the lance. This time was different; this time God had taken one of their sisters, and Rivera had to work hard, calling on his training, to not let his voice break when he read from the Mass of the Dead.

"Eternal rest grant to her, Lord, and let perpetual light shine upon her. May she rest in peace."

After they buried Mercedes, the *familia* spent the night under that tall oak tree. The caravan brought them food, and the men offered them blankets for the chilly night falling around them. There was no fire to keep them warm; no one thought to build one. They huddled together using the warmth of the *familia* to get them through the night.

Petra held onto little Josep, wrapped up in the shawl of his mother and pressed against his *tia*'s empty but warm breasts. Felipe sat next to Petra, and when he put his arm around her, she did not move away. She settled into the closeness of him, and that is how she stayed all through the night, never moving away. Not even for a moment.

The ground around them was covered with fallen leaves and tiny acorns. Felipe reached out and picked up one of the acorns at his side. It was bright green—so new and freshly fallen. The other ones around it were ripe and ready, brown like the soil they fell upon, but this one was still young and not ready yet to fall. A perfect acorn in so many ways. Felipe slipped it into his pocket and decided he would keep it there until he found a home again, until he found that land that would be his—and Petra's. When he found it, he would plant the little acorn there. And Mercedes' tree would give shade to their children one day.

Felipe was sure of it.

When the sun came up, the Luna family was back with the caravan, the first to mount up their horses and the first who were ready to ride on.

Mercedes was gone but never to be forgotten.

Adelante, siempre adelante.

FIFTY-SEVEN

Mercedes had taught her little Josep well.

That baby was a good eater.

The only problem was Mercedes' *tetas* were not there anymore to feed him. That baby pecked, pushed, and buried his face into that bosom of his *tia* Petra and still she did not offer them to him.

And so he cried!

From sunup to sunset, each step they took along the way, each new piece of land they covered, was filled with the sounds of that hungry little baby crying for his *teta*.

Petra was beside herself; there was nothing she could do.

No other woman could help either. Sola and Beatriz had no babies anymore, and the three women from Sinaloa whose *tetas* had been full at the start of the journey were now dry, and their babies ate what everyone else ate. All had been weaned, and no woman among them had what little Josep cried for—the milk that had been stolen from him with the death of his mother.

Still, the women all gathered together and tried this thing and that—a little water with sugar they gave the infant Josep, soaking it in cheesecloth and squeezing a drop into his tiny mouth. But he cried even more—this was no *teta*! They emptied a *bota* and filled it up again, brewing a weak tea of chamomile and letting the baby suck at its tip. Josep wailed even louder.

This, too, would not do; the breast is what he wanted. What he needed was his mother's milk!

Night and day that baby cried, screaming at the top of his lungs. No one could sleep; everyone was exhausted. Domingo cursed himself and sobbed at the sound of the son he had always wanted so badly. But at what cost had he paid? He clung to his little girls and worshipped them in a way he had never done before. Petra could only hold little Josep close, wrapped in the shawl of her sister, and pray that a miracle would find them. That somehow they could come across a goat, or a cow maybe to milk, and little Josep could stop his crying. But there was nothing on that *camino* to help feed that baby. No farmland and no ranches. No livestock to be found anywhere around them. Just wilderness as far as the eye could see. And the closest mission was still three days away.

By the next morning Josep had grown quiet.

He was pale and limp in Petra's arms, and he could barely turn his head away when the women tried to give him the sugar water in the *bota*. Little Josep was dying, and there was nothing anyone could do about it.

All of the caravan knew this.

Only Petra would not face the truth.

When the women offered to hold little Josep to lighten her burden, she refused and held that little baby even tighter. This was Mercedes' son, and she would cling to him as long as she could. It was her job now to be his mother, and he belonged in her arms and no one else's. She held on tightly to the reins of her horse with one hand, and with the other she held onto little Josep, his tiny head tucked in close against her heart, and the beat of it calmed him and helped him sleep. No other woman in the caravan could take care of him like Petra—a woman who had the same blood, the same scent as his mother.

Petra rode like this all day long, and when the caravan stopped as the sun was slipping from the sky, she did not stop her horse like the others. Instead she kept going forward.

Martín galloped after her and caught up, riding at her side. "We have to set up camp for the night."

Petra ignored him and didn't halt her horse.

Martín reached out for her reins, but she yanked them from him.

"This baby needs milk!" she said. "I won't stop until he can get it!"

There was nothing Martín could say to change her mind, and he knew this. Instead, he spurred his horse and rode back to the caravan to tell Rivera.

The captain said that with an escort, if Petra and the baby traveled through the night, they would reach the mission at San Luis Obispo by daybreak. "There's livestock there," Rivera said to Martín. There would be milk. If the baby survived. "If he dies, at least the mission priest can baptize him," Rivera added.

It was the only hope for little Josep.

There was no moon that night to show them the way.

Rios was the only one who had traveled this road before, and he rode at the front, with Martín, Felipe, and Domingo abreast of Petra as they followed the *camino* to San Luis Obispo de Tolosa. They stopped only once, at the beginning of their journey, so Petra could hitch up her skirt, tucking it into her waistband to ride with both of her legs around her horse instead of sitting sidesaddle like a proper *española*. Riding like this, she could gallop her horse the way she had done when she was a little girl, the same way her Martín had taught her, the way she loved—with the wind at her face and as fast as any man could ever ride. In this way, she could keep up with the men and push them to ride even faster.

Onward they galloped into the night.

Onward to San Luis Obispo.

FIFTY-EIGHT

They reached the mission by dawn.

Petra was off her horse at the front of the chapel before any of the men could even offer her a hand to help her dismount. Hurrying up to the massive wooden doors of the sanctuary, she pounded with all her might, shouting for the priest to come.

Never has a cow been milked so quickly.

Father Caveller pulled at the *tetas* of that animal himself, collecting the milk as fast as he could into a bowl for the baby. That clay bowl was barely a third full when Petra snatched it from under that animal and brought it quickly to Josep's lips. Pressing it gently against his mouth, she tipped it so that he could taste it. But the baby's eyes barely opened, and his lips did not part for that creamy white offering.

He would not drink it.

Felipe took off his *bota* and poured the cow's milk inside of it, rubbing a few drops on the tip. He handed it to Petra who carefully slipped the tip into the baby's mouth, pressing on the leather sides and squeezing a drop into Josep's mouth. But the milk dribbled out from the baby's lips and slipped down his chin. He would not swallow; he would not nurse from it.

By now, everyone at the mission was gathered around outside the stables—a handful of *soldados* surrounded by dozens of Stishni, a tribe of the Chumash people. All eyes were on Petra and the infant in her arms. They could see Domingo, crying softly at the side of his sister-in-law, and Martín, Felipe, and Rios, with their hats in hand, all broken men in their helplessness.

There was only one priest at San Luis, and he would need the help of one of his soldiers for what he had to do next. Padre Caveller asked Sergeant Rincon, a pious man and one who always assisted him at Mass, to make ready the holy waters of the baptismal font inside the chapel. It would be far better to baptize this child while he still had time on this earth and before dying with Eve's sin on his soul, dooming him to everlasting life in limbo. Baptism was the only answer left for poor little Josep.

But when the priest tried to guide Petra out of that stable, she would not move. He took her arm gently, but she slapped him away. Once again, she tried to get that little baby to take the milk from the tip of the *bota*. And once again, that baby refused.

There isn't a woman alive whose womb would not ache at such a sight.

The women of the Stishni felt this way as they watched on, outside the wooden stable gate. One of the oldest of them, a tiny woman, darkened from the sun and still dressed in the old ways—in deerskin wrapped around her body with bits of seashells tied into her long hair—did not let the gate stop her. She moved, without fear, into the stable and over to Petra and little Josep.

The *soldados* did nothing to stop this old *indio* woman, who now shuffled her way over to Petra. They knew her as Momoy, an elder of the tribe, an *antap*—one chosen from birth to guide and give wisdom to her people. The *soldados* at the mission knew her well and were smart enough to stay out of her way if they wanted to keep the rest of the *indios* at the mission and working in the fields. Words from her were heard much better than any words the *españoles* could say.

Momoy stood at Petra's side and looked at the little infant in this stranger's arms. From the color of him and his dry cracked lips, she could tell he was starving. And yet this mother-of-his was not offering him her breast, and she wondered why. It was confusing to her and made no sense. Momoy stepped closer and took a moment to look at Petra and to study her—this was the first *española* she had ever seen. She wondered if this was, in fact, a real woman, one with breasts, or simply another *soldado* dressed like a woman, dressed the way the *padre* wanted all her people's women to dress. Reaching out she touched Petra's chest, looking for those breasts.

Petra stepped back from her quickly.

Martín pulled his pistol.

But Momoy was fearless, and she paid no attention to this soldier who now pointed a gun in her direction. She had found her answer—this *was* a woman—a woman with breasts. But they were not full with milk, and this child was starving because she was not its mother. Momoy quickly moved her hands and brought them up to her lips, making a sign by touching them.

"Eat" is what she signed, and then she pointed to the baby.

Petra did not understand her, and her eyes filled with tears.

Momoy could see the helplessness there and the sadness too. There was nothing this *española* could do to help feed this little baby. Momoy understood this now, and she did not hesitate to act. Reaching for little Josep, she tried to take the baby into her own arms, but Petra would not be separated from the child and shook her head no.

Martín was there at Petra's side in a heartbeat, with his pistol pointed at Momoy.

"No guns, please!" Padre Caveller begged him. "She's one of the elders. These people listen to her! If you hurt her, we will lose their trust—and their souls too."

Damn these *chingado* priests and their goddamn souls! Martín was sick of these men who dressed like women and were too soft in this world. These *putos* in their skirts did not understand that to show these animals kindness only showed weakness, and the only souls that would be lost would be their own.

"Tell her not to touch the baby," Martín commanded the priest. He would not lower his pistol until he heard the words spoken.

Father Caveller did as he was asked, speaking to Momoy in Chumashan, words that he had learned and that Momoy and her people could understand. When he told her not to touch the child, she obeyed by lowering her hands. But when he asked her to leave the baby, to go back to the other women of her tribe, she looked directly at Petra and would not move away.

Do you want this? Do you want me to leave you alone? Alone with this dying child?

This is what Petra saw in the woman's eyes. There was no question about it. She did not need to hear the words to understand this woman. If there was a way to save this baby, Petra did not know of it. She could only pray that this woman did.

"Lower the gun," Petra told her brother.

Martín hesitated.

But Petra did not hesitate at all.

She stepped forward to Momoy, and as she moved, she turned her back to Martín. The gun now pointed directly at Petra and not at the old *indio* woman. Into Momoy's arms, Petra placed little Josep.

Martín had no choice but to lower his pistol.

The name of their village was Tixlimi, and it was right next to the mission.

There were dozens of houses—round-topped and built on willow poles, covered with cattails, or tules. This was where the

Stishni families lived. They worked on the mission, farmed the land, and when the day was done, this was their home. Momoy guided Petra through the village, as she carried little Josep in her arms. Stopping in front of one of the houses, she stooped lower and entered it, with Petra following her.

Inside, a young Stishni woman named Lihui sat in front of a fire, using a mortar and pestle to pound and grind a mash out of acorns. She was a widow since two winters ago, when her husband had been killed hunting black bears in the mountains. The soldiers had used their rifles to try to protect him, but the bear's reach was too quick and the damage to the Stishni hunter was done before the bullets finished off the animal. The spirit of Lihui's husband still remained, in the child she brought into the world a few months after his death. On her back was strapped a woven straw basket with a toddler inside of it, a little girl who was standing up and just big enough to peek over her mother's shoulder.

Momoy came into the house with Petra at her side and said something to Lihui as she knelt down next to her by the fire. Petra stood awkwardly and watched as the two women spoke. Momoy used her hands, showing Petra she should sit with them, and Petra joined both of them at the fire. The young woman was a little frightened by the sight of Petra. She could see that Petra wore the same kind of clothes the *padre* had given many of the Stishni women to wear—a simple white blouse and a long black skirt. Momoy and some of the older women did not wear this outfit, but Lihui did, so they were dressed the same. Still she did not know Petra, and this made her careful and shy.

Momoy calmed the young woman by speaking softly with her and by showing her little Josep, who she held in her arms. She moved the shawl away from his face, so Lihui could see the child better, so she could look into his eyes. He was so helpless and so pale. And when Lihui looked closely at that little baby, she did not see *español* or Stishni. Her breasts began to ache, and they did not know the difference. When she looked over at Petra and saw the tears in her eyes, she was not frightened anymore of this stranger. And when Petra did not reach for the baby, to offer her breast and to feed him, Lihui knew that this baby was not hers. That this baby was truly all alone in the world.

Lihui reached out for Josep, as her own child reached out and played with her mother's hair. Lying there in her arms, Josep was quiet and ready for death. Pulling down the top of her blouse, Lihui freed her breast and brought Josep closer.

His eyes were shut and his head was turned away, but Lihui reached out and gently stroked the infant's cheek. Slowly she did this, and slowly Josep turned his head to face her breast. When he did, the young mother brought him to her nipple, touching his lips with it; and the nearness of him brought down her milk, a small drop kissing his lips. The baby opened his mouth, and Lihui brought the nipple to him. As she pressed it forward, little Josep latched onto it, and as the milk flowed, he began to nurse.

It was the best meal of his life.

FIFGY-NINE

A day later the caravan arrived.

The people couldn't believe their eyes when they saw little Josep. Fearing the worst, they had expected to see a freshly dug grave on the grounds of the mission. Instead they found a little baby busy at the breast. Filled with life, fussy and crying, little Josep was ready to take on the world.

With her own child toddling at her feet, Lihui sat outside near the cooking ovens and nursed little Josep. She had not been separated from him since the moment Momoy had put the infant in her arms. She did everything with that baby slung to her chest with Mercedes' shawl, keeping him close to her heart all day and night.

And Domingo stayed there right by her side. So close to her she almost tripped over him when she went to bring water from the creek that morning. He followed her everywhere she went, whether she wanted him to be there or not. Thanks to her *tetas* and her kindness, Lihui was stuck with him.

Rios watched the three of them, with Petra, Felipe, and the rest of the caravan, taking supper at long tables on the mission grounds. "This is how it is done in the mother country," Rios said as he nodded in the direction of Lihui, who sat with Domingo and his girls, with baby Josep at her breast. "No well-respected lady allows a baby to feed from her. Such a thing is low and common and not fit for a woman of decency," he added, bothered by the thought of it. "The best of families always use a wet nurse," he told them. "I never knew my mother's milk," he added with great pride.

"I wish that I had," Petra said softly. She seldom thought about her mother or how much she missed having one. Martín had made sure she was never sad and never wanted for anything. That had always been his job, and life had always been easy for Petra. But everything was so different now.

"It's too bad you have to use a savage for this and not one of our own people," Rios said, simply.

The word was sharp and brutal.

Savage.

For Petra, it was like hearing the word for the first time. In the past, when it had come from Martín's lips, it had been a word just like any other word. As easy to say, and as common too. But now that word had lost all its meaning. She could never think of Lihui as a savage, only as the woman who had saved her nephew's life.

Petra looked across the table at the lieutenant. There was something in the way he had said the word—quickly and easily—that made her pause; she gazed upon him in a way she had never done before. Maybe it was the way he was sitting, or the light through the sycamore trees that sheltered them with shade, or perhaps without his hat he looked younger, without the wisdom of age on his face. He was pretty like a child, without worry, without sense, without knowledge. He didn't look quite as tall as he had looked the first time she had met him. His shoulders seemed less broad and his eyes, so blue, were not quite as blue as she once thought they were. Petra was not sure she could get lost in them anymore. The way he looked as he had spoken this word made him suddenly different in her eyes, not like a God anymore, but like something much smaller. Too small to hold her attention the way he once did.

Petra wanted to say something, to answer him, but something held her back—a fear perhaps of speaking up. A fear of losing the way Rios gazed upon her and made her feel like she deserved a special place in the world.

"That woman saved Josep's life. She's not a savage."

Felipe said this quietly, without looking up from his meal.

This is what Petra had wanted to say but could not find a way to say it. Felipe had been brave enough to speak up, and his courage did not go unnoticed. Petra turned to look at him, and Rios saw this happen.

"You're a mule boy, what do you know?" Rios said, laughing at Felipe. He would not be bested by a peasant recruit. "You eat whatever food we give you, you do whatever we order you to do; you have no money in your pockets, no ambitions, and no education. You're just as savage and ignorant as the barbarians that live on this land. You're the perfect *soldado!*" Rios smiled when he said this, and the smile that once was so charming seemed not so charming anymore.

Petra waited for Felipe to speak again, to defend his name and his honor. But his uniform silenced him; there was nothing he could do or say to an officer. He could only obey. Felipe simply lowered his head and finished his meal quietly, as any good private would do.

"Go do your work, mule boy. Go clean the shit out of the stables," Rios ordered, dismissing Felipe by turning his attention away from the recruit and back to his meal. Felipe felt the anger rising inside of him, and he tasted its bitterness. But he would not act upon it. He would not become less of who he was because someone simply tempted him to become it. Instead he tipped his hat at Rios, saluting him as a good soldier would do to any officer, and he rose from the table, going off to do as he was told.

Rios turned his attention back to Petra.

"My dear," he said softly to her. "You will never have to bother yourself with such a lowlife as Garcia, once I bring you to Barcelona. You will be cherished and protected always, as you so rightly deserve. I will make certain of it." Reaching out carefully—so no one could see or think ill of it—Rios gently brushed his fingers against Petra's hand. And though she still felt that deep ache between her legs at the touch of him, the words he had said about Lihui were felt just as strongly and with a pain that was new to her.

Rio's words had tempered her longing.

When the caravan moved out, Domingo stayed.

It was never a question for him whether to continue on to Monterey or to stay with his son. This was the child he had waited so long for, the son whose price was paid for by the life of his wife. When Martín had told him no, that he must go on with the caravan, Domingo had challenged him by putting up his fists, willing to be beaten down again. That kind of sacrifice Martín respected. This father was willing to fight for his child and stay. He could only give Domingo his blessing and let him do what he had to do for his own family.

The bigger *familia* would have to let him go.

The twins and little Maria too stayed with their father. Domingo could not bear to be separated from any of his children. Now that he had almost lost one of them, and Mercedes had taught him the cruelties about death, he would keep all his children within his reach. He understood now how each one of them—his son, and his girls—were the most precious parts of his life.

It would be the first time the Luna family would be separated, but it would not be the last. Mercedes had wanted all of the family to stay together, but she was not there anymore to make certain that happened. And because she was gone, the family did not have her strength to keep them all together. For the first

from the tree, a branch that

in front of the mission and
aloa, as their family and the
the *camino*.

at them. She rode sidesaddle
they were going, but still she
ing the strong back of Rios as
the one she had followed, the
ay. But for the first time since
mething she had never done
end of the caravan, searching
d her.

the back—alone now, with-

hing Petra.

way.

SIXTY

The air chilled with the threat of winter.

The caravan followed the San Luis Creek up a *cuesta* to heights touching the clouds. The *camino* was narrow, and the drop to the valley below was far and frightening. But the pull of Monterey on the people was stronger than ever, and with every step they took they knew they were getting closer. To the end of the *camino* and the beginning of their dreams.

Petra rode next to Beatriz and Sola, with Marco on a pony at her side. But without Mercedes there in front of her, with a wink or a laugh to lift up her spirits, she felt truly alone. Her family had always made her feel untouchable—she was protected from every little slight and hurt. Even when the flood had come to Sinaloa, *her* family had been spared. God smiled on them because they were Lunas, and Lunas were better than everyone else. That's what she had always been told while growing up. Life had always been sweet for her. It was the only taste of the world that she had known.

But now she knew better.

The *camino* had shown her the truth. It had filled her heart with such beauty, with sights so different and new: the sweetest of birdsongs and the brightest of flowers, the smells in the air, and the look of a land like nothing she had ever experienced before.

It gave her a longing and pushed her to go forward, hurried her steps and made her want more. But the longer the *camino* went on, and the farther it went, something else came along with it.

Life.

With all its glory and all its thorns.

You could move from one place to the next, but life always came with you. All of it, not just the beauty but the thorns too. And the thorns were something Petra had never counted on or known before.

That night, after the tents were set up and Petra was alone, she could not close her eyes or fall asleep with the same sense of security. The world seemed different to her now, and she wondered if she would ever feel safe in it again. These doubts gave her a new kind of longing—a need to settle, to stay in one place, to build a life strong enough to handle the thorns.

Some nights on guard duty went more quickly than others.

This night for Felipe was long and slow. They were camped on the bank of the Salinas River in the long valley that would soon end at Monterey. He wondered what kind of a life would be waiting for him there and if Petra would be a part of it. All those nights on guard duty he had let his mind wander to thoughts of Petra. He had spent long hours thinking about her, trying sometimes to give her up, to let Rios step in and take his place. She didn't look at him the way she looked at Rios, and some nights he would have a good talk with himself and say, "Move on. Let her go." But no matter how hard he tried, his heart would not listen, and his patience would overrule his mind whenever his mind told him to give her up.

Rios was wrong about him; Felipe *did* have ambitions. His heart was full of dreams, and every one of them was a child waiting to be born. His family had been his whole world. Now it was up to him to rebuild that world, to make a new life in California. He wanted more sons and daughters than he could count, so many children he would be busy all his days building rooms for them, growing food to fill their bellies, and teaching them how to grow up strong and good. And he wanted Petra to be their mother, to give to them the same joy she gave to him—simply by walking on this earth.

As Felipe was thinking these thoughts, he did not notice the fog creeping into the night. It spilled slowly into the valley, clinging to the ground and hiding everything from sight. Fingers of it stretched out, long and hungry; the fog was wrapping around everything in its path. The shrubs and the *camino* disappeared from sight; the tents of the caravan slipped into it, and the livestock were shrouded from view. Only the stirring of the animals, the sounds that they made, revealed where they were hidden, covered in the blackness of night and the blanket of fog.

An owl screeched loudly somewhere, and Felipe's eyes searched for it. But when he looked out he could see nothing, only the fog. The owl screeched again, and the sound brought Felipe to his feet. It was an odd sound to be hearing, so quickly after the first time. Something about it was different. He didn't know what, but he knew that sometimes men, too, could make this sound. He had heard stories of the Yaquis, and the Pimas too, imitating animals when in battle one needed to be heard but not revealed. Sometimes these sounds could come from a man's throat, and his father always warned him not to trust what he couldn't see.

Felipe's eyes searched in vain in front of him, but he could not see a thing. The fog clung to him, and as he moved forward slowly, carefully, his ears led the way as he listened for any sound that could clear his path. He could hear the water of the river to his left, and he followed it, letting it guide him forward, his feet stepping carefully along the grassy bank. To his right, he could feel the presence of the trees that he knew stood close to the edge of the river, protecting him from a breeze that rustled their leaves.

Onward he kept moving, listening to every sound in the darkness. Behind him were the tents of the caravan and the night sounds of the people—the snores of the men, a child waking from a nightmare, a crying out as a couple moved with each other, coming together in the darkness.

The owl called out again.

Louder and closer this time.

Felipe stopped and followed the sound with his body. It was just in front of him and he took a step forward towards it.

And that's when he fell.

Slipping on the wet grass, he tumbled forward, head over heels, falling down the embankment and landing in the moist river soil at the edge of the water. Felipe lay there for a moment, the fog still pressing against his body, as he tried to get his bearings before standing. The water flowed past him, so closely he could almost stretch out his arm and touch it. Standing slowly and keeping the river to his back, Felipe tried to look through the fog as he moved carefully back towards the edge of the embankment, to the willows above him.

Suddenly there was movement off in the trees. A scurrying in the darkness. Running. A rustling in the night. Felipe stopped and listened, focusing on where the sounds were coming from. They were a few yards ahead and to his left. So silently Felipe stood, his heart wildly beating.

Whispers broke the silence. Low and quick. Were they real? Or the wind blowing through the willows? Felipe moved forward, slowly. Softly. There, he heard it again. A voice. A word. He found the sound just in front of him, above the bank, in the trees there. Words. Low and breathless.

"*Te adoro.*"

I love you.

Felipe stopped and his heart wanted to break out of his chest. He knew this voice. His eyes searched, scanning the fog in front of him. He put his hands out, stretching out his arms and moving forward carefully to find the edge of the embankment. When he reached it, he grabbed hold of the wet grass growing there and raised himself higher to look over at the trees. As he did, the fog seemed to part a little, and he could barely make out a tree here and there, the fog flowing around them, circling their trunks and weaving its way through the branches.

The rustlings in the dark grew stronger. And that voice.

"*Te adoro.*"

Felipe's eyes searched for that voice, finding it finally as the fog started to slip back, revealing two figures pressed up against the trunk of a willow tree. They were barely visible in the fog as it wrapped its arms around them, clinging to their bodies that were naked in the night and pressed hard against each other. Together they moved as one, their faces unseen as their bare legs and arms entwined, hungry for each other. The broad back of the one on top glistened in fresh sweat and lingering fog, as the long dark hair of the other flowed free. That flowing long hair, so black and so beautiful.

Felipe's breath quickened at the sight. He could not look away as he watched that beautiful long hair stream down those broad shoulders and naked back of the other. Watching on in agony, he waited to see that face, hoping he was wrong. Knowing his heart would stop if the truth he feared was the truth revealed. Waiting for Petra's face to be seen and praying it was a lie. That the fog was playing with him and just being cruel.

The couple moved together—face to back—coupling there in the shelter of the darkness and the fog. And when the man moved his face back, so loving and so urgent, that's when Felipe could see him. Clearly and without a doubt.

The man was Rios. It was his voice Felipe had recognized. "*Te adoro,*" he had murmured, and once again now he said it, turning his beloved to face him, to hold in his arms. It was then that Felipe saw the truth.

It was not Petra who was his lover.

It was Simon.

SIXTY-ONE

Out of the fog walked Felipe.

Simon was the first to see him, and the shock on his face made Rios turn quickly to look. The two men stood naked in front of him, until Rios reached for his clothing. Without his uniform, the lieutenant was lost, with no rank to protect himself.

"You shouldn't be out here," Rios said to Felipe, as he pulled on his pants and slipped on his shirt, acting as though nothing had happened and no one had witnessed it. "It's too far from camp." Once dressed, his power started to come back to him, and he hid himself behind his command. "Go back to your post."

But instead of turning and following the orders of the lieutenant, Felipe stepped forward, moving closer to Rios. Reaching down, he made a point of picking up Simon's clothing and holding his pants and shirt out to him. Simon took them and began to dress. With fear in his eyes, he looked over at Rios, not knowing what he should do.

"You need to go back to your post, Garcia," Rios said again, his words stronger and more certain.

Felipe did not move. "You are in no position to give me a command," he told Rios, without hesitation. No longer did the private have to answer to the lieutenant. Now, there, in the middle of the night, there was no such thing as rank. Felipe had the power over Rios and he knew it.

Rios knew it too.

"This fog can be very confusing," the lieutenant said, searching for an excuse. "It can play tricks on you. You think you understand what you see, but it's not the truth at all."

"I know what I saw."

Rios took Simon by the arm and forced him to kneel in front of Felipe. "This man tempted me!" he said. "He followed me out here in the darkness. I did not instigate this! He's the one at fault for doing this to me—for taking advantage of me like this. It's unspeakable! It's an unnatural sin!"

Felipe was not moved by Rios or by his lie.

"Will you report him?" Felipe asked, simply.

Rios hesitated.

"Or do you want me to tell the captain?"

When Rios didn't answer him, Felipe turned away and started to walk back to the camp.

Simon waited for Rios to say something, to stop Felipe. But the lieutenant was quiet.

"Please! Don't turn me in!" Simon called out to Felipe. "They will kill me!"

Felipe stopped and looked over at Rios.

"He's right." Rios said. "If Rivera learns about this, they'll hang him."

"And will they hang you too?" Felipe asked, already knowing the answer.

They wouldn't.

"I will say he tempted me . . . For my honor and my commission, I must say it. They will not kill an officer of the king."

Felipe walked over to Rios and faced him. "But you'll have to watch as he hangs."

It was true. And this truth was more than Rios could bear.

"He's a good guide. I'm asking for your understanding," Rios said softly. "I've never caught him stealing or sneaking food. And he's not once tried to run away. I will do anything I can to keep him by my side." Rios was trying to cover up his real reason for protecting Simon—that he cared for him, that he could never betray him.

Felipe leaned in closer to Rios, feeling the power he now had over him.

"I'm the perfect *soldado*, remember? That's what you said to me. If my officer tells me this is an unspeakable act and a sin, how can I not report it? Give me a reason to look away. To forget what I saw."

Rios hesitated, looking over at Simon, who now stood fully dressed but shivering as the fog embraced him. Felipe had Rios where he wanted him. The lieutenant had no choice but to face him, honestly, man-to-man, shedding his command to open his heart to him.

"What do you want?" Rios said, in barely a whisper. "What do you want from me to keep your silence and to save him?"

"Stop making Petra promises you can never fulfill," he said.

"I give you my word this would never have happened if she and I were together."

"Don't sacrifice Petra to find out if that's the truth or not."

"I do love her," Rios said, hoping that Felipe could understand. "I would honor her always."

"Honor her and let her go." Felipe waited for Rios to say something, to say yes to what he was asking. But the lieutenant said nothing at all. Turning away, Felipe started back to the camp.

"You don't have it in you, Garcia!" the lieutenant called after him. "You're not the kind of man who can send someone to his death. If you tell the captain, you'll be killing him! And that's not who you are!"

Felipe kept walking, his steps steady with purpose. What Rios didn't understand was this wasn't just anything Felipe wanted from him. This was Petra—his life.

And he would do anything to protect her.

SIXTY-TWO

There was one last mission before the caravan reached Monterey.

San Antonio de Padua sat at the foothills of the Santa Lucia Mountains at a place called Telhaya by the Salinans, who had always known this land as their home. Now almost two hundred of them had been baptized and lived with five *soldados* and one priest at this last stopping place before the final stretch of the Camino Real.

Felipe was not so quick to seek out the captain and tell him what he had witnessed the night before. His word would not be easily trusted by Rivera, and he thought maybe Rios would keep his distance from Petra, honoring Felipe's challenge by leaving her alone and letting her go.

But what he saw the next day did not give him hope.

While the caravan had stretched out in a single file, on its way into the Valley of the Oaks that led to the mission, Rios had ridden at the front of the pack. But as they approached Mission Creek, the lieutenant left the formation and found his way down the line to where Petra rode, all by herself.

"When will we reach Monterey?" she asked, as Rios pulled his horse up next to her, riding at her side. Petra was tired and he could see that in her face.

"We stop here for tonight, and in two days we'll be there."

"Is it beautiful in Monterey?"

Rios laughed. "Just mud and more mud. And when you don't notice the mud, that's because the fog comes and hides it from you," he told her.

"It's not beautiful like Barcelona?" Petra asked.

Rios shook his head and smiled.

"No rich palaces or the scent of oranges in the air?" she asked, remembering what Rios had shared with her about the city and its splendor.

He looked over at her with a kind of sadness. "There is absolutely nothing in Monterey to give you happiness." They rode side by side for a few moments.

"Will you be going back soon to Barcelona?" Petra asked him. It was a question asked with more than just a little curiosity.

"Why do you ask?" he said, hoping her answer was one that he wanted to hear—that she didn't want him to go back to Barcelona without her at his side.

Petra looked around at the land they were riding across: the grove of oak trees off to their left and the creek, like a wound cutting through the earth, off to their right. There were freshly planted cornfields in front of them, and *indios,* dozens of men, women, and children working there, cutting down the cornstalks and piling them together, harvesting the crops for winter. Two of the mission *soldados* stood under the shade of the largest oak tree. With pistols on their hips and whips in their belts, they shared a *bota* between the two of them as they watched the *indios* work, without a break, under dark and threatening skies.

Petra was bothered by the sight.

There were so many *indios* on this land and so few *españoles.* The *indios* had frightened her on that beach, the one before San Diego; those warriors with their stones and arrows, angry and shouting, didn't want them there. She had welcomed the sight of guns in the hands of Martín, Tomás, and the other men. But in San Luis it had been different. The women there had saved Josep's life—the life of an *español*. There was no shouting, no anger, no stones or arrows to frighten them. It didn't seem to matter who was who and what difference there was between them. There was plenty of land, and together it could be shared, as one tribe with another. But Petra wondered if it could always be this way? Or if the whips and pistols would win, and one or the other of them would be destroyed. In body, or in soul.

"A person might get used to this land and find herself never leaving it," she said, looking over at Rios. "Unless she had a good reason to leave. Or someone who would take her with him."

It had never been Petra's decision that brought her there. It had been Martín's. Mercedes and Tomás too had wanted to come to this place where they were strangers, where no one welcomed them, and where there was no place they could call home. Her *familia* had made the decision, not Petra. But the decision to stay or leave could be hers alone—a choice made by her for the first time in her life.

Rios could be her reason to leave.

Felipe's eyes were on Petra and Rios for the rest of the day.

He watched as the lieutenant helped her gently dismount from her horse. And he studied the way Rios guided her with his arm over to her family. The lieutenant helped her unpack her things from the *burros*, carrying what she needed and helping her settle in at the tents. Every time Felipe looked, there was Rios close to Petra.

And he felt a darkness filling him up inside.

When it was time for the caravan to supper at the back of the mission, Felipe was quick to sit with the family and next to Petra. He looked across the mission grounds, his eyes meeting the eyes of the lieutenant.

Rios kept his distance. The lieutenant ate with Rivera, staying close to the captain, and Petra did not turn his head once.

After the meal was over, Rios went his way and Petra went hers. The two were not seen together for the rest of the day.

When darkness entered the valley, Felipe finished feeding all the horses and *burros* that were corralled together on the mission grounds. Locking up the wooden gates, he started off to begin his guard duty. All of the tents of the caravan were now grouped together outside the walls of the mission, families inside of them, with shadows of the lantern flames flickering through the canvas.

Felipe went over to his tent to say goodnight to Petra. Opening the canvas flaps, he looked inside into darkness.

The tent was empty.

Petra was not there.

The creek was full and running fast, and Petra followed the sound of it, careful of her footing as the moonless night did nothing to help her find her way. With her heart pounding, she did not falter or fear; forward she went into a joy she could not name. No one was watching her. No one was protecting her. Her honor was her own, and she was free to do with it as she wanted. It was her choice. Finally, hers.

Someone caught her by the waist.

Rios turned her quickly to face him.

Petra couldn't help it, but she laughed. She was light-headed for a moment, looking for a way to steady herself. She never had the chance because Rios wrapped his arms around her and brought her to his chest, holding her closely.

"You want more than what's here, don't you?" Rios whispered, brushing back a strand of her hair. Petra closed her eyes and listened to him. "I would share with you everything beautiful in this world," he promised her, holding her in the darkness. "If you come with me, I will be everything to you," he said in a voice that was soft and comforting.

She looked up into the lightness of his eyes, which even the darkness could not hide. "My *cortèjo*?" she asked, smiling and teasing him. "But not my husband."

"You'd be free to marry anyone you want," he said to her. "But someone of a better class than who your brother made you marry. A count, perhaps? Or with your beauty, even a prince. A prince who would understand that a husband can never give a woman the true adoration she craves like a *cortèjo* can and who would gracefully look the other way when we're together."

Rios reached out and gently touched her cheek.

Petra felt that ache open up inside of her again, wanting more but not knowing what.

"You will be the only woman in my life," he said to her sweetly. "And I will send my coach to fetch you, sneaking you away and pampering you with anything you desire. On my honor, you will never want for anything."

"What if I want you to be my husband?"

Rios smiled but did not answer.

Petra took his hand in hers, away from her cheek, and held it against her breast.

"To have you close," she said. "To have you at my side always. Not to be beckoned or to have a coachman call for me. To be one with you forever. And to have your children."

This was the one promise that Rios knew he couldn't make to her. If Petra's happiness depended on having children, he would need to find another way to honor her, to make sure her happiness could be fulfilled.

"If you want children, you will have them," he promised her. "I will make sure of it."

Rios brought her hands up to his lips, and he kissed them tenderly.

"Go back to the camp now—before they miss you," he told her.

And his words sent her back alone into the night.

SIXTY-THREE

Petra did her best to sneak back to the camp without being seen. With the stars watching her, she hurried back up from the creek to the caravan of tents within the mission grounds. It was only when she reached her own tent that she hesitated a moment, sensing something in the darkness. Maybe it was her conscience that gave her pause, that made her turn to look across the grounds, to the front of the mission and to the steps there at the entrance. A figure stepped out of the doorway. It was dark and his features could not be seen. But there was something sad in the way he moved, in the slowness of his gait, and the slant of his shoulders heavy with disappointment.

Petra knew right away.

It was Felipe.

They stood apart from each other for what felt like a lifetime, separated by the darkness and too afraid to speak. She could feel his pain, and it frightened her how much it hurt her. It confused her, too, and took away the joy she had been feeling. Why did just the sight of him do this to her, when all she wanted was to be free?

Petra never had the chance to ask him.

Rios appeared, coming up from the creekside.

And when Felipe saw him, he knew what he had to do.

⌒

Rivera missed his family, especially at night.

He had the responsibilities of his command and the traveling along the *camino* to keep him company during the day. But at night he was tired and alone, and the sounds of the families around the campfire, talking softly or singing with the strings of a guitar, made him long for his wife's voice and the presence of his sons.

The captain usually kept to himself in his tent, but when they stayed at the missions, the *padres* kept him company. They filled his head with praise and his belly with oak-barreled brandy the Franciscans had brought with them from Loreto—brandy that helped Rivera forget all the joys he had left behind with his family in Guadalajara.

On this night, he had taken a little bit more of the grape than on other nights.

Martín was at his side, guiding him back to his cot in the soldiers' quarters. "I'm making you a sergeant in Monterey, Luna," Rivera told him, his steps not the steadiest. "You come back with me to San Diego and we'll hunt down those bastards who burned down the mission. We've got to teach them who's boss!"

They stopped at a crudely made wooden hut with a roof of clay tiles instead of straw. "Three goddamn times they sent arrows of fire to burn down these structures. So you see here, what we did..." Rivera pointed to the roof. "Clay tiles to stop the fires. You outsmart these *diablos* and you win!"

If not for these *chingado indios*, his wife would be with him, Rivera was sure of it. She would have made a good home for him in Monterey, giving him comfort and peace of mind. But these people frightened her with their nakedness and their strange ways; and she refused to live among them.

"You bring your wife and children with you to San Diego," Rivera told him. "No matter what your wife says!"

"I have my sister I have to look after," Martín said, taking advantage of the brandy and the captain's indulgence.

"She's got her husband to take care of her, doesn't she?" Rivera asked.

"Garcia is my sister's husband in name only. It's not a real marriage," Martín told him. "We are hoping Father Serra will grant an annulment in Monterey."

"In that case, you bring your sister too. Keep your family close!"

Felipe now appeared, coming out of the darkness. Standing at attention, he tipped his hat, saluting the captain.

"You're on guard duty, Garcia. Why aren't you at your post?" Martín snapped.

"I need to speak to the captain," Felipe said, not backing down.

"Make it quick," Rivera said, ducking his head to enter the low doorway of the hut.

Inside, Rivera sat on his cot and pulled off his boots, tiredly. Felipe entered the quarters and stood in the doorway.

"I would like to report something I witnessed on guard duty," Felipe began. And once he began, his mouth started to go dry, tasting a shame that was rising inside of him.

"What's the problem, Garcia?" Rivera said, with a yawn.

"I saw something last night, and I want to report it."

Before Felipe could go on, the door to the hut opened and Rios appeared.

It's one thing to talk about a man behind his back, but to face him and say words that will sentence him can sicken the soul. The sight of the lieutenant made Felipe go silent.

"Why isn't this man at his post?" the lieutenant asked.

"He says he has something to report from last night," Rivera said. "But Garcia's tongue is slow tonight, and all he's doing is wasting my time. Maybe you can get him to talk."

Rios moved over to Felipe, standing face to face with him.

"What happened last night that you want to report?" Rios asked. If his heart was beating a little faster and fear was in his throat, his face did not betray it, and no one other than God would have known. "If you want to report something, speak up, Garcia," he challenged him.

Felipe tried as hard as he could to find a way to speak the truth. But this truth was not like any other; it was sharp and brutal, a truth that would murder Simon as easily as if Felipe himself plunged a knife into his back. This one sin—witnessed by him—could give life to another sin, one more contemptuous than the first, and more deadly. His words would be responsible for a man losing his life. And in his heart Felipe secretly questioned what he dare not speak: Was what he witnessed really a sin? How could he be sure? How could loving another person be as vile as taking a life? How could loving anyone ever be a sin? In his soul, he felt it wasn't. How could he find the words, then, to say that it was? To condemn Simon to death, simply for loving.

"You're wasting the captain's time!" Martín said sharply.

"I know why he's hesitating," Rios began, searching for a way to save himself, striking first before Felipe could strike. "Garcia fell asleep on guard duty last night. I caught him."

"How could you be so stupid!" Martín spit out the words.

Rivera was on his feet now and in full command. And the brandy that had calmed him no longer was doing the job.

"Is this true? Did you fall asleep on duty?" Rivera asked, sternly.

Felipe looked straight into Rios's eyes, and it was there that he found his answer. The lieutenant had been right: Felipe didn't have it in him to condemn a man to death. He could not take what he wanted by sacrificing a person's life. Felipe could not change who he was: a good man. And he'd have to accept whatever consequences came along with being one.

"Yes," Felipe said. "I fell asleep."

Rivera was swift and commanding. "I warned you before, Garcia. You've betrayed my trust one time too many. Neglecting your post is a punishable offense. If we were at war, I would take you out right now and shoot you." The captain was all business. The safety of the caravan had been compromised and the recruit had to be taught a lesson.

"You're under arrest," Rivera said, turning away from him.

Martín stepped over swiftly to Felipe and took his pistol from the holster on his belt. He removed his dagger too, stripping the recruit of all his weapons.

Felipe touched the brim of his hat and saluted the captain.

There was no way out of this.

SIXTY-FOUR

When an *español* broke a rule, there was hell to pay.

It was a long time ago, and what is cruel today was then as ordinary as the sky above us.

Felipe had to be punished, and that punishment had to be witnessed by all the people. That is how it was done, how rules and laws were learned by these *gente de razon*. If you spit in the face of reason, you sinned. And for the big sins, you had to pay the price in public. When a man was caught stealing and he was tied up and put in the stocks, that would teach him to never use his hands again for stealing. Seeing this man suffer for the wrong he did would teach everyone who watched him being punished never to commit such a sin. That is how the people learned, from the smallest *español* to the oldest.

On the day Felipe was punished, the whole caravan was gathered together to watch. Mothers and fathers held toddlers in their arms, so all could see Felipe and learn from him. Rules tied them together, made them strong, and gave them the will to push forward—to build this new world for themselves and for their children yet to be born. Breaking a rule was like breaking the backs of all the people, hurting them and slowing them down from the work that had to be done. It was a sin against them all, and the people understood this. For this reason they watched, and no one looked away.

The priest was the only one to question the captain about such a drastic punishment on the consecrated grounds of the mission. This was a military matter, and it was best done in one of the fields, away from the sacred dwelling of the Lord. The *indios* could watch—the priest wanted that—so the savages could see that *españoles*, too, needed to learn how to be good followers of Christ. In this way, the *indios* would be taught how to be just like them. But it should happen out in an open field, where the blood would not stain the adobe.

They marched Felipe out to a meadow behind the corrals and away from the mission. The new grass was green from the late autumn rains, and it was still covered with the early morning dew. Felipe's hands were tied behind his back with thick leather straps, and he was without shirt or shoes, as two *soldados*, their hands in the crook of each of his elbows, walked him to the center of the meadow that was bordered by sycamore trees. The sun was low in the sky, and gathered there underneath the shelter of the trees were the people of the caravan, close enough to see, but far enough away to keep their distance.

From out of the people stepped El Capitán, with the lieutenant and Martín at his side. The three men walked out to the center of the meadow to meet Felipe face-to-face.

Petra, with Sola and Beatriz at her side, watched with the others. Sola had begged her not to come; the other people would understand. Felipe was her husband, and he had shamed her. It was not just his own humiliation a man suffered; the honor of his family was also stained. But it was exactly for this reason that Petra wanted to be there, to stand up front and to see with her own eyes. If they would all suffer because of Felipe, she wanted to understand what he had done and why he had done it.

Petra had witnessed a sight like this before. When she was a small child, one of the village men had almost killed another man with his knife after finding that man in his home with his wife. She had watched as this man had been punished—leather ripping into his flesh—and his cries had made her sick to her stomach at the time. Martín was the one whose arms had pulled her close, and he had covered her face so she would not see anymore. He cleaned Petra's vomit from her dress and stroked her hair gently, and his voice took away from her the images of that violence that had sickened her so.

But now Martín would be the one to do violence and not be the man to comfort her.

The soldiers in their heavy blue uniforms, dressed and protected in wool from the morning chill, all faced Felipe, who was wearing only pants, naked except for the disgrace that he was forced to wear. His skin was taut and pale, covered with tiny bumps from the touch of the cold.

Petra felt the chill and shivered for Felipe.

Rivera stepped in closer to his recruit and pronounced sentence in a clear and booming voice so all could hear.

"For negligence of duty to the Crown and to the people of Nueva España, for falling asleep while on guard and risking the lives of the people of this expedition, Felipe Santiago Garcia, I hereby sentence you to fifty lashes by the whip. Under the sanctity of the King's Seal of España and in front of God and these witnesses, I so command it."

Rivera took a step back and waited.

Martín removed the whip from his belt and walked over to Lieutenant Rios. It would be the lieutenant's honor to perform the sentence on the prisoner, and Martín handed him the whip. Rios motioned to the two soldiers holding Felipe to step away from the prisoner. When they did as he had asked, Rios moved closer to speak to him privately.

"You may kneel down if it helps you with the pain," Rios told him kindly.

Felipe remembered Calixto, and he did not speak. He stood and did not kneel.

The lieutenant circled around Felipe to face the back of

him, and when he did, that's when he saw Petra at the front of the gathered crowd. The sight of her made him stop. He didn't want her there; he wanted her to look away. He wanted to protect her from this thing that was not beautiful, that was stripped of all grace and elegance, guarding her from the sight of it, keeping her pure and innocent. But instead, he would be the one to do the deed, to unleash the brute inside of himself that would draw the first blood. It was his duty, and he had to do it. Gazing upon her, he twisted the leather handle of the whip in his hand, and he could feel Petra slipping further away from him. With this one regret, he let loose the whip and struck Felipe with the first blow.

"One!" Martín called out, keeping count as the leather found its mark on Felipe's back. "Two!" Martín shouted, and the lieutenant flung the leather tip against the skin. Rios snapped the whip again and again, and each time Martín cried out the count, and with every count Felipe's naked back received a blow, the whip snapping through the air and slapping the flesh.

With each blow, Felipe was silent. Not a murmur, not a cry, not a whimper. He met each strike upon his body with no resistance and no giving in. He placed himself above the pain. And the only evidence of every blow was the red-raised flesh on his back after each strike had landed. Only his skin betrayed him, not his cries—for there were none. The more Rios snapped the whip, the stronger Felipe became. He stood there, his shoulders never drooping, his face never changing. If he felt shame, he never showed it. In fact, he seemed to stand a little bit taller after every blow, as his pride grew within him.

This was not the purpose of a whipping.

Such a display of courage was not good for the people to see.

Rios had his rank to protect. If he was perceived as weak, he would lose the respect and obedience of his men. He had no choice but to speed up the blows and to make them fiercer. He put his whole weight and muscle into the thrust of that whip, snapping it with all his strength. By the twenty-fifth blow, the skin of Felipe's back broke open and blood began to show.

Still, Felipe was silent.

By the thirty-fifth blow, with blood running down Felipe's back, Rios paused and looked over at El Capitán. Never had these two officers seen a man take such a beating as this and not show some sign of weakness or plead for mercy.

Petra could not take her eyes off Felipe. His silence emboldened her and gave her a strength she had never known before. His courage touched her. His goodness had finally reached her. Defiantly, she watched as Rios, sweating now and unsure how to go on, looked at his captain with uncertainty. Her eyes found his, and they dared him not to strike more blows.

For a moment, Rios obeyed her, and the whipping stopped.

But Martín stepped forward quickly and took the whip back from the lieutenant.

Rios did nothing to stop him.

Raising the whip, Martín snapped it hard and fast against Felipe's back. In quick succession, he counted off the numbers, loudly, hurriedly, and with great pleasure.

"Thirty-six! Thirty-seven! Thirty-eight! Thirty-nine!"

Still, Felipe stood there, silently, the blood slipping from his back and running down his pants. He did not bow his head; his legs stayed strong and he did not bend or give in as Martín hit him over and over again, without pause, without care, shouting out the count, number by number, until the last and final blow.

"Fifty!"

The last strike hit him the hardest. And only then, once the sentence was finished, did Felipe drop down to his knees. It was at that moment that Martín took advantage of the situation, hurling the whip for one extra blow, with all his strength and all his hatred against this man who dared to challenge him for a love he could not even name. The blow struck Felipe with a vengeance, and he fell down hard, first to his knees and then face first into the dirt. His strength left him and he lay there, a beaten man.

Martín raised the whip once more, and he was about to strike Felipe again, but the only person who could possibly stop him shouted his name from the crowd, holding back his hand.

It was Petra.

"Martín!" she yelled at him. "Martín!" she pleaded. Out of the crowd she ran, hurrying across the meadow to Felipe. Kneeling down next to him, she stroked his hair gently, comforting him with her voice and her touch.

"Stand up, Felipe," Petra said to him softly. "I'm here, and I will help you." She spoke to him in the gentlest of voices, as she reached out her hand to his. Petra's words were like honey to him, and her touch was healing. She brought the strength back to his legs, and the will to his arms. With her hands to guide him, he stood up on his feet slowly, standing there tall and proud once again.

Without shame. Without humiliation.

Petra helped Felipe walk across the field, guiding him carefully with her arms. Rios watched the two of them walk across the meadow together. And that's when he knew.

He had lost her.

SIXTY-FIVE

Petra never left Felipe's side.

They would travel another two-and-a-half days on the road to Monterey, and wherever Felipe went, Petra went too. When the caravan left camp on that morning of the whipping, Petra was the only one of the people of Sinaloa to have anything to do with Felipe. She helped him put on his shoes and guided his arms into his shirt, watching in agony as the wool touched the open flesh. She brought him his *tortillas* and hot chocolate for breakfast and made sure he ate to keep up his strength. And she rode by his side at the back of the caravan, far from her family and ignoring Martín's orders to move up to the side of Sola and Beatriz.

"Get back to the family!" he had shouted, circling Petra with his mount as she rode defiantly on her horse. "Go back and join the family!" he had ordered her.

The louder Martín yelled, the more deaf she was to his voice. Eyes forward, with her hands gripping the reins and no longer riding sidesaddle, Petra rode her horse as close to Felipe's horse as she could manage. Martín had no choice but to give up and take his place at the front of the caravan next to the captain.

Petra would not leave Felipe.

And when night fell, she would be there too. Felipe had been ordered not to stand watch at nights anymore. Instead, he was commanded to sleep in his tent.

Rios had ordered it.

A soldier who fell asleep on guard duty might do it again. What other choice could Rios make? And he knew exactly when he made this choice what he was doing. It was a sacrifice he was making for the pure love of a woman he could never have. For Felipe, too, he was doing it. For the words Felipe never said. For the secret that he had kept. For saving Simon's life.

This was Rios's command.

"Tomás, take your brother-in-law's post and guard the camp at night," he had ordered. "Let Garcia spend the nights with his bride. Maybe she can keep him up and awake at night, eh?" Rios had said, with a laugh that men often share. And with that laugh a piece of his heart broke away with it, as he let Petra go forever.

That day of the whipping the ride on the *camino* afterwards seemed to go on forever. Felipe tried not to show his pain, as Petra rode her horse close to his side. But when they stopped in the late afternoon and set up camp for the night, she saw on the dark blue of his uniform the crimson marks of blood seeping through the wool. And she could tell just how much Felipe hurt. He tried to pretend he was fine, and Petra played that game for a while. They sat by themselves for supper, and they didn't speak a word.

Once night fell and the tents had been put up, everyone gathered around the campfire. Someone strummed a guitar, and someone else joined in with a violin. People began to sing, and the children chased one another in the shadows.

But Petra and Felipe were not among them.

By the light of their own campfire just outside their tent, Petra bathed the wounds on Felipe's back. She would not take no for an answer, and Felipe, in his pain, could not bear to struggle alone anymore. She first dampened his shirt with warm water she had heated on the fire. Pouring a little of the water from her cupped hands, she loosened the dried blood from the cloth on his back, carefully peeling it away from his skin, stripping it slowly from the open wounds. She winced as she looked at what had been done to him—at the raised and bloody marks. Using a ripped piece of hem from her cotton slip, she carefully dripped the water on his back, gently cleansing him. Breaking open a small piece of aloe vera she had gathered on their travels, she squeezed out its cooling gel so it ran down his back and eased his pain.

It was the closest Petra had ever been to Felipe.

Or to any man.

And as she cared for him, she felt that wound between her legs begin to ache with that same pain she had felt with Rios. How strange, she thought, to be feeling this now. She tried to will that ache away, and yet it grew stronger with each moment that her hand reached out, caring for him, cleaning his wounds, and healing him.

Petra looked at his naked back, and for the first time noticed how it had filled out since they had started this journey, how it had widened at his shoulders and narrowed at his hips. It was the back of a man now and not a boy still growing. Felipe had always been that boy who never spoke to her but whose eyes watched her walk across the village square, even as he tried to stay invisible. He had always been a part of her world, part of what was so ordinary about it. And because he was so ordinary, she had grown used to him. She had stopped seeing him.

Until now.

Now he was different—he moved differently in the world than she did. And she knew now he was something other than she was, and it was this otherness that she wanted, that she craved, that she desired with her body and her heart. Now his shoulders were thick and his arms were strong, and as he sat facing away from her, she fought the urge to reach out and touch him, not to nurse him or to care for his wounds, but to make that ache between her legs grow stronger until she could be lost in it. Lost and taken.

She did not understand what she was feeling. And where was Mercedes now to explain it to her when she needed her the most? Mercedes had always had the answers, and when she didn't have them, she made them up, and that was fine too. There was no one to help her now but this man in front of her, whose back was so wide and so strong it only made her want to touch him and touch him now, with no answers, no questions, no reasoning at all.

The ache within Petra was felt too by Felipe. He understood more than she did what was happening, but understanding was not something he cared about at the moment. With every touch of her he wanted her to touch him even more. And God help him, he wanted to touch her back. His skin cried out for it, and he could not stop himself from making a sound that slipped from his throat that was low and wanting. More than a sigh, and brother to a moan.

Petra heard him and her hand paused. She could see his skin shivering from the cold, or was it from her touch?

Felipe's head was bent forward in front of her and his neck was long and strong. Petra could not help but lean closer, and in an instant she kissed the nape of his neck where his hair curled, dark and thick. One kiss, so gentle and new.

Felipe turned slowly and faced Petra. They looked at each other, their faces lit by the flames of the campfire. Their fate was sealed then; it was as if they had known each other forever but only seen each other now, for the first time.

Petra could not wait to taste him, to touch him with her mouth, and she pressed her body forward against his naked chest, brushing her open lips against his. Felipe's heart leapt inside of him and, for a moment, he thought he would surely die. Only she could save him and he reached out his arms, circling her body tightly against his, as if his life depended on her heart to keep his beating.

They were on their knees now, face to face, two bodies pressed together as one.

What they did not know, they learned together that night, letting their bodies teach them a little at a time. Their clothes came off, and together they moved as one. Felipe could not get his fill of her; with every touch, he sought to touch her even more. His hands stroked her skin, from the length of her neck to the curve of her breasts, and when his hand found itself lower, her impatience took over and she guided his hand the rest of the way to that wound that only he could heal, that was there for him, ready and open. And when that ache within her could not possibly hurt any more, Felipe joined her there, and in a moment she felt her body open and her soul was sailing in the clouds. And for the first time she understood God.

Petra was home now.

This man was her family.

SIXTY-SIX

The next day they arrived in Monterey.

As November began in pouring rain.

For twelve miles the caravan had followed the *camino* along-side the Monterey River, until the group reached Buena Vista. Leaving the river on the right, they headed through the hills and dales, westward through lush, fertile countryside—beauti-ful land the travelers barely noticed. The storm blinded them, so they couldn't see the sloping hills at their sides and the gentle rise of the *camino* as they rode forward. They didn't see the wild huckleberries growing at the side of the road, nor did they smell the scent of lavender and sage filling the air. They barely noticed a forest of towering pines, and the smell of the ocean was hidden by the fragrance of wet, muddy earth. Only as they came to the top of a plateau and the pines ended did they realize there was a magnificent bay stretched out below them, waiting there to wel-come them home.

The people from Sinaloa were soaking wet, their clothing clinging to their bodies, as they rode into Monterey. Whatever joy they felt that day, as they arrived hungry and exhausted, came from finally being able to stop their travels. After fif-teen hundred miles on the *camino,* and almost six months of traveling, they had survived the journey. They had made it to

Monterey. This was the place that was to hold their dreams, that would allow them to start again, to rebuild their lives.

But paradise Monterey was not.

The presidio waiting for them could barely hold up under the torrent of water crashing down from the sky. Only the tiny chapel and the quarters for the officers and the priests were made out of adobe. The rest of the buildings were put together with poles and hardened mud with sod roofs, which were now crumbling from the rain. The plaza in the center of it all was not safe for man or beast; it had become a river of brown that splashed against the sides of the buildings. This was where the caravan would have to set up their tents, since their quarters had not yet been built. In time, they would be the ones to build them. Monterey was not yet big enough for the arrival of fifty-two settlers. It would have to grow, and the people would grow with it.

But God must have been smiling when He saw that caravan come into Monterey because by the time the travelers had climbed down from their horses, the rain was beginning to stop. The sun struggled with the clouds, trying to peek through those grey skies, lighting up the day. With its rays came possibilities. And the feeling that this place was a good one.

The people of Sinaloa were met by the people of Monterey, and some of the ones who came out to meet them were new there themselves. A ship had brought fresh recruits just three months earlier, and along with those recruits had come a carpenter with his wife and family. A physician too was there, with his two daughters and his *señora*. The women of Sinaloa were now no longer the only *españolas*. Altogether, there were now 170 *españoles* in all of Alta California, including the 52 people from Sinaloa.

And more would be coming.

The new settlers brought with them babies yet to be born.

Beatriz had known since San Gabriel that she carried a child, and three other women from the caravan would keep the

Monterey physician busy that coming spring, bringing those little ones into the world.

But not all the babies would be born there.

There were four other missions that needed recruits, as did the San Diego presidio. The people from Sinaloa would soon be spread across California like seeds cast away by the wind, following their *soldados* as they were sent from Monterey back to San Diego, San Luis Obispo, San Gabriel, and San Antonio, and to newer missions yet to come. Families kissed their loved ones farewell and never dwelled again together, separated by the vastness of the lands of California.

And this, too, happened to the Luna family.

Within a fortnight, Rivera would mount his horse once again and head back to San Diego. At his side was Martín, with Rios as his lieutenant, Simon as his aide, and Tomás riding at the back. Victor too was dressed in the uniform of the king, and Marco had his own horse, riding ahead of the women, protecting them as only a newly turned seven year old could do. The mud had not even thickened from the storm that had accompanied them there before all the Lunas were mounted up and ready to leave Monterey.

Leaving Petra and Felipe behind them.

Rios was the first to say good-bye—and it was not easy for him.

He walked his horse over to Petra and reached a hand down to her. She took it and did not care who saw them together or what might be said, the good or the bad. She tried not to think of Barcelona, or of all the pretty pictures in her head that he had put there. A part of her wanted to go with him, that part of her that he would never know.

Rios smiled, knowing he would always carry the thought of her with him wherever he went. But the pain of losing her was hard to bear, and the weight of it took away any pretty words he could think to say. When tears threatened to reveal his feelings, he spurred his horse and went forward, joining Simon once again and the caravan of travelers.

Martín struggled harder at letting her go.

He wanted Petra to go with them, and he tried to insist upon it, threatening and cajoling her the night before they left. At dinner he had Sola beg her, and Beatriz asked her to come along to help with the baby that would be coming in a few months. "Family stays with family" is what each and every one of the Lunas said to Petra. It had always been their plan, Martín reminded her, and he used his own two sons, Marco and Victor, to make Petra cry, to make her feel like she was abandoning them.

But everything Martín tried failed to move Petra.

Felipe was staying. And that's where she would stay too.

She was different now; Martín could sense it, in the way she moved and in the words she spoke, and he knew in his heart that he was the one being abandoned, the one being left behind. That was a void that would have to be filled. Where once there was love for her, now that place would be filled with anger and spite. And when they all rode out of Monterey, the Lunas waved to her and shouted their good-byes. Each one had tears in their eyes but smiles and hope for Petra. And for Felipe too.

But Martín rode forward, eyes on the future.

And he never turned to look back at his sister.

SIXTY-SEVEN

It would be comforting to say that life for Petra and Felipe was always good.

But that wouldn't be the whole story, and it wouldn't be the truth.

Felipe and Petra stayed long enough in Monterey for Petra to realize she was going to have a baby. But Felipe was soon transferred to Mission San Antonio, and the baby was born there—a boy they named Carlos Ramon, who they called Carlitos. Before the boy's first birthday, Felipe was transferred again, this time to San Luis Obispo where two more children—both daughters—were conceived. The first was born at San Luis Obispo, and the second one made her appearance at San Gabriel, where Felipe was sent next. That second baby was still at the breast when Felipe was transferred once again to the new mission of Our Lady—Misión de Nuestra Señora. Every time the family had settled in at a new mission, it was time to pack up and move again.

Other soldiers, if they followed orders and did what was expected, stayed in one place and grew in rank and prestige. But Felipe was not that kind of soldier.

The whipping he had been given at San Antonio had not broken his spirit. It had made him stronger. And more stubborn. Felipe had never learned that obedience outweighed doing what was right and what was good. He would not blindly follow orders. The other soldiers that had come from Sinaloa were able to move up in rank and eventually found a few more coins in their pay—that is, if they were paid at all, since they only were paid when the coffers were filled. All of the big promises made to them as recruits—the land and livestock, and handsome new uniforms, never found their way to the lowly soldier. Including their monthly pay. If they weren't paid, they learned to make do with what little they were offered: some flour, rice, or beans perhaps, or a small piece of land to grow vegetables. But if you were an officer you could expect much more. Acres of land for a *ranchero*, fields filled with cattle, and a reputation that could bring a man riches and respect.

None of this was enough for Felipe; he would not change who he had become as a man. When he was asked to do something he knew was wrong, he thought of Calixto and he grew silent like him, in words and in deeds. He was the one soldier who would not follow a command if his heart told him not to. Despite any riches that would have been his had he done what was asked of him.

Sometimes *indios* ran away from a mission, and soldiers were ordered to go after them. Felipe was always the last man to mount his horse. He had become an expert rider, but in a chase against escaping *indios*, Felipe always seemed to fall far behind the rest. When those *indios* were found and the soldiers had to drag them back to the mission, Felipe's soldiering skills were suddenly found wanting. If he was commanded to tie the hands and feet of the captured *indios* with leather straps, well, he followed the orders but made sure those ties weren't tied all that tight. And if those *indios* managed to free themselves and run away, well, maybe Felipe's horse was a little tired that day. If Felipe saw the *indios* escape into the woods and was asked which direction they had run, well, maybe the sun had been shining too brightly in Felipe's eyes and he pointed in the wrong direction. In this way, Felipe resisted what he felt in his heart was wrong.

People said he was stubborn or stupid. Or possibly both.

No *comandante* wanted to keep him. So they sent him to another mission. And another one after that.

Babies were conceived at each and every mission.

Felipe just smiled and considered himself blessed. And no matter how many times they moved, or how far they traveled, Petra found courage in his happiness, comfort in his touch, and yes, beauty in his arms.

That's when the next baby would come.

In all, Felipe and Petra would have twenty children—that's a fact, and you can look it up in the history books if you want. Petra gave birth to ten girls and nine boys. Now, it's true that doesn't add up to twenty.

One of the boys is not listed.

You won't find his birth written down in the archives of the Mission of Our Lady—the mission where he was born. There's no record anywhere of his birth, and the reason for that is this: History is written by the ones who win, and the victors only tell you what they want you to know. Not the whole truth.

That's why this story of Felipe is so important.

These words you are about to read are the whole truth.

This part of the story needs to be told.

The mission at Nuestra Señora was brand new when Felipe and Petra arrived with a two-year-old son, one daughter just walking, and one still at the breast. There were only six soldiers there, living on a dry patch of land, not close to any water. Years later the mission would be abandoned, but when the *padres* first came there, they had too much hope in their eyes and it clouded their vision. What they saw was a land with many natives using it; they didn't understand that they used the land for a season or two and then moved on to more fertile lands.

The Chalones were friendly people, and they were curious too. They didn't run away when the first strange-looking men came to them, with brass buttons on their chests and with mates that were four-legged, that ran quickly like the wind. Only later, when Petra arrived, did they understand that these strangers also had women, that they didn't mate with their horses, and yes, they had children too. But by then they had learned many other things about the *españoles*.

That not all of them were good.

Together, the *españoles* and the *indios* built up the mission; the soldiers and the *padre* taught them how to use tools, how to grow crops, how to build a chapel and quarters for the soldiers.

They also built dormitories for the young *indios*—for the unmarried women and men who would be kept separate from one another. The dormitories were locked at night, especially the ones where the young women slept. The *padre* wanted no problems with any of his soldiers. He knew that men on their own could be tempted, and when tempted, they could sin. For this reason, he locked the women away at night, protecting them as any good father would.

He also didn't want the women to run away.

One young girl had run away three times already. They had first found her at the creek when the weather had turned icy cold. It wasn't difficult to bring her back to the mission, where she found a warm fire in the cooking pit and a good woolen blanket to cover her nakedness. She was a beautiful girl; they thought she must have been at least twelve, with wide, brown almond-shaped eyes. She didn't understand a word they spoke to her, but she looked at their lips and their eyes and thought that these men seemed kind. They offered her some beads and something warm to drink. And because they didn't know her name, they called her Dulce, because she loved the sweets they would give her, pieces of candied fruit and dried honey.

It wasn't difficult to keep her there in the beginning, when the weather was cold and when they treated her with such kindness. She was good with the other *indios*—the ones that would wander into the mission and, seeing her, would speak in their language. She always brought them closer to the *padre*, and he made friends with them. But when the weather turned warmer, one day she ran away without warning.

Two of the soldiers at the mission went riding out after her. When they brought her back the next day, she was different. Sadder. The light had gone out of her eyes, and she wouldn't look at anyone like she did before. She stayed by herself and not with the others. She tried to run away two more times and by the third time, when they caught her again, that's when they started to lock the dormitory. For Dulce's own good. She was a daughter of God now; Jesus was there at the mission and not anywhere else she could possibly run. This was where she belonged, said the *padre*. So they locked the doors at night to protect her for her own good.

After that, Dulce stopped trying to run away.

This had all happened many months before Felipe and Petra arrived at the mission. In fact, Petra never had a chance to meet Dulce. But Felipe had met her the first night they arrived at Our Lady.

Night duty always fell to the newest of the *soldados*. Felipe only had time to set up Petra and his three little ones in a lean-to close to the back of the mission. The corporal had warned him to make sure his family stayed close to the mission grounds. The *indios* had been sneaking in at nights to steal baskets of grain from the warehouse, and there was little of it to take as it was. Supplies were low, and the *españoles* had not had fresh meat in weeks. It was in the hottest days of summer and there was a drought so crops had not grown, and without supplies they could easily starve. Everything had to be rationed.

The *indios* too were suffering and so they would grab what they could from the *españoles* and run away. Sometimes taking with them a horse or two, and riding like hell into the night.

After the attack at San Diego, word had been sent from one mission to the next: This is what can happen. This is what the *indios* are capable of doing. Be careful, or lose everything. The soldiers grew tougher and more afraid.

Felipe was told all this that first night he was on duty with two other soldiers—one a young boy of fifteen named Fernando, and the second, an old widower named Javier. The boy was nervous; it was his first night on guard duty, and he was afraid of the dark. Javier kidded him and called him a mama's boy, and when Fernando told him to shut up and he didn't, the boy leapt at him, grabbing him by the throat and squeezing for all his life. If Felipe hadn't pulled the boy away, Javier would have been sleeping with the angels that night. Fernando was not a young man to tease, and Javier learned the hard way that all teasing should stop.

After that, the three of them sat together in uneasy silence.

The night was quiet until the moon was just above them. That's when they saw several shadows running across the mission grounds. Javier saw them first and shouted. Pulling out their pistols, Javier and Fernando ran across the grounds after the figures, with Felipe running behind them. They chased them away past the adobe walls, and Fernando raised his pistol high and shot once after them.

The night again was quiet.

The figures were gone.

But as the three soldiers made their way back into the mission grounds, they heard running coming right at them. When they looked, they saw a figure carrying something away. A bundle or a basket. Someone was stealing from the mission. Fernando raised his pistol and shouted, "*Alta!*" He called out loudly for the person to stop, and when he didn't, the boy shot his pistol. Not to be outdone by a young buck, Javier raised his gun too and fired off another round.

The figure stopped and crumpled to the ground.

Felipe was the only one who didn't fire, and he was the first to reach the fallen figure in the darkness.

That is when he met Dulce. The first bullet had entered her cheek and looked so small, like a tiny red beauty mark, really. But the second bullet had entered her chest, and she was dead from it, eyes open and blood spreading across the front of her. She was lying on her back, with her arms holding tightly a bundle wrapped in a blanket.

A baby.

Dulce wasn't stealing—she was running away with her baby.

Killing can grip a man in many ways. Javier was sick and vomited at the sight. Fernando was anxious, his nerves on fire, excited by the new power he felt.

"Shoot it!" he said to Felipe. "Kill it!"

"Are you crazy?" Felipe said, looking at Fernando as though he were mad.

When Felipe did not move, Fernando pulled his dagger from his belt and lunged towards the baby. Felipe jumped on Fernando and knocked him hard to the ground, slapping the knife away and pinning the boy down. He cocked his own pistol and held it at Fernando's head.

"I've never used one of these on a man before, but I will now," Felipe told him. And by God, he meant it.

Javier stepped in. "What difference does it make?" he said to Felipe. "The mother's dead. The baby's a bastard. They kill them themselves when they don't want them. I've seen them do it. They bury them alive! We'd be doing it a favor, putting it out of its misery."

Felipe did not wait to hear any more of this shit. He threw his pistol far into the night and picked up the blanket with the baby inside it. Holding it close to his heart, he hurried away into the darkness and away from the soldiers.

Petra was asleep when Felipe appeared. Her children she cradled with her body on a mattress of straw covered by canvas and blankets that she had brought from her old life. She could barely see her husband as he came into the lean-to, ducking his head as he moved, taller than the rest, as always. She saw he had something in his arms, but she couldn't see what it was. Only when it cried did she understand: Felipe was carrying a baby.

The child wasn't much older than a newborn. Just a few weeks old. Petra sat up, and when Carlitos started to stir, she shushed him with a hand on the small of his back, and he settled down again and curled closer to her. Her daughters, Celia and Gabriella, lay close together on their mother's other side, facing each other as they slept.

Felipe kneeled at the side of the bed and uncovered the naked baby for Petra to see.

It was a boy. A very small one at that. He had a mop of black hair that stood straight up in the air, going this way and that. And he was angry. Crying so strongly with his little fists tightly balled and kicking his legs with all his might.

"Where did you find him?" Petra asked Felipe, in a surprised whisper.

"His mother is dead. They wanted to kill him," Felipe said softly, when he could finally find the words. Petra just looked at him in disbelief. Felipe stopped before he could tell Petra the rest of what had happened. He wanted to save her from knowing the truth.

Petra didn't want to know the rest. The why or the what wasn't important to her. The baby was all that mattered. The sight of the child and his sounds filled her breasts, and the milk moved to her nipples. The warm flow of her milk spread across the front of her gown, and she reached out for the baby, bringing him closer to her, holding him gently in her arms. She didn't think twice about what to do next. She had seen it before and learned from it. It had opened her up like it was doing to her now. This was a baby that needed help to live, and there was a debt that needed to be repaid.

Petra pulled the top down on her gown and offered the child her breast. She stroked his cheek as she had seen Lihui do for Josep. Petra ran her finger gently from cheek to tiny mouth as she pressed his little face close to her breast. The baby's head turned in that direction and met her nipple with his mouth.

And that is how it happened.

That's the truth, and now you know it.

Felipe and Petra tried hard to find someone who knew Dulce or knew who the father was. But no one offered a name; if anyone knew anything, no one said a word. The mission *indios* wanted nothing to do with the baby. The *españoles* wanted even less to do with him. Fernando and Javier were sent on to other missions, and the *padre* acted as though nothing had ever happened. As long as the child was baptized and his soul saved, that's all that mattered to the Church.

No birth was ever listed. Only a baptism.

With Felipe and Petra named as his parents.

We will never know his real last name or the birth name of his mother. But he became a Garcia the day Felipe and Petra chose to save his life. And his children, too, became Garcias. One branch of the family tree just as strong as the rest.

He was named Teodoro Calixto Garcia, but everyone called him Teo. His mother was a Chalone, and no one knows if his father was an *español* or a native Californian. He was always known by the land where he was born.

A Californio.

Every family has a story and this one is ours.

I, Rosa Garcia Gonzales de Adrian, swear to it.

Teo Calixto was my grandfather.

That truth is filled with pride, and with sadness too. It is two sides of the same coin that was forged out of cruelty and ignorance. Cruelty is passed from one generation to the next, until others come along to claim it. The *españoles* who treated the *indios* as less became treated as less by the ones who followed. The hatred in words and deeds cast upon the first people of this land would one day ricochet back to its owners. "Savage" and "animal" were replaced by "spic" and "greaser." That's the way it goes in the world, all through the ages.

But even in the worst of times there will always be a little goodness. Good people like Felipe will do what they can to stop the cruelty and get on with their lives. All we can do is tell their stories and learn the truth along the way.

When I am gone, this story must go on without me.

You must be the next to tell it.

Remember Felipe. And pass it on.

Acknowledgments

I owe a special thank you to Monica Orozco, PhD, Executive Director of Old Mission Santa Barbara, former Director of the Santa Barbara Mission Archive-Library, who provided a creative cocoon for my researching and imagining *Californio*. I am indebted to Fr. Carl Faria, Archivist for the Diocese of Monterey, and also Dr. Randy Bergstrom, Department of History, UC Santa Barbara. A special thanks goes to Dr. Daniel Krieger, Professor of History, Emeritus, California Polytechnic State University, and past President, California Missions Foundation, along with Liz Krieger. Thanks also to the first readers of *Californio*: Philip Levien, Harriet Proval, Marie Favro, and Pamela Wells.

I'm grateful to Ryan Quinn for his 18th Century map of the expedition, Debra Prescott Waterfall for her photo that captured "Felipe" in the Santa Barbara Fiesta parade, Robert Faulkner for the cover, Cheryl Nicchita for her editing, and The Book Designers for their beautiful pages. Many thanks to my *parientes* for their support: Suzi Calderon Bellman, Lynn Adams, Isa Wel, Mary Moreno, Debra Prescott Waterfall, Lee Beckom, and the late Mike Perry.

Finally, a special thank you to my uncle, Daniel Craviotto, for the inspiration of his genealogical research. What had always been a mystery to me while growing up was suddenly revealed in his meticulous gathering of names, dates, and locations that were passed on to me after his death. My only wish is that I could've thanked him for giving me the framework I needed to create the characters of *Californio*. Like Rosa, he too handed down the stories of those who came before us, and I will always be indebted to him for his curiosity, persistence, and love for family.

About the Author

DARLENE CRAVIOTTO has worked professionally in the entertainment industry for over twenty-five years. After co-starring with Kathleen Quinlan and Bibi Andersson in the critically acclaimed film, *I Never Promised You a Rose Garden*, a car accident prematurely ended her film-acting career, and Ms. Craviotto turned to screenwriting.

Hired as the executive story editor for the David Jacob's CBS series *Married: The First Year*, she also simultaneously wrote for *Dallas*. Turning to long form projects, Ms. Craviotto wrote the NBC television film, *Angel Dusted*, co-starring with Jean Stapleton, and Helen Hunt. Craviotto also co-wrote *Sentimental Journey* for CBS, starring Maureen Stapleton and Jacqueline Smith. Next followed *Love Is Never Silent*, an adaptation from the acclaimed Joanne Greenberg novel, *In This Sign*, for the Hallmark Hall of Fame. Starring Phyllis Frelich, Ed Waterstreet, and Mare Winningham, the film won numerous awards including an Emmy Award for Outstanding Drama Special, and also garnered Craviotto an Emmy nomination for outstanding writing. Other awards for the movie included the Amade Unesco Award; the Christopher Award as best television film, as well as Humanitas and WGA nominations for outstanding writing.

Ms. Craviotto's feature film, *Squanto: A Warrior's Tale*, starring Mandy Patinkin, Michael Gambon, and Adam Beach, was released by the Walt Disney Studios and won a Movieguide Award when it was selected as one of the "Ten Best Family Films" of the year.

For the stage, Craviotto wrote *Pizza Man*, winning both the L.A. Dramatist Award and Dramalogue Award as best new play of the Los Angeles season. Published by Samuel French, *Pizza Man* has been translated into nine languages, and has been produced all over the world.

Ms. Craviotto's first venture into non-fiction narrative was "The Pediatrician Visit," anthologized in *A Cup of Comfort for Mothers and Sons*, published by Adams Media. Her memoir, *An Agoraphobic's Guide to Hollywood: How Michael Jackson Got Me Out of the House*, was published by Front Door Books in 2011. Ms. Craviotto is married, has two children, and lives in Goleta, California. She is an 8th generation Californian. You can read more of Darlene Craviotto's stories at darlenecraviotto.com.